DAVID DICKINSON was born ~~in~~ Cambridge with a first-class hon~~ours~~ the BBC. After a spell in radio he transferred to ~~television~~ on to become editor of *Newsnight* and *Panorama*. In 1995 he was series editor of *Monarchy*, a three-part examination of its current state and future prospects. David lives in London.

Praise for The Lord Francis Powerscourt series

'A kind of locked bedroom mystery … Dickinson's view of the royals is edgy and shaped by our times.'

The Poisoned Pen

'Fine prose, high society and complex plot recommend this series.'

Library Journal

'Lovers of British mysteries will enjoy Powerscourt's latest adventure.'

Booklist

'Dickinson's customary historical tidbits and patches of local color, swathed in … appealing Victorian narrative'

Kirkus Reviews

521 046 15 3

DEATH OF A PILGRIM

DAVID DICKINSON

ROBINSON
London

Constable & Robinson Ltd
3 The Lanchesters
162 Fulham Palace Road
London W6 9ER
www.constablerobinson.com

First published in the UK by Constable,
an imprint of Constable & Robinson, 2009

This paperback edition published by Robinson,
an imprint of Constable & Robinson, 2010

First US edition published by SohoConstable,
an imprint of Soho Press, 2009
This paperback edition published 2010

Soho Press, Inc.
853 Broadway
New York, NY 10003
www.sohopress.com

A copy of the British Library Cataloguing in Publication
Data is available from the British Library
US Library of Congress number: 2008034617

UK ISBN 978-1-84901-097-9
US ISBN 978-1-56947-623-9

Printed and bound in the EU

1 3 5 7 9 10 8 6 4 2

For Chris and Karen.

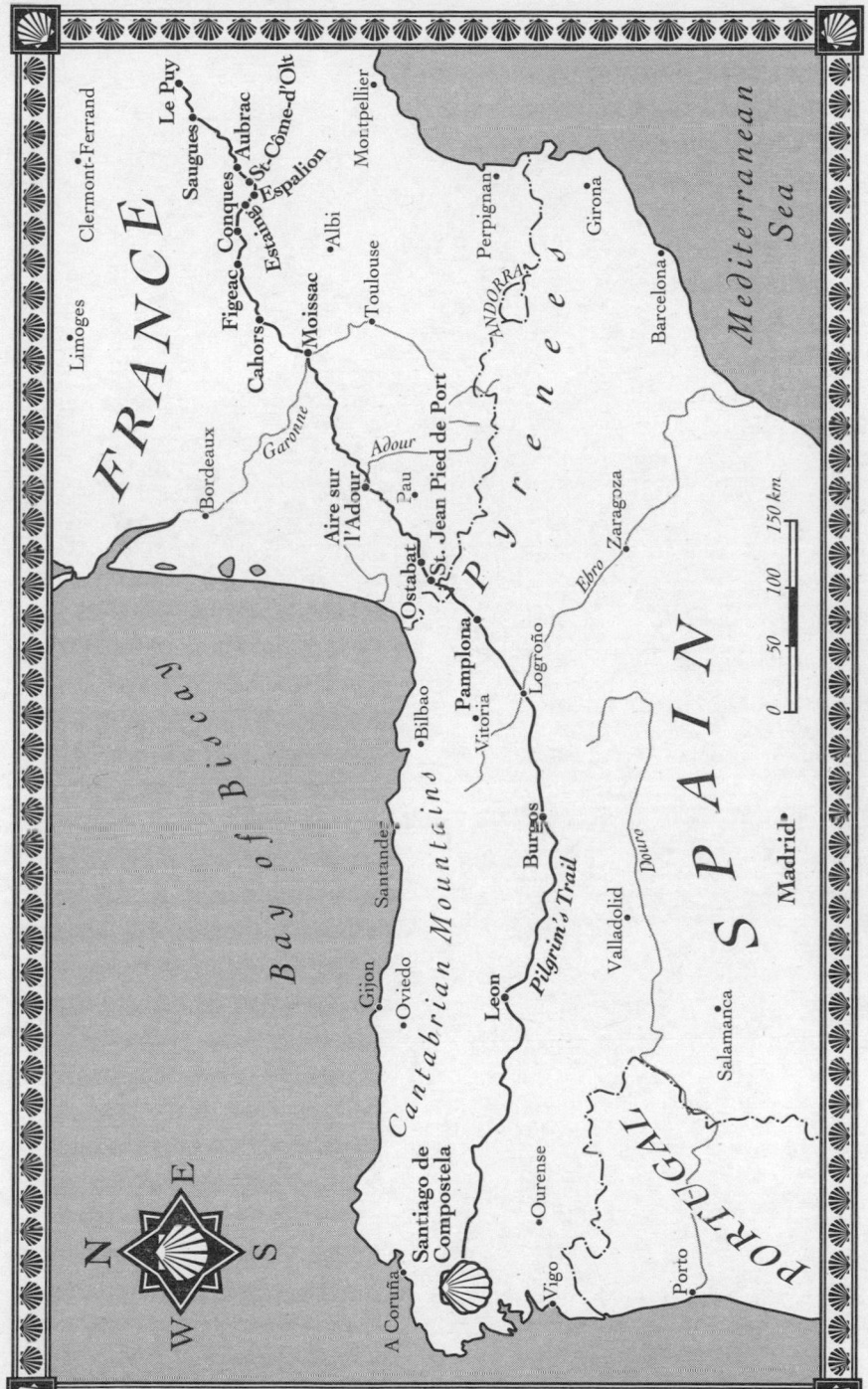

PROLOGUE

The message carved in stone is very simple. It tells of a choice, a choice between eternity and salvation, a choice between paradise and the torments of the damned, a choice between heaven and hell. The work is divided into three horizontal sections. In the centre stands the largest figure of them all, Christ risen from the dead and wearing a long tunic with a scarf of white wool embroidered with black crosses, usually reserved for the Pope and certain church dignitaries. Above him is a cross carried by two angels holding a nail and a spear. His right hand points upwards and to his right. There a procession of the chosen ones, the Virgin Mary and St Peter, carrying the keys of the kingdom, lead the elect into paradise. On the strips of stone that divide the panels there are Latin inscriptions. For Peter and Mary and Abraham, seated with the other victors in this religious race, the message is clear: 'Thus are given to the chosen who have won, the joys of heaven, glory, peace, rest and eternal light.'

On the other side of the work there is neither peace nor glory nor eternal light. Christ's left hand points to the left and sharply downwards. Beneath him is a panel enclosed by two doors, one ornate and graceful with two keyholes for the locks, the other with heavy metal supports and no keyholes. The chosen are led by the hand to heaven's gate, but in front of the gateway to hell diabolical monsters pummel the damned and force them into the vast open jaws of Leviathan:

in the words of the Book of Isaiah, 'Sheol, the land of the damned, gapes with straining throat and has opened her measureless jaws: down go nobility and the mobs and the rabble rousers.' Presiding over hell is Lucifer, Prince of Darkness, with a hideous grimace, bulging eyes and short hair pleated to resemble a crown. To his left a miser or a thief has been hung up with a pouch of hoarded or stolen money wrapped round his neck, killed by the weight of his own greed. To his right a messenger devil is whispering into Lucifer's ear the news of the latest torments in his kingdom. Lucifer's legs are adorned with serpents and his feet are pressing down to hold a sinner being roasted on a brazier. In the panel above, an abbot is holding on to his crozier, prostrate in front of a deformed and bestial demon. In his net the demon has captured three other false monks and is preparing further torture. Behind him, a heretic, his lips shut and a closed book in his hand, is having his mouth crushed while a demon devours his skull. To the right a false banker or money-changer is about to atone for his sins. A demon is melting the metal in a fire. He is tilting back the false banker or money-changer's head and preparing to make him swallow the liquid of his infamy. A king has been stripped naked and a demon is preparing to pull him off his throne with his jaws. A glutton has been hung upside down with a pulley and forced to vomit his excesses into a bowl while another fiend prepares to beat his feet with an axe. There is a couple taken in adultery and fornication, possibly a monk and a nun, now tied together for ever with a rope joining their heads at the neck. The sins of pride and power are here in stone. A knight in an expensive mailcoat has been forced upside down by a demon pushing a pole into his back. Another seems to be trying to tear his arms off. A scandalmonger, forced to sit in a fire, the flames licking round his waist, is having his tongue pulled out. A glutton with an enormous belly is going head first into a piece of kitchen equipment, a cauldron or a boiling casserole. Love of money, love of power, love of women who

are not your wife, love of gossip are all portrayed here, surrounded by demons with fire and snakes and pulleys and
axes and prongs to welcome you into hell. 'The wicked', the
inscription proclaims, 'suffer the torments of the damned,
roasting in the middle of flames and demons, perpetually
groaning and trembling.'

These scenes are carved in the tympanum, the space above
the doorway, in the Abbey Church of Conques in southern
France. They were put in place early in the twelfth century,
possibly around 1115. For a couple of hundred years they
would have acted as inspiration and warning, threat and
reward, to the tens of thousands of pilgrims passing through
Conques on their journey to Santiago de Compostela, the field
of stars on the north-western coast of Spain, final resting place
and shrine of St James the Apostle, which was the ultimate
destination of one of Europe's most important pilgrimages. As
they came into the great square in front of the church in
Conques the pilgrims would have stared in awe, and possibly
terror, at this visible representation of the likely fate of all their
souls in the world to come.

And now, in this year of Our Lord 1906, another group of
pilgrims, bringing perhaps the same hopes and the same
vices, are preparing to set out on the same pilgrims' path to
Santiago and stand in front of the great tympanum at Conques.
For them, as for their predecessors eight hundred years
earlier, the inscription at the bottom of the sculpture still rings
true: 'Oh sinners, if you do not mend your ways, know that
you will suffer a dreadful fate.'

PART ONE

NEW YORK—LE PUY-EN-VELAY

Be for us, a companion on the journey, direction at our crossroads, strength in our fatigue, a shelter in danger, resource on our travels, shadow in the heat, light in the dark, consolation in our dejection, and the power of our intention; so that with your guidance, safely and unhurt, we may reach the end of our journey and, strengthened with gratitude and power, secure and happy, may return to our homes, through Jesus Christ, our Lord. Apostle James, pray for us. Holy Virgin, pray for us.

Pilgrim's prayer, Cathedral of Le Puy

1

A bell was ringing, somewhere close. As the man struggled towards consciousness he thought he was deep, deep underwater. A ship was sinking slowly beneath him, heading straight down for her last resting place on the sea bed. Maybe it was one of his ships. Ghostly figures, their clothes streaming behind them, were struggling towards the surface through the murky water. Other figures, the fight abandoned, were falling backwards towards the ocean floor. Still the bell rang on. Now the picture in the man's mind changed. He was in a coal mine. The bell meant danger, a rock fall perhaps, or a collapsed shaft. Miners were running as hard as they could towards the way out, trying to escape before they were buried alive. Maybe it was one of his mines.

Then the bell stopped. The clanging was replaced by a loud knocking on the bedroom door. The man woke up and peered at his watch. It was a quarter to three in the morning.

'Sir, sir, it's the telephone, sir! It's the hospital, sir!' The butler's voice was apologetic, as if he felt hospitals had no right to disturb his employer at this time of night. He was still suspicious of telephones.

'Of course it's the bloody hospital, you fool,' shouted the man, beginning to pull on the clothes he had dropped on the floor the night before. 'Who else would telephone at this time, for Christ's sake? What did they say?'

'You're to come at once, sir. I've ordered the carriage.'

'God in heaven!' said the man. 'I'll be with you in a moment.'

This man didn't answer telephones. He didn't open letters. In normal times he didn't tidy his clothes away. He didn't clean his shoes. He paid other people to perform these mundane tasks for him. They marked, these triumphs over the trivia of modern life, the milestones on his journey to unimaginable wealth, his town house in New York, his mansion in the Hamptons, his yacht, his servants, the great industrial empire, the mountains of money sleeping in the vaults of the Wall Street banks.

As the carriage rattled through the empty streets of Manhattan, Michael O'Brian Delaney thought bitterly that he would happily give them all away in return for just one thing, the life of his only son.

Michael Delaney was in his late fifties. He was slowly turning into a patriarch. He was over six feet tall and with a great barrel of a chest. Dark eyebrows hung over brown eyes that were liable to flash with anger or excitement. His hair was brown, turning silver at the temples. He radiated a vast energy. One of his employees said that if you could somehow plug yourself into Delaney you would light up like a candelabrum. Oil paintings of a more peaceful Delaney adorned the boardrooms of his corporations.

By the time his carriage drew up at the hospital entrance there was only one candle burning, to the left of his son's bed. The little ward looked out on one side to the night streets of Greenwich Village, on the other to the main ward for the terminally ill in St Vincent's Hospital. Not that the nuns or the doctors ever referred to the ward in terms of terminal illness. It was St James's Ward to them. All the wards on this floor were named after one of the twelve apostles. Only in private did some of the less religious nurses refer to it as Death Row. As Delaney tiptoed into the room on this November evening, nearest the main section an elderly nun, her entire working life spent in tending the sick and the dying on these wards, sat perched lightly on a chair and stroked a young man's hand, as if her caress could prolong his stay in these sad surroundings.

'Thank you so much for coming, Mr Delaney. We felt we had to call you. We thought the end might be near, you see, but the crisis seems to have passed. He is no better, of course, but at least he's still with us.'

'Thank God,' said Michael Delaney, and sat down on the other side of the bed. These were familiar surroundings to him now, the dim lighting, the crisp white of the sheets, the antiseptic pale green paint on the walls, the picture of a saint – Delaney didn't know which one – on the wall above the bed, the faint smells of soap and disinfectant, the light rumble of the trolleys outside taking away the dead on their last journey to the morgue, or bringing fresh consignments of the dying into the terminal ward. But he could not sit still for long. He was restless, now leaning forward to peer into the young man's face, now pacing on tiptoe over to the window and staring out into the snow swirling round the streets of his city.

This elder man was the father of the patient lying unconscious in the bed. Michael Delaney was one of the richest men in America. The patient was his only son, James Norton Delaney, and the doctors were convinced he could not last more than a day or two. He was suffering from a rare form of what the doctors thought was leukaemia but knew little about. He was eighteen years old, James Delaney, and this evening he was lying on his left side. He had been on the other side when the father sat on vigil until ten o'clock the evening before. Perhaps, the father thought, the nuns had turned him over to make him more comfortable. James was a couple of inches shorter than his father's six feet two. He had, as Michael Delaney recognized every time he looked at him, his mother's pretty nose and his mother's mouth. Only in that high forehead, Michael Delaney thought, had he left his own print on the face of his only son. The young man's forehead was lined and wrinkled as if he had added thirty or forty years to his age. He was deathly pale. The light brown hair, almost straw in colour, straggled dankly across the pillow. His father had lost count of the number of days his James had been in this isolation ward on his own now. Four? Five? Days and nights blended into one another; the vain hope that those light brown eyes might open, that the lips in his mother's pretty mouth might part and speak even a few words, was dashed as the ritual timetables of the nurses and doctors measured out their patients' days. Still there was no movement. Delaney leant down and kissed his son very lightly on the forehead. Every time he did this he wondered if it would be the last time his lips touched a living creature rather than a corpse.

Shortly before seven o'clock in the morning the order changed in the Hospital of St Vincent. The elderly nun was replaced by a younger one. Delaney was conscious of shadowy figures flitting silently to their places along the main ward. The Matron of the hospital materialized by his side and led him away.

'You must have a change for a little while,' she whispered. 'Come with me.'

She led him through a series of passageways, the walls now pale blue and filled with paintings of the Stations of the Cross or scenes from the Gospels. Then she slipped away and he nearly lost her. The Matron, Sister Dominic, was a considerable force in St Vincent's. Almost all the male patients she met, even the very sick ones, were absolutely certain that she had chosen the wrong profession. Think, they said to themselves, of those translucent pale blue eyes. Think of that face with its delicate features and that soft blonde hair. Think of that figure, alluring to some of them even through the folds of the habits of her order. Quite what the right occupation for Sister Dominic might be they had no idea, but central to it, in the male view, was non-nunnery. No veils, no wimples, no rosary beads, no strange garments, no prayers, let her be just another example of that great institution, American womanhood, available for courting, wonder, romance and, for the lucky one, love and marriage. Often the male patients would dream about Sister Dominic, coming slowly back from drugged sleep after visions of nights spent in her company. Matron herself was well aware of these strange currents of male interest, even male desire, that flowed invisibly around her person. She prayed regularly that God would punish her every time she thought about her appearance. There was one quality, central to her personality, that most of the male patients did not see. Her faith was the most important facet of her life. And she had a deep, intense, very personal calling to heal the sick. Sometimes she would tell herself that somebody in her care was just not going to be allowed to die. It would be too unfair. Sister Dominic never told any of her colleagues about these missions of salvation. When all her efforts failed she would repair to her bare cell and weep bitterly until she was next on duty, sometimes refusing to eat or sleep for days at a time. Failure did not come easy to the Matron of St Vincent's Hospital.

'Where are we going?' Delaney whispered.

'We are going to the chapel,' she replied. 'We are going to pray.'

The man stopped suddenly. He told her he had forgotten how to pray. Bitterly he remembered the times he had ignored all forms of religious instruction as a boy and had played truant, the church services where he had deliberately ignored the words and the responses, the Sunday mornings he had managed to flee from the Church of the Blessed Virgin and gone to hang around the waterfront, the beatings from his father for not taking his faith seriously. He remembered too his father shouting at him that one day he would be sorry he had not paid attention to the priests. One day the sins of his past would come back to haunt him. Well, Judgement Day had finally arrived, here in this place where the sheets were changed twice a day and crucifixes and rosary beads were as common as top hats on Fifth Avenue.

Matron told Delaney he should not worry about the praying on this occasion. She would find him something else to do. She asked him to wait for a moment outside the main entrance to the chapel. When she came back there was a ghost of a smile about her face. She led him into the little church, for so many of the nuns the very heart of the hospital. There were enough pews to hold about forty people. All of them were filled, mostly with kneeling women. All of these Sisters, she told him, had come to pray for his son James. It was a special effort for a special young man. When Delaney asked her what he had to do, she gave him a box of matches. She pointed to the great banks of candles inside all the side chapels and below the paintings on the walls.

'You must light these,' she said, 'and as you light each one, you must pray to God in his mercy to save the life of your son. Do not worry if we have gone before you have finished. You must light them all and then return to the bedside. Later on this morning I am going to find you a priest or a chaplain to teach you how to pray.'

With that Matron knelt to the ground in the pew beside him. Delaney turned to the candles to his left and began lighting them very slowly. Please God, spare the life of my son James, he said to himself, feeling coarse and awkward as he did so. Gradually, as he repeated his prayer, he began to weep. The tears poured down his face and would not stop. Sometimes they would drop on to his match and extinguish the possibility of lighting another symbolic message before it had even begun. The nuns took little sideways glances at the weeping tycoon but left him to his ordeal. At eight o'clock the Sisters began to peel away, walking quietly back to their nunnery or their places on the wards. Matron sent word to a Father Kennedy, asking him to come to the hospital and to James Delaney's ward later that day. Michael Delaney had not finished yet, though one wall was a blaze of light, dancing off the faces of the saints or the waters of the Lake of Galilee. It was so strange for Delaney, asking an unknown and invisible

God to save the life of his only son. His was not a world made up of these religious or metaphysical certainties. His was a world of balance sheets, of strike-breaking, of amalgamations, of mighty trusts, of personal enrichment, of power, power over the lives of the thousands of people who worked for him, power over the local politicians who might need a subvention to help them through their next election, power over grander politicians, aspirant statesmen perhaps, whose need for invisible assistance was often as great as their hunger for high office. Alone in the chapel with his matches and his candles he thought of Mary, the boy's mother, who had died three years before. She too had come to this last resting place of Manhattan's Catholics and been tended by the nuns until she died. There had been, he shuddered slightly, a great deal of pain. It was a mercy, they said, when she was called home. Delaney didn't think it had been a mercy then and he didn't think it was a mercy now. This God person, he reckoned, reaching up to the top of a sconce almost out of reach, He had a lot to answer for. If He took James as well, Delaney thought, he would write God out of his account books, sell Him off to a competitor, even at a knockdown price, put Him out of business, close this God outfit down once and for all.

Just before nine o'clock all the candles were lit. Delaney sat down in one of the pews and looked around him. He tried to remember the words but they had gone. Hail Mary, that meant something, he was fairly sure of it. The same went for Our Father. But of what those nuns said as their knees rested on the stone floor he had no idea. He turned back at the door and looked one last time at the candles. He wondered if their light would go out before his son's life. Suddenly his brain took off into a strange mixture of his own world and the very different world of the hospital. Did they have enough candles here at the hospital? Did the other hospitals? This was something he, Michael Delaney, could do. His mind set off on a journey round the economics of candle production, possible advanced production techniques that could reduce the cost of

manufacture and the numbers of employees, candle trans-
portation routes and freight rates, distribution of candles
round the churches and hospitals of New York. Would it be
cheaper to amalgamate candle supply into general delivery
lines of food, linen and so on, or simply have one outfit
responsible for distribution? What about the competition in
candle land? Could he buy them out? Could he drive them
out of business?

As Delaney pondered these questions on his way back to
the ward a whistle blew less than a mile away at one of New
York's great railway stations. A mighty passenger train moved
slowly out on its way to Chicago. The train was nearly full
and promised to be a busy one for the stewards and the cabin
staff. This railway line was one of many owned by Delaney's
companies. This section of his three and a half thousand
railway employees across the eastern seaboard of the United
States was clocking on for work on the normal ten-hour shift
with no breaks, which would see them travel halfway across
a continent. And, in the rear part of the train, there was a
steward who rejoiced in the name of Patrick or Paddy Delaney,
a cousin of the proprietor on the Irish side of the family
though the two had never met.

The boy had hardly moved in his bed when his father
returned. The new Sister on his left was also stroking his
hand. Delaney paced up and down the room, staring into the
face of his son, doing more planning for his schemes for a
candle monopoly, then peering out of the window. Sometimes
he cried and wished he knew the words of the prayers. Ten
o'clock, then eleven o'clock passed, and by noon Delaney's
train with his cousin on board was well into upstate New
York. Occasionally a doctor would come in and look at the
young man, feeling his pulse and taking his temperature by
the heat on his forehead. None of the doctors had seen a
version of the disease like this. They were acutely conscious
that any new treatment might not cure the young man. It
might kill him instead.

Shortly before one o'clock a priest appeared and took Michael Delaney aside. You must go home and rest now, the priest told him. You do not need to rest for a very long time, but you must maintain your strength for what might happen. I, Father Kennedy, will meet you here in the chapel at seven o'clock this evening. The nuns will have finished their services by then. Please, I will stay with the boy a while.

Delaney's carriage and Delaney's coachman had waited for him outside St Vincent's. The coachman spent his time playing cards with the porters or reading one of his ever-growing collection of magazines about motor cars. Mercedes Benz. Ford. Chrysler. Cadillac. Bugatti. The coachman was very fond of his horses but these names took him to another world where he sat proudly at the wheel of a mighty machine and drove his master up and down the eastern seaboard, hooting his horn at recalcitrant pedestrians, a muffler round his throat and a chauffeur's cap upon his head. As they made their way slowly through the crowded streets they were overtaken by a couple of fire trucks, their insistent bells shrieking and echoing round the thoroughfares. Sitting inside his carriage, Michael Delaney remembered that other bell which had woken him up earlier. He thought suddenly of the numerous funerals he attended as his contemporaries in the Wall Street jungle died off in their prime. Delaney never missed one of these sad occasions, come, his enemies whispered, to make sure that another of his competitors had really been removed from the earthly market place. He recalled the words in one of the addresses, usually full of sentimental rubbish about the dead man, now transformed from a rapacious capitalist into a virtual saint and generous benefactor of the poor: 'Ask not for whom the bell tolls, it tolls for thee.' Were these bells ringing for him? For his son? Michael Delaney huddled into his greatcoat and tried to pray.

The Archbishop of New York used to say that the net wealth of Father Patrick Kennedy's flock was about the same as that of a medium-sized country like Sweden or Portugal. Delaney was a parishioner of his, a very occasional worshipper at Mass, like so many of his kind, but a generous contributor to church charities, like so many of his kind. Quite simply, Father Kennedy was the parish priest in the richest part of the richest city in one of the richest countries on earth. He was popular with his congregation, Father Kennedy, with his charming voice and elegant manners from the Old Confederate State of Virginia. In his youth Father Kennedy had been slim, ascetic almost, a devoted reader of the works of Meister Eckhardt and St Thomas Aquinas. He was about five feet ten inches tall with a Roman nose and his blue eyes were then fixed on another world. The temptations of the flesh did not reach him in his rich parish, but the temptations of the table made an impact. Middle-aged now, he was known to his critics as the Friar Tuck of Manhattan. He glided through the Fifth Avenue drawing rooms with his polite smiles and his anecdotes from his time in Europe a decade before. Father Kennedy was very successful at drawing new converts into the bosom of Mother Church, and as most of his recruits were as rich as everybody else in the parish, St James the Greater increased yet further in wealth until cynics in poorer parishes referred to it as St James the Richer.

Father Kennedy worried a great deal about the very rich. He saw all too clearly that the leisure of those who lived off the interest on their money, or even, in some cases, the interest on the interest, without needing to work at all, could be corrosive. Souls could be lost in the fripperies of the season as easily as they could in the brothels and the gambling dens of the Bronx. He worried a great deal, Father Kennedy, about camels and their ability to pass into the kingdom of heaven. Three times he had asked to be transferred to a parish in one of the slums of New York. Three times the church authorities had refused. The Archbishop always maintained that remaining in Manhattan would be good for Father Kennedy's soul. The truth was somewhat different. Father Kennedy was the greatest benefactor of the poor in the whole of New York. Not personally, but through his parishioners, who would contribute funds for the education or housing of the poor, for the support of the destitute, for building new churches where none had been before. It was all so easy. The rich just reached for their chequebooks as they might hold out their hands for a glass of champagne at a Fifth Avenue soirée. After watching this waterfall of charity dollars for years Father Kennedy himself had become cynical. They're trying to buy their way in with false currency, he thought. God doesn't want their money, he wants their souls. So, while he never stopped the cascade of charity, he was beginning to think about deeds rather than dollars as the way to improve the spiritual health of his flock.

Michael Delaney's staff pressed anxiously around him as he returned to his mansion. None dared to ask the question they most wanted to – how was James? Was he still alive? The young man's father refused all offers of refreshments except for a large glass of bourbon and took himself off to bed. He slept badly. He dreamt he was in a cemetery looking at his wife's grave, the two marble angels he had had erected a year after her burial towering above the marble tomb. But now, by her left side was another tomb, to his son, passed away in the month of November 1905. This month. Then he noticed what was happening by her right-hand side. Four gravediggers were excavating a third burial place for another Delaney. It could only be himself, last of the line. There was no inscription yet on his grave, he realized. He might have years to go still. With that comforting thought he woke up to a darkened city at a quarter to six in the evening.

He was early at the chapel in St Vincent's Hospital. Somebody had removed the guttered candles and replaced them with fresh ones. Delaney began to light them, remembering to say the words the Matron had told him earlier that day.

Father Kennedy came and sat down with Delaney in the very first row, a large silver cross in front of them. Just repeat the words after me, he said to Delaney, that's all you need to do for now. They started with Hail Mary.

Two doctors, one middle-aged and one very young, were examining James Delaney. The nurse had moved unobtrusively to the back of the room. They agreed that he looked a little better, that the terrible chalky colour of the previous day was less pronounced.

Father Kennedy and Michael Delaney had moved on to the Lord's Prayer. Forgive us our trespasses as we forgive them who trespass against us . . .

And so a strange ritual evolved. Early in the mornings Delaney would pray with Father Kennedy in the chapel and relight the candles while the doctors looked at his son. He would wait by the bedside during the day and early evening, departing occasionally to care for his business or buy out a competitor. One of the nuns would sit on the other side of the young man and stroke his hand. Delaney now had reading matter, a missal provided for him by Father Kennedy. He also had a special prayer of his own. It was, he knew, somewhat unorthodox, owing more to contemporary business practice than to the Gospels. If God would save his son, he would, in return, make a mighty offering to God. The nature of the offering was to be determined by Father Kennedy, who smiled delphically when told about the Delaney Compact. Early in the evening all the nuns and Matron would pray for James for half an hour. His father would light the candles and say some of the new prayers he had been taught by Father Kennedy. As the priest watched the intensity of Delaney's concern, the depth of his grief, he wondered if there might be other grounds for sorrow and remorse in his past, now mingling with anxiety for his son James.

As Delaney became a part of this medical world, so different from his own, he found his eyes roaming the wards and the corridors for a sight of Sister Dominic. Even in her formal Matron's clothes, he thought, you could still discern the woman underneath. Lust began to flow through him as the medicines and the drugs flowed through the veins and arteries of the patients. Damn it, man, he said to himself, not here, not now. All your life you have followed your basic instincts. The temporary delights of fulfilment have all too often been followed by recriminations and remorse. This is neither the time nor the place for such base thoughts. Here, above all else, you must focus on the life of your son, James. But it was no good. His lust did not grow weaker. It grew stronger. Fantasies filled his mind, of those clothes falling to the floor, of his holding such a beautiful creature in his arms. Matron, for her part, was not insensitive to what was happening to Michael Delaney. She knew. She had seen this phenomenon all too often before. She took great care to pay even less heed to her appearance. That, had she but known it, inflamed Michael Delaney further, clothes slightly out of place, hair not properly tucked in yielding up yet more erotic thoughts. Sister Dominic did change her ways in one respect. Every evening when she and her Sisters prayed for James Delaney in the little chapel, she prayed for Michael Delaney too.

Then the doctors moved. For over a week they had monitored every medical detail they could measure about the condition of James Delaney, still lying motionless in his hospital bed. Neat folders recording his current state were tucked away in the cupboard beside the bed. The following day was a Saturday. They asked Delaney to a meeting in the library at ten o'clock in the morning. If he wished, Father Kennedy could accompany him. Matron was to attend too. All that evening the nurses and the Sisters looked at the Delaneys with great pity. All too often they had seen mothers and fathers or husbands and wives coming out of that that room, holding on to each other in desperation, weeping their way down the corridors and out into the fresh air. The library was the place the doctors brought close relatives when they had to tell them that their loved ones were about to die.

2

The library of St Vincent's was on the top floor of the hospital, looking out over the tall buildings of the city. A storm was brewing outside, angry bursts of rain battering at the windows, gusts of wind blowing the hats off the pedestrians and rattling and shaking the cabs as they made their way around the streets. As Delaney and Father Kennedy filed in for their ten o'clock meeting that Saturday morning, the senior doctor, George Moreland, waved them into a couple of comfortable chairs by a low table in the centre of the room. Dr Moreland was a graduate of La Salle University, summa cum laude, and had graduated Phi Beta Kappa from the Harvard Medical School. He was six weeks off his fortieth birthday. He was short and his hair, to his great regret, was receding rapidly. His colleague, Dr Stead, was ten years younger with exactly the same medical pedigree as his superior. Together they represented one of the most formidable medical teams in their field in the United States.

'Thank you so much for coming at such short notice,' Dr Moreland began, a slight smile moderating his look of extreme gravity. 'Believe me, I can only imagine how difficult a time this must be for you, Mr Delaney.'

Delaney was trying desperately to stop himself looking at Matron's eyes. 'Not at all,' he replied. 'I am so grateful for all you are doing here for my James.'

'I'm afraid I am going to be frank with you this morning,

Mr Delaney,' said Dr Moreland, who had to steel himself for these difficult encounters with a small shot of brandy before they started. 'I want to put a proposition before you. You know by now, of course, of the difficulties we have with James's condition. We believe it to be some form of leukaemia, but we do not what form, what shape it is taking. His illness does not a have a name. If it did,' he pointed at the lines of books that lined two whole walls of the room from floor to ceiling, 'there would be articles about it in places like the *Lancet* or the *New England Journal of Medicine* or the *Proceedings of the Harvard Medical School* which line the walls here. But there is nothing. We are working in the dark, groping our way to some form of treatment that might effect a cure. So far we do not believe we have found the answer.'

Delaney brightened slightly. 'If it would help, Dr Moreland, I could endow a Chair for the study of this strange disease at the university here in the city. Or I could establish a Foundation to look into it.' This world of self-interested philanthropy was one he knew all too well.

'Please, please!' Dr Moreland held up his hand. 'Your offer is most kind and most generous but I do not feel this is the right time or place to raise such questions. We are concerned with one life here, a life that is, as we speak, ebbing slowly away a couple of floors beneath us.'

Michael Delaney winced. Wealth was not going to save him here as it had saved him so often in the past.

'You see, Mr Delaney,' the younger doctor cut in, 'we know so little. If I could draw a very imperfect example from your own world, let us suppose that you are going to build a new railway line across some difficult mountains.' The young man did not see fit to mention it, but his father was the senior engineer on the Kansas, Topeka and Santa Fe Railroad. 'When you come to work up your plans, you have a pool of knowledge to draw upon: surveyors who have mapped similar lines in the past, engineers who can estimate the optimum route to avoid the high places where possible, men who have designed the rolling stock and the engines to carry the trains most efficiently across the difficult terrain. Others have trod the path before you. But with James, we have nothing at all, no maps, no charts, no previous experience. We have been changing James's treatment all the time. Nothing seems to work. Very slowly, little by little, he is becoming weaker every day.'

There was a distant peal of thunder and a flash of lightning lit up the New York skyline for a brief second. Delaney, Matron thought, sneaking a surreptitious glance at the man in case direct eye contact should set him off again, was looking miserable, more miserable than she had yet seen him.

Silence ruled briefly in the library. It was Dr Moreland who broke it. 'I hope I have tried to make it clear to you, Mr Delaney, right from the beginning, how little we know. In the medical profession,' he glanced briefly at his colleague and at Sister Dominic, 'we wear these white coats to impress the patients and their families. Sometimes we carry medical instruments with us, hanging around our necks. The Sisters and the nurses are dressed in special uniforms to imply they too have special knowledge. At Harvard, my old university, you see the professors wearing their gowns with scarlet hoods lined with fox and ermine and their dark mortarboards to impress on the students that they too have special knowledge. I once saw a formal assembly of lawyers processing through the Royal Courts of Justice in London with wigs and robes and emblems denoting who was Master of the Rolls and so forth. Fancy dress implies fancy knowledge. I cannot speak for the lawyers or the academics, Mr Delaney, but in so many medical cases we have no claim to special knowledge. In the case of your son James we have, in fact, almost no knowledge at all.'

'I'm sure that's not true, Dr Moreland.' said Delaney. 'You are most distinguished in your field, the pair of you.'

Dr Moreland brushed the interruption aside as if he were swatting a fly from his forehead. 'Let me cut to the point,' he said, leaning forward to look Delaney in the eye. 'There is a choice to be made here. Only you can make it. I am not sure I would have presented you with such a choice were you not such an eminent man.'

'What is the choice?' asked Delaney very quietly as another blast of wind rattled the windows.

'If we carry on with the current treatments, then I think your son will die very soon. I could be wrong. Our knowledge is so limited. We have been making things up as we go along. If we stop the treatment altogether, then again, he might die very soon. But he might recover. Our drugs may be doing him more harm than good. We just don't know. That is the choice, Mr Delaney. Continue as we are and he may die – if you pushed me hard, I would say it is very likely. Stop them, and there is a chance, only a chance, mind you, that he might recover.'

Father Kennedy spoke for the first time. 'What a terrible choice. I pray that God will guide you in the right path.' Matron threw caution to the winds and smiled at Delaney.

The man was silent for a moment. 'Can I ask you a couple of questions, Doctor?' he said, sitting forward in his chair and twirling his hat in his hands. 'Let me thank you for a start for being so honest. In your opinion, is stopping the drugs the only chance of saving James's life? Is there any other way? And when would you start, or maybe I should say stop?' He sent an agonized look to Dr Moreland. 'I mean, if you did it, how soon before you would know if it was working, that James was beginning to recover? Or to put it another way, how long,' Michael Delaney fought back the tears, 'how long before he dies?'

Dr Moreland answered immediately. 'I cannot promise you anything, Mr Delaney. I cannot promise that stopping the drugs is the only way to save James's life. There might be other ways, but we have tried all we know. As to how soon we should stop the treatment and begin to treat your son with non-treatment, as it were, I think I can give you an answer. We should do it as soon as possible. The young man grows weaker. His ability to fight the disease lessens by the day. The longer we wait, the less likely the non-treatment is to succeed.'

'Do you mean', said an aghast Delaney, 'that you want me to make the choice now? Here, in this room?'

'I do not wish to rush you in any way,' said the doctor, leaning back and looking at Father Kennedy, as if appealing for help. 'It is a most terrible choice. Only you can make it. But I emphasize what I said before: the sooner we start, the better our chances. Which, as I hope I have made clear, are not very good in the first place.'

Michael Delaney rose to his feet. He walked very slowly to the window. He was still fiddling with his hat. He stared out at the rain cascading down the windows, the dark clouds racing across the sky, the busy streets of the city outside in a healthy world.

Sister Dominic found the whole encounter had a terrible fascination. So many times she had watched families and loved ones almost literally torn apart by the doctors' words in this room. But she had never seen a man of such wealth and power face such a situation before. She wondered what he would do. Silently she began saying Hail Marys. The younger doctor, Dr Stead, was trying, yet again, to work out how long it would take for death to happen or recovery to begin if the treatment were to stop. Father Kennedy was planning to slip away quietly after this meeting and fetch the little box from his house, the little box that would enable him to administer the last rites. He should, he told himself bitterly, have brought it earlier. Dr Moreland was running the discussion back through his mind, hoping that he had made the position clear. Delaney thought of his dead wife and what advice she would give about the life of her only son. He thought of his own parents, now long gone, who had watched young James tottering across the floor on his first faltering steps and had been in the front of St Patrick's Cathedral as he took his first communion. Delaney's dead remained silent. No answers came from beyond the grave.

At last Delaney spoke. He turned back from the window and returned to his chair to face the two men who had presented him with what he mentally referred to as the Devil's Alternative.

'Very well, gentlemen,' he said firmly, 'I do not think I have much choice. I ask you to stop the treatment. I ask you again, how long do you think it will be before you can detect changes for better, or . . . ' He paused for a moment. 'Or worse?'

'The next treatment was due to be administered in just over an hour's time,' said Dr Moreland. 'I do not know how long it will be before we know something. Dr Stead and I will take it in turns to sit by the bedside until we have resolution one way or the other. Matron will see to whatever special nursing needs we may require. I would advise you to take a little rest just now, Mr Delaney. Any changes might start in three or four hours. It might take twenty-four hours or even more. We do not know. But we will prepare as best we can for all eventualities.'

'Thank you,' said Delaney.

'From this moment on,' said Father Kennedy, 'we are moving outside the knowledge of these good doctors here. We are all in God's hands now.'

Michael Delaney returned to the hospital shortly after half past two. He brought with him a small bag containing a change of clothing and a large bottle of Jack Daniels. His coachman watched him turning into the main corridor of St Vincent's. Then he took from underneath his seat a couple of European motor magazines that had recently arrived in New York. In some respects, he thought, the French and the Germans and the British might be ahead of the Americans in terms of design and engine construction. The coachman found that hard to believe.

The death watch party, as Delaney mentally referred to them, were already in their positions in the little ward. By the left-hand side of the bed, looking at it from the door, was a nurse, one section of her rosary beads hanging out of her pocket. Just behind her sat Dr Moreland, a couple of files on his lap and a pencil in his right hand. Next to the nurse sat Matron, her rosary beads in her lap, her lips moving silently, one tress of blonde hair which had escaped from her cap lying across the top of her forehead. Opposite the nurse sat Delaney, the hat still twisting in his hands. By the window stood Father Kennedy, staring out at the storm outside and the tiny rivers running down the front of the buildings. Above the bed, in a plain frame, was a reproduction of an earlier painting of a saint, dressed in brown with a brown background, his elbows resting on a table, his hands stretched out in prayer, the fingertips touching.

The nurse kept her head very near the bed. If you looked closely, Delaney realized, you could see faint breathing movements, slight swellings in the sheet as the boy's chest rose and fell. Maybe the nurses had tucked him in extra tight, Delaney thought, so they could watch the movements better. He suddenly remembered telling James about the death of his mother. It had been in the drawing room of his great house, the lights burning brightly, a fire roaring in the grate and the continuous rumble of a great city on the move just audible from the street outside. Delaney had comforted the boy as best he could. Even though they both had known she was dying, it was still a terrible shock. He recalled James telling him, months after the event, how he, James, had felt numb for weeks. Sad, of course, tearful, naturally, but the most memorable feeling was numbness, a cold feeling that ran right through you as if you had swallowed some ice cold mixture. But he wouldn't be able to tell James about this death, Delaney realized. James wouldn't be here.

'It's all right to talk, as long as we're quiet, Mr Delaney,' said Dr Moreland in a voice scarcely above a whisper. 'Some people think it might even help, that when the patients hear human voices, they know they're still alive. Or you can take a little break with a walk in the corridor.'

'How do we . . . ' Delaney began and then paused, groping for the difficult words. 'How do we know if James is getting better? Or worse, for that matter?'

'I cannot give you precise guidance,' said Dr Moreland. As Delaney looked closely at the doctor, he saw that the top left-hand corner of his folder was covered with tiny drawings of golf clubs. Woods, irons, putters, they were all there. Maybe this was how Dr George Moreland usually spent his Saturday afternoons, out on some green golf course by the sea, sinking his putts with the same authority that he brought to his patients in the hospital. Not, mind you, Delaney thought, looking out of the window, on an afternoon like this.

'It's the breathing, Mr Delaney, that's one thing that can help us. If the breathing becomes shallow, or the gaps between breaths become longer, then I'm afraid that we would regard that as bad news. But often even that simple observation can be wrong.' He sent Delaney a small, rueful smile.

Delaney found himself hypnotized by the praying figure on the wall, hanging directly over his son's head, the pale, ascetic face, the fingers joined in prayer. He wondered who he was. He beckoned Father Kennedy into the corridor.

'That fellow on the wall,' he said, 'the one above James. Do you know who he is, by any chance?'

Father Kennedy smiled. 'That fellow, as you call him, is one of the most important saints in the Catholic firmament. He's called St James the Greater. He was one of the disciples, one of the fishermen.'

Delaney had investigated fishing once as a possible source of profit, and found it disappointing. There were, in his view, too many variables, bad weather, leaking boats, unreliable fishermen. Now a temporary bout of flippancy overcame him, out here in the corridor of a hospital where his son might be about to die.

'Why was he called the Greater? Was there a Smaller one? A Thinner? A Fatter perhaps?'

23

Father Kennedy had seen these temporary flights of fancy all too often in his long vigils by the bedsides of the dying.

'I think he was called that to distinguish him from another St James, known as St James the Less. But, come, we should return. I shall tell you more about him later, if you wish.'

The afternoon wore on. The nun and the Matron continued their prayers. Dr Moreland moved on to tennis rackets on his folder, his eyes checking on his patient every couple of seconds. Father Kennedy was composing a sermon about the workings of God's grace in his head. Delaney found a quiet corner of the corridor where he could take occasional consolation from his bottle of Jack Daniels. Every half-hour or so he tiptoed into the chapel and lit more candles. Outside the light faded and the storm raged on. Nurses came and went, bringing hot tea and sandwiches, pausing on their way out to say a prayer for the young man in the bed underneath St James the Greater.

The hours passed impossibly slowly. Delaney could see no change in the condition of his son. The blue eyes he knew so well were still closed. The light brown hair still lay ruffled on the pillow. His colour was still very very pale, a white that was almost the same shade as chalk. But he was still breathing. At seven o'clock Matron took Michael Delaney back to the little chapel. He had lit all the candles by now. The room was full, standing room only at the back. There must have been fifty or sixty people in there, mostly nuns with some auxiliary staff. All of them, Matron whispered, were there to pray for the life of James Delaney. Matron didn't say that she was using all the weapons she knew of in her fight to keep the boy alive. And that if there were weapons she knew nothing of, she would use those too, if only she could find them. Delaney wondered about the power of prayer. Certainly he had never availed himself of it in his long business career. It had never occurred to him. Great business deals, he felt, depended on more mundane, possibly, in his present surroundings, more sordid factors: profit, or the possibilities of it, the cost of borrowing money, the size and potential for growth of the particular market. But Delaney closed his eyes and prayed along with all the others for the life of his son.

Shortly before nine o'clock the storm grew ever fiercer. Brilliant flashes of lightning shot past the windows. Claps of thunder sounded from the skies. The rain still pounded on the windows. Father Kennedy, the sermon in his head on the workings of God's grace nearly finished now, wondered if this was an omen. Was his God, Yahweh the ever living, sending a sign that James Delaney was close to death now? Were the young man's days and nights in his wilderness of pain and suffering coming to an end? Looking out of the window at the raging tempest outside, he thought that the fanciful and the superstitious might think that the end of the world was nigh. Was James's passing going to be marked by this display of the power of nature, and, for Father Kennedy, of the power of God? He checked that his little box with all the necessaries for performing the last rites was still at his feet.

Dr Moreland had been replaced by the younger man, Dr Stead. He brought with him a medical journal which he read from time to time, making notes or marks in the margin with a silver pen. By eleven o'clock the storm outside showed signs of abating in its fury. James Delaney was still breathing. The doctor beckoned to the elder Delaney and to Father Kennedy and Sister Dominic to follow him to a little room off the main ward that served as a nurse's office. Timetables, rotas and pictures of the Virgin lined the walls. He motioned them to be seated.

'I thought I should bring you up to date on our thinking about this case,' he began. Michael Delaney felt a moment of resentment. His son was more than a case. 'James', the doctor carried on, 'is still with us. We do not know how long it will take for the drugs to pass out of his system. Certainly their power is less, considerably less, than it was twelve hours ago. Our hypothesis, and it is only a hypothesis, has been that if the withdrawal was going to kill him, it would probably have done so by now.'

'Does that mean, Doctor,' said Delaney, the hat spinning ever faster in his hands, 'that he is going to recover, that he's getting better?'

Dr Stead had heard this note of hope against all the odds many times before. 'I don't think we could say that. Not yet. Not now. At this point the absence of bad news is almost good news. That is all I can say, I'm afraid. It's too soon for hope, for the present.'

Delaney pressed him. 'I understand your qualifications, of course I do. But would you say that his chances of recovery are better now? Better than they were, I mean?'

The doctor looked down at his journal. 'I would not wish to give you false hope. But if you pressed me, I should say that the answer is yes. Or probably yes. Our knowledge is so limited. Forgive me, but I have been looking at a recent article in my medical journal here about the process of dying. It is, if you like, a timetable of the way death comes over the body. It is concerned with diseases similar to, but obviously not the same, as James Delaney's. It suggests to me that if he were going to pass away, he would have done so by now. I emphasize the word "suggests". We could be wrong.'

Delaney was still looking for comfort. 'Should we be more hopeful now? Is the worst over?'

The doctor shook his head. 'I could not agree to that at this moment. The crisis is not over. It may yet be ahead of us, I don't know. But the breathing has become slightly more regular in the last two or three hours. His colour may be fractionally better. That is good.'

'And what', Delaney went on, 'would you have us do now? Should we stay with him through the night?'

'That is entirely up to you. I think I would say that you should go home and rest before you come back. Lack of sleep is well known for causing lack of judgement. You have to weigh in the balance the possibility of his leaving us while you are away against the need to remain strong for the days ahead, as you certainly have done up till now, Mr Delaney. Dr Moreland or I will stay on duty by the bedside.'

'I see,' said Delaney. 'Thank you so much for keeping us in the picture.'

Father Kennedy added his weight to the doctor's opinion. 'I too think you should go home, Michael. I'm sure we can leave the young man in the hands of the medical staff. And, of course, in the hands of God.'

Delaney made up his mind quickly. In his own kingdom of finance he was famous for it. Father Kennedy accompanied him down the long corridor that led out of the hospital. They would both return in a couple of hours.

'Father, can you tell me some more about that saint on the wall? I've been looking at him all day. St James the Greater, you said he was called?'

'Fisherman, disciple, martyr,' Father Kennedy replied. 'He was beheaded for his beliefs by Herod Agrippa, grandson of the biblical Herod, in about 44 AD. Legend has it that his body was taken to the north-western coast of Spain in a stone boat. His remains were discovered centuries later.'

'And what was he made a saint for?' asked Delaney, pausing suddenly.

'If you were a disciple and a martyr,' said Father Kennedy, 'it was virtually certain that you would become a saint some day. In fact, St James the Greater became much more famous after his death than he had been in his life. They made him the patron saint of Spain, for one thing. In the countries where they speak Spanish or Portuguese, the name Santiago is the same as our James. There are cities and churches and statues of him all over the Iberian Peninsula and in South America. During the centuries when the Spanish were trying to expel the Moors from Spain, the story goes that Santiago would appear on the battlefield on a mighty horse, wielding a great sword and urging his troops on to victory. "Santiago Matamoros!" was the battle cry of the Spanish soldiers. "Santiago the Slayer of Moors!"'

'You implied, Father,' said Delaney, resuming his walk towards the main doors, 'that his military powers were one of the reasons for him becoming famous after his death. Are there others?'

'Oh yes,' said Father Kennedy. 'A great city grew up close to the place where the body was found. A great cathedral was built in his honour and in his name. It became a place of pilgrimage in the Middle Ages, one of the most important pilgrimages in Christendom. Jerusalem and Rome were the most important sites, but Jerusalem was not a healthy place to go to at the time of the Crusades and Rome was in the hands of the barbarians. Thousands and thousands of pilgrims from all over Europe made the journey.'

Father Kennedy paused and looked Delaney in the eye. 'I think we may have witnessed a miracle here tonight, my friend. If that is the case, and your son James survives, as I believe and pray he will, we must put it down to the intervention of St James the Greater, praying for your son in his picture on the wall.'

'And what was the name of the city with the cathedral?' asked Delaney.

'The city? I forgot to tell you. The city is still there. It is called Santiago de Compostela, James of the field of stars.'

As the two men passed out into the wet night the bells of New York began to peal the midnight hour. It was Sunday in Manhattan.

3

James Delaney didn't die on Sunday. He was still alive on Monday.

Always now, Delaney had a special prayer of his own as he roamed the corridors of the hospital and watched over his son. On Tuesday James opened his eyes and smiled weakly at his father. The snows and rain of November turned into the snows and rain of December. Early that month the doctors told Delaney his son was getting better. They were perfectly honest with him, saying that their ignorance of the disease worked both ways. They hadn't been sure in the past that they knew how to treat his illness. Now they were not sure why he was getting better. All they could say was that doing virtually nothing seemed to work best of all and they proposed to continue with that course of non-treatment. Five days before Christmas they pronounced James Delaney out of danger. It would be a long time yet, they said, before he could come home. Delaney offered the hospital unlimited funds to study the disease that had nearly carried off his boy, saying he didn't see why anybody else should have to suffer as much as he and his son had done. He presented monies for a five-year supply of candles for the chapel in new designs approved by Matron and Father Kennedy. He wondered then if he had fulfilled his obligations to God and man. All through the month, as the Christmas trees and Christmas decorations filled the shop windows and New York prepared to celebrate the birth of Christ, Michael Delaney was haunted by the image of St James the Greater, the brown saint in his brown background praying with fingertips joined, on the wall above his son's bed. A strange idea haunted him too, an idea he could not shake off. Two days before Christmas he invited Father Kennedy to join him for a festive drink.

Father Kennedy had been telling all his parishioners about the miraculous recovery of James Delaney. It was, he assured them, a blessing from God and St James the Greater. He had amended his sermon on the workings of God's grace around the theme of the Miracle in Manhattan, as he referred to it. He was going to preach the sermon after Midnight Mass on Christmas Eve.

The Father had been thinking a lot about Delaney's pact with his creator. Such pacts, he knew from personal experience, were sometimes found in families struck with terminal diseases and desperately trying to buy a reprieve for their loved ones with the promise of some unspecified future conduct. He knew, Father Kennedy, that he could ask for a new hospital, new schools, fresh charities to support the starving and destitute of New York. But all Michael Delaney would have to do would be to hand over the money. There would not be any sacrifice, for Father Kennedy had private intelligence of the relative wealth of the New York patrician classes in his parish which told him that Delaney was one of the richest of the rich, a millionaire's millionaire.

'Come in, Father,' said Delaney, 'come in! Would you care for a glass of John Powers?' Father Kennedy nodded and settled down in a chair by the fire.

All through his son's illness Delaney had lost weight. His shirt collars grew loose. His trousers sagged at the waist. He discussed with his valet the possibility of buying a whole new wardrobe to suit his new figure. The man advised him to wait. Now, very slowly, he was beginning to fill out again.

'I've been thinking about my deal with God, Father.' Delaney plunged straight into business. He made the Delaney Compact sound like a commercial contract, a takeover perhaps, or the sale of some of his blocks of New York real estate. 'And I've been thinking about that St James the Greater man and the pilgrimage to Santiago.'

'I am glad you have been thinking about such matters, Michael. It may do some good to your immortal soul.'

Delaney resisted the temptation to say 'To hell with my immortal soul.' He pressed on.

'Can you tell me some more about the pilgrimage, Father? Has it died out completely, or do people still go on it?'

Father Kennedy had no idea what was coming next. He wondered if Delaney was going to offer to buy up the city of Santiago, or to turn the memory of the pilgrimage into a subsidiary of one of his great companies.

'Well,' he began, 'it hasn't died out completely, the pilgrimage. But it's only a trickle, a tiny trickle of what it used to be. It takes a long time, you see, to walk from one of the starting places in France all the way to the far corner of Spain.'

'I've been thinking, Father, and I want to put a proposition to you. It may sound strange. You may think I'm mad. But what about this? Why don't I and selected members of my family go on this pilgrimage? I'd pay for them all, of course. It would be a thank-you to God, don't you see? For my James's life.'

Father Kennedy thought another miracle had come to Manhattan. Deeds in the service of the Almighty were going to replace the bankers' drafts to New York's charities. It is easier for a camel to pass through the eye of a needle than for a rich man to enter the kingdom of heaven. The good of the Delaney soul, for a while at least, was going to replace the good of the Delaney wallet. Maybe Michael Delaney would get to meet St Peter up above after all.

'What a splendid idea, Michael! I'm sure our Lord would approve. Would you like me to think about some of the details, possible starting points and so on? Do you have any idea of when you would like to set off?'

31

'Not in this weather certainly,' said Delaney. 'I don't know if James will be strong enough to do the whole thing – if we go, that is. I'd have to hire somebody to work out the details. Easter perhaps? Early summer? To start, I mean.' Delaney was not an expert on European weather patterns but he thought it might be easier to make the journey once the rains and storms had gone.

'Easter might be good, very propitious to start a pilgrimage at one of the greatest festivals of the Christian year.' Father Kennedy thought of the amount of prayer power, nun power, candle power expended on the salvation of young James Delaney. Surely this would be a fitting recompense.

'And would you come with us, Father? To be our spiritual guide? I don't know very much about pilgrimages, you see. I can dimly remember the garish cover of a book in one of my school classrooms called *The Pilgrim's Progress*. Will we visit the Slough of Despond? The City of Destruction? Will we see those strange places on the way? Would we dally in Vanity Fair?'

'I think those places are metaphors, if you like, of the mental state of the particular pilgrim at any particular point along the route,' said Father Kennedy with a smile. 'There were many reasons for pilgrimage in those earlier times. Some went to seek forgiveness for their sins. Some went as part of a pact with the Lord. Some went seeking spiritual enrichment in the long journey and the adventures that would surely befall a traveller on such an expedition. Some, no doubt, went partly for fun. It was a holiday, as it were, as well as a quest. Plenty of different food and wine to sample on the way to Santiago, the city of James after whom your own son is named.'

Father Kennedy spent a morning in the New York Public Library in the days after Christmas. On New Year's Eve he was back in his usual seat in the Delaney drawing room with another glass of John Powers whiskey. He brought various suggestions with him. Their great trek – for Father Kennedy had decided that he would accompany the pilgrims for part of the way at least – could start from the town of Le Puy-en-Velay in the Auvergne in southern France, one of the traditional setting-off places for the pilgrimage, and proceed down through France to Spain and the great cathedral in Compostela. Le Puy and the other starting places like Vézelay, he told Delaney, were like medieval railway stations in the busiest times for pilgrimage in the Middle Ages, a cross-over point for converging pilgrims coming from Germany and the countries of the East who were funnelled down through Le Puy-en-Velay on to the route to Compostela. An earlier version of Grand Central Station in New York perhaps. Father Kennedy didn't expect them to walk all the way. Sometimes they would be able to take a train or a boat. Horse lovers would be able to ride for part of the journey.

Contemplating the scale of the enterprise, the vast distances, the enormous expense, Father Kennedy wondered, as he had wondered in the hospital, about the scale of Delaney's response to the salvation of his son. He didn't think disproportionate was the right word to describe it – it is not every day after all that a man's only son is rescued from death's embrace. And yet. And yet. Was Delaney trying to buy a clean slate for all the sins of his previous life? Were there hidden crimes, now buried deep in the Delaney past, that he wished to atone for? Was the pilgrimage a gesture to the past as much as to the present?

Michael Delaney had evolved a number of maxims for the conduct of his affairs, developed over his many years in business. Always pay your men enough to stop them from striking. In his early days he had been involved in a lockout, with blackleg labour and picket lines and hired detectives, and it had nearly finished him off. Always try to buy out your competitors – nothing succeeds like monopoly. Always invest in the latest technology, it will pay for itself in no time. For the management positions at the top of the organization, always look for the very best men in America. Quality managers, Delaney believed, would never let you down. Even he had never drafted a job advertisement quite like the one inserted for the pilgrimage in the *New York Times*. Organizer Required, it said, for pilgrimage to France and Spain, Europe. Duties to include finding as many members of the Delaney clan as possible in Europe and America, route planning, hotel reservations, liaison with church authorities. Fluent French essential. In return he obtained the services of one Alexander Eliot Bentley, son of a French mother and a doctor father from Rye, New York, graduate of Princeton and Yale Law School, aged twenty-four years.

From the start Alex Bentley regarded the whole thing as an improbable joke. He thought they might get as far as France, but he doubted if this strange collection of Delaneys who passed through his basement office in the Delaney mansion on missions of inspection and research would ever get to the Spanish border, never mind the final promontory beyond Santiago that rejoiced in the name of Finis Terre, the end of the world. But he persisted. He wrote to Irish Delaneys in Donegal and Ballyhaunis, in Macroom and Mullingar, in Westport and Wicklow and Waterford. Across the Irish Sea he wrote to Delaneys in Hammersmith and Kentish Town, in Birmingham and Liverpool. Across the Atlantic he wrote to more of the clan scattered across the eastern seaboard and the Midwest of America. On the wall opposite his desk in the basement Alex Bentley constructed a family tree of Delaneys that grew at the rate of four or five entries a week, each one carefully inscribed in Bentley's immaculate copperplate. Next to the family tree was his pride and joy. This was a map of the route of the pilgrimage that snaked out from just below the high window, worked its way in a wiggly line down the wall, then turned right once you crossed the Pyrenees by the edge of the carpet and carried on to Santiago. Le Puy-en-Velay, La Roche, Aumont-Aubrac, Espalion. You could, Alex Bentley thought, almost hear the rivers gurgling the sounds of the names, the Lot, the Truyère, the Dourdou, the Celé. Estaing, Espeyrac. Conques, Figeac. Symbols were added to the route as he completed his preparations on every stop of the journey, little signs for hotels, signs for railways, signs for places with acceptable roads. Limogne-en-Quercy, Cajarc, Montcuq, Cahors, Moissac. Names were added to the map as it travelled beneath the window towards the Pyrenees, names of priests and abbots and mayors in all the little towns they would pass through. St-Martin-d'Armagnac, St-Jean-Pied-de-Port, Roncesvalles, Pamplona, Burgos.

4

The little train, its three carriages full of French and Americans, pulled slowly out of the station in the town of St-Etienne in southern France and began the long climb up into the hills. In the front of the first carriage sat Michael Delaney and his party, on the last leg of their journey towards the starting point of their pilgrimage, Le Puy-en-Velay in the Auvergne. Alex Bentley was very excited, peering out of the window at the rivers and forests they were travelling past. This, for him, was the culmination of months of planning, finding as many Delaneys as he could in Ireland, England and the United States, trying to establish that these were genuine Delaneys, not some freebooters come to scrounge a holiday in Europe at his employer's expense, inviting them, if suitable, to join the pilgrimage. Now he was coming to see the fruits of his labour.

One grave doubt about his own position was gnawing away all the time in a corner of his mind. He couldn't understand much of the spoken French. He could read the newspapers. He could understand the great advertisements plastered along the sides of the boulevards. But when they spoke to him, these living Frenchmen, he grasped very little. If he was honest with himself, he knew he could latch on to the occasional word or phrase but complete sentences eluded him. They sped past him like an express train, a torrent he could not, for the moment, comprehend. They could have been speaking Hottentot to him, or Ancient Greek. Alex Bentley's grandmother, who had taught him French, had died when he was only six years old. His mother had always spoken to him in English. The knowledge seemed to have vanished from his mind, as if a conjuror had spirited it away. For most of his expensive education in French literature and culture he had been concerned with the words of dead Frenchmen. Alex Bentley could remember huge chunks of Baudelaire and Rimbaud. He could read Flaubert and Stendhal, Balzac or Zola as easily as he read the baseball scores. He could have written leaders about the Dreyfus Case for *Le Monde* or elegant diplomatic memoranda for the French Foreign Office in the Quai d'Orsay. But at one of the greatest universities in America he had spoken no French at all. He had written his essays in English. His lectures were in English. The professors spoke to him about French literature and its glories in English. But when the taxi drivers or the hotel porters of Paris spoke to him in French, he could only guess at what they were saying. He wondered if he should tell Michael Delaney.

Father Kennedy had endured an unhappy crossing of the Atlantic. Even though the great liner they sailed on from New York to Le Havre did not give them a particularly rough passage, the Father was seasick all the way. At first he consoled himself with the thought that it would pass, that after a day or so the illness would abate, and that he would be able to walk the decks like the other passengers and gaze at the vast mystery of the ocean. He dimly remembered reading a book about Nelson which reported that the great Admiral himself suffered from *mal de mer*, as the French doctor on board called it, for the first few days as he sailed off from Portsmouth or Plymouth to wage war in Egypt or the West Indies. But then, for Nelson, it passed. For Father Kennedy, it did not pass. He had consulted his small travelling library of religious books but could not find what he sought. There appeared to be no patron saint of seasickness to whom he should address his prayers. The liner's library did not help either. It contained no religious volumes at all. So he spent virtually the entire crossing lying on his bunk, trying not to move.

There were five other Americans in the party. One, Michael Delaney's cousin Maggie, had been a last-minute entry. She was single, in her early sixties, with thinning hair that was nearly white and a semi-permanent frown on her face. She told everyone who had ever asked that she was married to Mother Church and that being a Bride of Christ was far far better than being joined to some man who might neglect you most of your life and occasionally perform acts of unmentionable violence upon your person. Michael Delaney couldn't stand the woman. He had sworn violently when Alex Bentley told him that she too wished to come under starter's orders for the pilgrimage. Bentley found it easier to communicate with his employer using sporting analogies. It had taken all Father Kennedy's diplomatic skills to persuade Michael Delaney to take her along. And, for once, the Father misjudged his example from the Gospels.

'Remember our Lord's words to the woman taken in adultery, Michael,' he had said. 'Go thou and sin no more.'

Delaney was on to him in a flash. 'Woman taken in adultery, Father? That old cow has never been taken in any kind of ultery with or without the add-ons. More's the pity. Might be better if she had been. Might have been better if she'd committed a few sins too. Can you imagine? That dried-up old bag coming with us thousands of miles across the world? God save us all. Sorry, Father.'

At length Delaney was persuaded that he had no right, even as the organizer and paymaster of this pilgrimage, to exclude certain of God's people merely because he didn't like them. So now Maggie Delaney, clad in a dark suit that was far too heavy for the climate of southern France in the middle of June, perched primly on the edge of her seat, and fingered her rosary beads. A couple of elderly Frenchwomen, who had inspected the Americans with ill-disguised venom and distaste, nodded to each other and smiled frostily as they looked at this transatlantic visitor. They too had rosary beads in their pockets or their bags. They recognized Maggie Delaney as one of their own.

Sitting on the same bench, but a few feet away, was a much younger Delaney, 'Wee Jimmy' Delaney. People often thought Wee Jimmy was an ironic nickname, for the young man stood over six feet four inches tall, with dark hair and a wavy moustache. He had been given the name because he was very small as a child, only shooting upwards between seventeen and twenty. By then it was too late to change the name. Wee Jimmy was a skilled steel worker from Pittsburgh, come on the pilgrimage, he told Alex Bentley, because it was free and he had always wanted to travel.

The train now seemed to be making heavy weather of the slope. Tall trees lined the route as the engine panted upwards and sent out great bursts of steam. The herons, standing to attention in the river, took no notice. Trains were now as familiar to them as fish.

Opposite Wee Jimmy sat another young man in his mid-twenties with light brown hair and very delicate hands. Girls, he had observed, often looked at his hands as if they would like to take them off him. Charlie Flanagan, a Delaney on his mother's side, was a carpenter by trade and he had spent the Atlantic crossing making a model of a ship from a piece of wood he had brought with him from his little workshop in Baltimore. He had worked right through the voyage, whittling away in a corner of the sun deck where he wouldn't create any disturbance. After every session Charlie would tidy up his shavings neatly and place them carefully in the bin. As they travelled further and further east across the Atlantic, word spread among the passengers and crew that a beautiful model ship was being created on the vessel and people came to watch him work, some of them mesmerized by the flashing blade as he shaped his wood. Indeed, by the end, he had a commission from the captain himself, a handsome commission too, for another wooden model, to be delivered shortly after his return from Europe.

Charlie came from a deeply religious family but his main motive for going on pilgrimage was to see some of the cathedrals and castles. Charlie would much rather have been an architect than a carpenter but he was one of ten brothers and sisters so there was little money.

Next to Charlie on the bench was a slightly older man, a handsome man in his early thirties, clean-shaven with curly brown hair and dancing dark eyes that were almost black. Waldo Mulligan, who told Alex Bentley he was a Delaney on his mother's side, worked for an important senator in Washington. For the last year and a half he had been conducting a passionate love affair with the wife of a colleague. He was trying to break it off. He was, he said ruefully to himself, trying to break his own heart. He had come on pilgrimage to beg forgiveness of his sins and the courage to start a new life without his darling.

Slightly alone, towards the middle of the carriage, was the last member of the American Delaney party, another young man, Patrick MacLoughlin, twenty-two years old with small eyes and a small nose, from Boston. He was studying for the priesthood and had signed up because he was convinced that the faithful of today had much to learn from the faithful of centuries past. Indeed he planned to go on a whole series of pilgrimages before he was thirty to help him in his ministry. He was very excited about kneeling down and praying in front of one of Le Puy's most famous objects, the Black Madonna in the Cathedral of Notre Dame. Patrick MacLoughlin looked forward to visiting religious relics in the same way other people might feel about going to major football matches or the Niagara Falls.

And Michael Delaney himself? He was wearing one of his louder suits today, a bright green check with a cream silk shirt and a bright red cravat. He was still wearing the same broad-rimmed hat he had worn on the liner across the Atlantic that took them back to the Old World. They had stopped for a night and a day in Paris on the journey south and Delaney had been most impressed with the layout of the centre of the place, those great boulevards radiating outwards across the city like spokes in a wheel. Delaney took himself on a short guided tour, astonished when he learnt that the choices for the duration ranged between six and eight hours in a single day. 'Take me round in three,' he said to his guide, 'and there's a bonus if you can do it in two.'

The Arc de Triomphe and the Champs-Élysées impressed him. The Louvre he found disappointing. Too many damned paintings in the place, he said to his guide. Why can't they put all the finest stuff in a couple of rooms at the front so people can pick up the best bits? No point wandering through all those wretched rooms or saloons as he thought they were called. Americans are busy people. Put the best things at the front and the people would pass through quicker. Quicker visits, in Delaney's view, could mean more visits. More visits would mean more money. Much better management all round. Notre Dame, he thought, wasn't a patch on St Patrick's Cathedral in New York. Napoleon's tomb impressed him, however. Anybody who could organize that many military campaigns would be certain to succeed in America. Not necessarily on Wall Street, with all those stocks and complicated bonds he felt the Corsican might not understand, but in any difficult business that needed proper organization, management by vertical integration. Oil, perhaps, coal, coke and steel, that would be thing. In a rare moment of fancy, Delaney could see himself, hand tucked inside his tunic in the best Imperial fashion, tricorne on his head, a faithful marshal or two by his side. Buonaparte Coke Works, he said to himself, Napoleon Steel, that would be a mighty fine name for a business.

The town of Le Puy is one of the most extraordinary sites in France. Located in the bowl of a volcanic cone, three enormous outcrops of rock shoot up hundreds of feet above the ground and give the impression that they might actually lift off into the sky. On the smallest of these giant fingers is the complex of buildings around the cathedral and its cloisters; on another is the huge statue of Notre Dame de France, made from hundreds of cannon captured at Sebastopol in the Crimean War, an enormous reddish pink Virgin clutching an enormous reddish pink child, their colour matching the shade of the slate of the roofs of the town, towering up into the heavens. And the third is the Chapelle of St Michel d'Aiguilhe, an enormous needle of rock with a belfry at the top lifting it even higher towards God and his angels, over two hundred and fifty feet above ground level. Even Michael Delaney was impressed. New York might have its tall buildings and the Statue of Liberty lording it over Ellis Island, but here they had three of the things, all occurring through the forces of nature rather than the energies of man. Alex Bentley thought they looked as if they might hurtle off into the skies, leaving Le Puy, the Auvergne and France far behind. Patrick MacLoughlin, the young man training for the priesthood, marvelled at God's work, sent to impress the humble sinners here on earth.

Their hotel, the St Jacques, was in the centre of the town. It boasted the heavy decorations of the Second Empire, with dark red paper on its walls and dark wooden banisters. The furniture was dark too, great armoires and secretaires and commodes cluttering up the public rooms. The bedrooms were dark, and the dining room, a vast area that could seat over a hundred and fifty gourmands at a sitting, was gloomy however many lights were turned on. You would never have thought that you were in the country that produced Versailles centuries before, with the light flooding in through those high elegant windows. The Hôtel St Jacques was where the respectable citizens of Le Puy would congregate for Sunday lunch, the doctors and the lawyers and the schoolteachers in their Sunday best, the wives showing off the latest fashions to arrive in the Auvergne, the children looking starched and polished in their frocks and sailor suits.

As the pilgrims dispersed to their rooms to unpack, Bentley and Delaney found some more pilgrims who had arrived earlier that day sitting in the bar. These were the Irish pilgrims. Two older men of about forty were sharing a bottle of wine. They had discovered something in common on the boat from England. The balding man was Shane Delaney, a railway worker trained in Dublin but now with a different railway company in Swindon. His wife, Sinead, was suffering from a terminal disease. The doctors said she had less than two years to live. Shane was coming on the pilgrimage at her request. 'I'm too ill to travel,' she told her husband. 'I've been to all the holy sites in Ireland and England now, so I have. I'd never get to that Lourdes place the priests all go on about, I'm too ill. I want you to go in my place, Shane. It's as near as I'm going to get to going myself, don't you see? Pray for me every step of the way now, pray that I may recover. Those doctors will never make me better, so they won't. Only God can do that. So you pray for me and my immortal soul and don't you go drinking too much of that French wine on the way. My sisters will look after me.'

The case of Shane's drinking companion, Willie John Delaney, was slightly different. He was short and single with a small beard and worked as a debt collector in north London. He was dying from an incurable disease. He had come to parley with God for his life.

On the other side of the bar two young men were sitting at a table well stacked with empty beer bottles. Christopher, commonly known as Christy, Delaney came from Greystones in County Wicklow. He had bright blue eyes and a great shock of sandy hair. He looked absurdly young, much younger than his eighteen years. His parents were comfortably off and he was going up to Cambridge to read history in the autumn. He thought he could learn some French and see some of the great sites of France. His mother, a deeply religious woman, hoped that the pilgrimage would be good for her boy's immortal soul. Already she had doubts about it.

His companion was about twenty-five, slim and wiry, brown eyes darting round the room to take in the details of his surroundings. Jack O'Driscoll was a reporter on one of the Dublin newspapers. His editor had given him leave of absence because he thought the experience might broaden his outlook. This pilgrimage, the editor – a pious man in an impious profession – told him, should make him a better reporter. He also offered to take some articles about the journey for his paper. Jack O'Driscoll was one of those fortunate people who seem at home in any surroundings. Before they came to the bar, he pulled out a battered document from his waistcoat.

'Chap on the paper gave me this,' he said to Christy cheerfully. 'He says it's all you need to order a drink in France. It's in a sort of pidgin French. Phonetics, I think they call it.'

'Oon bee air,' said Christy doubtfully. 'Oon bee air?'

'That's a beer in French,' said Jack. 'You've got to run the words together, mind you. Hold up two fingers for two beers and so on.'

'Are you sure?' said Christy.

'I am sure,' said Jack. 'If you want to impress them with your knowledge of the French language, this is what you say when you need a refill. On core oon bee air.'

'On core oon bee air,' Christy sounded more confident now. 'How do you pay when you get to the end, if you follow me?'

'Easy,' said Jack, pointing to the last entry on the piece of paper. 'Say "com bee yon?" You've got to put the question mark at the end of the "yon" now, or it won't work.'

Miraculously the O'Driscoll method of ordering beers worked well. Christy took the plunge and ordered rounds three, five and seven. They even ordered two more beers for Michael Delaney and Alex Bentley when they joined them and the introductions were made.

The pilgrims dined well that evening in the Hôtel St Jacques. Alex promised them even better fare the following night when the chef was going to cook them an Auvergne meal with some of the specialities of the region. The next day the pilgrims were to inspect the town and generally make themselves at home in France. The last little band of pilgrims, the ones from England, were to arrive in the morning.

The head waiter made his dispositions carefully the next evening. He sectioned off part of his dining room. The tables were reorganized so that one long table ran across in front of the kitchen entrance, flanked by two others. The tables were adorned with dark red candles and crisp white tablecloths and napkins. Three types of wine glasses were lined up to the side of each place setting. Bottles of white and red were placed at strategic intervals along the tables. Through a judicious use of sign language, acquired during his years of service with the French Army in North Africa, he managed to extract from Alex Bentley a seating plan for the occasion, name cards in Bentley's immaculate copperplate adding formality to the scene.

From his position at the centre of the top table Michael Delaney surveyed his flock shortly after half past seven. There was just one empty space, a pilgrim who had not arrived to take up his station, praying in the cathedral perhaps, or fallen asleep in his room. They were sampling, suspiciously at first and then with growing delight, the chef's *amuse-bouches*, tiny tasters of croutons with a lemon and garlic flavour topped with small pieces of pickled vegetable or dried fish. On Delaney's right sat Father Kennedy, Alex Bentley to his left. He observed that Alex had mixed up the Irish and the Americans but left the English sitting in a group. Delaney had met them all that morning.

Sitting at the far end of the table to his left was a shifty-looking man of about thirty-five years with a small moustache and a greasy jacket. Girvan Connolly would have described himself as a merchant in his native quarters of north-west London. Others would have said he was something more than a stall-holder and something less than a shopkeeper. He dealt in things, pots and pans, wool, second-hand clothes, plates and knives and cups, buying them in bulk cheaply wherever he saw a bargain and trying to make a living off the profit. But business did not always go well for Girvan. Many of his suppliers had not been paid. Some of his customers found that the goods quite literally came apart in their hands. There were rumours that one or two of them were going to come and sort him out. In Kentish Town people knew what that meant. Free board and lodging for three months would be a godsend. So Connolly had pressed his remaining funds on his wife and fled. He doubted very much if his creditors would find him in Espalion or Figeac, Roncevalles or Burgos. He was on the run.

The great doors behind Delaney opened at this point and three steaming silver tureens of soup were carried in proudly by the waiters. It smelt of the countryside, of little farms up in the hills, of vegetables ripening under the sun. Alex Bentley had translated the details of the menu from the head waiter. He informed the company that this was known as Shepherd Soup. It had, he said, been cooked to this formula by shepherd mothers and shepherd wives for centuries up there in the vast desolate spaces of the Aubrac they would travel through in the coming days. From there it had passed into the culture of the wider Auvergne. The principal ingredients were the famous Le Puy lentils, flavoured with meat bones, carrots, turnips, swedes, local potatoes, a few chestnuts and whatever other delicacies the chef might have to hand. It went down very well with the dry white wine.

Beside Connolly, Delaney watched a forty-year-old Christian Brother in his black gown begin the attack on the soup. Brother White, Brother James White, taught Religion at one of the leading Catholic schools for boys in England. He felt the call to pilgrimage, as he had felt the call to join the Brothers all those years before. He knew he could do no other. He persuaded his abbot to give him leave of absence.

The waiters were clearing the empty plates now, filling up the glasses. Opposite Brother White was a prosperous gentleman of about fifty-five years, wearing a business suit with a flower in his buttonhole. He was quite short, and round, with a kindly face, looking as if he might be a sympathetic bank manager or a friendly headmaster. In fact, Stephen Lewis, a Delaney on his mother's side, was the senior partner at Daniel and Lewis, the leading firm of solicitors in the little town of Frome in Somerset. His children were grown up. His wife was more interested in the garden than in routes of pilgrimage. Stephen Lewis had two reasons for coming on this journey. He had always been passionate about railway travel. He did not intend to dirty his expensive boots walking across the dusty roads of France and Spain. Bentley had fixed it so that he could travel most of the way by train, and they would, he knew, be different sorts of train. Stephen Lewis could have told you about the different gauges operating in the two countries, the different sorts of engines that would pull the passengers, the different bridges they would cross. He had the *Baedeker Guide to European Train Travel* by his bedside. Lewis's second reason was much more irrational. He sold a lot of insurance policies in his office in Frome, looking out at the sluggish river and the dirty façade of the George Hotel where the stagecoach used to leave for London before the railways came. This pilgrimage was a form of insurance policy. It would, he felt, buy him a credit entry in God's bank, a favourable note in the celestial account book that might mean that the days the Lord his God gave him here on earth would be long and healthy. Beside him was the empty seat, the name John Delaney standing out in Alex Bentley's handwriting. The empty place troubled the pilgrims. It was as if there was a hole in the table, a gap left in a face where a malevolent tooth had just been extracted by the dentist.

Father Kennedy had enjoyed the soup. He took a second helping. He was fond of his food, Father Kennedy, punishing himself from time to time with days of fasting, but he never seemed to last out the full week he had promised himself at the start. Now the doors into the kitchen were opening again. Great dishes of vegetables were being brought in and placed

47

on the tables. Then the three waiters reappeared, each bearing an enormous earthenware pot. Even with the lids firmly on, the smell began to percolate through the dining room. One pot was placed in the centre of each table and the waiters whipped off the lids simultaneously. Steam now rose up to join the cooking aromas and the pilgrims peered forward to inspect the contents, a stew in a light brown sauce with all kinds of appetizing things floating on the surface.

'This', Alex Bentley began, reading from a note in front of him, 'is a delicacy of the region. Its name is *potée* or pork stew, and the original recipe comes from a local poet. This', he looked up brightly at his audience, 'is what it says: "Take a cabbage, a large succulent cabbage, firm and close and not too damaged by frost, a knuckle of pork with its bristle just singed, two lumps of pork fat, two good lumps, some fat and thin bacon on the turn but only just, turnips from the Planèze, Ussel or Lusclade."' The waiters were ladling out great helpings of the stuff. The young man Christy Delaney thought the recipe sounded more practical than poetic. Shane Delaney thought, disloyally, that this looked far better than anything his Sinead had ever produced in all their years of marriage. '"Add to the pot"', Bentley went on, '"a well-stuffed cockerel or an old hen, a knuckle of veal, a rib of beef. Put the meat in the pot, a goodly amount, don't be afraid, add some water, not too much, and some red wine and stew gently over a wood fire for four to five hours."'

There was a brief ripple of applause and then the pilgrims fell to, comparing notes on the taste and taking comforting gulps of their wine. It was Jack O'Driscoll who first noticed that something was wrong. He was sitting closest to the other set of doors that led out into the entrance foyer and he could hear raised voices. He thought one of them might belong to the hotel owner. Whatever else he was doing, Jack reflected ruefully, he didn't think the man was ordering a beer. Then the doors opened and the proprietor walked in, rather sheepishly. Nobody likes their guests being disturbed in the middle of the finest meal in the hotel repertoire. But it was his companions, a large elderly Sergeant of Police and two constables, who caused the decibel level to rise as the pilgrims gasped and asked each other what on earth was going on.

'Silence!' boomed the Sergeant. Alex Bentley thought he had grasped that bit. But most of what followed he did not, though the words he did understand filled him with horror. The Sergeant spoke for over a minute in thick guttural French. Then he looked round the room, waiting for a response. He spoke again, in a louder voice than before. Everybody looked at Alex Bentley.

'*Je ne comprends pas*,' he managed to blurt out at last, 'I don't understand.' The Sergeant spoke again. He stamped his large foot. He shook his fist at them. Michael Delaney thought the man was swearing at them. Then the Sergeant spoke in a quieter tone to the proprietor.

'Did you catch anything of what he said the first time?' Michael Delaney whispered to Alex Bentley.

'I think he said something about a dead man, about a corpse,' Bentley murmured back.

'Christ in heaven!' said Delaney and looked out towards the party at the door. The hotel man was pointing now, in the general direction of Michael Delaney and his companions on the top table. He's identifying us as the people in charge, Delaney guessed. The burly Sergeant beckoned to them to follow him and spoke some more words, very loudly and very slowly. Father Kennedy was reluctant to rise from his seat. He didn't want to leave his delicious stew. It might have gone cold by the time he got back to it. He followed the others slowly out of the dining room, the smell as heady as ever, the pilgrims open-mouthed, Girvan Connolly refilling his glass while he thought nobody was looking.

The Sergeant took them across the hotel entrance and through a door to the side of reception. He closed the door carefully behind them. Lying on a trolley beside the proprietor's desk, papers and receipts spilling over on to the floor, an old map of Le Puy on the wall, was what looked like a body totally covered from head to foot in a couple of blankets.

He shouted some more words in French. Then he pulled back the blankets briefly to reveal the mutilated corpse beneath. The face had been battered out of all recognition. One arm was hanging from his shoulder. Dark stains of dried blood covered his clothes. Then the Sergeant covered him up. He handed a wad of papers to Michael Delaney, pointing three times to his own breast pocket and then to the dead man to indicate that these had been found on his person. Great waves of sadness washed through Michael Delaney as he looked at the train tickets to Le Puy, at the names of the hotels, including the one where they now stood. There was a map of the pilgrim route to Santiago, sent by Alex Bentley to all those coming on pilgrimage. This corpse on the trolley was his cousin, John Delaney from England. The missing guest had turned up at last. But he hadn't come for a feast. He'd come for a funeral.

5

Father Kennedy began praying. *'Pater noster qui es in caelis*, Our Father who art in heaven . . . ' The Sergeant and his men closed their eyes. Michael Delaney continued staring sadly at the dead man's papers. Latin, Alex Bentley thought, the last universal language left. Maybe it would be easier to conduct the whole thing in Latin, the trial, if it came to that, adorned with Cicero returning from the dead in his finest toga to entertain the jury with his florid prose for the prosecution. When prayers were over, the Sergeant grabbed Michael Delaney by the arm and pointed to the map.

'St Michel d'Aiguilhe,' he shouted three times. Delaney stared at him.

'He's drawing our attention to that great pinnacle of rock, St Michel, sir,' said Bentley. 'Maybe that's where he died, the poor man.'

As if he had understood, the Sergeant drew a fat finger very slowly almost all the way to the top of the pinnacle. He had been making climbing noises with his feet. Then his finger dropped suddenly down the side.

'Tombé, peut-être?' he yelled.

'He fell, perhaps?' said Bentley, trying to put a question mark into his voice.

'Ou poussé!' The Sergeant turned round and pushed one of his men firmly in the back.

'Or he was pushed,' said Bentley.

'*On ne sait pas*,' the Sergeant said in a quieter tone with a Gallic shrug.

'We don't know.'

'*Alors*,' the Sergeant went on,

'Anyway,' said Bentley, feeling he was becoming proficient in translating one word at a time.

' . . . *le monsieur ici* . . . '

' . . . the gentleman here . . . '

' . . . *est trouvé au fond de St Michel*.' He pointed now at the very bottom of the rock, stabbing his finger into the surface of the glass repeatedly. '*À huit heures ce soir. Il est mort, naturellement*.'

'I think he's saying the body was found at the bottom of the rock at eight o'clock this evening, sir, but I'm not sure.' Alex Bentley felt you could have understood what had happened from the sign language alone. Maybe he hadn't done as well as he thought.

'*Aussi* . . . ' The Sergeant brought something out of his trouser pocket. He pointed twice to a jacket pocket and twice to the dead man. He handed the object over to Delaney. It was an Atlantic scallop shell, symbol of the pilgrim journey to Santiago for over a thousand years.

'I think they found it in the jacket pocket, sir.' Delaney held it in his hands. The dead man hadn't even started on his pilgrimage.

Delaney led them back to the dining room. He made signs to the Sergeant that he was about to speak. One constable had been put on guard duty at the door. The pilgrims were turning into prisoners.

'Friends, fellow pilgrims,' he began, 'I have some terrible news to give you. I have as yet, very few details. John Delaney,' he pointed sadly at the empty chair, the unopened napkin, the cutlery still in the correct position, the wine glasses untouched, 'John Delaney is dead. I believe the body was found at the bottom of the most distant rock pinnacle from here, the one they call St Michel.'

The pilgrims crossed themselves. Maggie Delaney hunted desperately for her rosary beads but couldn't find them. She made a grimace and started praying anyway. Stephen Lewis, the solicitor from Somerset, wondered if there were legal angles to come he could assist with. Then he reflected sadly that he didn't know very much about French law. He didn't think there were any French speakers in Frome. Probably there weren't any English speakers in Le Puy.

'For now, I think we should wait here until we can discover what the French authorities propose to do.'

Michael Delaney was a veteran of strange meetings, of meetings sulphurous and meetings argumentative and meetings violent. One of his competitors had once enlivened proceedings by pulling a gun on the Delaney company secretary. But he didn't think he had ever been in one as unusual as this. For the moment he was calm. The Sergeant was now sucking on his pencil and inspecting them all silently. The other constable had stationed himself by the kitchen doors as if to prevent escape through the stoves and pots and pans. And it was from the unlikely quarter of the kitchens that assistance came.

The head waiter was fairly sure that Alex Bentley was much happier with written rather than spoken French. He had after all translated the written menus very quickly earlier that day. The head waiter remembered a tribesman who was fluent in French for some reason, a legendary translator during the head waiter's days with the military in the Maghreb who had lost his tongue in some tribal vendetta. But his knowledge of Arabic and French was unimpaired. The French officers would make their prisoners write down their statements or their confessions in Arabic. Sitting cross-legged in his tent the man with no tongue would write the translations down in French and hand them over to his employers.

He wrote a brief message to Alex Bentley. He heard, but did not understand, the translation.

'Our friend here has a suggestion, sir,' said Alex. 'He will ask the Sergeant to write down in French what he wishes to say. I think I'll be able to translate most of that all right. Then you tell me in English what you want to say and I'll write it down in French. It might work, sir.'

Michael Delaney stared at him thoughtfully. 'Might take a lot of time. Never mind. Let's try it.'

The head waiter and a colleague departed briefly to the rest of their dining room and returned carrying a medium-sized table able to take four chairs. They brought a large writing book whose pages, Alex Bentley noticed, were not blank or ruled but filled with those impenetrable squares the French are so fond of. Alex wrote a brief message for the Sergeant. The Sergeant looked at him for a moment as if he thought the American was mad and then a slow look of recognition dawned on him. He grabbed a pen and began to write very slowly, pausing regularly to suck the bottom of the pen. French composition had never been his strong suit at school. Alex Bentley noticed that just as people shouted louder when speaking to foreigners, the Sergeant was writing in extra large letters. The pilgrims watched, spellbound. Girvan Connolly thought it would be permitted to refill his glass again; alcohol was always useful in the absorption of shock. Father Kennedy was staring sadly at his plate of congealed stew. It would never be the same now. At last the Sergeant stopped and passed the book over to Alex Bentley.

'This is it, sir,' Alex Bentley began, pausing every now and then to look down at his page, 'the Sergeant here is operating under the assumption that this may be a suspicious death. People in Le Puy, he says, don't go around pushing each other over the edge of St Michel. Nor do they go round throwing themselves off it. Most of them never go near the place. There hasn't been a death of any kind, murder or suicide, up there for at least twenty years. For the time being, we are all under suspicion, all of us here in this room. Nobody, for the time being, is allowed to leave Le Puy. Nobody is allowed to leave the hotel. The process of interviewing all the suspects, as he calls us, will begin in the morning, one person at a time.'

There was a moment of stunned silence. All the pilgrims began to talk at once. Jack O'Driscoll had been watching Michael Delaney very carefully all evening. Jack had made extensive inquiries about Delaney before he set off and knew the man had a fearful temper. After this piece of news, he felt, Delaney might be about to blow.

Michael Delaney banged his fist on the table. 'Quiet, please, quiet! Alex,' he shouted, 'this is monstrous! Monstrous! It's intolerable! We've come on a pilgrimage, for God's sake. Why can't we bury the poor man and move on? Haven't they got a policeman in this place who speaks English? Tell him I want to speak to the Chief Police Officer in the morning.'

Alex wrote as fast as he could. The reply was short.

'You're not going to like this, sir. He says the Chief Constable will not be available in the morning. The Sergeant is going now. He says he's late for his supper. It's always bad for his digestion, the Sergeant says, to be late for his supper. His wife doesn't like it either. He will see us here in the morning. His two men will be on duty here in the hotel all night, sir. To make sure nobody leaves.'

As Alex Bentley finished speaking, the Sergeant rose slowly to his feet and marched out of the room. One of his constables took up a position in the centre of the doors leading to the hotel foyer and the outside world. Delaney restrained himself with difficulty. He downed a glass of red wine at breakneck speed. A French priest, presumably the local curé, came in and began talking quietly to Father Kennedy in a corner of the room. Brother White joined his companions of the cloth. Wee Jimmy, who was closest to them, thought they were conversing about the funeral in a kind of prayer book Latin.

'Well, I'll be damned,' said Michael Delaney at last. 'Let's try and approach this thing in a businesslike manner.' It is one of the many differences between the French and the American character that the French attach great value to collective action. Fraternity. The Americans are suspicious of the state, and all in favour of individual initiative, of citizens taking responsibility for their own lives, rather than depending on others to do it for them.

'Damn French police,' Delaney began. 'Useless, completely useless. If I don't do anything else I'm going to get my own man to look into this death. Pinkerton's, Alex, what chance of Pinkerton's here in this dump?' Michael Delaney had an account with the great detective agency Pinkerton's in New York, enabling him to spy on his competitors all across the United States.

'I doubt if there are any Pinkertons to be found anywhere in Europe, sir.'

'Damn! We've got to find the top man,' said Delaney firmly, 'top private investigator fluent in English and French, able to drop whatever he's doing and start immediately. Money no object. Anybody got any ideas?'

He turned to Father Kennedy. God might have some ideas. Plenty of contacts, God. 'Your friend there, Father. Does he speak English?'

'I'm afraid not, Michael,' said Father Kennedy. 'We're conversing in Latin here.'

'God in heaven,' said Delaney. 'Alex, can you take your ouija board over there and ask the man to help us find this bilingual detective. Tell him to ask his bishop, for God's sake. And ask the bishop to ask his archbishop if he doesn't know. Not sure where we go after the archbishop. Anybody else got any suggestions?

Oddly enough, it was the youngest member of the party who had the best idea. He might have been only eighteen years old but Christy Delaney was a very intelligent young man. His parents moved in sophisticated circles in Dublin.

'Why don't you ask the Ambassadors, sir? Telegraph them in the morning. Ask them to find you such a man.'

Delaney, unusually for him, didn't understand at first. 'Ambassadors?' he said, looking at the young man in rather a patronizing way. 'Ambassadors plural? Why plural?'

'Sorry, sir,' said Christy, 'I didn't make myself clear.

Telegraph the American Ambassador in Paris and the American Ambassador in London. They may not know the name of such a person but they will certainly know someone who will.'

'Excellent, by God!' said Michael Delaney. 'Well done indeed. I'll do it first thing in the morning.' He wondered about offering the young man a job in the Delaney organization on the spot.

As the pilgrims made off towards bed, Father Kennedy was the last to leave. The food had all been cleared away. Looking wistfully at the doors leading to the kitchen he wondered what he had missed for pudding.

The French telegraph system was busy the following morning. Alex Bentley sent Delaney's messages to the two American Ambassadors very early in the day. The priest sent word to his superiors. The Bishop of Le Puy was concerned not just about the death of a pilgrim in his diocese but about the damage that could be done to the good name of the town and its cathedral and the practice of pilgrimage itself. When he had dispatched his pleas for help to his brothers in Christ, the Archbishops of Lyons and Bordeaux and the Cardinal Archbishop of Toulouse, he sent word to the beleaguered pilgrims in the hotel. The Church, he assured them, would pray for their safe journey onwards in every service in the cathedral from this morning on. He himself proposed visiting the pilgrims in their hotel and, if possible, organizing some sort of service for the soul of the departed Delaney.

The American Ambassador in Paris, Bulstrode P. Wilson, had been in post for a number of years now. He knew France well. He thought he had dealt with every difficulty his fellow countrymen could encounter on their voyages to the strange lands of Europe. Pilgrims were new to him. He sighed wearily to his assistant that morning. 'Get me the Minister of the Interior on the phone,' he said, 'then the President's Private

Secretary. And now I think about it, I'd better speak to the British Ambassador when I've finished with them.'

The Archbishop of Lyons did not speak English. He knew of no detectives. Privately he did not approve of these foreigners coming to France and murdering each other on French soil. To the Bishop of Le Puy he conveyed his inability to offer assistance on this occasion. The Archbishop of Bordeaux wanted very much to help these pilgrims for they and their successors would pass through some of his diocese on their way to Compostela. Honour and fame would attach themselves to his archbishopric. His congregation could only benefit, materially and spiritually, from the passage of these devout souls. But the Archbishop knew no English, he knew no policemen, he could only guess what a private investigator actually did. He too sent his regrets.

In the hotel the pilgrims were remarkably sanguine. Delaney had wondered if there would be a call to rebellion, people wanting to pack in the whole thing and return home. Father Kennedy reassured the doubters that they were doing God's work. Alex Bentley and his notebook began the long process of translating for the Sergeant, returned to the St Jacques shortly after ten in the morning, as he began the interviews with every member of the party. Charlie Flanagan found himself another fine piece of wood in the hotel woodshed and began another carving. Jack O'Driscoll and Christy Delaney went to work on improving their French by ordering more beers in the hotel bar.

The Cardinal Archbishop of Toulouse was a more worldly sort of churchman. He was a secret devotee of the works of Sir Arthur Conan Doyle. In his mind's eye, for he knew Le Puy well, he could see Sherlock Holmes, cane in hand, striding up the little path that led up to the summit of St Michel, Dr Watson panting at his heels. The Cardinal was a veteran of ecclesiastical politics. He liked to think that his work in God's cause had led to the election of the previous Pope. His enemies – and he had many – called him a plotter and an intriguer. He preferred to think of his activities as guiding his colleagues who might suffer from confusion and uncertainty into the right path, into voting for his candidate. The Cardinal hoped to live long enough to take part in the next Conclave to elect another Pope when the current one was called home. Maybe he should stand himself. The quest for this detective touched a distant chord with the Cardinal. Somewhere, he knew, at some international gathering not very long ago, he had met a fellow Prince of the Church who had talked to him of such a man, but he could remember for the moment neither the name of his colleague nor the name of the investigator. He sent word that he was making inquiries and praying for God's guidance. He would be in touch.

Whitelaw Reid, the American Ambassador Extraordinary and Plenipotentiary to the Court of St James's, had enjoyed a long and distinguished career in journalism and politics. He had served as the special representative of the US Government at the coronation of Edward the Seventh. He had been Ambassador in Paris before his present posting. He too summoned his assistant. 'Get me the Commissioner of the Metropolitan Police,' he said. 'Tell them it's urgent. Tell them they're to pull him out of whatever damned meeting he's in and bring him to the phone.'

Sir Edward Henry, the Commissioner, came on the line straight away. He listened carefully as Reid put forward before him the little he knew.

'You've come to the right place, Mr Ambassador,' he began. 'I believe we do have such a man in this country, though I do not know if he is available at present. Let me fill you in on his career. He served in the Army as an intelligence officer. Then he took up work as an investigator. He was involved some years ago – this is for your ears only, Mr Ambassador – in some delicate work involving the household of the then Prince of Wales. He was sent by Prime Minister Salisbury to reorganize Army Intelligence in the Boer War. He's solved murders in the world of art and in a leading West Country cathedral. Recently he was dispatched by our Foreign Office to look into the mysterious death of a British diplomat in St Petersburg where, as you know as well as I do, he will have had to speak French. He's charming, he's clever and he has a very attractive wife.'

'What's his name?' said Reid.

'Our friend is called Lord Francis Powerscourt. I have been looking for his address for you while we speak. He lives at 24 Markham Square, Chelsea.'

'Commissioner, I am more than grateful. If there's anything my country can do for you in return, just let me know.'

'Just one other thing, Mr Ambassador,' said the Commissioner. 'If you want a second opinion, could I suggest you get in touch with Lord Rosebery, our former Prime Minister? He's long been a great friend of the Powerscourt family.'

'Thank you, sir,' said the Ambassador. 'Thank you so much.'

'Right, young man,' Ambassador Reid turned to the languid young man beside him, 'this is what I want you to do. Take a cab. Go to 24 Markham Square. Find me Lord Francis Powerscourt and bring him straight back here. Immediately. You got that?'

'Yes, sir,' said the young man, heading for the door at considerable speed.

'You'd better take him this cable so he can see what's going on.' James Whitney took the message from his master and hurried off through the wet streets of London. It was shortly after eleven o'clock in the morning.

Lord Francis Powerscourt was sitting in his favourite armchair by the fireplace in his upstairs drawing room reading a pamphlet by the suffragettes. He was just under six feet tall with curly brown hair and deep blue eyes that inspected the world with interest mixed with irony. He found some of the suffragette arguments quite convincing. His wife Lady Lucy was looking at the catalogue for a forthcoming auction of antique furniture. There was a loud knock at the front door and Rhys, the Powerscourt butler, slipped into the room.

He coughed. Rhys always coughed. 'There's a young man to see you, sir. From the American Embassy, sir. Mr James Whitney.'

The young man strode into the room and shook Powerscourt and Lady Lucy firmly by the hand.

'Please forgive me for rushing in like this, sir, but my mission is most urgent. Ambassador Reid has sent me here to bring you to him at once. It's terribly urgent, sir.'

Powerscourt smiled at the young man. 'Am I being kidnapped by American forces, Mr Whitney? May I not learn something of what all this is about?'

'My orders are to bring you at once, Lord Powerscourt. I have a cable for you to read on the way. My cab is waiting.'

'Well,' said Powerscourt, 'I will come with you. You will remember, Lucy, the circumstances of my departure, virtually taken prisoner by our young friend here.' With that he kissed her goodbye and was escorted off towards the American Embassy.

As they rattled along in their cab Powerscourt found himself fascinated by the little he learned from Delaney's cable. The case interested him. A band of pilgrims marching towards a holy shrine as people had done in centuries past to Canterbury or Rome. Some of these towns on the route he knew already, Conques and Figeac and Cahors. He had always wanted to see the cloisters at Moissac. Roncesvalles in the Pyrenees spelt high romance with the death and the *Chanson de Roland*. Pamplona, he thought, had something to do with bulls.

'Lord Powerscourt.' Ambassador Reid had risen from his desk to greet his visitor. 'Thank you so much for coming so promptly. Thank you indeed.'

'I had little choice, Mr Ambassador,' said Powerscourt with a smile. 'Your young man here virtually carried me off at gunpoint.'

The Ambassador laughed. 'Tell me, Lord Powerscourt, now you have read that cable you know about as much as we do. What do you think of it?'

'I think the immediate position is difficult, Mr Ambassador. They can be very obstinate, these French policemen, and the French bureaucracy is never quick. Maybe Mr Delaney needs to put his hand in his pocket.'

'What do you mean, put his hand in his pocket?' said the American quickly. He didn't want to see his Embassy and his country dragged through the courts of Le Puy on charges of bribery and corruption.

'I don't mean pressing notes into the hands or the pockets of this Sergeant and his men, Mr Ambassador,' said Powerscourt with a smile. 'I was wondering about a contribution to the restoration fund of the cathedral, maybe. These ancient buildings swallow money whole, as you know. Another contribution or even the endowment of a charity to look after the widows and orphans of the local police force, something like that, perhaps?'

Whitelaw Reid had known as soon as he heard the Commissioner's description that this was his man. Now he was certain.

'Lord Powerscourt,' said Ambassador Reid, 'let's not beat about the bush. Will you take the case?'

'I will,' said Powerscourt.

'Excellent,' said the Ambassador. 'May I tell Delaney the news?'

'You may,' said Powerscourt.

'Is it too soon to ask how soon you will be able to depart?'

'Well,' said Powerscourt, 'let me see. I would like, with your permission, to bring my wife along in the first instance. Her French is better than mine. Two translators will be better than one. I have one or two commissions I would like to perform before we go. I wish to brief my companion in arms Johnny Fitzgerald about the case and to leave him here for now. It may be necessary to pursue various inquiries here or in

Ireland about the background of some of these pilgrims. I hope we could set off this afternoon, Mr Ambassador.'

'Very good, Lord Powerscourt, that all sounds in order. May I thank you again for taking the case on. Let me quote the words of your poet John Bunyan, if I may, with yourself in the role of the pilgrim:

> He who would valiant be
> 'Gainst all disaster,
> Let him in constancy
> Follow the Master.
> There's no discouragement
> Shall make him once relent
> His first avowed intent
> To be a pilgrim.

'May I wish you God speed, Lord Powerscourt.'

'Thank you,' said Powerscourt. 'Who knows? Perhaps we shall meet true valour on the way.'

6

Michael Delaney thought his pilgrims were bearing up remarkably well as they neared the end of their third day of incarceration in the Hôtel St Jacques. They knew that a miracle worker called Lord Francis Powerscourt and his wife were travelling through France at breakneck speed to help them. Father Kennedy had organized little prayer meetings in his room for interested parties. Patrick MacLoughlin, the trainee priest from Boston, was a regular participant. Shane Delaney, the man on pilgrimage for the life of his wife Sinead, had written her a long letter. In his first draft he waxed lyrical, for Shane, on the subject of the food. Then he could hear his wife's voice in his ear: 'What in God's name do you think you are doing, Shane Delaney, here's me dying now in a rainy Swindon, and all you can do is tell me about the feasts of French food in some place I can't pronounce, all stuffed out with that disgusting garlic, no doubt. You're not on some bloody holiday, Shane Delaney; if you've got nothing better to do while you're stuck in this hotel, get down on your bloody knees and pray for me. That's what you're there for, in heaven's name.' So Shane had torn that version up and composed another letter which might not have been one hundred per cent accurate, but would surely save him from the wrath of Swindon. He talked of regular prayer meetings with Father Kennedy. He said he was going to pray for her in front of the Black Madonna in the cathedral. He mentioned, towards the end of his letter, which nearly filled a page, that the Bishop of Le Puy would be coming to visit them in the next day or two. Sinead had always had a weakness for the church hierarchy, monsignors better than priests, abbots better than monsignors, bishops better than nearly everyone else. Shane Delaney did not mention the death of John Delaney. If he had, he was sure, he would be summoned home on the next train.

Waldo Mulligan, the man who worked for the senator in Washington, had come on pilgrimage to break off an affair he had been having with a colleague's wife. The woman's name was Caroline. To his horror he found during these days in the hotel that Caroline had followed him across the Atlantic. He saw her slender form and dark hair disappearing round the corridors of the Hôtel St Jacques. At night she came to him in his dreams, turning into a wraith and vanishing when he reached out to touch her on the other side of his bed. He didn't know what to do. He found that the hotel bar had a good supply of Irish whiskey and Waldo would sit by himself in some dark corner twirling his drink round the glass and nursing his broken heart.

Christy Delaney and Jack O'Driscoll had been making good progress in their French language lessons at the other end of the bar. They could now order glasses of red or white wine, cognac or pastis. They had advanced to Thank You and Good Afternoon and Good Morning and Good Evening. In his spare time Jack had begun writing his account of recent events for his newspaper. He kept it factual. Jack always remembered the grizzled chief sub-editor on his first paper, the *Wicklow Times*, telling him, as he struck his red pencil through the offending words, 'We don't want any of your bloody adjectives here, and we don't want any of your bloody adverbs either.'

Brother White, the Christian Brother who taught at one of the leading Catholic public schools for boys in England, seemed to all who looked at him or spoke with him to be a man at peace with himself. Inside he was in turmoil. He had a secret, a rather terrible secret. Brother James White liked beating boys. He enjoyed it very much. He could still remember the very first caning he had administered years before. It had been on a Saturday afternoon in the summer term and the boy had failed to hand in his maths homework three days in a row. Outside he could hear the shouts of the cricketers as they appealed for leg before wicket or caught behind. Before the first stroke, the boy's body stretched taut leaning over a chair, Brother White felt a small frisson passing through him. His first three blows, he remembered, had been wide of the mark, landing on the top of the legs or the very bottom of the back. The last three had struck home, the whish of the cane alternating with the whimper of the victim. From then on, Brother White beat as many boys as he could. He had a wide selection of instruments now, hidden in his cupboard, the thinnest cane reserved for the occasions when he wanted to inflict the maximum pain. He had tried to stop. He had prayed for guidance. It was no good. Once he had beaten an entire class in the course of an afternoon as they failed to own up to breaking a window. On very rare occasions, he beat boys he really disliked with their trousers down and with his thinnest cane. That always gave him special pleasure. He was always careful not to draw blood. It was now fifteen days since he had last beaten anybody. That last victim had left his room with tears running down his face, only turning at the door to catch the look of guilty pleasure that had spread all over Brother White's features. I'm like an alcoholic now, he said to himself sadly, all I can think of is the next beating. Alone in his spartan room in the Hôtel St Jacques in Le Puy-en-Velay, Brother James White found himself remembering his favourite beatings as others would remember favourite evenings at the theatre or visits to the National Gallery.

The chef, Michael Delaney would have been the first to admit, had been a major contributor to the bonhomie of his pilgrims. A succession of delicious dinners had been served with delicate tomato soup or coarse local pâté, roast guinea fowl or navarin of lamb, *tarte tatin*, which the chef felt sure his visitors would never have tasted in their places of culinary darkness. Father Kennedy rather wished he could stay for ever, or at least until the chef had exhausted his repertoire. Even then, the Father felt, he could have happily gone back to the beginning and started all over again. The head waiter had been varying the seating plan, tables of four alternating with tables of six or eight. They were all working their way through a *tarte aux myrtilles* when the doors were flung open by the proprietor, and a tall man with curly brown hair in a dark blue travelling cape and a woman with a very elaborate hat strode into the dining room.

'Please don't get up,' said the man with a smile, as chairs began edging backwards amid a rustling of feet. 'My name is Powerscourt, Francis Powerscourt, and this is my wife Lucy.' He offered her forward as one might offer a trophy to the winner of the Derby.

'Why,' said Michael Delaney, 'welcome, Lord Powerscourt, Lady Powerscourt! Welcome indeed! I have had these two spaces on either side of mine ready for you for the past two days.' He pointed to two empty chairs, places set, as a single place had been set for John Delaney days before. 'Do you need food? Are you hungry?'

Powerscourt assured him that they were in no need of food and asked for introductions. When he asked Lady Lucy later that evening how many names she could remember from this first encounter, she managed twelve. Powerscourt had got stuck on nine. Lucy was always better at remembering names than he was. He claimed it was because she belonged to such a large family and would be cast into outer darkness if she could not recall the name of some distant cousin from the depths of Shropshire. As Powerscourt shook hands with the pilgrims he was saying to himself, One of you is a murderer. Is it you? But answers came there none. Maggie Delaney simpered over Lady Lucy for some time, delighted to have another woman on the premises. When the pilgrims returned to their *tarte aux myrtilles*, Powerscourt and Lady Lucy joined Delaney and Alex Bentley and Father Kennedy at a table set back from the others.

'Tell me, Mr Delaney, what has happened since you sent your telegram?'

Delaney grimaced. 'Not a lot, if I'm honest with you, Lord Powerscourt. We're still locked up here. We're not allowed out at all. Nine people have been interviewed so far. Alex here does his best but it's very slow work.'

Alex Bentley explained the bizarre method of translating they had been forced to adopt.

'A book, do you say, Mr Bentley? Are the questions and the answers written down in the same book?'

'Yes, they are,' said the young man.

'And where is the book now? Does the Sergeant take it away with him when he leaves?'

'He does, usually. But he left it behind today. I think he was in a hurry. He said something, I think, about his wife's mother coming over.'

'So do you have this book in your room, or the room where the interviews take place?'

'I do.'

'Could you copy it before morning, before the Sergeant comes back?'

'Of course,' said Alex Bentley, and rose to begin the process of turning himself into the scribe of Le Puy.

'Don't go yet,' said Powerscourt. 'Having access to that information could make my life easier, Mr Delaney,' he added. He didn't say that he would have access through the book to what nine of the pilgrims had told the authorities about where they were on the day John Delaney died. He leant forward and helped himself to the last slice of the *tarte aux myrtilles*. Lady Lucy declined. Father Kennedy watched it go rather wistfully. He thought he had enough room for one more helping.

'Let me tell you, gentlemen, my current thoughts. I have been thinking about this situation on the train. In one sense, there is a paradox at the centre of affairs. You have employed me, Mr Delaney, to find out who killed your cousin John. If you are an investigator, what could be better than to have all the suspects cooped up in one place? They can't go out. They're in a sort of sealed box where the investigator can have access to them whenever he wants. But that doesn't suit your particular circumstances. You are here on pilgrimage. You want to move on, all of you.'

'Of course we want to move on,' said Michael Delaney with feeling. 'The question is, how do we do it?'

'Well,' said Powerscourt, 'the first thing is to speed up the process of translation. Lady Lucy or I will translate tomorrow for the Sergeant for a start. You see, I don't think these people can be persuaded to let you go until the due processes have been completed. I'm not familiar enough with French police procedure to know what is meant to happen next. But I think the time has come to take the initiative.'

Michael Delaney cheered up at this point. He had always believed that in business, if you didn't take the initiative, somebody else would do it for you and you would lose the deal. Alex Bentley was wondering if this Lord Powerscourt might not be as formidable an operator in his special field as Delaney was in his.

'Tomorrow morning — ' Powerscourt began, and then stopped as the rest of the pilgrims began drifting out of the room. He turned to face them. 'Gentlemen, Miss Delaney, my apologies, I noticed a facility for posting letters in the hotel entrance on my way in here this evening. Have any of you actually posted a message to what we might call the outside world? If you have, would you be so kind as to let me know before you leave the room?

'Tomorrow morning', he continued, looking back at Michael Delaney, 'I have interviews booked with the Mayor of Le Puy, with the Chief of Police in the town and with the Bishop. I telegraphed from Calais to a young man who works for the American Ambassador in London and asked him to arrange them. I think the Mayor may be the key, they're very influential people in France, these Mayors. With your permission, Mr Delaney, I propose to mention money to them. Obviously it will be your money. Do you have any objections?'

'None at all,' said Delaney with a smile. The man had only just arrived and already he was talking about bribing a bishop and a Chief of Police. This was progress indeed. This Powerscourt could have a great career in American business. Alex Bentley didn't think anything as crude as bribery was going to be employed. He felt Powerscourt was holding back as much as he was divulging about his plans.

Powerscourt noticed two pilgrims hanging back rather sheepishly by the door. 'Excuse me, Lucy, Mr Delaney,' he said, and walked over to join them. As he talked to the first one, the second drifted off to a far corner of the dining room.

'Delaney, Lord Powerscourt, sir, Shane Delaney from Swindon in England, sir. I'm very sorry sir, but I wrote a letter to my wife, Sinead. She's dying, you see, sir, of some incurable disease and I'm here to take her place. She's too ill to travel. She can only just get down the road to her mother's, if you follow me.'

'My sympathy goes out to you and your wife,' said Powerscourt solemnly. 'May I ask what the letter said? In general terms, of course.'

'Well, sir, in the first version I talked about the food a lot. Your man the chef here is a wizard in the kitchen, as you will see. Then I thought she might get mad at me, filling my face with fancy cooking while she's dying slowly back there in Swindon. So I tore that one up, sir. The one I did send I just talked about praying with Father Kennedy and the Black Madonna up there in the cathedral and how the Bishop might come and see us. That's all, sir, cross my heart and hope to die.'

'You didn't mention the death of John Delaney at all?' asked Powerscourt.

'Good God no, sir. She'd have had me on the next train home if I had, so she would.'

Powerscourt smiled and said no harm would come of it. Jack O'Driscoll was unrepentant about writing an article for his paper, which included a lot of detail about the death. But, he assured Powerscourt, he hadn't sent it yet. Indeed, he hadn't finished it. 'The trouble with stories like this, Lord Powerscourt,' said Jack in his most man of the world voice, 'is that the readers expect a proper ending, so they do. They don't like being left hanging in the air.'

Powerscourt nodded his agreement. He said he could see the difficulty. But he made the young man promise that he would only send the article after he, Lord Powerscourt, had seen it and approved it. Jack O'Driscoll showed unusual maturity for a young reporter. 'Of course, Lord Powerscourt, I can see that. I wouldn't want to get in the way of a murder investigation, if this is a murder investigation. That's much more important than a newspaper article.'

As Powerscourt watched Jack O'Driscoll take the stairs two at a time he thought he had found another weapon in his quest, one that might prove much more potent than the young reporter knew. And then he remembered, one or other of the two people he had just spoken to might be a murderer.

'Francis,' said Lady Lucy later, in bed reading a book about pilgrimages, 'you're not really going to bribe these people in the morning, are you?'

Her husband was staring at the ceiling, his mind far away. 'What's that, Lucy?' he said, returning to earth. 'Of course I'm not going to bribe them. Not in the orthodox way at any rate. We have to convince the authorities, Lucy, that it's their idea, or in their best interests, to let the pilgrims go, not ours. We have to work things so that they think they have thought of it first.'

'And just how are you going to do it, my love?' said Lady

Lucy, taking temporary possession of her husband's left shoulder.

'Well,' said Powerscourt, 'it might work out like this . . . '

Early the next morning Lord Francis Powerscourt wrapped his dark blue cape round his shoulders and set off for a quick look round Le Puy-en-Velay. He bought two large black notebooks in a Maison de la Presse, a French newsagent, the pages filled with those irritating squares. He checked out the Town Hall – the Hôtel de Ville – the French tricolour flying from the flagpole, in the Place du Martouret, a handsome square with a plaque that told him that the guillotine had been installed here during the Revolution between March 1793 and January 1795. Forty-one citizens had been put to death in this little town. The memory of the French Revolution was everywhere, Powerscourt thought. It might have happened over a century before but the footprints were still there, all over the Republic it had created, wading through blood and terror.

There was a gasp in the dining room of the Hôtel St Jacques when Powerscourt took off his cape and sat down to breakfast. He was wearing full military uniform, the black trousers and scarlet jacket of a colonel in the Irish Guards, medals marching across his chest, gold epaulettes on his shoulders. Lady Lucy smiled when she saw the effect. She thought her Francis looked very handsome. Charlie Flanagan dropped a croissant on the floor. Christy Delaney was in the middle of ordering more *pain au chocolat* and coffee from a pretty waitress, and his newfound French deserted him.

'It's for the Sergeant,' Powerscourt assured Delaney. 'Pound to a penny he was in the military before he joined the police. Uniforms always impress other people in uniform. Mine's more important than his. Colonel in the Irish Guards beats French police sergeant any day of the week. So he's supposed to think I am, so to speak, the superior officer.'

Michael Delaney laughed and clapped Powerscourt on the back. 'Well done, man. I'm sure that will help with our policeman friend.'

'This is the original interview book,' said Alex Bentley to Powerscourt and handed over a large notebook. 'I have the earlier notes upstairs.'

'Excellent,' said Powerscourt and hurried across the room to greet the Sergeant who had just appeared.

'*Enchanté*,' he said in his best French accent. 'I am delighted to meet you, Sergeant. I am so sorry we have caused you so many problems here with our inability to speak French.'

The Sergeant muttered something inaudible, mesmerized by Powerscourt's medals.

'You are a soldier, monsieur?' he managed finally. He had known of a milord detective coming but not that he was a full colonel milord with campaign ribbons.

'Was, Sergeant, was, those days are behind me now, alas. Never mind, once a soldier, always a soldier, eh? Have you served your country in war as well as peace, Sergeant?'

The Sergeant replied that he had indeed served, in the Army in North Africa, and had risen to the rank of lance corporal after seven years' service. Promotion, Powerscourt felt, might be quicker in the police rather than the military. He pressed on, anxious to make the maximum benefit of his advantage.

'May I have the honour of presenting my wife, Sergeant? Lady Lucy Powerscourt, Sergeant Fayolle.'

Lady Lucy bowed slightly and then shook the man's hand. The skin, she felt, was rather coarse.

'I hope to have the honour of translating for you later today, Sergeant,' Powerscourt went on, 'but this morning I propose that Lady Lucy should do it. She is a most experienced translator, my friend.' Powerscourt patted the Sergeant on the back at this point. 'Why, only this year she translated at a joint meeting between members of your Assembly and our members of Parliament in London on the subject of African colonies, a most delicate subject, as you know.'

Lady Lucy blushed slightly. Francis had told her that morning that he might invent a previous translating career for her if he felt it would help. The Sergeant looked at Lady Lucy and reflected sadly that she was much more attractive than his own Colette whom he had left scowling at her saucepans earlier that morning. Damn it, the Sergeant said to himself, not only did the man have the scarlet uniform of a full colonel, but he had a wife to match as well.

Powerscourt was anxious now for the translation to start. New circumstances called for a new location. A small section of the dining room had been cordoned off, the rest closed in case of eavesdroppers. He led the Sergeant and Lady Lucy to their seats. Alex Bentley, who had appointed himself knight errant to Lady Lucy for today, if not for the rest of his life, brought the relevant paperwork and the list of people to be interviewed that day and sat down beside Lady Lucy. Powerscourt withdrew. Delaney winked at him. 'Fine piece of business there, Lord Powerscourt. Reckon we've got the Sergeant on the back foot now. Let's hope we can keep him there.'

'Wish me luck,' said Powerscourt, drawing on his cape once more. 'I'm off to meet the Mayor, official representative of the Third Republic. *Liberté, Égalité, Fraternité*, that's the motto for the day!'

Powerscourt wondered if the Mayor would have a pair of tricolours leaning against each other in his office. There they were, by one of the great windows looking out over the square. M. Louis Jacquet, the Mayor of le Puy for the past fifteen years, was a tubby man with greying hair in his early fifties. He had a small moustache and searching blue eyes. By profession he was a butcher, and although he had handed over much of the running of his business to his eldest son, he still kept a keen interest. The shop, Jacquet et Fils, Bouchers et Vollailers on the Rue Raphael, prospered greatly for the *citoyennes* thought it might be more advantageous to purchase their *gigots d'agneau* and their *filet de boeuf* from the Mayor than from his competitors.

Compliments were exchanged, on the military service, on the beauty of the town, on the Colonel's colours and the ancient traditions of Le Puy.

'Please allow me to present my credentials,' said Powerscourt, extracting a typewritten letter, written on very expensive notepaper, from his pocket. The missive assured its readers that Lord Francis Powerscourt had a most distinguished record as an investigator in Great Britain. On a number of occasions, it continued, he had given exemplary service to his country. The letter asked the recipient to afford Lord Francis Powerscourt every possible assistance for he was a man of integrity and judgement. The signature at the bottom was Sir Edward Grey, His Britannic Majesty's Secretary of State for Foreign Affairs. Powerscourt had obtained the introduction on the day he left London. Since I was almost killed on the Foreign Office's business in St Petersburg last year, he had said to himself, then the least they can do is to write me a letter.

'You bring heavy artillery with you,' said the Mayor, handing it back to Powerscourt. 'Pray tell me, how I can be of assistance?'

'I need advice, Mr Mayor,' said Powerscourt. 'I need the benefit of your experience here in this town. On the one hand, we have the pilgrims, this strange collection assembled here from two continents by Mr Delaney. I think we should remember that the whole thing has been organized by Delaney as a thank-you to God for saving the life of his son. You know, no doubt, about the dead man, fallen or pushed from the rock of St Michel. You know the pilgrims are cooped up in that hotel, unable to leave until the police interviews are completed. You know the pilgrims want to bury the dead man and move on to their pilgrimage. So, that is one set of facts, as it were.'

The Mayor nodded. 'On the other hand,' Powerscourt went on, 'we have the position of the police. They have to investigate the death, or, as it may be, murder.'

'Please forgive me for interrupting,' said the Mayor. 'Do you think it was murder, Lord Powerscourt?'

Powerscourt felt suddenly that considerable weight would be attached to his answer. He had no alternative but to tell the truth as he saw it.

'I do not, as yet, know the full facts, Mr Mayor. It seems to me perfectly possible that he fell. I hope to make the climb myself this afternoon or tomorrow. But I would not rule out murder, not at this stage.'

'Pray continue,' said the Mayor.

'I was speaking of the position of the police. They are looking for a possible killer. Why should they let the pilgrims go? Why not keep them locked up in the Hôtel St Jacques until they find out the truth? There is deadlock here.'

'I have been concerned about this affair ever since I first heard of it,' said the Mayor. 'I am concerned, above all, for the good name and reputation of Le Puy. My father too was a butcher, here in this town. He was also Mayor. So was his father before him. I would not have you believe that the Jacquet butchers are a sort of *ancien régime* here but we do go back a long way. During the Revolution a company of butchers, including one of my ancestors, saved the Chapel of the White Penitents up there by the cathedral from destruction. We Jacquets have always been proud of that.'

'Could I throw in a couple of other facts that might be relevant?' asked Powerscourt. 'The first concerns this man Michael Delaney. I scarcely know him but I am empowered to speak for him this morning. These American millionaires, as you know, Mr Mayor, are men of almost unimaginable wealth. As they grow older they start to give their money away. They found libraries. They set up charitable foundations in their names. They amass great collections of paintings which they may leave to the nation.'

'Are they trying to cheat death, do you suppose? To gain immortality by other means?'

'Yes, I think that is very well put. Our Mr Delaney wishes to leave money to Le Puy. I do not know if he intends to scatter his gold across the pilgrim path like the scallop shells of old. A donation for the upkeep of the cathedral is in his mind. And some gift to the town to be made through the good offices of your own office, Mr Mayor. Maybe some assistance to look after the widows and orphans of the police force.'

'None of which can happen', Louis Jacquet cut in quickly, 'if Mr Delaney remains a prisoner in the Hôtel St Jacques.'

Powerscourt nodded. He thought he would play his ace of trumps. He hadn't been sure until now. 'Pilgrims made Le Puy rich, as you know far better than I, Mr Mayor. Pilgrims paid for the cathedral and all those fine buildings in the upper town. You must have wondered if this Delaney pilgrimage, bizarre in its origins, unfortunate, maybe even cursed in its beginning, might mark the start of a revival. Maybe pilgrims will choke the streets in future as they did in the Middle Ages. Le Puy would become even more prosperous. But I am not convinced they would come if they thought they might be locked up in their hotel for days at a time. Pilgrims might go elsewhere, they might start in Vézelay, or further south in Arles. And one last thought for your consideration.' Here it came, the Ace of Spades, as black as the Black Madonna in the Cathedral of Notre Dame. 'There is a young man in the Delaney party who is a newspaperman, a reporter. He is writing an article for his paper in Dublin. I have not seen it but I fear its publication would not do much for the reputation of this town abroad. They are all incensed, the pilgrims, about what they see as the incompetence of the police. I have asked him not to send it without my permission but I may not be able to hold him back for ever.'

'Thank you for being so frank,' said the Mayor. 'It is a most tricky problem.' He stared out of his window into the Place du Martouret outside. 'Let me ask you a most improper question, Lord Powerscourt. I give you my word that your answer will not go beyond these four walls where we sit now. You are known as a man of integrity. Let me ask you for your opinion, your advice, if you were not a man of integrity. Please pretend to be Machiavelli for a moment, if you would.'

Powerscourt thought very fast. Should he decline the gambit? Should he take it? He looked briefly at a portrait of the current President of France, Armand Fallières, on the wall. History would come to help him. He took the gambit.

'When I was young, Mr Mayor,' he began, 'I was fascinated by two of the great cardinals who gave such wise, if devious, advice to their kings, Cardinal Richelieu and Cardinal Mazarin. Even looking at their portraits you could tell that they too were Machiavellian in their approach. I speak now as Cardinal Mazarin. This is what I think he would say. Get rid of the pilgrims as fast as you can. Suppose the police do find the murderer, if there is one. There will have to be a trial. Do you want these witnesses to take up permanent residence in the Hôtel St Jacques? Do you want the English and American newspapers writing articles about St Michel, Crag of Death? Horror Strikes in Holy City? Let the murderer be found in some other place, some other town. Let *them* have the problems of solving the crime and the problems of the prosecution. Put the wretched pilgrims on the first train, carriage or horse you can find and bid them God speed.

'Once they know they're going,' Mazarin Powerscourt was getting into his stride now, 'you can start on Michael Delaney. He would feel grateful, would he not, for the liberation of his friends. Take him for every charity you can think of. Separate him from as many dollars as you can. Sleep easier in your beds. The problem is not with you any more, the problem is en route to the little town of Saugues, next stop, I think, on the pilgrims' way.'

Powerscourt laughed. 'How was that, Mr Mayor?'

Louis Jacquet laughed. 'Very good, Lord Powerscourt. I think you're in the wrong profession. You should have been a politician. There's still time, mind you, there's still time.'

Back in the Hôtel St Jacques things were moving fast. With Lady Lucy as translator and Alex Bentley as transcriber the witnesses were being polished off at remarkable speed. Lady Lucy was using all her wiles on the Sergeant, a little smile here, an occasional request for assistance with a particular word there, interested queries about his grandchildren in the intervals between witnesses. The Sergeant was captivated. Had she but known it, Lady Lucy was surrounded on both sides by admirers, though the Sergeant did not fit the description of knight errant as well as Alex Bentley. Father Kennedy was surprisingly nervous as he gave his account of the day of John Delaney's death. Brother White was monosyllabic, thinking perhaps of all the possible beatings he was going to miss during his time away on pilgrimage. The clearest witness was Stephen Lewis, the solicitor from Frome in Somerset. He had only had occasional dealings with the criminal classes of Frome. One of his colleagues looked after those, but he knew what was required, clear and unambiguous reporting of his activities that day, refusal to be drawn into any speculation about any of the other suspects, a pleasant and open countenance. As she listened to them all Lady Lucy thought that any one of them could have been a murderer. All their statements, even a few days after the event, were woolly about exact times. The Sergeant even allowed the last interview to run on beyond the sacred hour of twelve o'clock, lunchtime for all God-fearing Frenchmen, and ended the morning session at four minutes past. There was only one interview left now, Michael Delaney himself, due at two o'clock sharp.

After he left the Town Hall, wondering if he had given too much away, Powerscourt climbed up the Rue Meymard and the Rue Cardinal de Polignac to the Bishop's Palace beneath the cathedral. It was uphill all the way to the house of God. His interview was short for the Bishop was old and frail and suffering from a heavy cold. Powerscourt introduced himself as an investigator working for Michael Delaney. He passed on

Delaney's wish to make a donation to a fund for the restoration of the cathedral. The Bishop was very grateful.

'I have to tell you, however, Lord Powerscourt, that I am more concerned with the souls of the pilgrims than I am with Mr Delaney's gold. We have made arrangements to hold the funeral of that poor soul in St Michael's Church behind the Hôtel de Ville every afternoon now for the past two days. But the police won't let us bury him. Maybe we can conduct the service tomorrow. Every day since I heard it, I have thanked God for the return of the pilgrims. I pray that these ones are but the first detachment of a mighty army of Christian soldiers marching to Santiago. Did you know that the very first pilgrim to Compostela was one of my predecessors, a Bishop of Le Puy in the tenth century? Remember that as you march out down the cathedral steps, young man. A thousand years of pilgrimage will be with you in spirit.'

Powerscourt asked if the Bishop hoped the pilgrims could start on their way soon.

'Of course I do,' the old man replied, 'but we have to render unto Caesar that which is Caesar's. The civic authorities must decide. I do hope they walk, mind you.' The Bishop looked very concerned about the walking. 'Somebody told me that some of these pilgrims are going to take the train or be ferried about in carriages like the fashionable ladies in Paris.'

Powerscourt thought he made the fashionable ladies of Paris sound like the whores of Babylon.

'Please tell them from me, young man,' he said to Powerscourt as he hobbled to the door to bid him farewell, 'tell them they've got to walk. It won't do their souls any good at all if they take the train. It really won't.'

7

Michael Delaney finished his interview at half past two. The Sergeant gathered up his papers and prepared to return to his police station. He told Lady Lucy that he would return in the morning to take her and Powerscourt to the St Michel rock. He wanted to show them the site of the incident in person.

Alex Bentley went to his room to write up his notes of the interviews. He wanted to make a good impression on the investigator from London. Princeton men could organize their data just as well as the young gentlemen from Oxford or Cambridge.

Powerscourt's interview with the Chief of Police was postponed. When he returned to the hotel he found a chess tournament in progress in the dining room. Charlie Flanagan had discovered that the Hôtel St Jacques had four sets of chessmen and vigorous battles were being fought all over the room. Willie John Delaney, the Irish pilgrim suffering from an incurable disease, was master of the board, dispatching all who faced him with a checkmate within fifteen or twenty moves. Lady Lucy was deep in conversation with Maggie Delaney in a far corner of the room. Maggie was holding forth on the subject of human wickedness. It made her very happy. If it wasn't bad enough that all these pilgrims were so burdened with guilt at the crimes they had committed that they had to travel across the Atlantic in a desperate quest for forgiveness, here they were now, virtually encased in the flames of hell. Maggie Delaney was convinced that John Delaney had been murdered. The wrath of God must surely come upon them. Lady Lucy told Powerscourt later that day that Maggie Delaney was a living example of how the contemplation of other people's sins can make you happy.

'Any news, Delaney?' said Powerscourt to Delaney. 'Did the Sergeant say anything before he left?'

'He did not,' said Delaney cheerfully. 'How about you? Have you given comfort to the enemy?'

'Well,' replied Powerscourt, 'I've been trailing my coat. I've virtually invited them to come here and help themselves to as much of your money as they can. In exchange for our release, of course. I hope I didn't overdo it with that Mayor. He's very shrewd, the Mayor. He's a butcher by trade, name of Louis Jacquet, and his family have been mayoring here since before the Revolution. I think somebody may be along to see us fairly soon; I could be wrong.'

Powerscourt was not wrong. Shortly after four o'clock a small anonymous-looking middle-aged man in an unremarkable suit presented himself at the hotel reception. He asked to speak with Mr Delaney and Lord Powerscourt. He was led to a table in the corner of the dining room, closed off from the chess players.

'Good afternoon, gentlemen,' Powerscourt translated. 'I am Pierre Berthon of the firm of *notaires* of Berthon Berthon and Berthon of Le Puy. We represent the interests of the Bishop and the Cathedral of Notre Dame.'

'Powerscourt,' said Powerscourt.

'Delaney,' said Delaney, shaking the *notaire's* hand very firmly.

M. Berthon took out a large black notebook from his bag and a silver pen from his pocket. Powerscourt saw to his astonishment that the page was not filled with squares. It was ruled. There were lines going across it. He had looked in vain that morning in the Maison de la Presse for such a thing. Did the lawyers of Le Puy have their own secret supplies of proper notebooks, denied to the rest of the citizens?

'I understand,' M. Berthon went on, 'that you gentlemen are anxious to leave Le Puy and continue your pilgrimage?'

'That is the case,' Powerscourt nodded.

'And that you would welcome the support of my lord Bishop in these proceedings?'

'Such support would be more than welcome, coming from such a distinguished quarter.' Powerscourt bowed slightly to the lawyer to show his respect for his employers.

'Tell the little man', said Delaney, keen to move things on, 'that it's not the Bishop who's holding us up, it's the damned police.'

'The Bishop bids me tell you that under certain circumstances he would be happy to assist your cause. I understand, furthermore,' Berthon pressed on, making an entry on his page with the silver pen, 'that you wish to make a contribution to the restoration fund of our cathedral here in Le Puy?'

'We do,' Powerscourt nodded once more.

'How much?' said Berthon.

Powerscourt and Delaney had discussed figures just before the lawyer arrived.

'Ten thousand francs,' said Powerscourt.

One of the notaire's eyebrows arched upwards in a quizzical fashion. He didn't say a word.

'Fifteen thousand,' said Powerscourt. Delaney had been making gestures with his fingers going upwards.

The eyebrow rose a fraction further. The question mark hung in the air. Powerscourt looked at Delaney who made a tiny upward gesture.

'Seventeen thousand five hundred,' Powerscourt increased his offer. He wondered flippantly if they could keep going to thirty or even forty thousand so the lawyer's eyebrow would disappear right off the top of his forehead.

The eyebrow managed yet another upward motion. The man must practise at home in front of a mirror, Powersourt thought.

'Twenty thousand.' M. Berthon recalled his eyebrow. He made a note in his book.

'Done,' he said with a thin smile. 'I accept on behalf of the Bishop and the cathedral, gentlemen. Perhaps you could leave a banker's draft at the reception here in the morning. I must go and tell my lord Bishop. He will be delighted. Those gargoyles have been troubling him for years. I am much obliged to you gentlemen. Rest assured that the Bishop will do all he can to assist your cause. Good afternoon to you both.' M. Berthon departed. A careful observer would have noticed that he did not seem to be going back in the direction of the Bishop's Palace or his own offices in the Rue de Consulat. He was going in a different direction altogether, towards the Place du Martouret and the Hôtel de Ville, headquarters of the Mayor.

Well, well, Powerscourt thought. God has opened the batting. Who's coming next? Mammon or the law? 'What did you make of our friend the Bishop's man and the Bishop's move?' he asked Delaney.

'Quite remarkable eyebrows the man had,' said Delaney, 'I've never seen anything like it. I've found over the years that's it's always best to start low on the money side of things on these kind of occasions. Once the other fellow thinks he's doubled his money, he'll settle for that. I bet our friend thinks he's done well. If I was a betting man, Powerscourt, I'd say that the next man up to the plate will be the Mayor or the Mayor's man of business. If I was playing their hand I'd keep the law till the end.'

Powerscourt and Delaney had already agreed that they would offer the Mayor something other than money. Twenty minutes after the departure of M. Berthon, about the time it would take for a man to walk to and from the Hôtel St Jacques to the Hotel de Ville with a five-minute meeting in between, another, younger man in his mid-thirties was escorted to the table in the corner of the dining room. He was wearing a dark grey suit with a plain white shirt and a rather loud tie.

Powerscourt didn't think Lady Lucy would have let him out of the house wearing such a thing.

'Jean Paul Claude, gentlemen, of the firm of Raffarin and Barre, *notaires* to the Mayor and the town of Le Puy. At your service.'

'Powerscourt,' said Powerscourt.

'Delaney,' said Delaney, delivering another of his bone-crushing handshakes.

Jean Paul Claude had a small notebook and a gold pen. 'I understand you gentlemen are anxious to leave Le Puy and continue your pilgrimage,' he began.

Powerscourt nodded.

'And I understand that you are anxious to secure the support of the Mayor in this enterprise?'

Powerscourt nodded again.

'I am pleased to be able to tell you that under certain circumstances, the Mayor would be willing to back you in this matter.'

Powerscourt wondered if they had all learned their lines together, these lawyers, sitting in the Mayor's parlour with the crossed French tricolours and the portrait of the President.

'What circumstances?' he said amiably.

'I believe that there has been some discussion about a possible contribution to the Mayor's office for the good of the town of Le Puy.' Claude thought things were going well so far.

'I think you'll find', said Powerscourt, 'that our thinking has changed slightly on that.'

'In what way?' said the lawyer, looking anxious.

'Well,' said Powerscourt, 'Mr Delaney here would like to bequeath something permanent to the town, something that would commemorate the name of the Mayor for generations to come.'

'What is that?'

'A fountain,' said Powerscourt, 'or rather two fountains. One at the north-east part of the town where the pilgrims enter, and one at the south-west end where the pilgrims set off for Compostela. Think how these pilgrims will bless the name of the Mayor in years to come when they can quench their thirst on arrival and have a last drink or fill their water bottles as they leave. It will be a lasting memorial. We envisage that they should be called the Jacquet Fountains with an inscription round the top with the name of the Mayor and the date of construction. Mr Delaney's name would only be mentioned in much smaller type at the bottom. Is it not a good plan?'

Claude knew in his bones that the Mayor would like such a proposal. He stuck to his script.

'*Et encore*?' he asked.

'*Encore*?' said Powerscourt.

'*Et encore*?' Claude stuck to his guns.

'Fellow's turned into Oliver Twist, Delaney. He's asking for more.'

'To hell with his encores,' said Delaney, 'this is way out of order. Perfectly decent offer, two bloody fountains, if you ask me. Is the cupboard completely bare, my friend? Do we have anything we could throw at them?'

'We do,' said Powerscourt.

'Throw it,' said Delaney.

'Mr Claude,' Powerscourt began, speaking as reasonably as he could. 'We are all men of the world here. I would remind you that we have in our party of pilgrims a young man who is a journalist on the *Irish Times*, one of the foremost newspapers in Ireland. Their articles are syndicated all over the world. He has nearly finished his story. He proposes to be highly critical of the police force here in this town. I'm sure you wouldn't want him writing that the Mayor was greedy as well.'

Silence reigned in the corner of the dining room. The hotel clock chimed in the entrance hall. Outside the rain beat down on the pavements of Le Puy

Jean Paul Claude turned the same colour as his tie, a rather disagreeable pink.

'This article,' he stammered, 'this article . . .'

'This article need never see the light of day, Mr Claude. We have an element of control over its publication. The young man need never hear about our encounter this afternoon. Why don't you go back to the Mayor and tell him about the fountains. "This fountain was given to the town and the pilgrims of Le Puy by Louis Jacquet, Mayor, in the Year of Our Lord 1906," the inscription might say. "I was thirsty in the desert and ye gave me drink." I'm sure we could find some such biblical quotation to give the thing resonance. Perhaps the Bishop would bless them once they're in place?'

'Very well, gentlemen,' said Claude, trying to rescue some of his dignity. 'I shall go back to the Mayor. Thank you for your time. We shall be in touch shortly.'

Delaney laughed when he heard what Powerscourt had thrown at them. 'Didn't know you had a newspaperman in your back pocket, Powerscourt. That should make the bastards sit up for a moment or two. If I want to give the damned place a fountain, why shouldn't I give the damned place a fountain? Don't see why I should hand over cash to the Mayor so he can build an extension to his butcher's shop where he can hang a few more sides of beef and store the local pigs' trotters.'

The gap between the departure of M. Claude and their next visitor was rather longer than the previous one. Perhaps the Mayor's party were having a council of war. It was just after half past five when the next visitor arrived. This was Inspector Jean Dutour, who numbered among his many roles that of representative of the police federation for the widows and orphans of serving or retired officers. He too said he understood that Mr Delaney wished to make a contribution to the fund. The conversation followed exactly the same path as that with M. Berthon, except the Inspector did not have a movable eyebrow. He regaled them instead with piteous tales of young police widows with tiny pensions and numerous children, virtually unable to feed their families, of retired constables whose wives had passed away and were scarcely able to look after themselves. He too settled for twenty thousand francs. He had an important announcement to make before he left.

'I am asked to inform you, gentlemen, that representatives of the police and the public prosecutor's office wish to see you in the morning. They propose that the meeting should start at nine o'clock. A very good day to you, gentlemen, and thank you again for your contribution.'

Before Inspector Dutour could leave, there was a knock at the door. Stephen Lewis, the solicitor from Frome, poked his head apologetically round the corner.

'Forgive me, Lord Powerscourt, Mr Delaney, I saw our policeman friend here arrive a few minutes ago. I wonder if we could ask him to clear up a procedural point about the French legal system. I think it has bearing on our particular circumstances. I was taught this years ago in college but I only remembered it this afternoon. Could you ask the Inspector who decides whether to proceed or not in important cases like murder or corruption in France. Is it the police, or is it somebody else?'

'Inspector,' said Powerscourt, 'could we ask you a general question about the working of the law in your country? You are perfectly free to decline, if you so wish. Mr Lewis here is a solicitor from England.'

'I'll try,' said the Inspector, more than happy to sing the superior virtues of the French system to that of the Anglo-Saxons.

'In important cases like murder or corruption,' said Powerscourt, 'who decides whether to proceed with a case or not? In our country it would be a matter for the police.'

'Not so in France, Lord Powerscourt. Here we have a different system. The lawyers call your system adversarial because two lawyers end up fighting it out in court. The French system is better, I think. It's called inquisitorial. In such cases as those you mention, the conduct of the case is in the hands of a judge called an investigating judge or an investigating magistrate. His job is to find out the truth. So it is he, not the policemen, who decides whether there is enough evidence to proceed with a case.'

'Thank you very much,' said Powerscourt and escorted the Inspector to the door.

Delaney was in belligerent mood when he returned. 'Do you mean to tell me, my friend, that we have been buttering up the wrong people? That we needn't have bothered with shelling out for the police widows and orphans as the police won't decide whether to let us go or not? Should we have gone after this investigating magistrate person instead? How do you fix them, anyway?'

'Don't think it would be easy,' said Powerscourt, 'fixing one of these characters, as you put it. They're probably meant to be completely independent like the judges on your Supreme Court, Delaney.'

'It's perfectly possible to fix a few members of the Supreme Court,' said Michael Delaney happily. 'They say some of the robber barons did it in a case involving a steel cartel back in the 1890s. Two years later relations of the judges who backed the robber barons began getting highly paid jobs in the subsidiaries of the steel companies. Nothing was ever proved, of course.'

'Was there not a perfectly valid reason why these people should have got jobs in the steel industry?' Stephen Lewis asked. Frome had seen nothing like this.

'Sure,' said Delaney. 'One of them was a hairdresser in the Bronx. Another taught primary school in South Dakota.'

There was one further development at twenty past seven that evening. A note arrived, addressed to Lord Francis Powerscourt. It informed him that the Mayor was delighted about his fountains.

There was a great air of anticipation in the dining room of the Hôtel St Jacques that evening. Powerscourt talked to Michael Delaney about his son James and his progress. Only that afternoon, Delaney informed him, there had been a cable from New York to say that James was almost fully recovered and hoped to join them later in the pilgrimage. The young men were in high spirits, wondering how far they would be able to walk in a day and if they would meet any pretty girls on the pilgrim path. Lady Lucy was doing her duty by Maggie Delaney once again. 'Look,' the old lady whispered, her finger travelling round the diners like the beam of a searchlight, 'one of these men is a murderer. It would have to be a man, wouldn't it? Oh yes. Now we have a further crime to add to our burden, the bribing of the civil and the religious authorities in this holy town. When we leave, if we leave, we'll be a travelling charabanc of sin, a mobile circus of iniquity!' Father Kennedy was making final plans for the funeral. He decided to get Powerscourt to ask the proprietor if it would be appropriate to hold a wake in the dining room.

The men of Le Puy, Michael Delaney thought, arrived for their meeting at nine o'clock in the Hôtel St Jacques the next morning looking like a posse from the days of the Wild West. There was The Lawman, a slim man of about forty years wearing the black robes of a French *juge d'instruction*. There was a priest, the local man who had conferred with Father Kennedy in the past, men of God so often at hand at the time of the final shoot-out in Abilene or Cheyenne. There was The Marshal, Mayor Jacquet himself, looking as though he might have hacked off a few flitches of bacon before breakfast. There was another Lawman, Jean Paul Claude, Deputy to the Mayor, in a lurid green tie.

The proprietor arranged four chairs in an arc in front of the pilgrims.

'*Pèlerins, pèlerine*,' the Mayor began. 'Pilgrims, Miss Pilgrim,' Powerscourt translated, 'thank you for your patience. I think we should hear first from Mr Toulemont, the *juge* in charge of the case of the late John Delaney.'

The *juge* took out a pair of pince-nez and looked down over his nose at his notes. 'It is for me to decide, gentlemen and lady, if this case should proceed. I have read the details of the interviews you all gave to the police. I have myself visited the site of the unfortunate incident. I cannot see any point in proceeding with this matter under present circumstances. There is no evidence that the laws of France have been broken. I have therefore decided that you may proceed on your pilgrimage.' A burst of applause rang out from the pilgrims. 'However,' the *juge* held up his hand for quiet, 'I do not think we should close the case completely. Fresh witnesses may come forward. People could change their minds. I do not think any of you should be allowed to leave France without permission. I have asked and been granted leave to ask for a bond, a form of bail, if you will. If anybody leaves without permission, or if you fail to register with the local police force wherever you may be once a week, the bond will be forfeit.'

'How much?' said Delaney from the back of the room.

'Fifty thousand francs,' said the *juge*, frowning at this rude interruption.

'Done!' said Delaney. 'I'll leave you a banker's draft at the reception.'

'Gentlemen, lady.' The Mayor was back on his feet. 'The matter is now closed. As of this moment you are free to leave the hotel and enjoy the sights of our town. I am asked to tell you that the funeral of John Delaney will take place at three o'clock this afternoon in the church behind the Hotel de Ville. Tonight the town of Le Puy would like to invite you to a banquet here in this hotel. The Mayor's office will pay and look after the arrangements. Tomorrow there will be a special pilgrims' Mass in the cathedral at nine o'clock, the service to be taken by the Bishop himself. Until this evening then. I wish you all a very good day.'

The pilgrims shot out of the room into the fresh air of the town, like children let out of school. Powerscourt saw Lady Lucy out of the corner of his eye, conversing happily with the Sergeant. Delaney was brooding at the back of the room, shaking his head sadly from time to time. 'It's not the money,' he assured Powerscourt, 'stock dividends and bond interest should clear that before lunchtime. I feel they've put one over on us somehow, that we've been conned. Me, Michael Delaney, beaten by a bunch of Frenchmen in berets.'

Powerscourt assured the tycoon that they hadn't lost, they had won. The pilgrims were leaving.

'Maybe we could have gotten to that judge person earlier. Maybe we were thinking too small.' The vast possibilities of the New World that had made Delaney so rich seemed to open out before him once more. 'What do you think it would have taken to fix the man? Flat in Paris? Château on the Loire, wherever that is? Women? He looked as though he could do with a woman or two, that judge, now I come to think about it.'

'I must go now,' said Powerscourt. 'The Sergeant is taking Lady Lucy and me to St Michel, the rock where John Delaney died.'

'Careful now,' said Michael Delaney. 'Don't fall off.'

The volcanic pinnacle of St Michel d'Aiguilhe is some distance from the cathedral and the pink Corneille Rock with its huge statue of the Virgin and Child. It disappears behind other buildings as you approach, reappearing in larger and more menacing form as you draw closer. The day was overcast, with dark clouds scudding across the sky and gusts of wind tearing at their clothes. The summit was some two hundred and sixty feet above ground with a tenth-century chapel at the peak and, as the Sergeant told them at the bottom, there were two hundred and sixty-eight steps to the top.

'There's a rail most of the way,' said the Sergeant, preparing to lead his party upwards. 'Hold on to that. If you're worried about heights, don't look down.' The Sergeant resolved to take special care of Lady Lucy. She might get blown away in the wind.

Powerscourt was worried about heights. He always had been. He had once been forced to come down the steps that led to the roof of Durham Cathedral sitting down after vertigo struck him at the top. Lady Lucy watched him anxiously as they set off.

'You will be careful, Francis, won't you?' she said to him. 'Turn back if you feel queasy. I can give you a full report later.'

Powerscourt worked out a plan he thought might take him to the top. It was, he knew, the sight of the drop that would set him off. The path clung to the outside of the rock, snaking its way round the edge of the volcanic outcrop towards the sky. There was always rock to look at on one side or the other. After a hundred steps or so they came to a little clearing. Lady Lucy asked her husband if he wanted to sit down. The drop on the left-hand side was clearly visible from the bench. Powerscourt shook his head. The Sergeant, all fifteen stone of him, was trudging steadily on, a few paces ahead of them. Powerscourt thought he was doing well. Look at the step. Look at the Sergeant's back. Look at the blessed rock to one side of you. Look at Lady Lucy. Don't look round. Don't look down. Don't look back. The rain was falling heavily now, the steps growing slippery. They passed another resting place with a bench for weary travellers. Again Powerscourt declined. He was panting now, sweat breaking out on his forehead. Just one step at a time. There. Now another one. One more. Don't look down. Don't look up. Don't look across. Keep your eyes on the rock to your left or right. We must be nearly there now. A dark bird shot past just a few feet away. Powerscourt slipped slightly but then regained his bearing. It's an omen, he said to himself. I'm going to be all right. Don't look down. Don't look up. Don't look sideways. Fix your eyes on the step, on the dark blue uniform of the Sergeant, on Lucy's feet. One step at a time. You're wearing brown boots today. The Sergeant's boots are black. The bottoms of the Sergeant's trousers are frayed. One foot in front of another. Keep looking at the rock.

He had long ago abandoned the rail and was huddling close to the rock on the left-hand side. In the past vertigo attacks crept up on him very slowly. There was always time to turn back and it would pass in a minute or two. The Sergeant did not look round. He could hear the other two coming up behind him. Lady Lucy was talking to her Francis now, very quietly. 'You've done so well, my love. You're nearly there. Don't rush it, we're nearly there.' We must have done over two hundred steps now, Powerscourt said to himself, and began counting from two hundred. Two hundred and five. Don't look down. Two hundred and eight. One step at a time. Two hundred and ten. To his right he saw for a fraction of a second the ground below, pygmies and dwarves moving along matchstick roads. He looked away. Two hundred and thirteen. Nearly there. Don't look back. Two hundred and fifteen. The sweat was pouring down his face now. There was still rock, blessed rock on his left. Two hundred and eighteen. The pinnacle tapered as it rose to the little chapel on the top. These steps are very worn. How did they carry all the building materials to the top a thousand years ago? One step at a time. Two hundred and twenty-one. Only forty-seven to go. One of my laces is broken. Don't look round. The rock to his right ran out. Don't look down. A gust of wind and rain hit him full in the face. Good. Don't look round. Don't look up. The Sergeant's trousers are dark blue. The bottom of Lucy's dress is grey. Two hundred and twenty-five. There is green moss clinging to the rock. Don't look down. Two hundred and twenty-eight. Keep your head down. Two hundred and thirty-one. Then he ran out of rock. There wasn't any rock on his left. There wasn't any rock on his right. Infinity loomed behind the rail. There was no warning. The vertigo hit him like a typhoon. The sky was spinning round above him. The chapel of St Michel was whirling away in the opposite direction. He felt his legs begin to go. The clouds, those dark grey clouds were accelerating above him, shooting into space. His head was going round faster and faster.

'Sergeant! Quick!' For a big man the Sergeant moved remarkably fast. Lady Lucy took one side of her husband, the

Sergeant the other. Powerscourt was reeling like a drunken man. He knew what he had to do. He had to throw himself over the side. He had to jump. Then this terrible spinning sensation, this total loss of control, might stop. He had to go. He flung himself desperately towards the edge. The Sergeant took him in a bear hug. For a moment Lady Lucy thought the two of them might plunge into the abyss. Then Powerscourt tried the other side. A really determined man, his wits cascading round his head like the colours in a child's kaleidoscope, could force his way over the left-hand side of the rock. Again the Sergeant just managed to hold him, Lady Lucy pulling desperately from the other side. Still the tempest in Powerscourt's brain raged on, people, buildings, rock zooming away from him, swirling round and round and round and round and shooting up and down and up and down. There was another struggle. There was a brief pause. Lady Lucy thought incongruously that if her husband's brain was stable he would be comparing this with the final conflict between Sherlock Holmes and Dr Moriarty at the Reichenbach Falls. Then the Sergeant whipped out his truncheon. He hit Powerscourt a very firm blow on the head. Powerscourt passed out two hundred and thirty feet above ground with his wife and a police sergeant for company. There were only thirty-seven steps to go.

'Sergeant!' said Lady Lucy and then she realized he might have saved her husband's life. 'Well done! How very clever of you to think of knocking him out!'

'I wasn't sure we could hold him,' said the Sergeant. 'This seemed the best thing.'

'What do we do now?' asked Lady Lucy. 'Do we wait for him to come round?'

'I don't think so, Lady Powerscourt. I think he might be off again if we leave him up here. I'll carry him down.'

In ten minutes the Sergeant and Lady Lucy had carried him down. In fifteen the three of them were installed in a little café at the bottom, waiting for Powerscourt to come round.

'I'm still here,' he said at last. 'I've got a very sore head. I know I had a terrible attack of vertigo up there.' He shuddered as he looked up at St Michel, dimly visible through the dirty windows of the café. 'I had this irresistible urge to jump off the rock.'

'The Sergeant knocked you out, Francis. Then he carried you down.'

'I'm very much obliged to you, Sergeant. I think you may have saved my life.'

As the Sergeant prepared to move off to more normal duties, Powerscourt held him back.

'I say, Sergeant, I've only just thought of this. Do you suppose that poor man John Delaney suffered from vertigo? If he'd gone up there on his own and been sent spinning round, he'd have fallen off or jumped off just like I nearly did.'

'Don't suppose we'll find the answer to that one, Lord Powerscourt. I don't see how we'll ever know.'

'I shall make inquiries in England,' said Powerscourt, resolving to send a message to Johnny Fitzgerald. 'If I find the answer, rest assured that you'll be the first to know.'

Half an hour later Powerscourt and Lady Lucy were in the Cathedral of Notre Dame, staring at the Black Madonna above the high altar. Alex Bentley had given Powerscourt some of the history of this strange artefact over breakfast that morning. The statue itself was small, less than three feet high. A black ebony Virgin with staring eyes was dressed today in a white robe embroidered with fleurs-de-lis and golden roses. Halfway down, a small black Christ, wearing a crown, peeped out from under the robe.

'Is it very old, Francis?' whispered Lady Lucy.

'The original was very old, Lucy. It was brought here by some Louis who was a king and saint in the late 1250s. Le Puy was famous as a Marian shrine long before that but this one up there really put them on the map. They say Louis was given it as a present by some prince in the Middle East. The Black Madonna brought the pilgrims to Le Puy. The Black Madonna was their special attraction. Nobody else had one. The Black Madonna made the town rich.'

'What happened to the original, Francis?'

'Ah well,' said her husband, 'the original perished in the Revolution. Some say she was burnt at the Feast of Pentecost in 1794, there's even a story that she was beheaded in the guillotine. You won't be surprised to hear the church authorities decided to bring her back in the middle of the nineteenth century. Maybe she could make Le Puy rich again. This is a copy of the first one.'

Lady Lucy wandered off to another part of the cathedral. Powerscourt moved forward, as close as he could get to the little ebony statue in her white robes up on the wall above the high altar. It was extraordinary how this tiny figure dominated the entire building, how your eyes were drawn to it from all over the cathedral. Powerscourt wondered what it would have meant to those pilgrims over six hundred years before. A black Madonna and a black Christ. That surely meant a black Joseph, black disciples, a black Peter, a black Mark, a black Matthew and a black Judas. Did it also mean a black God in a black heaven with black angels and black cherubim and black seraphim? And where would thirteenth-century minds have thought this black kingdom was? Did they know where Africa was? Probably not, he thought. No wonder people flocked to Le Puy in their tens of thousands even now to see the Black Madonna carried in glory through the streets of Le Puy on special religious festivals. She came, quite literally, from a different world.

As they were leaving a young priest pressed a note into Powerscourt's hand. It came from the Bishop. There was a prayer enclosed and a short message. 'Dear Lord Powerscourt,' it said. 'Tomorrow, after Mass, I shall read this, the pilgrim's prayer, for all making the journey to Compostela. It is very beautiful. I would not like to think that the people who are most meant to hear it will not understand it. Could you therefore stand by the pulpit and translate for the benefit of our English friends?'

Powerscourt nodded to the young priest. 'Please tell the Bishop that I shall be honoured.'

Shortly before nine o'clock the next morning the pilgrims and the rest of the congregation were in their seats for the Pilgrims' Mass. The dinner the night before had been a great success with speeches from the Mayor and Mr Delaney and a spectacular crème brûlée from the chef. It had been washed down with Châteauneuf du Pape, hidden away in the corner of the hotel cellars for special occasions, which Powerscourt thought was one of the finest wines he had ever tasted.

Alex Bentley had placed the pilgrims in order of their method of transport by the west door of Notre Dame. At the end of the service, he had told them, when the Bishop reached the door they were to file out in pairs, the young ones who were going to walk first, the more sedentary pilgrims behind. On the other side of the nave Powerscourt noticed that there was a good cross section of the citizenry come to see them off. The Mayor and some of his staff were in the front row. Behind them the Sergeant with six of his police colleagues for company. And behind them the staff of the Hôtel St Jacques come to say goodbye to the guests they had served so well. Even the chef was there, in plain clothes.

As the Mass flowed on Powerscourt realized that at last the pilgrims and their hosts were speaking the same language. When the service was over the Bishop, clad in his purple robes, made his way slowly into his pulpit and up the steps. Powerscourt, his copy of the prayer in his hand with his own translation underneath, stood to attention at the side.

'*Ici nous avons . . .*' the Bishop began.

'Here we have', Powerscourt spoke slowly so his voice would not sound too hurried, 'a pilgrim's prayer that we believe goes back to the Middle Ages. It has been said over countless pilgrims as they leave this cathedral to go to Compostela. This prayer is for all of you today.' Powerscourt paused. The Bishop carried on.

'Dieu, vous avez appelé Abraham . . .'

'Lord, you called your servant Abraham out of Ur of Chaldea and watched over him in all his wanderings; you guided the Jewish people through the desert: we ask you to watch over your servants here who, for love of your name, make the pilgrimage to Santiago de Compostela.'

The pilgrims' eyes were shooting between the Bishop and his translator at the bottom of the pulpit steps.

'Be for us, a companion on the journey, direction at our crossroads, strength in our fatigue, a shelter in danger, resource on our travels, shadow in the heat, light in the dark, consolation in our dejection, and the power of our intention; so that with your guidance, safely and unhurt, we may reach the end of our journey and, strengthened with gratitude and power, secure and happy, may return to our homes, through Jesus Christ, our Lord. Apostle James, pray for us. Holy Virgin, pray for us.'

The Bishop came down and shuffled slowly towards the west door. One of his acolytes followed, carrying a selection of objects on a silver tray.

Wee Jimmy Delaney and Charlie Flanagan were the first to leave. The Bishop blessed them. The acolyte handed each one a copy of the pilgrim's prayer and a scallop shell, symbol of the pilgrimage to Santiago de Compostela for a thousand years.

Waldo Mulligan and Patrick MacLoughlin followed, then Shane Delaney and Willie John Delaney, Christy Delaney and Jack O'Driscoll, Girvan Connolly and Brother White, Stephen Lewis and Maggie Delaney, Father Kennedy and Alex Bentley. Michael Delaney on his own brought up the rear. Powerscourt hurried Lady Lucy away to see the pilgrims leave. For the traditional route was down the steps by the west door, along a corridor, through a mighty ornamental gate and then down one hundred and thirty-four steps to the Rue des Tables at the bottom. They stood at the top of the steps and watched the pilgrims, some awkward, some relaxed, set out down the same steps into the same street on to the same route as their predecessors eight centuries before.

PART TWO

LE PUY—SAUGUES—ESPALION— ESTAING—ESPEYRAC

Who so beset him round with dismal stories
Do but themselves confound – his strength the more is.
No foes shall stay his might; though he with giants fight,
He will make good his right to be a pilgrim.

Since, Lord, thou dost defend us with thy spirit,
We know we at the end shall life inherit.
Then fancies flee away! I'll fear not what men say,
I'll labour night and day to be a pilgrim.

John Bunyan

8

'I do wish we had Johnny Fitzgerald with us, Francis.' Lady Lucy was staring sadly at the dark red covering on the walls of their bedroom, a fleur-de-lis pattern fading away, occasional marks from grease or spilt liquids staining the surface. 'He's always been here on the most difficult cases.' She and Powerscourt were back in the Hôtel St Jacques preparing to compile a list of the pilgrims and their whereabouts on the day John Delaney died. It was, Powerscourt had said, time to begin the work that brought them to the Auvergne, the unmasking of a killer.

'I'm sure Johnny's time will come, Lucy. I've got to cable him about John Delaney, as you know,' Powerscourt said, placing the big black notebook he had bought in the Maison de la Presse on the little table by the window. 'Now then, you've got all your notes there and the ones Alex Bentley took in the interviews with our friend the Sergeant? Let's begin with the Americans.'

'Do you think they're all suspects, Francis?'

'What do you mean, all?'

'Well, do you include that nice young man, Alex Bentley? Father Kennedy? Michael Delaney himself?'

'For the purpose of this exercise, Lucy, we include the lot. I'd even include the cat if they'd brought one. I'm going to give each one a page to themselves. That way we can enter more information as we go along.'

'Here goes,' said Lady Lucy, pulling out a page of notes in Alex Bentley's finest hand. 'Maggie Delaney, spinster, in her early sixties, resident in New York City, religious fanatic, cousin of Michael Delaney.'

Powerscourt was writing away. 'Fanatic a bit strong perhaps, Lucy? On the religious front, I mean.'

'No,' said Lady Lucy with feeling. 'You've not talked to the woman as much as I have, Francis. Fanatic possibly too weak if you ask me.'

'Very good,' said her husband and entered the word in his ledger. 'Do we know what sort of cousin? First? Second? Some sort of larger number twice removed?'

'Not clear. She only left the hotel once in the morning, she told the Sergeant. She went to buy some religious material in a shop on the Place du Plot. I've seen that place, Francis, it's full of indescribably vulgar religious knick-knacks. Like you get in Lourdes only there's no excuse here.'

'I see,' said Powerscourt. 'What did she do in the afternoon? Prayers in the cathedral? Confession with one of the younger clergy?'

'Not so,' said Lady Lucy triumphantly. 'She spent the afternoon in her room, reading works of religious devotion.'

'God help us all,' said Powerscourt. 'Next?'

'Father Patrick Kennedy, aged about fifty, parish priest to Michael Delaney, accompanied him, he told the Sergeant, in the dark days of the son's illness. He spent the morning going round the cathedral. He climbed the Rocher Corneille and the St Michel. He went back to the hotel for lunch. He rested in the afternoon.'

'Not surprised he took a rest if he did all that lot in the morning. The good Father must have been exhausted. Anything else we know about him?'

'Great weakness for food, especially puddings, I've watched him at the table.'

Powerscourt put that in too. You never knew what might be relevant.

'Alex Bentley, aged twenty-four. New England family. Educated Princeton and Yale Law School. Secretary and general factotum to Michael Delaney. Went out once in the morning to take a coffee in the Rue des Mourgues. Otherwise worked in his room on the details of the pilgrimage.'

Powerscourt looked up from his writing. 'Related to Delaney in any way? Or just a hired hand?'

'Hired hand,' said Lady Lucy. 'Rather charming sort of hired hand, I should say.'

'Next?'

'Wee Jimmy Delaney, aged about twenty-five, steelworker from Pittsburgh. Unspecified cousin of Michael Delaney, distance of ancestry unknown. Went first to St Michel Rock with Charlie Flanagan, then they went to the cathedral. After lunch they went to the Rocher Corneille and took a walk round the upper town. They returned to the hotel around four thirty.'

Outside they could hear a heated exchange between one of the kitchen staff and a butcher's boy delivering meat from an enormous pannier on his bicycle. It appeared that the wrong cut of beef had been delivered to the Hôtel St Jacques. The shouting match went on for about five minutes. The butcher's boy seemed to have lost the battle.

'Charlie Flanagan, aged early twenties again, carpenter from Baltimore, cousin of Michael Delaney on his mother's side. His version of events is identical, almost word for word with Wee Jimmy's. Do you think that is suspicious, Francis?'

'No, I don't,' said Powerscourt. 'Alex Bentley was writing this down. He may have made their versions word for word because he remembered the other one. Anything else we know about this Charlie?'

'He makes models out of wood,' said Lady Lucy. 'They say he did a beautiful one of the ship they crossed the Atlantic in.'

'Next?' said Powerscourt.

'Waldo Mulligan,' said Lady Lucy. 'Works for a senator in Washington. Looks slightly haunted some of the time. I saw him one afternoon drinking whisky in the bar all by himself. Like Father Kennedy he went to the two Rochers and the cathedral in the morning but in the reverse order. He stayed in the hotel in the afternoon. Possibly in the bar, but he didn't say.

'Our last American is Patrick MacLoughlin, aged twenty-two, training for the priesthood in Boston. He went to the cathedral in the morning and the Rocher Corneille in the afternoon. He didn't go to St Michel at all.'

'Didn't he now,' said Powerscourt thoughtfully. 'I wonder why. I'd have thought that St Michel would have a greater appeal than the Rocher Corneille, Lucy, wouldn't you?'

'Maybe he's scared of heights, Francis. I've met one or two people round here who aren't overfond of tall rock pinnacles.'

Powerscourt laughed. 'Next, my love?'

'We've got the Irish now, but the first one lives in Swindon. Maybe he's just moved there recently. Shane Delaney, early forties, works on the railways. On pilgrimage for his wife who's dying of some frightful disease and isn't well enough to travel. Spent the morning praying in front of the Black Madonna. Spent the afternoon on pilgrimage to various bars in the town with Girvan Connolly. Back at the hotel about half past four.'

Powerscourt remembered his conversation with Shane Delaney about his letter home.

'Willie John Delaney, the man who is dying from an incurable disease. Didn't feel well after the travelling, he says. Spent the day in his room, most of it asleep.'

'I've always thought it could be a great advantage for a murderer to be dying of some frightful disease,' said Powerscourt. 'You could kill off all your enemies one by one. With any luck you'd be dead before they brought you to trial.'

'Francis! What a horrible thought!'

'It's a fairly horrible way to go, being pushed off that damned rock out there,' said Powerscourt. 'Who else has ventured forth from the Emerald Isle, Lucy?'

'Christopher or Christy Delaney. Aged eighteen. Going up to Cambridge in October. He went to the cathedral and the two rocks in the morning. He spent the afternoon reading a book set by his tutor at the university, Clarendon's *History of the Rebellion*.'

'God help him,' said Powerscourt. He too had had to read Clarendon before going up to Cambridge. Perhaps the syllabus hadn't changed at all.

'One last Irishman, Francis, Jack O'Driscoll, aged about twenty-five, related on his mother's side. Newspaperman. He wandered round the town in the morning, stopping for one or two beers, and took in the sights in the afternoon. He says he left St Michel about half past four in the evening but he's not sure. It could have been five.'

'Isn't that the last time we have for anybody leaving there, Lucy?'

'I think so,' said Lady Lucy. 'Only four to go now, Francis. Three really if you take away John Delaney.'

The marching pilgrims had made good progress. They had reached the village of St-Christophe-sur-Dolaison, some five miles from Le Puy, with a bakery, a bar and an ancient church in red stone topped by an open belfry with four bells on top. A horse with a very large cart was tethered right outside the bar. It looked as if the horse knew the place well. The barman, a cheerful soul with a bright blue apron on his front and a black beret on his head, waved happily at the pilgrims. The religious element pressed on towards their goal, unwilling to be diverted. Indeed Brother White, who had read widely before coming on pilgrimage, detected in the barman none other than Mr Worldly Wiseman from the town of Carnal Policy, determined to make Christian give up his pack and stray from the path to the Wicket Gate. Father Kennedy had felt very tempted by the éclairs in the bakery window but did not wish to draw attention to himself by stopping. Patrick

MacLoughlin followed the others as they walked straight out of the little square with the bar and headed for St-Privat-d'Allier.

But the other pilgrims needed no encouragement to sit down outside the bar. Jack O'Driscoll ordered eight beers. All of them stretched their legs as far in front of them as they could.

'Will you look at these boots of mine, for Christ's sake,' said Girvan Connolly. 'I bought them for a song from a man in a market stall in Kentish Town. They've more or less fallen apart.'

Sure enough, as the pilgrims peered at the boots, they could see that the outside sections had become detached from the soles. In a few more miles they would have disintegrated completely. Charlie Flanagan, carpenter by trade, whipped a strange-looking instrument from his pack and some string-like material from his pocket and carried out instant repairs.

'There, Girvan,' he said doubtfully, 'those should take you to journey's end today. I wouldn't count on it, mind you. That sole isn't strong at all.'

'Does anybody know how much farther we've got to go today?' asked Wee Jimmy Delaney. All the pilgrims had been given maps. All had looked at them carefully in the early stages of the march. Some had turned them upside down for better appreciation of the route. Some had peered at their map from the side, or the bottom, or the top. One or two had got down on the ground and tried to make sense of them that way. Shane Delaney had thrown his away. Only Waldo Mulligan and Christy Delaney were able to read them properly, and this gave them great prestige in the group. Neither of them had been asked to pay for the first or the second or the third beer consumed so far in St-Christophe-sur-Dolaison's bar.

'Another ten miles or so. We go out of this place and turn left,' said Waldo Mulligan firmly.

'How long till we get there, wherever there is?' said Willie John Delaney.

'I should think it's about four hours,' said Christy Delaney cheerfully. 'We'll be there in time for tea.'

'Tea be damned,' said Jack O'Driscoll. 'I asked the barman in the St Jacques about this St Private place or whatever it's called. I think he said it had absolutely no redeeming features, none at all. Except, the man said, it had some of the finest red wine in the Auvergne.'

'Girvan Connolly, Francis, mother's side, aged thirty-five or so. Described as merchant from Kentish Town. It's not clear why he's on pilgrimage at all. Spent the day with Shane Delaney. Fond of a drink, our Mr Connolly.'

'How do you know that, Lucy?'

'I saw him out of the corner of my eye yesterday evening. Our friend Girvan was forever topping up his glass when he thought nobody was looking.'

'Well spotted, Lucy. Next?'

'Brother White, late thirties, teaches at one of England's leading Catholic public schools. He spent most of the day in the cathedral, Francis. He was praying in front of the Black Madonna, he says. Other people who went to Notre Dame say they saw him there.'

'Why would you spend most of the day praying to the Black Madonna? Does she have any special educational powers, as far as you know?'

'I don't know the answer to that, Francis. But there's something rather horrid about Brother White. I can't put my finger on it just yet.'

'Then we have the late John Delaney himself. Cousin again of Michael Delaney. He went to St Michel and the Rocher Corneille in the morning, and the cathedral in the afternoon. The last sighting we have of him was about four thirty when two of our pilgrims saw him going into the hotel.'

'And nobody saw him go out after that?'

'No,' said Lady Lucy. 'You're going to like this last one, Francis. Stephen Lewis, mid-fifties, mother's side again, solicitor from Frome in Somerset. Come on pilgrimage for the sake of his immortal soul and because he likes trains. Our Mr Lewis, if his story is to be believed, and I think it is, did not go to the Rocher Corneille. He did not climb the two hundred and sixty-eight steps to the chapel at the summit of St Michel. Nor he did he go up or down the one hundred and thirty-four steps that lead up to the Cathedral of Notre Dame.'

'So what did the man do, in heaven's name?' asked Powerscourt.

'Mr Stephen Lewis, solicitor, from Frome in Somerset, went to the railway station in Le Puy. He looked at the engines for some time. Then he took a train south, travelling first class he tells us, to the next port of call, a stop called La Bastide St Laurent Les Bains. It's on the Nîmes line, apparently. Our Mr Lewis took lunch in the Hôtel Bristol in the main square, some local pâté with *cornichons*, duck à l'orange, and returned to Le Puy on the 2.55, arriving just before half past four. He said he didn't have time for coffee or he'd have missed his train.'

'He may have had a more interesting day than the rest of them,' said Powerscourt cheerfully. 'I don't suppose anybody can corroborate any of that?'

'Well,' said Lady Lucy, 'one or two people did see him coming back into the hotel. They report that Mr Lewis was carrying a book of timetables.'

'Excellent!' said Powerscourt. 'A little bedtime reading, no doubt.'

'I've forgotten one person,' said Lady Lucy, 'Michael Delaney himself. He went briefly to the cathedral in the morning. He didn't go to either of the rocks. During the afternoon he was in the hotel, working on the plans for the pilgrimage with Alex Bentley.'

'Well, Lucy,' said her husband, rising from his little table and pacing about the room, 'these witness statements are about as much use to us as the smile on the face of the Sphinx. This is what I think we should do tomorrow. Could you have another word with our friend Maggie Delaney before she leaves in the carriage? If Michael Delaney has any great sins in his past she may know something about them. Could you see what crimes she comes up with? And ask her about how all these people are related. I'm going walking tomorrow with the young ones and the men of God. Let's see what they've got to say for themselves on the pilgrim trail and the — '

Powerscourt stopped suddenly in mid-sentence. He looked at Lady Lucy. 'Wait here a moment, darling. I've been a fool, a stupid, stupid fool.' He headed for the door.

'Where are you going, Francis? What's the matter?'

'Only this, Lucy. Here we have all these statements about people coming in and out of the hotel. All of them refer, unless I'm very much mistaken, to the front door. What about the back door? Side doors? Fire escapes? Balconies? We may have been looking in the wrong direction altogether.'

Jack O'Driscoll and Christy Delaney were in a great hurry. They were both very thirsty, completely parched as Christy put it. They had left their own party far behind. They sped past the religious brethren who had stopped to pray at a wayside shrine to St James. As they drew near to St-Privat-d'Allier a passer-by would have noted that Jack kept writing a couple of phrases in a small notebook which he passed to his companion.

'I think this is it,' he said finally, as they passed an ancient mill on the side of an old bridge.

'Oon boo tile van rouge, seal voo play, that should do it.'

'Oon boo tile van rouge, seal voo play,' Christy repeated.

'Good,' said Jack.

'And I presume on core stays the same?'

'On core oon boo tile van rouge seal voo play might be better,' said Jack.

'*Bien, très bien,*' said Christy.

Powerscourt returned from his inspection of the entrances and exits to the Hôtel St Jacques in sombre mood.

'It's hopeless, Lucy, quite hopeless,' he said to his wife. 'The place has got more ways in and out than a honeycomb. Round the back there are two back doors, not locked during the daytime, a rickety fire escape, and rooms on the ground floor all of which have windows that open wide enough for a man to get out. All this work', he waved helplessly at the notebook, 'is rendered null and void. Anybody could have got in and out without being seen. All of that evidence is all right for the front but not for the back.'

'What do we do now, my love?' asked Lady Lucy.

'God knows,' said her husband.

Lady Lucy Powerscourt was taking morning coffee the next day with Maggie Delaney in a corner of the dining room at the Hôtel St Jacques. She noticed that her companion ladled in three spoonfuls of sugar.

'Can you tell me how you are related to Mr Michael Delaney, Miss Delaney?' she began brightly.

'That walking heap of wickedness?' Maggie peered crossly at Lady Lucy as if she had just taken the name of the Lord in vain. 'It goes back to our grandparents, I don't know the precise details. I've tried, of course. But it isn't easy to find out what happened in Ireland in the famine years. There's a story that Delaney's father did something incredibly wicked in a place called Macroom, wherever that is, something to do with the workhouses. I wouldn't be surprised. Like father, like son.'

'So when did your own particular interest in your cousin and his activities begin?'

Maggie inspected Lady Lucy once more. 'Twelve years ago, it would have been. Somebody on the parish committee for the reclamation of fallen women mentioned that he'd seen the Delaney name in the papers. That's when I started to read those money pages in the newspapers.'

'Money pages?' said Lady Lucy. Had Maggie been picking up tips on domestic thrift, *How to Make Your Household*

Budget Go Further and *Keep a Happy Husband*? She had not.

'I believe the proper term is the financial and business pages of the *New York Times*,' she said primly.

'You read those pages every now and again, Miss Delaney? That's very advanced, if I might say so.'

'I do not read those pages every now and then, as you put it,' said Maggie Delaney crossly, 'I read them every day. I have great files of them at home, sorted year by year, going back to 1894.'

Lady Lucy would have been the first to admit that she was not a regular reader of this material. She hardly ever looked at them at all, moving on to higher things like the accounts of forthcoming auctions, or society weddings that might feature members of her family. She dimly remembered row upon row of numbers, of company reports, of the details of the flotation of new companies on the London or New York Stock Exchanges. For some, perhaps, there was romance in all these dry figures.

'And what was the first evidence you found about Mr Delaney's activities?'

'His crimes, you mean,' said Maggie Delaney. 'The first evidence? There was so much of it, so many sins. Did you know that somebody wrote a book about Delaney's crimes round about that time?'

'Really?' said Lady Lucy, 'What was it called? Did it do well?'

Maggie Delaney laughed. Or rather she cackled and a look of twisted triumph passed across her face. 'The book was called *Michael Delaney, Robber Baron*.'

Lady Lucy thought the author hadn't minced his words. 'I see,' she said. 'Was it perhaps not a very flattering portrait? Of Mr Delaney, I mean.'

'It was not flattering, oh no. The author had got hold of the details of most of Delaney's crimes over the previous fifteen years. It would have been very powerful. Two hundred pages of Delaney's sins, bound for ever in a hardback cover.'

'But what became of it, Miss Delaney? You make it sound as if something happened to the book. Did you manage to read it?'

'Nobody, as you put it, managed to read it. When Delaney found out about it – he must have heard people were making inquiries about him – he went straight to the publishers. He bought every single copy just as they were about to start sending them out to the bookshops. Then he had them all destroyed, pulped is the term, I believe. He paid the author all the royalties he would have earned if he'd sold every single copy and a bit more to keep his mouth shut. And the author's mouth has remained shut from that day to this. I tried to find him, of course, the author, but he's vanished. That was the end of *Michael Delaney, Robber Baron.*'

Lady Lucy wondered if the author too had been pulped, like his books. Another crime for Maggie Delaney to put on her cousin's charge sheet.

'If you will excuse me, Lady Powerscourt,' Maggie Delaney was gathering up her prayer book and rosary beads, 'perhaps we could continue our conversation over lunch. I must go to the cathedral to pray in front of the Black Madonna.'

An improbable image rose to the front of Lady Lucy's mind. She could see Maggie Delaney sitting at a table in her little apartment in New York, the walls lined, no doubt, with religious pictures of the Holy Land and the saints, the business pages of the *New York Times* in front of her. She had a pair of scissors in her hand and was cutting out selected paragraphs to be inserted in a large black file. Chicago meat prices. New York Stock Exchange closing prices. Timber futures. Report from London. Steel stocks firmer.

Powerscourt had ridden over to St-Privat-d'Allier and abandoned his horse at the hotel, hoping to catch up with some of the pilgrims on their march to Saugues. A party of schoolchildren in crocodile formation passed him in the village square on their way to the church, escorted by a couple of nuns. The locals stared at him with that rude and never-ending stare reserved for foreigners and people from the next village. The road was climbing now, climbing upwards towards the vast empty plateau of the Aubrac. Small farms were littered across the landscape, the occasional cart trundling past him. Two birds of prey, buzzards he thought, were performing great acrobatic swoops in the pale blue sky, waiting for a glimpse of lunch before hurtling to the ground at unimaginable speed. He found Girvan Connolly, the man who described himself as a merchant from Kentish Town, sitting beside a great rock, swearing.

Pilgrimage was not being kind to Girvan. Those two young men, Christy Delaney and Jack O'Driscoll, had stopped their consumption of St Privat's finest red fairly early the evening before. It had, Girvan realized now, been a mistake to carry on drinking the stuff with Willie John Delaney, the man dying from an incurable disease. That pilgrim had leaned over to Girvan as he opened their third bottle and announced thickly, 'You know the old saying, Girvan, my friend? Eat, drink and be merry for tomorrow you die? In my case that's almost literally true. This bloody incurable disease I can't pronounce could take me away tomorrow, so help me God. So I may as well have a glass while I can. I can't drink to my health so I'll drink to yours instead.' And with that Willie John Delaney launched a steady campaign down the third bottle.

Not only did Girvan have a hangover. His feet, in the cheap boots he had bought from a man in the market at Kentish Town, were hurting. Charlie Flanagan's repairs were holding out but only just. When he had tried to ask by sign language in the village that morning if there might be a cobbler in the place, they had shaken their heads and pointed vaguely in the general direction of western France. Now here was this detective person arrived from nowhere and looking very cheerful. Nothing, Girvan knew, is more annoying to people with hangovers than their fellow citizens being cheerful around them.

'Good morning, Mr Connolly,' said Powerscourt. 'Are you having trouble with your boots?'

Girvan pointed sadly to the offending objects. 'They're bad now,' he said morosely, 'they're going to get worse.'

'I've got a very thick pair of socks in my pack somewhere,' said Powerscourt. 'Would you like to borrow them?'

The socks seemed to improve things. The two men set off along the path.

'Your business must have been doing well back in London, Mr Connolly, for you to be able to take the time off to come over here.'

Connolly laughed bitterly. 'I wish it was,' he said.

Powerscourt said nothing. He wondered if Girvan Connolly might tell him things out here in the wilds of the French countryside that he would never mention in the more crowded quarters of the hotel. He waited as a party of cows were driven in front of them into a neighbouring field.

'The thing is . . . ' Connolly began. He was tired of the lies, the lies he had told his wife, the lies he had told to the various bailiffs who had come to call at his run-down house, the lies he had told to his fellow pilgrims. He felt a sudden irresistible urge to tell the truth in the same way people sometimes tell their entire life stories, sins and all, to complete strangers on transatlantic liners or long train journeys.

'It wasn't going well at all,' he said, looking not at Powerscourt but at the woods in front of them.

'I'm sorry to hear that, Mr Connolly,' said Powerscourt.

Then his woes poured out of Girvan Connolly. The trouble with the business, the plates and the cups and saucers and the saucepans not selling as well as they should. The little loan taken out to tide them over. The slightly larger loan at a slightly higher rate of interest taken out to buy the consignment of cheap sheets and blankets that would restore his fortunes when sold off in the market stalls of Kentish Town.

116

Further trouble when early customers reported angrily that the sheets virtually disintegrated on washing. Yet another loan, larger still, to pay off the first instalments on the earlier loans while there was still time. And then no moneylenders left to advance him credit to pay off the loan that had accounted for the purchase of the wretched sheets and blankets. His creditors threatening to come round and sort him out. All of this poured forth like a torrent of disaster.

'I see,' said Powerscourt. 'What a run of bad luck, Mr Connolly.' He didn't think any of these troubles would give Girvan Connolly cause to murder one of his fellow pilgrims. He carried on, 'So what, pray, is the condition of your creditors now, Mr Connolly? Do they know you are here? Do they know they may have to wait longer yet for the debts to be repaid?'

Connolly was speaking very softly now. 'They don't know I'm here,' he said. 'Nobody knows I'm here. At least I hope they don't.' He looked behind him rather desperately but there were no moneylenders on the path behind, lining up for the kill.

'Tell me this, Mr Connolly, what is the grand total that would be needed to clear your debts today? You'd better add in something for the interest racked up since you've been here.'

'Fifteen pounds? Twenty pounds?' said Connolly.

Powerscourt thought that meant twenty-five.

'Could I make a suggestion?'

'Please do,' said Connolly.

'Why don't you speak to Michael Delaney about it? He might be able to help. Twenty or twenty-five pounds seems a lot to you, but to him it's a drop in the ocean. You're family, after all. He might be very happy to help.'

'Thank you, Lord Powerscourt, thank you so much.' Ahead they could just see a group of pilgrims bathing their feet in a stream. Powerscourt had always thought there would be no single reason that had brought this disparate group of people to the Auvergne, some of them travelling over four thousand miles to get here. Religion and piety would serve for some. Guilt would account for others, and love of travel and the excitement of adventure in unknown lands. He thought of the variety of pilgrims in Chaucer's *Canterbury Tales*, the different stories of the Miller and the Franklin and the Pardoner and the Wife of Bath. Thinking about Girvan Connolly, he hadn't expected to find among these pilgrims a man on the run from his creditors.

'I've only just remembered this one, this crime of Delaney's.' Maggie Delaney seemed to have gained fresh strength from her visit to the cathedral and the Black Madonna. She and Lady Lucy were taking lunch in the Hôtel St Jacques, a dish of veal today with sweetbreads in cream accompanied by sauté potatoes and carrots. Lady Lucy loathed the feel and the taste of sweetbreads and hid hers under a cairn of potatoes. 'This,' Maggie Delaney continued, 'was the crime that set him on the path to riches, may God have mercy on his soul.'

'What did he do then?' asked Lady Lucy, preparing to make another mental note to tell Francis about when she met up with him later that day.

'He arranged to buy a railroad with another man. I think the man was called Wharton. He, Wharton, I mean, put up most of the money. Delaney swindled him, I don't know how. Wharton, poor man, lost the lot!' With that Maggie Delaney speared three sweetbreads on to her fork and popped them into her mouth.

'What happened? Surely Mr Delaney must have got caught? Shouldn't he have been arrested for fraud or something like that?'

'Every day, Lady Powerscourt, every day the man should be arrested for fraud or something like that. There was a great court case. Delaney hired better lawyers. He's always hired better lawyers than his opponents. He got off. Isn't that terrible? I doubt if God will forgive him.'

'What happened to the man Wharton?' asked Lady Lucy. 'Did he recover?'

'As far as I know, he never recovered. Very bitter he was apparently, very bitter.'

Francis will like this story, Lady Lucy said to herself, he'll like it very much indeed.

Michael Delaney was not aware of the catalogue of his sins being rehearsed in the dining room of the Hôtel St Jacques. He was using his last afternoon in Le Puy to walk up to the cathedral. The party travelling by carriage was due to set off for Saugues at four o'clock that afternoon to meet up with the pedestrian pilgrims. Michael Delaney was thinking about his son James. He thought of his boy many times a day. He remembered with a shudder the deathly colour on his face as he fought with death, lying motionless on that hospital bed. He remembered how pale and wan he had been for weeks afterwards, the tottering steps when he began to move about again, like a toddler learning to walk for the first time. He remembered how healthy James had looked when they had said farewell with a long embrace on the ship preparing to take Delaney back to the Old World. He wondered what James was doing now. Playing golf, he suspected, with that elegant swing the older members admired so much. Maybe he was sailing with his friends, the wind in his hair and the spray racing along the sides of the Delaney yacht. He had only bought it for James.

Michael Delaney felt a proprietary pride as he entered the Cathedral of Notre Dame. This, after all, was another of his buildings now, or it would be when twenty thousand of his francs had been spent. He wondered briefly about hourly rates of pay for French workmen, the cost of building materials, the profit margin the contractors would charge even when working for the Church. He gave up. There were too many unknowns for him to estimate how much work could be done with his money. But some small part of it would be his. Future visitors would point to some section of nave or chancel and

119

tell each other, 'That was repaired thanks to the generosity of an American called Michael Delaney.'

He had not thought much of the Black Madonna the first time he had looked at her on his fleeting visit a few days before. He thought even less of her now. Why was she so small? Why couldn't they get themselves a decent-sized statue like the pink Virgin on the Rocher Corneille, fifty-two feet high, not counting the base? A visitor to Notre Dame with bad eyesight sitting halfway down the nave wouldn't even know the thing was there. It would be invisible, a black hole rather than a Black Madonna. He wandered over to an enormous painting dating from the year 1630 on the wall. It showed a great procession of town worthies going into the cathedral to commemorate the lifting of a plague that had carried off ten thousand citizens of Le Puy. In the top right-hand corner a group of hooded White Penitents were entering the cathedral. Behind them a group of monks in brown, then another group of monks in grey. Behind them a great party of religious, dressed in their more colourful vestments, escorted the Bishop, a bearded prelate with an oriental look about him, carrying his crook. Then, in the centre of the painting, a group of consuls dressed in red with black underneath and broad white collars were carrying the Black Madonna protected by a canopy above her. Ranged to the right of them were further groups of citizens wearing the robes of their guilds or their orders. Delaney felt sure that these consuls and the other citizens were the leading men of Le Puy in their time, merchants probably, men of business, come to join with their colleagues from the church in proper celebration, thanking God for their deliverance. Delaney felt sure that he would have been in this painting had he been alive then. A consul, he thought, a leading man. He rather liked the look of those red robes.

Maggie Delaney would not have believed it, but Michael Delaney had been thinking about God too. He always thought about God when he thought of his James for the one had saved the other.

Michael Delaney's God was not a great patriarch like Moses parting the Red Sea, bringing the Ten Commandments down from the mountain top, leading an unruly people towards the Promised Land. He wasn't the Christ figure who preached the Sermon on the Mount and said blessed are the meek for they shall inherit the earth. Michael Delaney didn't have much time for the meek, life's losers in his book. Nor was his God an immanent presence in the world like the Holy Ghost, bringing God's grace to his subjects. Michael Delaney's God was the Chairman of the Board. He, Delaney, Michael Delaney like to think, was Managing Director of the outfit. Above him, remote, wise, all-seeing and all-knowing, was the Chairman. God.

On his way out Michael Delaney passed a statue. It showed a saint, dressed in brown with a broad-brimmed hat on his head. He carried a satchel or scrip slung round his neck and hanging by his waist. In his right hand was a large staff reaching up to the top of his hat, and in his left, a book of scripture. The bearded face seemed to Michael Delaney to be saying welcome. For this was St James the Great, the saint of the pilgrims who walk to his shrine and his memory in the Cathedral of St James in Santiago de Compostela. It was the same saint who had watched over James Delaney in his hospital bed all those months before.

9

The walking party were still crossing the rocky Margeride Mountains, a damp pastureland speckled with broom and with great granite boulders sticking up out of the ground, stone sentries left on duty from an earlier age. The farmhouses here were squat with small windows and doors and steep roofs to cope with the snows of winter. Saugues itself, their destination for the night, was, Powerscourt noted, a handsome town with many old houses including an English Tower, a great fortress of forbidding grey stone said to be have been the base for bands of marauding English brigands in the twelfth century. Like Le Puy, Saugues had a fraternity and a chapel of White Penitents who paraded round the town on Maundy Thursday in white robes with the hoods pulled over their faces and a couple of other penitents, barefoot, dressed in red, carrying a cross and the instruments of Christ's passion. The hotel owner serenaded all who would listen with stories of the Beast of Gevaudan, a deadly creature from two centuries before who caused a reign of terror all across the region, killing women and children, decapitating them, sometimes eating them. Was it a wolf? Or some alien creature that had survived unmolested in the forests before coming out to kill?

The pilgrims progressed from Saugues across a mountain landscape dotted with medieval towers and simple stone crosses. Powerscourt and Lady Lucy were walking now, trying to draw out from the pilgrims any stories of their past or the history of the Delaney family that might help find the reason for the death of John Delaney.

Lady Lucy was walking with young Christy Delaney who had looked, she noticed, quite disturbed as the hotel owner told them of the marauding Beast of Gevaudan. She asked him what he had thought of the story. Christy Delaney laughed.

'It reminded me of my grandmother,' the young man told her.

'Your grandmother?' asked Lady Lucy incredulously, unable to discern a connection between man-eating wolves and human grandparents.

'Sorry, I'm not explaining myself properly,' said Christy. 'When I was little we often used to go to my grandparents' house. They used to leave me and my sister in this unused drawing room on the first floor. It smelt, that room. The whole house smelt, of damp and mothballs and dirty clothes. My grandmother didn't believe much in washing, you see, never had. Every now and then, either in that drawing room or when we were upstairs in our horrid little bedroom, she would come and tell us stories. She was especially fond of Little Red Riding Hood and she was particularly good at horrible voices for the wolf and those eat you all up bits of the story. She would lean over the bed, smelling, like the house, of damp and dirt and mothballs, and more or less shout at you. I always wanted to hide under the bedclothes but I knew that would be rude.'

'So you stayed still and got scared?' asked Lady Lucy.

'I did,' said Christy Delaney. 'Very scared.' He was thinking that Lady Lucy reminded him of his mother. 'But I don't think it's anything relevant to your husband's investigations, Lady Powerscourt. Mind you, she did tell us all kinds of other stories when we were older, the Big Bad Wolf.'

'The Big Bad Wolf?'

'That's how my sister and I referred to our grandmother. Anyway, I don't suppose these stories have much truth left in them, they've been handed down the family rumour factory for so long.'

Lady Lucy thought young Christy showed a true historian's scepticism about his sources. It would serve him well, she felt, among the dusty libraries and the eccentric dons of Cambridge.

'What did the stories say, Christy, even if they were unreliable?'

'The main incident, around which all the others seemed to revolve, involved a comparatively rich Delaney refusing to help other, poorer Delaneys in the famine years. The poor ones were said to have died in the workhouse, but lots of people were said to have died in the workhouse in those times. Thousands and thousands of people were dying all over Ireland '

'God bless my soul,' said Lady Lucy, 'is that all that is known? No names?'

'No names that had reached the Big Bad Wolf,' said Christy Delaney.

'Let me ask you another question,' said Lady Lucy. 'Do you think John Delaney killed himself?'

'I do not,' said the young man firmly.

'Why not?'

'It'd be a very painful way to kill yourself, Lady Powerscourt. You wouldn't be dead the first time you hit your head or your leg on a rock on the way down. You probably wouldn't be dead the second time either. You could bounce all the way down to the ground and still be half alive when you reached the bottom. You'd lie there, maybe, blood pumping out all over you, waiting to pass away from your injuries. Surely that's not a good way to kill yourself. The Romans used to slit their wrists in a bath of hot water, didn't they? They thought, those Romans, that that was a painless way to die. They just got weaker and weaker until they went. The bath water must have been a very odd colour by the end, mind you. So that's why I don't think he killed himself, Lady Powerscourt.'

'So what should we be looking for, do you think?'

'There's only one thing all these people have in common, Lady Powerscourt. Whether they're from Ireland or England or America, they're all Delaneys. There must be some mystery in their past that could explain the murder of John Delaney.'

'What sort of mystery?' said Lady Lucy.

'That's for your husband to find out,' said Christy Delaney cheerfully. He had often thought of a career as an author after he left university. 'Be a good title for a book, don't you think, Lady Powerscourt, *Delaney's Dark Secret*.'

Between St-Alban-sur-Limagnole and Aumont-Aubrac they came down from the mountains and crossed the river Truyère, flowing fast towards the great gorges that bore its name. Now they were in more alien territory, the Aubrac plateau, the most southerly of the volcanic uplands of the Auvergne, grazing country with vast stretches of pasture enclosed by dry stone walls. Higher up the dwarf beeches carried the scars of harsh winters and a long line of conifers along the side of the roads protected them against snowdrifts. There were still fragments of buildings left standing which had provided food and shelter for the pilgrims in the Middle Ages. Ruined donjons and medieval keeps bore witness to more shadowy figures from distant times, the Knights Templar and the Hospitallers of St John. The skies were huge up here on the Aubrac Massif. On a clear day you could see thirty or forty miles. Herds of cattle or sheep were brought up to the plateau to graze in the summer. The shepherds lived in strange dwellings called *burons*, home to cattle and pigs as well as humans, where the shepherds made Laguiole cheese which they stored in their cellars. But it was, even on a sunny day, a place where the solitude was almost oppressive. Looking out at the great expanse that surrounded them, most of the pilgrims fell silent. For many on the long road to Compostela the passage of the Aubrac, with the heavens stretching away towards infinity and the eternal quiet all around, was the most memorable part of the entire journey. 'There is the Aubrac,' a French author wrote, 'a lofty belvedere both bare and sublime, more lunar, more outstretched, more windswept than the paramos of the Andes.'

Powerscourt was talking with another of the Irish pilgrims as they crossed this extraordinary landscape, Willie John Delaney, in his early forties, the man dying of an incurable disease. Willie John's illness had left him completely bald. In his past life, he told Powerscourt, he had been a builder in Westport, County Mayo, home to another pilgrimage, to the summit of Ireland's Holy Mountain, Croagh Patrick on the last Sunday in July every year.

'And have you left a wife and family behind?' asked Powerscourt.

'I have not, thank God,' said Willie John, 'there'll be no wife and children left behind when I go.'

'Do you know how long you've got?' asked Powerscourt.

'It could be next week, it could be three months, that's what Dr McGreevy said to me in his little surgery on The Mall before I left now.'

'Do you find the pilgrimage helpful?' asked Powerscourt.

'I do and I don't, if that's not too Irish an answer for you. I've been praying a lot, you see. I'm never quite sure about praying, are you, Lord Powerscourt? You know how it is when you've got a bad connection on these telephones. Maybe the other end isn't plugged in right or the girl on the switchboard hasn't put you through in the proper manner. You can't hear what the other person is saying, there's just a fuzzy noise on the line. Sometimes praying is like that for me, Lord Powerscourt, you've just got a bad line. God isn't linked up properly. He can't hear you. You can't get through. You know that little Black Madonna back there in Le Puy?' Powerscourt nodded. 'I had a terrible thought the second time I was on my knees in front of her. Some little voice in the back of me head was saying, It's only a doll, Willie John, it's only a doll like you could buy a child for a birthday or Christmas and the little girl could make different outfits for the doll to wear, just like they have for the Black Madonna with those different sets of clothes for different seasons of the Church's year. I couldn't even manage a Hail Mary after that.'

'But you implied that there were times when prayer was helpful, Willie John,' said Powerscourt.

Willie John Delaney stopped and leant on his staff for a moment. He pointed his arm in the general direction of the sky. Way over to their right, dots on the landscape, a herd of Aubrac cows were making their way slowly into fresh pasture.

'I've never seen anywhere like this in my entire life,' said Willie John. 'I've seen most of the great barren spaces, littered with mountains and lakes and sodden peat, in the west of Ireland, but nothing like this here.'

He pointed up at the great canopy of sky, stretching away to impossibly distant horizons. 'God's here,' he said, 'I'm sure of it. It's so quiet here He doesn't need the telephone. I thank Him for allowing me to see Him in this landscape of His majesty, God's own country.'

Powerscourt asked if there were any details of Delaney family history which might help him in his inquiries.

'There's enough stories about the past of the Delaneys to fill an entire library,' said Willie John. 'I don't think it would be helpful to you, Lord Powerscourt, if I regaled you with the family gossip. Most of it is almost certainly wrong.'

They passed La Roche and Chabanes-Planes, la Chapelle de Bastide and les Quatres Chemins, they passed Nasbinals and its eleventh-century church with the basalt walls. Outside Nasbinals they climbed up over five thousand feet on the road to Aubrac itself, a little town almost as high as the high point on the road. This was bandit country, famous in the past for marauding wolves and wild boar and brigands. Over the next four miles the path dropped fifteen hundred feet to St-Chély-d'Aubrac.

Johnny Fitzgerald had been busy on Powerscourt's behalf in London. He had to find information about Brother White and the dead man John Delaney. Johnny had smiled when he read Powerscourt's request to find out if the man suffered from vertigo. He had helped his friend down from innumerable high places in his time. Johnny's only surprise was that Francis was still foolish enough to try once again to reach some lofty and isolated place. Surely, Johnny said to himself, he must know himself better by now than to try again. It was bound to end in failure.

He picked up the trail of Brother White by asking Powerscourt's brother-in-law William Burke, a mighty power in the City of London, if there were any banking or counting houses likely to employ old boys of the school where Brother White taught. Burke had been astonished when he learnt of Michael Delaney and his pilgrimage, for Delaney's fame and his fortune had spread to London many years before.

'If you'd told me that the great Michael Delaney was going on a pilgrimage halfway across France and Spain, Johnny, I'd have said it was about as likely as the Pope coming here and taking a post as a junior clerk in some insurance business. Never mind. I'm sure I can find a couple of Brother White's old boys for you, that shouldn't be any problem at all.'

The following evening, shortly after six o'clock, Johnny had bought the first round of drinks in a pub called the City Arms, just off Lombard Street, close to the Bank of England.

'I gather you're looking for information about that bastard Brother White,' said the First Old Boy, whose name was Robert. 'He's not dead by any chance, is he?'

'Not yet,' said Johnny.

'Pity, that,' said the Second Old Boy, whose name was Patrick. 'He should have been dead years ago.'

'What was the trouble with the Christian Brother?' said Johnny.

'Flogger White?' said Robert. 'Just that, he loved beating people, the bastard.'

'Trousers up, trousers down,' said Patrick, 'it made no

128

difference. He once beat an entire class in an afternoon. Think about it. Any normal person would have been exhausted by the end of that. Not Brother White, oh no. He was as fresh at the end as he was at the beginning. He enjoyed it, you see. You could tell by looking at his face afterwards. The bastard was always smiling, as if he'd just scored a goal.'

'They say he has a special collection of canes, about fifty of the things,' Robert went on, warming to his theme. 'He'd ordered up some pretty evil specimens from the Far East where they go in for beatings and that sort of stuff.'

'He'd have used a cat-o'-nine-tails if the school would have let him, those things they had in the Navy years ago,' Patrick continued.

'Bastard,' said Robert. 'Somebody should have flogged him good and proper.'

'He'd probably have enjoyed that,' said his friend. 'Some fellow who left last year said he'd seen White coming out of a classy prostitute place where they beat you for as long as you want.'

'Did nobody ever complain?' asked Johnny, returning from the bar with fresh drinks.

'Some American Ambassador complained years ago, a chap told me,' said Patrick, taking a great draught of his second beer. 'His son got flogged in the usual White fashion. Next day Ambassador and Mrs Ambassador turn up at the headmaster's door. Complaint not accepted. Running of the school a matter for the school authorities, not for outsiders, however distinguished.'

After four rounds of drinks Johnny thought he had the general drift of Brother White's activities, the boys bent over chairs or leant up against the wall or stretched out over some piece of equipment in the gym where the Brother could have a good run up towards his victims. The old boys were astonished to learn that their former teacher had gone on pilgrimage.

'Maybe he's gone to ask forgiveness for his sins,' said Robert.

'Let's hope God's gone deaf,' said his friend.

Johnny let a couple of days go by before he moved on to the case of the dead John Delaney, one-time resident of Acton in west London. He began his campaign in the Crown and Sceptre at the bottom of Church Street, a short distance from the Delaney residence. They knew him only slightly in there, they said, crossing themselves vigorously at the mention of the dead man, he would drop in occasionally on a Saturday afternoon. The King's Head in the High Street had heard neither of Delaneys nor of corpses. But the Fox and Hounds, hard by the underground station, was a fountain of information. Here Johnny learnt the name of his wife, the number of his children, the amount he drank on his regular visits, never more than two pints of beer, why, the man was virtually teetotal according to informed opinion in the Fox and Hounds. He was building up a steady business in the little community, Johnny was told, always offering slightly lower rates than his competitors and giving discounts for regular clients. John Delaney and his family were all devout, attending Mass and sending the children to classes for their first communion. There was, the regulars told him, nothing about Delaney which could make anybody want to kill him. Johnny thought it interesting that nobody was surprised John Delaney had gone on pilgrimage. But as to why he might have been killed on his journey they had no idea. It was a mystery to the youngest and the eldest habitués of the Fox and Hounds.

When Johnny had heard what John Delaney's job was he had to force himself to keep a straight face. And as he hastened towards the City to send a telegram from a Delaney outpost in Gracechurch Street he wondered how his friend would react when he heard of the collapse of one of his theories. Johnny decided to keep the bad news till the end.

'Don't worry about the number of words in your message,' the young telegraph operator in the Delaney offices told him. 'If Mr Delaney thought it would help, he'd send the whole bloody Bible down the wires.'

'Brother White known as Flogger White. Likes beating boys. Wide variety of horrible canes. Don't make any mistakes, Francis, when he's hearing your amo amas amat. John Delaney v. respectable citizen. Wife, two children. Churchgoer. Suggest you ask Croesus Delaney for contribution for widow and orphans. Not likely to be suffering from vertigo. Man was a window cleaner. Regards Johnny.'

The scenery changed when the pilgrims set out from St-Chély-d'Aubrac. They left behind the vast plateau with the wide open skies and the cattle and entered a softer world of French agriculture, great woods of beech and chestnut beside the road, the occasional vineyard. After four hours or so the advance guard could see the Lot, known here as the Olt, the name for the river in the ancient French language of Occitan, and the little fortified town of St-Come d'Olt. Powerscourt admired the three former gateways in the old wall that led into pretty streets with houses dating back to the fifteenth and sixteenth centuries. Some of the buildings still had the covered balconies installed centuries before. The sun was sparkling on the river, arrived here from St-Geniez-d'Olt, Ste-Eulalie-d'Olt and St-Laurent-d'Olt and twisting its way through the high cliffs towards Espalion, Estaing and Entraygues-sur-Truyère en route to its marriage with the Garonne many miles away.

There was a bizarre theological argument in St-Côme-d'Olt in front of the twisted spire of St Come and St Damien. Jack O'Driscoll, displaying the curiosity for which newspapermen are famous, had bought himself a guidebook. He didn't understand most of it but odd words made sense.

'That's a Flamboyant Spire,' he said proudly, pointing to the crooked structure on top of the church.

'No, it's not,' said Patrick MacLoughlin, the trainee priest from Boston, who did not have the benefit of a guidebook, 'it's crooked.'

'I think you'll find it's called a twisted spire,' said Father Kennedy, munching on an enormous pastry he had just picked up from the boulangerie.

'You couldn't worship God in a church with a twisted spire.' Patrick MacLoughlin stuck to his guns. 'It's like having a crooked nave or a crooked altar. It's not right. When did you last see one of these things in America?'

'America doesn't count in matters like this,' said Jack O'Driscoll, peering at his Baedeker for guidance, 'place hasn't been there five minutes. Not like round here.'

'Boston's jolly old, very old indeed. There aren't any twisted spires there.'

'See here,' said Jack, pointing triumphantly to a date in his book, '1552, it says here for the construction date of our Flamboyant friend, the only people running round near Boston then were those Red Indian fellows covered in war paint and living in funny wigwams and sending smoke signals to each other.'

'What do you say, Father? Could you worship God properly in a church with a crooked spire?'

Father Kennedy was reluctant to take on the role of arbiter in the matter. He was staring sadly at his hand. Only a minute ago there had been a pastry there. Now it seemed to have disappeared.

'I think you will find, young Patrick,' he replied, licking his fingers for the memory of what had gone, 'that you can worship wherever you wish. It is the mind of the congregation that is important, not the nature of the surroundings.'

Patrick MacLoughlin snorted and went off to inspect the river. Father Kennedy thought he had just enough time for a return visit to the boulangerie. There might not be another establishment like it for miles.

They marched on, the river dancing and sparkling through the rocks, to another ancient site of pilgrimage, the town of Espalion, graced with an ancient bridge the pilgrims of centuries before had crossed on their long march to Compostela. And here Alex Bentley's organizational powers came into their own. For he had corresponded with the local boatyard, asking if they could make some rowing boats available to his party, liable to arrive in a given ten-day period. They were to leave the boats at Entraygues further down the river. And so ten pilgrims, the Powerscourts, Alex Bentley and Father Kennedy divided themselves among four boats, three crews of four and two in the last. Maggie Delaney, Stephen Lewis and Delaney himself were travelling by carriage and were due to meet up with them in the hotel at Estaing that evening.

Alex Bentley, his rowing days at Princeton and Yale coming back to him, was in charge of one boat with Lady Lucy sitting opposite him in the front and Christy Delaney and Waldo Mulligan at the stern. Bringing up the rear were Father Kennedy and Patrick MacLoughlin, two in a boat meant for four. At first all went well. They rowed past the tanners' houses with stones sticking out of them at various levels so that hides could be scrubbed whatever the height of the river. They went by an old palace perched on a rock with a couple of pepper-pot towers. Then trouble came at the rear. Patrick MacLoughlin had protested his complete incompetence at any known form of sporting activity, so Father Kennedy, very reluctantly, took the oars. The only time Father Kennedy used his two hands together was in raising the chalice at Mass. This proved inadequate training for rowing down the Lot. The clerical figure, still dressed in black, was incapable of synchronizing the two oars together. One would drop feebly into the water and the Father sometimes forgot to stroke it through the water. The other oar, nominally under the control of Father Kennedy's left hand, usually failed to make contact with the Lot altogether. The result was that his rowing boat, far from following the others in a straight line, careered off towards the right and began going round in circles. The river at this point had fields above it rather than the vertiginous rocks that tower over it near Entraygues, but there were still plenty of large rocks lining the banks. Patrick MacLoughlin at least had the presence of mind to call 'Help' as loudly as he could.

'Bloody fool, can't even row straight,' said Charlie Flanagan in the third boat.

'Christ, he's going to crash into that great boulder in a minute,' said Wee Jimmy Delaney, resting on his oars.

Alex Bentley felt responsible. Why hadn't he made sure that a responsible person was in charge of that boat? He aimed his craft at a point where he should intercept the stricken religious and be able to tow them to safety. Father Kennedy's craft continued its progress, lurching this way and that like a drunk on his way home. He made to dip his left oar in once more and missed completely. The impetus almost carried him out of the boat. Patrick MacLoughlin steadied his superior and settled him back on the thwarts. A couple of locals got off their bicycles on the path and stared at the scene, roaring with laughter.

'Don't do anything now! Don't try to row whatever you do!' Alex Bentley was drawing close now. 'I'm going to throw you a rope. Hang on to it, for heaven's sake. I'll pull you back to the middle.'

It took four unsuccessful throws before Father Kennedy managed to grasp the rope thrown from Alex Bentley's boat. At last, the tow line secured, the rowing party were able to proceed. The gaping locals abandoned their mirth and their sightseeing and proceeded on their way. Overhead the birds still whirled, swooping down to perch on the sides of the river. The water, Powerscourt noticed, trailing his hand in the Lot, was very cold. Soon they could see the medieval bridge of Estaing and the mighty castle of the lords of the manor of the same name. On the slopes high above the river the Estaing vines were slowly growing back to full health and maturity after the ravages of phylloxera a generation before. Alex Bentley's hotel, the Lion d'Or, sat beside the bridge, flanked by two wings that had once been part of a monastery. That night each pilgrim was able to sleep in his own cell.

'It's so peaceful here, Francis, don't you think?' Lady Lucy was leaning over the ancient bridge and staring into the water. A couple of fish passed slowly by beneath her. 'You don't think anything else is going to happen, do you? Any more murders, I mean?'

'I wish I knew,' said Powerscourt, staring intently at a heron on the opposite bank. 'If there is a killer in this party, my love, he won't care if he's in the Doubting Castle of Giant Despair or the Delectable Mountains. All the other pilgrims are marching towards their final destination and resolution of their sins in that cathedral at Santiago de Compostela. The killer, if there is one, is marching towards the elimination of his enemies.'

Any pilgrim still awake in the small hours of the morning after an enormous supper of beef stew and almond tart, washed down with carafes of the local red wine, would have seen a strange sight by the side of the hotel. A hooded figure was pushing some package in a wheelbarrow towards the banks of the river. When the figure reached the pontoon where the rowing boats were tied up, he took his parcel out of the wheelbarrow and placed it carefully in the bottom of one of the boats. He borrowed a rough tarpaulin from another vessel and placed it over his package. Then the hooded figure took a knife from his pocket and cut the rope that secured the rowing boat to the bank. He waded out towards the centre of the river, pulling his stolen rowing boat behind him. When he thought he had found the point where the current was strongest, he steadied his craft in the centre of it. He reached into his pocket again and took out two objects. One he placed at the very front of the boat. The other he slipped under the tarpaulin. Then he gave the rowing boat a firm push to send it on its way towards Entraygues, Cajarc and Cahors. The hooded figure watched as the boat twisted its way along the currents of the Lot until it had passed out of sight. Then he waded slowly back to the bank and removed his trousers. He sent these too into the middle of the river with a great heave. Then he walked slowly back towards the hotel. The stars were bright above the water. An owl was hooting from further up the river in the direction of Golinhac on the other bank. There were still three hours before dawn.

10

A frantic hammering on his bedroom door woke Powerscourt shortly after half past six the next morning.

'Monsieur milord,' panted Jacques the hotel owner, 'you must come at once! At once, I say. There has been a catastrophe here, in my hotel!'

Powerscourt noticed a slight glow in the man's cheeks as if he had already been taking comfort from the local red. God in heaven, he said to himself, it's not yet seven o'clock.

'Whatever is the matter, monsieur?' said Powerscourt, buttoning his shirt and wondering if half the pilgrims in their cells had been visited by the Exterminating Angel.

'You must come, monsieur milord. I will show you. It is terrible!'

Powerscourt could hear Lady Lucy asking sleepy questions about where was he going so early in the morning as he sped down the stairs and out into the fresh air of Estaing. Jacques led him to the pontoon where the rowing boats were tied up.

'See, monsieur milord!' he said, pointing dramatically to the cut rope where a rowing boat had been tethered the evening before. 'One of these boats has been stolen! I gave my word that they would be safe in my keeping to that villainous fellow Berthier who keeps the yard at Espalion. I signed a piece of paper promising to pay a great deal of money if any of them was lost. It is more than all my life savings, monsieur! But what was I to do? I was not to suppose that any of these pilgrims here would turn into rowing boat thieves in the night!' Jacques stared angrily at the cut rope. Then another terrible thought struck him, possibly even more serious than the loss of the boat. 'And what will Charlotte say? What indeed! I am ruined, monsieur milord, ruined! What a way to start the day!'

Powerscourt remembered the innkeeper's wife, Charlotte, shouting at her husband the evening before to tear himself away from the bottle and supervise the serving of the supper. She was a formidable woman, he thought, round of figure, round of face, fierce of countenance, obviously the true mistress of the hotel. On one point at least Powerscourt could offer instant reassurance.

'Calm yourself, monsieur, calm yourself. The missing boat may be found. It may turn up later today. But if it does not, Mr Delaney will recompense you for its loss. I'm certain he will contribute enough to pay off Mr Berthier from Espalion.'

'Mr Delaney, the elderly American gentleman? Not one of the younger Mr Delaneys, but the old one? He has enough money to pay off Berthier?' Jacques the hotelkeeper sounded suspicious, as if men of such improbable wealth were not to be found on the banks of the Lot. Powerscourt assured him that Delaney could probably buy most of southern France if the mood took him. Relieved that his money troubles appeared to be over and another onslaught from Charlotte postponed, Jacques took his leave of Powerscourt, saying he had hotel business to attend to. He did not tell his guest that his business lay in a back pantry off the kitchen where he had a secret supply of *vin rouge* hidden at the back of a broom cupboard.

Powerscourt bent down and took the rope in his hand. The cut was very clean. This was no hacking job with a blunt instrument. Whoever came down here in the middle of the night came fully prepared with a sharp knife to hand. What else had the thief brought with him? Had he simply climbed into the boat and floated off downstream like the Lady of

Shallott? Powerscourt cursed himself for his folly and his delay and ran at full speed towards the pilgrims' bedrooms. Were they all there? Or had a single pilgrim abandoned the party to make his own way on the next stage of the journey?

The six cells to the left of the main hotel building were all occupied, pilgrims complaining at being woken or greeting him cheerfully as they dressed. Powerscourt stopped in the fourth cell on the other side. This had been the temporary home of Patrick MacLoughlin from Boston, just twenty-two years old and training for the priesthood. Powerscourt felt sick as he remembered the young man saying the day before that he was completely useless at any known form of sporting activity. Maybe that had been a lie, a preparation for this flight down the river in the middle of the night, but Powerscourt didn't think so. Patrick MacLoughlin was gone. There was only one set of circumstances, Powerscourt thought, which could unite the departure of MacLoughlin and the departure of the boat. Powerscourt raced into the Lion d'Or. He told Delaney to make sure nobody moved out of Estaing. He borrowed the innkeeper's horse and sped down the road by the side of the Lot. He prayed to God that he was wrong.

M. Berthier of Espalion's rowing boat had a fairly uneventful career after its unexpected departure from the hotel in the middle of the night. The river glided along in the middle of its gorge, the water almost black, the cliffs rising steeply on either side, the tall trees standing firm and upright against the night sky, the local wildlife peering curiously at a boat travelling down their river without any visible means of human propulsion. It stayed in the centre of the current for a long time, twisting its way past tiny beaches and the occasional small island. Shortly before dawn a breeze arose and this was enough to nudge the boat off course. It wandered off to the right and stopped by a group of rocks, close to a tiny bay much favoured by the local fishermen, a couple of miles from Entraygues-sur-Truyère. As Powerscourt was fastening his shirt buttons in the hotel an elderly angler called Maurice Vernais was settling himself into his usual position by the riverside. He had a couple of rods, a large basket to hold his fish, for Maurice was ever an optimist, and a smaller basket containing his breakfast, his lunch and an enormous bottle of wine. Maurice had long believed that the best way to achieve domestic harmony was to be out of the domestic environment for as long as possible. Had he but known it, his wife, Marinette, shared his opinion, only wishing that her husband could fish all night as well as all day.

Maurice saw the rowing boat, turning slowly away from him. Nothing would be more likely to disturb his fish. '*Merde*,' he said to himself and marched out in his waders to give the boat a good push. The boat swung round and came back to rest in virtually the same place it had been before. '*Double merde*!' said Maurice. This time he seized the front of the boat and waded out into the middle of the Lot until he felt he had reached the heart of the current. 'Off you go,' he said, pointing the prow downstream and giving it a firm shove. He resolved to have a leg of chicken and a large glass of wine shortly to fortify himself after his ordeal. Then he settled down and prepared his rods for the day. At no point had he raised the tarpaulin to inspect the contents of the boat.

The river Lot enters the little town of Entraygues from the south-west and passes under a medieval bridge. The rowing boat passed under the middle arch of this bridge, borne along by the centre of the current, and passed a nondescript road with a couple of shops. To the right a little street led up to the town square, a handsome place shaded by plane trees with room for weekly markets in season and sporting the inevitable bakery, butcher's and bar. To the left, across the river, the hills rose steeply towards Espeyrac and Conques. The town of Entraygues takes its name from the Occitan *entre aigas*, between the waters, and it was this meeting of rivers that stopped the rowing boat's progress. Racing down from its gorges to the north, passing beneath another medieval bridge, the river Truyère joins the Lot just after a ruined castle on the left. The force of the Truyère carried M. Berthier's boat off course right across the combined river. It came to rest on the opposite shore from the town, parked on a bank of rough stones, just out of sight from Entraygues on the opposite side. And there it remained. It's a fisherman, gone further downstream, said any locals who looked at it in the early morning. By noon it was still nestling by the side of the river. Oddly enough, Entraygues marked the first spot where the Lot was navigable upstream in medieval times, ancient vessels called *gabarres* carrying produce west along the Lot and the Garonne on a ten-day journey to Bordeaux. But for the little rowing boat, property of M. Berthier of Espalion, there was no more navigation that day. It was beached. The more fanciful citizens wondered if the owner had simply gone to sleep inside his craft after an early start with his fishing rod. The bells from the church tower were pealing the Angelus when a couple of small boys, just released from school for lunch, approached the boat.

Powerscourt made inquiries in the town square. A rowing boat? A rowing boat cut loose from Estaing in the middle of the night? Goodness me, monsieur, we do not have such things here in Entraygues. The man behind the bar looked closely at Powerscourt and wondered to himself if the English monsieur had taken too much armagnac the night before. Armagnac, the barman firmly believed, was always liable to produce hallucinations the next morning if taken to excess. Perhaps, he suggested, the thief had put the boat on his cart and driven off with it. The people in the bakery wondered if some fisherman might have taken it and hidden the boat in the ground just behind the river. It was the butcher, a cheerful soul engaged in the dismemberment of a great side of beef, who gave Powerscourt the best advice. There were always, he told him, some old fellows fishing on the banks of the river,

141

and they usually arrived there very early in the morning to get away from their wives. Had Powerscourt seen any of these characters on his ride from Estaing? Had he been travelling fast? Perhaps he should retrace his steps at walking pace. Maybe the fishermen would have seen something.

Twenty-five minutes later Powerscourt came upon the figure of Maurice Vernais, holding firmly on to his rod and glancing sadly at the empty basket meant to hold his catch.

'Forgive me, monsieur,' said Powerscourt, 'could I be permitted to ask if you have been fishing here all morning?'

Maurice Vernais stared at Powerscourt. Then he spat expertly into the sand at the edge of the river. 'What business is it of yours if I have?'

'I just thought you might be able to help me, that's all,' said Powerscourt, feeling that this interview might take longer than expected. 'I'm looking for a missing rowing boat.'

'Rowing boat, frigate, battleship, it's all one to me,' said Maurice, pulling in his line and preparing to recast.

'But did you see a rowing boat, monsieur, on this stretch of river, earlier today?'

'Happen I did and happen I didn't,' said Maurice, flicking his line well out into the Lot.

'That's a very pretty cast,' said Powerscourt. 'I'm sure you'll catch something soon. Now tell me, did you see a rowing boat or not?'

Maurice Vernais repeated his spitting gesture. Powerscourt felt it was less than helpful.

'Nothing to do with me, monsieur,' the Frenchman said, fiddling with his line and deciding to have another large glass of *rouge* when this irritating foreigner had gone away. 'None of my business. Nor yours neither, I shouldn't wonder.'

Powerscourt decided there was only one answer. He reached into his pocket and drew out a wad of notes. Maurice Vernais eyed them greedily for he and his Marinette had very little money, depending on the fish caught in the Lot for much of their diet.

'I wonder if I could make some small contribution towards your fishing expenses, monsieur,' said Powerscourt, holding out a fistful of notes but not actually handing them over. Payment, he decided, would be by results. 'Rods and things are very expensive these days.'

'That's a fine collection of money you have there,' said Maurice, holding out his hand.

'Not so fast, my fisherman friend, not so fast.' Powerscourt drew his hand with the bribe close to his chest. 'If I feel you are not telling the truth, then there is no money. Do you understand? Now then, did you see a rowing boat drifting down the river early this morning?'

'I did,' said Maurice Vernais finally, greed overcoming the natural instinct of the French peasant to be as unhelpful as possible. 'It must have been about seven o'clock. The damned boat was stuck on those rocks over there.'

'And what did you do?'

'It was interfering with my fishing, so it was. Hard enough to catch fish anyway without damned rowing boats getting in the way. I gave it a good push, so I did.'

'Was that all you did?'

'Good push didn't work. It came back to rest where it had been before. So I waded out and put it back into the current. Damned boat should be in Entraygues or even beyond by now.'

'Did you see what was in the boat, monsieur?'

'Why should I care what was in the boat, for God's sake? I come here to fish, not to inspect the insides of people's rowing boats like some devil of a tax man.'

'Was the boat empty? Could you see the bottom?'

'Damned boat had a tarpaulin drawn up all over it. Couldn't see what was inside. It was pretty heavy, mind you. I could tell that when I shoved it into the current.'

'Are you telling me that you didn't even take a peek under that tarpaulin? The cargo might have been valuable, after all.'

'Nothing to do with me. I've told you that already. Now

why don't you give my money and shove off. You're disturbing the fish, for Christ's sake.'

With some reluctance Powerscourt decided the man was
telling the truth. He handed over some notes and set off back
to Entraygues in pursuit of something buried beneath a
tarpaulin. As he regained the main road he heard a shout of
triumph from the river bank. Maurice Vernais had caught his
first fish of the day.

Jean Pierre Roche was a curly-haired youth just past his tenth
birthday. His friend Auguste was slightly smaller with a gap in
his front teeth. 'Race you to that rowing boat on the stones,' said
Jean Pierre, setting off at once for he knew his friend was faster
than he was. Sure enough, Auguste overtook him towards the
end of the hundred-yard dash to the stricken vessel.

'I win,' said Auguste proudly, touching the side of the boat
in confirmation of his victory. They bent down and peered
inside. More or less all they could see was the tarpaulin.

'What do you think is underneath?' said Jean Pierre.
'Smugglers' stuff, maybe? Perhaps it belongs to some gang of
smugglers operating in secret all over southern France.'

Auguste removed the heavy stone that held it down and
pulled back the tarpaulin. They stared at Patrick MacLoughlin,
his head lying to one side, dressed in the black garments of
the novice priest. MacLoughlin did not speak.

'He's asleep,' said Auguste, 'better leave him alone. I'm
hungry. I want my lunch.'

Jean Pierre did not think the man was asleep. He had seen
death recently in his own home, a grandfather who went to
sleep in his chair after Sunday lunch and never woke up. That
had been a year ago and Jean Pierre never forgot the strange
pallor that spread over the old man's face. Gingerly, his hand
shaking slightly, he reached inside and felt the face of Patrick
MacLoughlin. It was cold, very cold.

'He's not sleeping,' said Jean Pierre, pulling the tarpaulin back over the corpse, 'he's dead. I'm going to tell Mama. She'll know what to do.' He started off at full speed back to his house. 'It's jolly exciting finding a dead person, don't you think, Auguste? Maybe we'll be let off afternoon school. I still haven't finished that maths homework.'

'Do you think there'll be some reward?' asked Auguste, keeping pace with his friend rather than overtaking him. 'I could do with some extra money.'

Madame Daniele Roche was deeply devoted to all her five children, but if you pressed her up against a wall she would probably have said that Jean Pierre was her favourite. He was so quick and so curious and so bright. But she would have been the first to say that his imagination sometimes got the better of him. Last year he had reported a sighting of a squadron of lancers trotting down the main street of Entraygues. He had been able to give a perfect description of the details of their resplendent uniforms, but no soldiers had visited the town that day. A month ago he claimed to have seen Charlemagne himself on a mighty white charger pausing in the middle of the medieval bridge and asking Jean Pierre for directions to Conques. So when her eldest son announced that he and Auguste had found a dead body in a rowing boat by the river she paid no attention at all.

'Come along, it's lunchtime, Jean Pierre. Auguste, you'd better run off home. Your mother will be worried.'

Jean Pierre made no move towards the lunch table where his younger siblings and his elder sister were preparing to tuck into a fragrant stew, made to a recipe from Jean Pierre's grandmother. Auguste too held his ground.

'Please, Mama,' said the boy, 'I'm not making this up, I promise you. There is a dead man in a boat by the edge of the river. I don't think he's French either. I think he's foreign.'

'And what would a foreigner be doing lying dead by the Lot in our little town? We hardly ever see any foreigners round here. Come and sit down, Jean Pierre.'

'Please, Mama.' Jean Pierre was holding on to her arm. 'You've got to believe me. I'm not making it up. He might be important, this dead man. Maybe the police are looking for him already.'

'Your father always says, as you well know, that respectable people like us should have nothing to do with the police.'

'Jean Pierre is right,' said Auguste, entering the lists on his friend's behalf. Mothers could be so unreasonable at times. 'I saw it too, the dead body, I mean.'

Oddly enough the support and testimony of Auguste weighed heavily with Daniele Roche. Jean Pierre was capable of any feats of fancy but she had known Auguste since he and Jean Pierre started school together. Solid, yes, she would have said, reliable, yes, but about as much imagination as a dried raisin. That was what made him an ideal foil for Jean Pierre.

'Well, maybe,' she said, beginning to relent, 'but you must eat your lunch first. Auguste, you're more than welcome to join us as you're so late.'

'Please, Mama,' said Jean Pierre, tugging at her arm. 'We must go now. It could be important. How would you feel if one of your children was lying dead in a boat and some mother refused to help because of a plate of stew?'

Daniele Roche restrained herself from pointing out that the only member of her family she could imagine being found dead in a rowing boat was Jean Pierre himself. She entrusted her children to the care of her eldest girl and followed the boys towards the boat. Once there she too touched the dead man's face. Then she crossed herself and knelt down to say a battery of Hail Marys. She sent the boys to run as fast as they could to tell the doctor, who lived on the far side of the town square, and the local policeman. The two of them, she thought, would be believed. Jean Pierre on his own would not be regarded as a credible witness. About forty minutes later the butcher's cart, with the doctor on board, could be seen carrying a package wrapped in a tarpaulin towards the doctor's surgery. The rumours were flying round Entraygues faster than the wind. The body of a top politician from Lyon had been found in the boat. Nonsense, said the more fanciful citizens, it was a mass murderer from Toulouse the police had been trying to apprehend for months. Rubbish, said the party that took its news from the boulangerie, everybody knew that the dead man was American, on the run from the terrible gangsters in New York City.

Lord Francis Powerscourt noticed the tarpaulin as he rode back into town on the Estaing road. He raced up to the melancholy party. 'Gentlemen,' he said, 'please forgive me. My name is Powerscourt. I am an investigator from England, currently attached to a party of American pilgrims, at present resident in Estaing up the road.' He lowered his voice slightly. 'One of these Americans is missing. If you have what I think you have under that tarpaulin, I may be able to identify it for you.'

Half an hour later the business was complete. Dr Lafont informed Powerscourt that the dead man had been strangled before being placed in the rowing boat. After Powerscourt's identification a label was attached to the dead man proclaiming him to be Patrick MacLoughlin, twenty-two years old, resident in the city of Boston in the State of Massachusetts, United States of America, an American citizen. The only other thing found in the boat, apart from the corpse, was a scallop shell, solemnly handed over to Powerscourt. A police sergeant had appeared. He informed Powerscourt that the local officers had all been informed about the pilgrims by their colleagues in Le Puy. An inspector was on his way from the neighbouring town of Figeac to take charge of the investigation. He requested that the pilgrim party remain in the hotel in Estaing and its environs until further notice. Here we go again, Powerscourt thought bitterly as he rode back. Who do we start bribing first? The Mayor of Estaing, whoever he might be? The local curé or his superiors from Conques? More contributions to the widows' and orphans' fund of the police force in Figeac?

'My God, Powerscourt,' said Michael Delaney when he heard the news. 'To lose two, as that perverted playwright put it,

147

looks like carelessness. I've taken to counting them every time I see them now, the pilgrims, I mean. I did a run-through at lunchtime when they all sat down here. Tell me, Powerscourt, do you have any idea what we are going to do? Do we have to start bribing the local worthies as we did in Le Puy? I find it hard to believe we can pull off the same trick twice. Have you, as yet, any idea what is going on?'

'I have no more idea who killed Patrick MacLoughlin than I do of who killed John Delaney back there in Le Puy. I'm sure it's the same person, that's all.'

'How many people did we have to start with?' asked Delaney. 'Sixteen? Now it's down to fourteen and we've travelled less than a hundred miles. At this rate we'll be lucky if there's anybody left alive by the time we reach the Pyrenees. It reminds me of a great friend of mine, used to be much richer than me but not any more. Horses were his thing. Four or five years ago he had the finest collection of racehorses in America. He was aiming to win as many of the premier events as possible, the Travers Stakes in Saratoga, the Kentucky Oaks in Louisville, the Belmont Stakes in New York. At the beginning of the season all his animals were in tip-top condition. Raring to race, he told me. Then they started to go. A fetlock here, a splint there, I'm not an expert on equine diseases, but whatever could lay you low if you were a horse his lot got it. By the middle of June they were all limping or hobbling or off their food or off their saddles or off their wits. Man never got over it. Sold all his horses on the first of July and took to stamp collecting. No bloody fetlocks there, Penny Blacks not likely to suffer from equine flu.'

Delaney paused and looked at Powerscourt. 'Sorry, I digress. What do you think we should do?'

'I think we need to have a meeting. I think we need to have a meeting with all the pilgrims and everybody. Obviously we all have to wait to talk to the inspector from Figeac. But I feel you should ask the pilgrims if they wish to go on. You have your very special reasons, I know, Mr Delaney, for wanting to continue. But the others may not want to. We have to give them the option of going home. I think we should put it to the vote.'

'Vote?' said Delaney suspiciously. 'Ask the pilgrims? Isn't that a bit democratic? Nothing wrong with democracy, of course, you just have to make sure your own candidates are the only ones allowed to stand.'

Powerscourt thought that the workers' councils so beloved of extreme left-wingers right across Europe might not get off the starting line on the Delaney factory floor. He held his peace.

Half an hour later the pilgrim company assembled at the far end of the hotel dining room. Already Powerscourt, as he told Lady Lucy later, was beginning to feel that he could happily go to his grave without any further assemblies in the dining rooms of French hotels. Delaney sat at the centre of a table to the front, flanked by Father Kennedy – always happy to be in hotel dining rooms – on his right with Powerscourt on his left and then Lady Lucy. Alex Bentley basked in the sunshine on the far side of Lady Lucy. The pilgrims sat in two semicircular rows in front of Michael Delaney.

A black hotel cat shot across the floor as Delaney rose to speak. 'My friends, fellow pilgrims,' he began, 'I have to tell you that another of our number has passed away. First there was John Delaney in Le Puy. This morning the body of Patrick MacLoughlin was found in Entraygues-sur-Truyère, the next town on the banks of the Lot, lying in the bottom of a rowing boat that had been dispatched downstream from this hotel. The authorities believe he had been strangled before his last journey. We have to stay here in Estaing to speak to an inspector from the French police. We are here tonight to consider what we should do next. I believe Lord Powerscourt has some thoughts he would like to share with you.'

Maggie Delaney was torn between a delicious mixture of joy and sorrow, joy that further affliction had come on her hated cousin, Michael Delaney, sorrow that a young man of God with so much life in front of him should have been taken away. She began to pray for the dead man's soul. Powerscourt had told Lady Lucy beforehand that he wasn't going to mince his words. He felt very strongly indeed about this question.

'Pilgrims, friends,' he began, 'I was called here to look into the death of John Delaney on the rock of St Michel. Now we have a second death. I have to say that I have no idea who is responsible for these murders. They are linked by one small thread. On both bodies was found a scallop shell, symbol and guide to the pilgrims to Compostela through the ages. And Alex Bentley tells me that the body sent in a boat to Entraygues may echo the arrival of St James the Great in northern Spain, where his body was discovered in a stone boat near a place on the coast called Padron. Be that as it may, both of these young men died horrible deaths. People have asked me earlier this evening if I think there will be any further murders on the route. I have to tell you I think it is very likely, that it is almost certain.'

Powerscourt paused. There was a murmur from the pilgrims. He glanced briefly at Lady Lucy for reassurance.

'One of you in this room here tonight is a murderer.' He spoke very quietly. 'It might be you,' his finger shot out towards the middle of the second row, 'or you or you or you or you.' His finger travelled along the entire length of the front row and continued across the top table to take in Father Kennedy and Michael Delaney himself. 'Only one person can feel safe in this company and that is the killer himself. Only he knows who he intends to murder next. Only he knows where he intends to do it. Only he knows when he intends to carry out his next murder. Do not console yourself with the thought that there may only be one more victim. We do not know. There could be two or three or four. The most dangerous place in any battle is in the heart of the front line waiting for an enemy attack. Tonight you are all in the heart of that front line. All of your lives are in danger.'

Powerscourt wondered if he had said enough. He carried on. It was a long time since he had felt so strongly about one of his cases.

'So what would my advice be? My advice is very simple. Call off your pilgrimage. Go home, separately I should advise, once the police have completed their inquiries. Go home and see your loved ones. Go home to safety for this gathering is currently one of the most dangerous places in Europe. Go home while you can. Go home while you are still alive. Go home before you are thrown off some huge volcanic rock or sent strangled in a rowing boat down the Lot. In this case discretion is not merely the better part of valour. Discretion is the only way to stay alive.'

Powerscourt sat down. Lady Lucy squeezed his hand. There was a long silence. Then Michael Delaney rose to his feet once more. 'Does anybody wish to speak?' he asked. Powerscourt wondered cynically if this was the first time in his life that Michael Delaney had asked for contributions from the floor. There was a rustling among the pilgrims.

'Begging your pardon, sir.' Shane Delaney from Swindon, the man with a dying wife, had risen from his chair, shuffling nervously from foot to foot. 'I think Lord Powerscourt forgets something. We're not here on some walking holiday, we're here on pilgrimage. Christian didn't turn back, sir, because of his troubles and temptations on the way to the Celestial City. He went on. I promised my Sinead, so I did, that I would carry out this pilgrimage on her behalf. I'm here because she's too sick to do it. It might save her life, so the priests told me, not a great chance but it might. I can't go back, sir. I'd be letting her down. I couldn't look her in the eye if I ran away. We have all these difficulties, like Christian. But I for one have got to go on. Like him.'

Powerscourt spoke from his chair. 'You don't think, Shane, that your Sinead would rather have you back in Swindon alive than dead in the south of France?' Even as he finished he wondered if his comment had been unwise. These were not rational people after all, no rational person would set out to walk the thousand miles from Le Puy to Santiago de Compostela and think it might save his wife's life. Forces other than reason and logic, so close to Powerscourt's heart, were at work here.

'I'm with Shane, so I am,' said Willie John Delaney, the man dying from an incurable disease. 'Forgive me for mentioning it, but my number is up in a couple of months or so whether I'm on pilgrimage or not. It's been a great comfort to me so far, this pilgrimage, sir, so it has. As the priests might put it, I think I'd make a better death as a pilgrim travelling with all these good people here, than I would if I ran away.'

There was a muttering of approval. Powerscourt felt he was going to lose the argument.

'I think we should carry on too.' Jack O'Driscoll, the young newspaperman from Dublin was on his feet now. 'You see, as most of you know, I work for a newspaper in Dublin. Before I left my editor told me the pilgrimage would make me a better person. I didn't know what he meant then. I think I do now. I think that as we've made our way here we've stopped being a collection of individuals. We're becoming a little community. In a perverse way the murders make that feeling stronger. I feel so close now to the other young people I've been walking with, closer than I do to my friends back home. I'm sure that these feelings will only get stronger.' Maybe it's like people who have fought together in battle, Powerscourt thought, it's like Johnny Fitzgerald and I, bonded for life. 'I'm only young,' Jack went on, 'and I don't have that many sins. But some of us must have great burdens we wish to lay down, sins we want forgiveness for, and we won't achieve any of that by running away.'

There was one last contribution from the pilgrims. Waldo Mulligan, the man who worked for a senator in Washington, the man running from a passionate affair with a friend's wife, rose to his feet. He was a more accomplished speaker than the others.

'I am not yet old,' he began, 'but I am one of those of whom Jack spoke a moment ago when he talked of people burdened with sins. I don't wish to advertise my sins here this evening but as the days have passed I have come to realize that it is not all despair and guilt, that the process of pilgrimage itself, the rhythm of the days, the aching feet at the end of the journey, the deep sleep that comes with so much exercise, is helping me towards some kind of understanding. There is a long way to go. I may never be forgiven my sins but I may learn to come to an accommodation with them. I do not believe that process would continue if I ran away, as the others put it. Lord Powerscourt was eloquent, very eloquent, in making the case for our quitting. But I believe the good that may come from continuing outweighs the bad. By quite a long way. I thank Lord Powerscourt for his views but I think we should carry on.'

There was a short silence. The waiters were laying the tables for supper at the other end of the room. Michael Delaney looked quizzically at Powerscourt as if asking him whether he wished to speak again. Powerscourt shook his head. 'Very well, gentlemen,' said Delaney, venturing into new democratic territory, 'I think we should put it to the vote. Would all those who think we should continue please raise their right hands.'

The vote was unanimous. Powerscourt had lost. The pilgrims had won. Later that evening he sat in a chair by the window in their bedroom and stared moodily at the Lot, gurgling and dancing on its way to the distant sea. 'We're on a Cavalcade of Death now, Lucy,' he said sadly, 'a caravan trail with murder at our side and death stalking behind us. I'll tell you what it reminds me of. You know those stories of great expeditions into remote parts of Africa or the interior of Australia. The explorers set off in high spirits, laden down with supplies that will last for years and the very best clothing and equipment that modern science can provide. They appear in happy photographs in the magazines before they go, assuring the readers that modernity will always conquer the wilderness or the outback or wherever it is they're going. Early reports reach the world they've left behind that progress is better than expected. The huskies or the sherpas or the native bearers or whoever is carrying all their stuff are doing well. Then nothing. And a further nothing. After a couple of years another expedition is sent out to find the first one. They come across a couple of bleached bones and a tin or two of food lying in the desert or the snow or the ice. All gone. All dead in the middle of nowhere.'

'You'd better come to bed, Francis,' said Lady Lucy practically. 'It's not as bad as that and you know it.'

'Wait and see,' said her husband morosely, temporarily locked into the role of prophet of doom.

'Francis,' Lady Lucy was sitting up on her pillows now, 'you're not doing yourself justice, you know. You were right down there, of course you were. But the pilgrims didn't agree with you. So why don't you think of something else, my love, and stop being so miserable.'

'Like what?' asked Powerscourt.

'How about this,' said Lady Lucy, 'why don't you start thinking about how you are going to keep them all alive?'

11

The police inspector from Figeac arrived very early the next morning. Powerscourt came across him having a quick cup of coffee with Jacques the hotel owner. Nicolas Léger was small for a policeman. Powerscourt wondered briefly if he had stood on tiptoe when they measured the height of aspirant police recruits. He was about thirty-five years old, Nicolas, with a cheerful face, quizzical brown eyes and hair that was beginning to recede inexorably up his forehead. This seemed to be a matter of considerable regret to the Inspector for he sent a hand up to the top of his head at regular intervals as if checking on the damage.

'Lord Powerscourt,' he said, 'what a pleasure to meet you. I heard about your adventures in St Petersburg from a colleague who spent some time attached to our secret service in the Place des Vosges in Paris.'

Powerscourt bowed. 'I apologize, monsieur, for the trouble we are all causing the French authorities here. I wish it were not so.'

'Do not trouble yourself, my lord. As long as people are living together they will go round killing each other at one time or another. That is what they told us in the police college. Murder is as much a part of life as love. Look what happened in the Garden of Eden after all. Whole thing started with Cain and Abel. Now then, what can you tell me about these pilgrims? Do you have any suspicions? In half an hour or so

155

when they are taking their breakfast I am going to search their rooms. Just a quick look, you understand. I have a couple of men coming shortly who can turn them inside out during the morning. After they have had their coffee I should like to talk to them all. Perhaps you would do me the honour of translating?'

Powerscourt said that he and Lady Lucy would take it in turns for the translating. It was tiring work. He told the Inspector the little he knew about the pilgrims and their different motives for making the journey to Compostela, ranging from a love of architecture to adventure and a quest for forgiveness of sins or a cure for terminal illness.

'Come, Lord Powerscourt, while the pilgrims rouse themselves perhaps you could show me the place where the boat was taken? I am most curious to look at one aspect of that.'

Powerscourt led him to the little jetty where the boats were moored. He had to walk as fast as he could for Inspector Léger seemed to be in a great hurry. Perhaps, Powerscourt thought, he was one of those who are always in a great hurry.

'These little rowing boats,' said the Inspector, making a lightning check on his hair, 'I spent far too much time in them on the river of Figeac called the Celé when I should have been at my studies when I was young. Now then.' He bent down to peer at the cut rope.

'That knife must have been very sharp, the cut is so clean,' said Powerscourt, anxious to show that he too had taken note of the rope.

'How did he do it, I wonder?' Inspector Léger picked up the end in his left hand and made a quick cutting movement with the index finger of his right. 'Like that perhaps. Pity we cannot tell if our killer used his left or his right hand. Our work would be nearly over if he was left handed, but no. God is not that kind to us today. But tell me, Lord Powerscourt, what did he do with the knife? Would these pilgrims be carrying round knives this sharp? Would he have pinched it from the hotel kitchen? Perhaps I should ask our friend the hotelkeeper who likes his red wine so early in the morning that his breath smells of it even before breakfast. Would you take such a knife back to the kitchens? Or back to your room? We shall see.'

'If our murderer was a careful murderer,' said Powerscourt, looking at the Lot flowing past them, 'he would have thrown it into the river. Even if it was found, there would be nothing to prove that it was the murderer who put it there.'

Inspector Léger too stared at the river. No sharp knives could be seen glinting on the bottom. 'Maybe I shall get my men to search the river after they have finished with the rooms. But come, Lord Powerscourt, you can tell from the noise that they are now sat down to breakfast. A quick search of their rooms, I think.'

The Inspector shot through the rooms like a man possessed. Drawers were opened, rucksacks searched, clothes felt and shaken. Powerscourt thought he was hoping to find the knife. In Jack O'Driscoll's little cell, he found a notebook which he thrust into Powerscourt's hand. 'What do we have here? Is this the great novel perhaps? A love letter, a very long love letter?'

'It's a diary,' said Powerscourt, riffling through the entries. 'There's an entry for every single day of the pilgrimage, some much longer than others.'

'Really,' said the Inspector, staring at the impenetrable English that filled the pages. 'I think we should ask if we can borrow it, Lord Powerscourt. Maybe you or your good wife would be so kind as to translate it for us.'

Then the Inspector found a knife. It was in a leather case placed beneath an exquisite carving of a model ship. Beside it was a new work, not yet finished, that looked as if was going to be a crucifix of elegant proportions when it was completed.

'The knife and the carving belong to a young American called Charlie Flanagan,' Powerscourt told the Inspector. 'He spent the Atlantic crossing carving a model ship. I believe he has a commission to make another one.'

'Feel how sharp this knife is, my friend,' said the Inspector, staring intently at the blade. 'I cannot see any shards of rope on it, mind you. But then the murderer would probably have wiped it afterwards.' He began riffling through Charlie Flanagan's clothes but found nothing of interest. In the Flanagan pack he found a large notebook with pages and pages of sketches. Powerscourt found himself transported back to the cathedral steps of Le Puy, to the bridge at Espalion and the great castle at Estaing. There were drawings too of pillars and stone coffins and the view along the Lot from just outside the hotel. Powerscourt remembered Charlie telling him that his real interest was architecture rather than carpentry.

'What a good eye the young man has,' the Inspector murmured, leafing through the notebook and checking on his bald patch once more. 'There's nothing incriminating here.'

Powerscourt was relieved to find that all Charlie's possessions were innocent. He rather liked the young man from Baltimore.

'Now then,' said Léger, 'before I speak to the pilgrims, I must speak to the man in charge in private, I think. M. Delaney, he is the man?'

Powerscourt led the way to a small office behind the dining room and brought in the American millionaire. Delaney looked as though he had passed a troubled night.

'Inspector,' he began, 'our apologies for causing you so much trouble. Rest assured that we will do everything in our power to assist you. Do we need to contact any of the other authorities round here?'

He's trying to find out if we have to start bribing people again, Powerscourt said to himself. He wondered briefly what it must be like to have unlimited amounts of money to spend. The Inspector's reply astonished them both.

'Do not think that we wish to detain you here any longer than is necessary, Mr Delaney. The local priest will be here soon to arrange for the funeral and burial of the unfortunate young man. I believe you have your own curé with you who can liaise with Father Cavagnac. He plans to hold the service tomorrow afternoon. After that you will be free to leave, to continue with your pilgrimage. I and my men will come with you, for I am based in Figeac which is on your route.'

Suddenly Powerscourt thought he could see it all. The Mayor of Entraygues, unwilling to enter into negotiations about a fountain or a series of seats for the elderly and the footsore on the banks of the Lot, saying to the police that he wanted these wretched pilgrims out of his town as fast as possible before there were any more murders. Father Cavagnac, keen to bury one as fast as he could before he had to bury any more. The local police force, unhappy with one murder, unwilling to wait for the next one, handing the responsibility over to the larger force in Figeac. Nobody wanted them. They were pariahs, modern lepers shunned by society, doomed to continue their bloody journey across southern France until they passed into the lands of the Spanish.

All that morning and into the afternoon Inspector Léger interviewed the pilgrims. Powerscourt and Lady Lucy translated. Not one of them had heard anything unusual in the night. All had slept straight through. They did not learn very much about the dead man, for he had not been popular and had not mixed very much with the others. The Inspector's men made a thorough search of all the rooms. They waded happily in the river for a couple of hours. They found nothing. Lady Lucy began translating Jack O'Driscoll's diary. The young newspaperman had been very careful about what he committed to paper after the events in Le Puy. In the late afternoon the Inspector summoned Powerscourt for a conversation in the hotelkeeper's sitting room.

'It's not easy,' he said sadly, sending his right hand on a doomed mission to find more hair on his head, 'this case, I mean. But then murders seldom are. I could go on talking to the pilgrims for days and days. One of them might crack but I doubt it. My men can make further searches but I do not hold out much hope. We might be able – I shall certainly keep trying – to find the murderer from evidence gathered here but without that knife, without anybody telling us anything, it is very difficult. We are always told to look for motive in these affairs. Who might want the victim dead, that sort of thing. I do not think the motive is to be found in Le Puy or in Espalion, or Estaing, or in Conques.'

Inspector Léger stared sadly at the frayed carpet on the hotelkeeper's floor. 'Where is it, the motive? You tell me, my friend, for I am sure you reached the same conclusion some time ago.'

'I did,' said Powerscourt, 'and this is what makes this case so very difficult. The motive is hundreds and hundreds, if not thousands of miles from here. It's in Ballina or Roscommon or Longford or Galway, or it's in Hammersmith or Kentish Town or in Birmingham or it's somewhere on the eastern seaboard of America in New York or Boston or Pittsburgh, the city of steel. But it's not in France.'

Shortly before dinner Powerscourt found Lady Lucy standing on the little jetty where the rowing boats were tied up. She was staring intently down the river. She smiled at her husband. Powerscourt thought she looked very beautiful this evening.

'Francis, my love,' she said, 'I've been wondering about that rowing boat. What would happen if you gave it a push from here? Would it float away downstream? Or would it just go round and round?'

'I don't know, to be honest, Lucy. Tell you what, why don't we try it? You sit in this one here and I'll give it a good push. Let's hope the hotelkeeper can't see us or he'll think another of these boats is being stolen.'

Powerscourt handed Lady Lucy into the vessel. She settled herself gracefully into the centre of the craft. Powerscourt bent down and untied the rope. Then he gave the rowing boat his best shove and sent it out into the river. After a few moments it lost momentum and drifted back into the side. Lady Lucy rowed herself back.

'I thought that would happen,' she said, looking up at Powerscourt from the middle of the boat. 'My grandfather told me all about currents in rivers when I was a little girl in Scotland. I can't have been more than six or seven at the time. He was very good to me, my grandfather, he always talked to me as if I were a grown-up. I think you should try wading out into the river, Francis, and giving me a good shove into the middle of the current.'

Powerscourt gazed rather sadly at his shoes and his trousers, come to adorn the valley of the Lot from the tailors of Jermyn Street in London. He waded out into the centre of the river where the current was strongest. After his strongest push, Lady Lucy floated away.

Powerscourt watched her go. 'Willows whiten, aspens quiver,' he whispered,

> 'Little breezes dusk and shiver
> Through the wave that runs for ever
> By the island in the river
> Flowing down to Camelot.'

'And at the closing of the day,' Lady Lucy carried on,

> 'She loosed the chain, and down she lay,
> The broad stream bore her far away'
> The Lady of the Lot.'

Lady Lucy was now moving downstream at something close to walking pace. She sat upright in her boat and stared straight ahead. She carried on with the poem, the words drifting out across the river bank.

> 'Lying, robed in snowy white
> That loosely flew to left and right –
> The leaves upon her falling light –
> Through the noises of the night

> She floated down to Camelot:
> And as the boat-head wound along
> The willowy hills and fields among
> They heard her singing her last song,
> The Lady of the Lot.

'Should I sing something sad, Francis?' Lady Lucy called back. 'Some sad song of lost love from the days of the Knights of the Round Table?'

'I think you should remember the end of the poem,' her husband replied. 'It bids you bon voyage.

> 'But Lancelot mused a little space;
> He said, "she has a lovely face;
> God in his mercy lend her grace,
> The Lady of the Lot."'

Lady Lucy rowed back and was helped up on to the jetty. 'Thank you, Francis, and thank you, Lord Tennyson, for your compliment. I'd quite forgotten that bit at the end. But tell me this. What would you do with your trousers, Francis, if you were the murderer? You couldn't bring them back to the hotel dripping with water and you could never dry them out before morning.'

'If it was me,' said her husband, looking ruefully at the water still dripping around his ankles, 'I think I'd take them off and throw them in the river. Probably have to do the same with the shoes and socks. The Inspector and his men didn't find any wet clothes on their search in the pilgrims' rooms. So they're probably downstream from here somewhere.'

They heard footsteps approaching rapidly from the direction of the Lion d'Or. Michael Delaney was coming to join them on the jetty. Powerscourt thought the American was radiating energy. You could almost sense it flowing around and through him, as if he had a secret generating plant inside his chest hooked into his nervous system. Maybe that was what you needed to become an American millionaire. Maybe they were all like that.

'Look here, Powerscourt, Lady Powerscourt, I want to ask you for your opinion. Can't say I'm very happy at the way we're virtually being thrown out of here but it's better than bribery. Bodyguards, what do you say to bodyguards? Party of a dozen or so, guard the pilgrims day and night, follow any wandering souls, intercept any further acts of murder. I could wire to Pinkerton's in New York to send us a dozen or so straight away. They'd be here in a week or ten days. Some of us should still be alive in a week or ten days.'

'I'm not sure that the French authorities would look very kindly on that, Delaney,' said Powerscourt. 'This is their territory after all.'

'Would they give us the same number of men, do you suppose? I could pay for them, after all, rent them out like taxis in Manhattan.'

'We'd have to ask the Inspector,' Powerscourt replied. 'He seems a sensible sort of man to me.'

'We've got to find a way to keep everybody safe,' said Delaney. 'I feel responsible for all these damned pilgrims. I asked them to come, for God's sake. We can't have them being picked off like birds at some great country house shoot in England.'

Lady Lucy knew what her husband was thinking. She prayed silently to Merlin and the gods of Camelot that he would not say that the only way to guarantee the safety of the pilgrims was for them all to go home.

'I'm going to talk to Alex Bentley after supper,' said Powerscourt. 'He did a lot of research into the Delaneys before you sent out all the invitations. I think he may know where all the Delaneys come from in Ireland. We could launch some inquiries there.'

Powerscourt did not say that he was planning to ask Johnny Fitzgerald to go to Ireland. He thought it unlikely that Michael Delaney was the murderer but you could never be sure.

'And I did have one thought, Delaney, which is risky,' Powerscourt went on, 'but it might solve the problem for us.'

'And what's that, my friend? I'll pay for whatever it takes.'

Lady Lucy found herself wondering if Delaney ever thought about the things money could not buy, love, maybe, hatred perhaps, possibly madness. Surely there were some things that could not be weighed in dollars.

'This wouldn't cost any money,' said Powerscourt. 'Suppose we let it be known early one evening that I know who the murderer is and that I propose to tell the French authorities the name of the killer in the morning. I would not have told anybody else who it is.'

'How does that help?' said Delaney.

'I can tell you how Francis thinks it would help, Mr Delaney,' said Lady Lucy, reading her husband's mind faster than the American and fighting back the tears that threatened to overwhelm her. 'The murderer would then try to kill Francis. To stop Francis exposing him, don't you see. So then it becomes a fight to the death between the two of them. I think it's a terrible plan, I really do.'

'I didn't ask you here in order to have you killed in the middle of the night by some crazed pilgrim,' said Michael Delaney. 'Surely that becomes a weapon of last resort, one that we never have to use.'

Later that evening Powerscourt took a walk along the river bank with Alex Bentley. He had decided to break one of his own rules. Earlier on he remembered telling Lady Lucy that he suspected every single person in the pilgrim party. Now desperation had made him abandon his resolution and take Alex Bentley into his confidence. Anybody who admired Lady Lucy as fervently as the young American must have some good in them.

'Alex,' he began, 'I want to ask your advice. If I want to make inquiries in England or Ireland I can do it easily. I have

come across a lot of people in my previous work, you understand, and I have a special friend who helps me in all my
investigations who is helping me there now. But I don't have
anybody in America. I could ask Mr Delaney to call in
Pinkerton's to assist us, but I think they would be answerable
to him rather than to me, if you see what I mean. Do you
know of anybody who would be able to make intelligent and
discreet inquiries on our behalf?'

The sun had gone down behind the hills. The water in the
river was growing darker now, almost black. There was
occasional rustling as the breeze ruffled the branches at the
top of the trees.

'Do they have to be private detectives, Lord Powerscourt?'

'I don't know why, but I've never really trusted most
private detectives, even though I am one myself in a way. I
feel they look for what their employer wants to hear all the
time.'

'As a matter of fact I think I do know such a person, now I
come to think of it. But he's a lawyer rather than a private
detective. They too are trained to report what their clients
want to hear a lot of the time.'

'But is he reliable, the person you're thinking of?'

'Oh yes, he's reliable all right. You see, he's my brother, my
elder brother. He works for a big law firm with offices in New
York and Washington, Adams, Adams and Cutler they're
called.'

'Does he come laden down with degrees like yourself?'
asked Powerscourt with a smile.

'I'm afraid he does. He didn't go to Princeton, though, he
did all his degrees at Harvard.'

Powerscourt thought Bentley made Harvard sound like a
rather disagreeable prep school where they didn't give you
enough food and the teaching was poor. 'My father wants me
to join the firm too. That's why I went to law school.'

'Would he be able to make inquiries for us? Does he know
about the pilgrimage and your work on it?'

'He certainly does,' said Alex Bentley. 'I told him all about it in New York. Franklin, my brother, was very entertained at the thought of his little brother travelling all over Europe with a lot of mad pilgrims and a New York millionaire. He always felt they must be a bit touched to take on such a journey. I'm sure he'd be only too happy to help. And I'm sure a lot of the senior people in the firm would know about all kinds of things that might come in useful to you.'

'Well,' said Powerscourt, sitting on a fallen branch and trying to skim some stones across the river, 'this is what I think you should ask him about. First, and this is very vague, does he know or could he find out anything suspicious in Michael Delaney's past, anything that might have given rise to a feud between different branches of the family? I've got a couple of clues, though they might be hard to follow up. Many years ago Delaney persuaded an older and a richer man to help him set up a railway company. Delaney fixed it so the other man was cheated out of his money. You could say Delaney swindled him though I'm not sure I would say that to Delaney's face. Where is this man? What became of him? Does he have any surviving relatives? I believe his name is Wharton. And my other query is equally tenuous, I'm afraid, and it too goes back a long way to 1894. Some newspaperman got interested in Delaney years ago, so interested that he wrote a book which chronicled what the reporter thought were all Delaney's crimes. A lifetime of sin in one volume if you like. Delaney bought the lot and had them pulped. The author has not been heard of since though he may still be alive. I would be most interested to know if any copies of that book survived. I would be even more interested in getting my hands on a copy if that were possible. It was called *Michael Delaney, Robber Baron*.'

'I'll send a wire to Franklin first thing in the morning, Lord Powerscourt,' said Alex Bentley cheerfully. 'Things are going to look up now. Two Bentleys are much better than one.'

Powerscourt too was sending messages early the next

morning. He wrote to Johnny Fitzgerald, asking him to go to Ireland as soon as possible, to the area around Macroom in County Cork which Bentley believed was the epicentre of the Delaney clan. Johnny was to search for any feud, fight or other wickedness which might have led one of the Delaney descendants to kill. Powerscourt said he thought Johnny should start in the days of the famine. They had already heard, he told his friend, some terrible stories about one lot of Delaneys refusing to help their relations who later died in the workhouse. There might be other, different crimes from the past that had returned to stain the present sixty years later. Time, he concluded his message, is very short. There could be another murder even before Johnny crossed the Irish Sea.

The dead of Entraygues-sur-Truyère wait for the Second Coming on a hillside above the little town. Beneath them the Lot and the Truyère join forces and head off towards the distant sea. On the other side of the river wooded hills rise to several hundred feet. To their right, at the top of a very steep gorge, the vineyards of Le Fel produce sustenance and consolation for the living. It was here, after the service in the little church, that Patrick MacLoughlin was laid to rest. All the pilgrim party were present on parade that afternoon having walked along the river from Estaing. The doctor was there and the butcher who had carried him from the river bank on his cart. Madame Roche attended as a mark of respect to the man her son had found dead in a rowing boat. Inspector Léger was present, spending most of his time, as Lady Lucy observed, looking intently at the faces of the pilgrims. Powerscourt had bought a new black tie, observing mordantly to Lady Lucy that he expected it would see a lot of wear in the days ahead. Father Kennedy was thinking how very young the dead man was. He prayed that earth's loss would be heaven's gain. Michael Delaney realized that the dead man they were lowering into the earth was only a couple of years older than his James, who had himself come so close to this sad ceremony only months before. Stephen Lewis, the solicitor from Frome in Somerset, found himself wondering if the dead man had left a will. He couldn't help it. He had been dealing with wills all his life. He wondered if he should offer his services to all the pilgrims in case they were next for the last rites and the funeral service. Business, Lewis thought grimly, might be brisk. Charlie Flanagan, the carving carpenter from Baltimore, had finished his crucifix the evening before. Charlie was not a superstitious young man but he kept his latest work in his trouser pocket where he hoped it would keep him safe. Looking at the earth being thrown over the remains of the dead man he wondered grimly if his next work should be a coffin. Then, with a shudder, he realized it might be his own.

The little town of Entraygues lay slightly off the official pilgrim route which crossed the river some miles from Estaing and went up into the hills to Golinhac and then across to Espeyrac. The road to Espeyrac, where the pilgrims planned to rejoin the trail, led over one of Entraygues' medieval bridges and up into the woods. Lady Lucy was walking this afternoon with Father Kennedy who hoped that periods of violent exercise like the present ascent would erode some of the extra weight he had been acquiring from the local cuisine. He shuddered with a mixture of guilt and delight as he remembered his second helping of crème brûlée the night before.

'Tell me, Father,' Lady Lucy began, 'did you get to know Patrick MacLoughlin well? You must have spent a lot of time in his company on the Atlantic crossing and on the journey so far.'

'Well, I talked to him quite a lot,' Father Kennedy replied, panting slightly. He wondered if this climb was ever going to end. 'I think he liked conversing with me, as a fellow practitioner in God's work here on earth. But I wouldn't say I got to know him well.'

'What did he talk about?'

'Well, he was very interested in pilgrimage and pilgrimages. You could say, I think, that he was interested in them in the way other people are interested in antique furniture or stamp collecting. He had great plans as young men often do. He wanted to go to Rome, and to Jerusalem in the footsteps of the Crusaders. Next year he was intending to walk from London to Canterbury on the track of Chaucer's pilgrims. If he could have found the route of John Bunyan's *Pilgrim's Progress* I'm sure he would have followed that too. He seemed to think the pilgrimages would help him in his ministry.'

'You don't sound convinced about that, Father,' said Lady Lucy.

'I'm not,' replied Father Kennedy. 'I think a spell in one of the poorer parishes of Boston or New York would have served as a more fruitful apprenticeship. I know I have the good fortune to serve in one of the richest parishes in New York City, Lady Powerscourt, but I have applied many times now to be transferred to a less wealthy location. Always I am refused. I don't know why.'

'I'm sorry about that, Father. It must be hard if you do not feel at home in your work. Did young Patrick talk about his family, his past at all?'

'All he ever said was that his mother was overjoyed when he was called to the priesthood. She was very devout. Patrick was an only child, you see. It was the father who complained about the grandchildren he would never see. That was all I can remember him saying about that side of his life. I believe the young think more about the future than the past.'

The road to Espeyrac turned right off the main road. The pilgrims were now on a narrow path that went up and down the hills in a series of sharp curves. Lady Lucy found herself thinking about Mr and Mrs MacLoughlin in Boston mourning for an only son lost twice, once to the call of the priesthood and once to the hands of a murderer. She wondered if they would ever make their own pilgrimage to see his grave on the hill above the Lot, looking out over the river and the valley and the woods on the far side. Her husband had been walking with Waldo Mulligan but Mulligan seemed to prefer his own company and Powerscourt let him go ahead on his own.

Waldo Mulligan knew he should have engaged Powerscourt in conversation. Anything would have been preferable to his own thoughts. But he remained locked inside his own head. Even trying to forget about Caroline, his mistress back in Washington, married to a colleague on the staff of the senator he worked for, involved thinking about her, he had decided. You could only stop remembering her once you had remembered her in the first place. And then there was that other, even darker shadow. He could recall every detail of the day he heard about his parents' death in a rail crash some six months before, the time of day, just after four o'clock, the clothes he was wearing, the dark blue suit with the white shirt, the weather, a light rain falling, what he had for lunch, a ham roll with melted cheese, his work, a routine meeting with the senator just about to start. And then several days later, opening the desk with his father's papers so meticulously filed going back nearly forty years and the shock that had changed his life.

At the front of the party marched one of Inspector Léger's policemen. Another one walked roughly in the centre of the group surrounded by Jack O'Driscoll and Christy Delaney trying to improve their French by learning some of the words you might use when talking to young French women. The Inspector himself brought up the rear, some twenty yards behind Powerscourt. In Le Puy-en-Velay, Powerscourt thought, the French police virtually locked us up inside the hotel. Here we are under a form of mobile house arrest. Certainly the murderer would find it hard to strike here, surrounded by the officers of the law.

Powerscourt was thinking about vendettas and how long they could last. Did they extend down two or even three generations? Would a family be able to maintain a hatred of their enemies that would stretch out over fifty or sixty years? In one of his earlier cases he remembered a vendetta in Corsica, but that had only just started. It certainly hadn't been running for decades. He dimly recalled the myths of the Ancient Greeks where people wreaked frightful vengeance on their foes across the generations. But they had often been cursed by the gods, ever random and even whimsical in their choice of victims. He looked at the party of pilgrims ahead of him. Which one was carrying a terrible secret with him? Was he, even now, here among the trees and the lowing cows and the sunshine, deciding on his next victim?

Still the road twisted up and down the hills. They passed smaller, overgrown paths that curved their way into the woods and forests. Stepping into one of them Powerscourt realized that he was in a totally green world. This was what everything would look like if the creator had made the skies green instead of blue. Powerscourt bent down and stepped further along the path, dodging the overhanging branches. There were so many different shades in here. Emerald, sea green, olive green, pea green, grass green, apple, mint, forest, lawn green, lime, leaf green, fir, pine, moss, viridian. Dark green, he remembered, is associated with ambition, greed and jealousy. Maybe one of the pilgrims was green at heart. He turned about and made his way back into the blue universe outside and almost bumped into the Inspector.

'They say there are wild mushrooms growing in these forests, Lord Powerscourt. Did you find any? And tell me, what do you think of our security arrangements? The killer would find it difficult to strike now, is that not so?'

Powerscourt resisted the temptation to say that the killer had struck on the last occasion in the middle of the night. 'Very fine,' he replied.

'I hope to keep some sort of guard during the hours of darkness as well,' the Inspector went on. 'I have to work it out with my men later. Maybe we shall take watches like the sailors do but without those damned bells ringing all through the night.'

Lady Lucy found herself walking alongside Wee Jimmy Delaney now, the steel worker from Pittsburgh. She reckoned he was nearly a foot taller than she was. He must be at least six foot four, she told herself, with big calloused hands and masses of black curly hair. His eyes were pale blue and hinted that there could be a gentler soul behind them than outside appearances might suggest. Wee Jimmy had a great staff in his hand which seemed a puny thing in his huge fist, like a matchstick.

'Are you enjoying the pilgrimage so far, Mr Delaney?' Lady Lucy asked brightly. 'Maybe enjoy is the wrong word, I don't know. People have so many different reasons for being here after all.'

'I like it very much, Lady Powerscourt. I like this rolling countryside hereabouts.'

Lady Lucy paused. She didn't quite know how to put the substance of her next question without sounding rude or impertinent or both. They walked on. A herd of light brown cattle stared at them from a neighbouring field. The stare, Lady Lucy felt, was exactly the same as the stare from the local French people, impertinent and lasting far too long. In the end Wee Jimmy solved the problem for her.

'You know, Lady Powerscourt,' he said, 'I haven't told anybody yet why I'm here, why I've come on the pilgrimage.'

Lady Lucy waited. The cows were still staring. They looked as if they could stare all day.

'It's strange, I think, how we hope we or our loved ones could be made better by walking all this way and going to church in Santiago de Compostela. It's not rational.'

'I'm not sure that religion is rational at all, Mr Delaney. We're meant to have faith and that really means believing in things that aren't rational at all.'

'I've got a little sister, Lady Powerscourt.' Wee Jimmy Delaney tucked his staff under his arm and bent down to speak nearer to Lady Lucy's height. 'She's why I'm here.'

Lady Lucy didn't want to ask if the girl was dying or

suffering from some other terrible problem. She waited, walking more slowly now.

A strange look passed over Wee Jimmy's face. Lady Lucy thought it combined compassion and anger at virtually the same time.

'She's deaf and she's dumb and she's blind. Has been since the day she was born, poor little thing. Four children before her, all perfectly healthy, three children after her, all perfectly healthy, all faculties in working order. My mother thinks to this day that she is being punished for some crime, only she can't remember ever having committed a crime the size of this punishment.'

'How old is your little sister?' asked Lady Lucy.

'Marianne? She's eight years old, she'll be nine on the Fourth of July. She's well looked after, all her brothers and sisters would do anything for her. She can still taste.' Lady Lucy saw a gentle smile on the face of the man from Pittsburgh. 'Every time you give her a piece of chocolate she smiles this lovely smile. And she can smell. She always knows when I've come in from the steelworks and haven't cleaned myself up yet. You see these hands, Lady Powerscourt.' Wee Jimmy held out his great clubs for inspection. 'You could tell that I work in something like a steelworks or a coal mine. It's very hard work. I don't mind. I do as much overtime as I can. Sometimes I carry on right through the weekends. I do it to take Marianne to the best doctors in Pennsylvania, God, they're so expensive, these doctors, but I don't care about the money. We've been to two specialists in Philadelphia but they can't do anything for Marianne. I'm saving up to take her to a man in New York they say is the best man in America.'

Lady Lucy tried to imagine what it must be like to be the mother of a child who could neither see nor speak nor hear. The knowledge that you had brought this person into this world must be with you every minute of every day, as if you had been cursed by God or whatever deities you believed in.

'Is that why you're here?' she asked quietly, looking up into Wee Jimmy's face. 'For Marianne?'

'Well, it is. I'm here, I suppose, as the representative of our family on this pilgrimage to pray that Marianne may get better. We don't want everything, you see. It would be unrealistic to expect all three faculties to come back, I think. Just something, however small, some improvement to take her a little way out of the eternal darkness and the eternal silence as my father puts it. It's strange, our family, Lady Powerscourt. All the children born in even years, 1890, 1892, 1894, are believers, like our mother is a true believer. All the ones born in the odd years, 1895, 1897 and so on, are more doubtful, like our father. They all go to church and so on, the odd-year Delaneys, but they don't believe like the rest of us do.'

'Was it a family decision, then, that you should come?' said Lady Lucy trying to hold a picture of Marianne in her mind.

'It was my father who suggested it, oddly enough. He'd heard about the pilgrimage and Michael Delaney paying for everyone. He said to me that we'd tried all these doctors, we'd probably have to try some more later on. "Science hasn't worked for us," he said, he's a great reader, my father, always getting books out of the library, "so let's try religion." Here I am, Lady Powerscourt, praying for Marianne in every church we pass and out in the open too.'

'Can I ask you a favour, Mr Delaney?' said Lady Lucy.

'Of course.'

'Can I pray for her too?'

The village of Espeyrac boasted yet another river, the Daz, now a thin trickle running down the valley below the hotel, the Auberge des Montagnes. The place did not have enough rooms so Powerscourt and Lady Lucy were to stay in a house owned by the hotelkeeper's brother a mile or so outside. A long track led up to it past a couple of empty houses and a number of barns. Powerscourt noticed the roofs, all of which, whether designed for man or beast, had a slight outwards curve at the bottom rather than running straight down to the gutters. It gave them a slightly feminine appearance as if the male builders had been thinking of their wives or their lovers or their mistresses as they worked.

'What a charming little place,' said Lady Lucy, disturbing a couple of goldfinches minding their own business in the little courtyard outside the house, and opening the front door with the hotel proprietor's key. The house was on four floors with an attic at the top and a fine sitting room. But it was the view from the terrace at the back that really delighted them, a view that could also be seen, in different sections, from various windows on the other floors. The countryside, a mixture of clumps of trees and rolling pastureland, spread out down towards a valley. Over to the left the spire of the Espeyrac church seemed to hold the picture together like the altarpieces in the paintings of Renaissance Madonnas. On the far side the hills rolled upwards again. Behind them, their own hill climbed to a rocky peak. Later that evening, before they made their way to the hotel for supper, Powerscourt and Lady Lucy walked back up the road towards Entraygues. A smaller road led off to the right at the top of a crest in the hills. The sun was going down fast. They watched, hypnotized, as the colours faded from the bottom of the valleys while the tops were still bathed in sunlight. The lower half of some of the trees was a black and white etching, the rest still coloured by the sun. Soon only the highest parts of the trees and the ground were bright. Shadow and dark grey were covering the rest of the landscape that rolled away in great folds in front of them. The sun eventually sank behind the top of one of the hills, a blazing ball of yellow and gold, gone to light up another part of the world. Powerscourt took Lady Lucy's hand as they walked down the hill to the Espeyrac hotel. They were both too humbled to speak.

In the Auberge they found themselves translating in an animated discussion between the hotel owner, Michael

Delaney and Alex Bentley. The hotel proprietor was expounding on the need for more pilgrims, more visitors, more money to pass through his little village. 'So many of the towns on the pilgrim route grew rich and ever richer from the proceeds of those pilgrims hundreds of years ago,' he said, the bright light of profit in his eye. 'When the wars of religion and that terrible man Napoleon came along it all got too dangerous for the people. But we have peace now. Why can't we do it again? Why can't the pilgrims come back?'

'Why not?' said Michael Delaney, scenting perhaps or playing with a possible business opportunity. 'Tell me, Alex, how many Catholics are there in France? How many in Spain? How many in Germany? And how many in America, for God's sake? Just think of the size of the potential market!'

'Millions of them,' said Alex Bentley, 'probably tens of millions across Europe and the United States. Enormous numbers.'

'It just needs some proper marketing, that's all.' Delaney was warming to his theme now. 'They say that the art of advertising is to make people buy things they never knew they wanted. Well, imagine what they could do with the pilgrim route to Compostela! Come save your soul in Spain! Forgiveness of Sins! Salvation of Souls! Pilgrim's Progress! Redemption on Route! French food on the road to God! French wines on the Pilgrim Path! Just think what those early Christians did in terms of marketing when all they had were those four little Gospels and some of them pretty hard to understand. They converted most of the bloody Roman Empire in a couple of hundred years. All done with no proper slogans. No billboards. No newspapers to place advertisements in, for God's sake. Surely modern American methods can do better than that.'

'My little hotel here might be full for most of the summer,' the owner enthused, doing complicated calculations of potential gains in his head. 'We might never be poor again. My Yvonne could have a carriage of her own!'

'Hotels?' said Delaney. 'A man might do very well with hotels. I could buy or build a whole chain right across the routes from France and Spain. All called the St Jacques with a statue of the saint fellow with his staff and his sandals right above the main entrance. I know a man in stonework up in Westchester County who could knock those off at a reasonable price. Discount for large numbers, of course. Scallop shells in every bedroom. Pilgrim food, maybe not, now I think about it, that was probably inedible and the Americans wouldn't eat it. We could have shops in all the hotels selling staffs and rosary beads and maps and special prayer books for the pilgrims. I'm sure some medieval professor could dig us out a lot of the old prayers the people said along the way. If not, the Jesuits or some order or another could run off a few for us at a good fee. And once you had the whole system up and running you wouldn't have to do another thing. The business would look after itself, it'd be like selling water in the desert. It could be tremendous, simply tremendous. Have to get the Church on side, of course. I'm sure Father Kennedy could work out how to buy a couple of bishops, maybe even a cardinal or two. God bless the pilgrims. Confession en route. Absolution in the cathedral in Santiago de Compostela. We'd probably have to work out an easier means of transport for the older citizens, mind you. Should appeal to the old, pilgrimage, when they're so close to the exit themselves. Not long to go now. Pilgrim's passport to the next world. Maybe we could get some of those liners to make special cruises from New York, dropping the elderly close to the final destination so they didn't have far to walk.'

Powerscourt and Lady Lucy were walking back to their little house in the hills when they heard footsteps behind them. It was Stephen Lewis, the solicitor from Frome. He paused every now and then to look behind him, as if to make sure he was alone. 'I had to catch you on your own, Lord Powerscourt, forgive me, Lady Powerscourt, I didn't want anybody listening in to what I have to say.' He paused.

'You can speak freely in front of Lucy, Mr Lewis,' said Powerscourt. 'She's tougher than she looks.'

'It's probably nothing,' said Lewis, panting slightly as they climbed up the hill out of Espeyrac, 'but I felt I should tell you all the same. It's only a fragment of conversation, but I think you ought to know about it.'

Powerscourt remembered that Lewis was a solicitor by profession. Heaven only knew what secrets he held about the inhabitants of Frome locked up in his office safe.

'The other evening, in the hotel at Estaing, I felt unwell last thing at night. I thought I'd try a glass of brandy to settle the stomach. That's often worked for me in the past. Maybe the local cooking is too rich for me. Mabel, that's my wife, always likes to put plain food on the table. Anyway, the bar was still serving customers and I took my drink out on to the terrace. The windows were open and I could hear two men having a heated discussion at the other end of the bar. They were quite drunk, the barman didn't understand a word of English, they had no idea I was there. I could only hear fragments of what they said.'

'And what were they talking about, Mr Lewis?' Powerscourt too looked back down the road. He could see nobody, only the dark shapes of the buildings and the outlines of the trees.

'They were having an argument, I think. That's how it came across anyway. I couldn't even tell who they were, the voices were so thick. But one of them said something like, "God, how I hate Michael Delaney." At least I think that's what he said and he said it twice. I finished my brandy and crept away. I didn't think they'd be very happy if they knew I had over-heard them, and they were drunk enough for anything.'

'Are you absolutely sure you don't know who they were, Mr Lewis?'

'I'm afraid I didn't. Would it be important if I had recognized the voices?'

'Oh yes, Mr Lewis,' said Powerscourt, 'it might have been very important indeed.'

12

Lord Francis Powerscourt was staring out of the open window of their bedroom in the house above Espeyrac. Lady Lucy was reading a book about French abbeys and cathedrals. The night air was soft and warm. The moon, three-quarters full, was shining out across the valley. Fields and groups of trees looked ghostly in the white light. Small creatures of the night could be heard rustling about on their nocturnal business in the woods to his left. The spire of Espeyrac church was crisp in the moonlight. A fox could be seen clearly, padding across the track that led back to the main road. All it needed, Powerscourt thought, was an owl. He had always been very fond of owls ever since the time he had made friends with one which lived in a barn behind his house as a small boy. The bird would stare solemnly at him for several minutes at a time before flying disdainfully away.

'Do you think it's important, Francis,' Lady Lucy laid her book aside, 'what Mr Lewis was saying on the road?'

'It could be,' said Powerscourt. 'It's a pity they were drunk, though. They might say something completely different in the morning, whoever they were. I think they put the wind up Stephen Lewis, mind you. He seemed very frightened when he looked back to make sure nobody was following us. And I don't think he's a man who would scare easily.'

'Well, you might well be frightened if you were one of these pilgrims. Two of them dead so far. I don't think I'd go on if I were them. But tell me, Francis, what do you think of this house? Isn't it just perfect with these marvellous views?'

Suddenly Powerscourt suspected what might be about to come. Lady Lucy was always thinking about buying houses in the way he thought about making centuries at cricket or his children being happy and successful when they grew up. Another onslaught might be imminent. It could start at any moment. He regarded these attacks as a mild form of disease. None of his sisters had ever suffered from them, although one of them had recently acquired a monstrous house near the sea front at Antibes. He would be told how good it would be for the children. They could learn French. They could ride with their father in the hills. Lucy herself would be busy making the necessary improvements to the property, new carpets here, a new kitchen there, different curtains. The air would improve all their health, far from the smoke and grime of London.

'I think it's lovely here, so peaceful,' said Powerscourt, leaning out to inspect a ginger cat that had just captured a small animal with a very long tail and was carrying the trophy away to some secret lair for a late supper. Then Lady Lucy disappointed him. There was no talk of property in the Aveyron. She merely said that she hoped there would be sunshine the next day. They were going to one of the most famous places on the pilgrim route, the medieval abbey at Conques.

Johnny Fitzgerald had only been back to Ireland once in more than twenty years, and that had been on Powerscourt's business the year before with the ancestor paintings disappearing from the Anglo-Irish houses. He stared out from his boat approaching the Irish coast, trying to forget the time in the 1880s he had looked at that view, the green of the hills to the south, the lighthouses and the Martello towers, the pall of smoke hanging over the slums of Dublin. Ireland had broken his heart all those years ago. Maybe not Ireland, but a certain Mary Rose Lennox, eldest daughter of Mr and Mrs

William Lennox of Delgany, County Wicklow. Johnny had first met her at a tennis party in Greystones and had been enchanted from the moment he saw her serve. She was of medium height, with light brown hair and blue eyes that shone with mischief or delight. Mary Rose hit the ball with remarkable force and was also possessed of a formidable backhand, usually, in Johnny's experience, the weakest point in the female armoury on a tennis court. He played against her in a game of mixed doubles later that afternoon and found he was so bewitched his game went completely to pieces. It was worse than fighting, he said to himself that evening, for Johnny was home on leave from service with the British Army on the North-West Frontier. He saw her twice more that week and from then on they were inseparable. They would ride out into the Wicklow hills and Johnny would tell her wild stories about the Indians and their strange customs, and the way the heat affected the English in such a variety of different ways, some of them becoming parodies of retired colonels in Cheltenham, others learning the native languages and becoming obsessed with the local history and culture. Looking out over the two rivers at the Meeting of the Waters at Avoca on a hot July afternoon, Johnny told her he loved her. The girl was used to the flattery of young men and merely laughed a pretty laugh. He told her again after a trip to the theatre in Dublin where Johnny was so bewitched he scarcely noticed the action on stage. All through those summer days he floated through time in an ecstasy of love, counting the hours until he saw her again. Standing on the beach at Brittas Bay, looking at the waves pounding on to the sand, an unseasonal wind bowling along the beach, whirling clouds of sand as they went, he asked Mary Rose to marry him. He could remember the scene as vividly as if it had been yesterday. Johnny had rehearsed his lines often, especially last thing at night.

'I love you so much, Mary Rose,' he said, putting his arm round her waist. 'Will you marry me?'

The girl laughed as she had laughed before. Then she saw that he was serious. 'Don't ask me now, Johnny,' she said, 'it's far too soon. We've only known each other a couple of months, if even as long as that. Don't rush me, please.'

Johnny squeezed her ever tighter and settled in for a long siege. Expensive flowers and exquisite chocolates were his weapons of choice. As summer faded into autumn he grew ever more conscious of the date of his return to his regiment at the end of September. Surely he must make her his own before then.

On the last evening of his leave they went for a walk by the lake in the garden of her parents' house nestling in the Wicklow mountains. Johnny asked Mary Rose to marry him once more. Once more she laughed. 'I've told you before, Johnny, I think it's too soon. I'll wait for you, of course I'll wait for you. It won't be long until you're back again.'

'You know perfectly well that I have no idea when I'll be back,' said Johnny rather sadly. 'Why can't you tell me now?'

'It's too soon, Johnny.' That laugh again. 'Don't let's spoil our last evening before you go.'

So they went back to the house. Mary Rose played selections of Irish ballads at the piano. Johnny would always remember her seated there, her back as straight as a guardsman on parade, a slight frown on her face as she made sure she played the right notes, the occasional brilliant smile in his direction, those blue eyes sparkling with pleasure as he sang the songs of old Ireland in his finest tenor voice.

The next day Johnny left early for the English boat. He thought of Mary Rose for thousands of miles, down the spine of England in whose armies he served, past the strange waters of the Suez Canal and the dusty roads of India until he rejoined his regiment. The shock came a couple of months after his return. Johnny had gone for an early evening drink in the Club and noticed that all the others present shuffled quickly out of the room as he came in. It was as if he had some contagious disease. Even the barman and the waiters had disappeared to their private quarters behind the drinks counter. Johnny stared around him. Everything seemed to be normal. A copy of *The Times*, arrived that afternoon from London, was lying on the table. Later, Johnny thought his colleagues had intended to leave him a clue. He noticed one of the announcements in the Marriages column of the newspaper had been underlined.

> OSBORNE:LENNOX. On 3rd October 1886, at Christchurch, Delgany, County Wicklow, by the Reverend John Hancock, Jonathan Henry Osborne of Macroom Castle, County Cork, to Beatrice Mary Rose Lennox of Delgany, County Wicklow.

At first Johnny couldn't believe it. He picked up the newspaper and carried it back to his quarters. There he lay on his bed and stared at the ceiling. After the third reading he found the tears streaming down his cheeks. How could she do this to him? Had she been pretending all those weeks? Had she been seeing this Osborne person all the time she was seeing him? Had she been secretly engaged to the Osborne all the time he had courted her with his love and his generosity and his innocence? What did he feel about Mary Rose now, for he felt sure he still loved her. Even an innocent like Johnny in these matters knew that love could not evaporate in an evening, that four lines in a newspaper column could not rearrange his emotional landscape, but that time and distance and propriety meant there was virtually nothing he could do. He thought about writing an angry letter, pouring out his grief and his distress, then changed his mind. The terrible deed had been done. With just two words in a church, 'I will,' Mary Rose Lennox had chosen a different path and a different future from his own. Over the weeks that followed Johnny threw himself into soldiering by day and drinking by night. His commanding officer took care to make sure that he was kept very busy. Twice he almost lost his life in skirmishes with enemy tribesmen. It was as if, he realized later, he had been trying to kill himself. Suicide disguised as death on the battlefield. On the second occasion his life was saved by a fellow Irishman, an officer in his own regiment. Over time the two men became very close. They fought together and spied together after they were both transferred to the Intelligence Services. The fellow officer's name was Lord Francis Powerscourt.

Memories and regrets for his failed love affair pursued Johnny down to County Cork twenty years later, still carrying out the instructions of the friend who had saved his life and his sanity all those years before. But one thought haunted Johnny Fitzgerald on this return visit to his native land. He could still see in his mind the black letters in the fateful announcement. Jonathan Henry Osborne of Macroom Castle, County Cork. Macroom was his destination on this quest for crimes and possible vendettas in the Delaney past. Would Mary Rose still be there? Would he recognize her? What would he say to her if they met in the street or in society? What would he say to her husband?

The village of Conques lay on a hillside, surrounded by trees. Time had hardly touched it. Modernity with its railways and its factories, its great shopping palaces and its telegraphs and its obsession with time had made very little impact. It was one of the few places on the entire pilgrimage where the pilgrim could imagine himself back in the Middle Ages. The pilgrim party entered by the old road over a tiny Roman bridge across the river Dourdou. The Inspector and his colleagues were offering lessons in the chequered history of the place. Conques, they said to whoever would listen, with Powerscourt and Lady Lucy translating at either end of the pilgrim column, had not always been a major centre on the pilgrim route. Sometime in the eleventh century an ambitious abbot hatched a daring plan to put his church, literally, on the map. He sent one of his younger monks to enrol in the community centred round the martyr's church at Agen. Here were held the remains and a famous statue of Ste Foy, an early Christian martyr beheaded by the Romans for her beliefs and the most celebrated saint of the time in medieval France. The abbot's instructions to his man were clear. He was to steal the lot, statue, relics, whatever he could lay his hands on, and bring them back to Conques. The young man waited and waited for his opportunity. Years passed. Daily at first, and then at ever decreasing intervals, the abbot of Conques would stare out at the road that led to Agen, hoping and praying for the arrival of the treasure. After seven years he gave up. But the monk had not. After ten years he saw his chance at last when the community was at dinner and the door to the room where the treasure was kept had, for once, been left unlocked. He stuffed the booty into a sack and fled back to Conques, travelling mainly by night to avoid capture and humiliation. The abbot was overjoyed.

The telling of this tale took them past the slate roofs and into Conques through the western gate, the Porte du Barry with its great red arch, covered with half-timbered houses. Up the steep slope they went, their boots slipping on the cobblestones. The preserved medieval houses looked small compared to the great church in the centre. Here, day and night, the monks had gathered for their seven services a day. Here behind the altar stood the reliquary statue of Ste Foy encrusted with jewels and cameos and intaglios donated by the pilgrims. And here above the doorway was the tympanum, a great semicircular structure depicting the Last Judgement where a majestic Christ ushers the elect into heaven and the damned into hell. Some of the sculptures on the road to Compostela are delicate, almost ethereal in composition, etiolated saints and ethereal evangelists gazing out at the passing pilgrims. The Conques tympanum is not among them. Its message is direct, simple, uncompromising. Follow the scriptures and you'll be saved. Sin and you'll go to hell. This was the blunt message of Conques. As the pilgrims stared up at the message, Charlie Flanagan, the young man from Baltimore who carved ships and crucifixes out of wood, took out a small black notebook and began making drawings of the figures. Powerscourt wondered if a tiny Lucifer or an Abraham would emerge in the days ahead.

A great crowd of schoolchildren enveloped them suddenly. They wriggled their way to the front of the crowd, slipping past the pilgrims, pushing them out of their way and scattering them across the square. The children seemed to have emerged from nowhere and began pointing excitedly at the little stone figures above. Heaven didn't seem to interest them very much. It was hell that appealed.

'Look at Lucifer with those mad eyes!'

'They're hanging one over there upside down!'

'See that one near the bottom! The devils are putting him into a furnace!'

'How about that couple below! They must have been very bad. They're tied together at the neck!'

'What about this hunchback devil? He's caught three monks in a sort of fishing net like my father uses!'

As their teachers appeared to restore order the morning air of Conques was split by a scream. It cut through the excited babble of the schoolchildren. Then there was a second. The teachers began to gather their children into a huddle under the main door. The pilgrims looked as if they had been turned into stone. Powerscourt turned and ran as fast as he could towards the noise. It came from the opposite end of the church. The Inspector was close behind him. At the far side of the radiating chapels that led out from the choir were a series of empty stone coffins that looked as if they might once have been inside holding the bodies of dead saints or warriors. They could be seen clearly from the street. One of them was no longer empty. Blood flowed out of it in streams and ran on to the grass and spilled over the flagstones below. It looked fresh, as if it had only started to pump out recently. A lone woman in the street carried on screaming. Powerscourt turned and sprinted back to the tympanum.

'The children,' he said to the teachers in a voice he tried to make as normal as he could. 'Get them out of here as fast as you can. It's bad back there, very bad. Whatever you do,' he pointed dramatically behind him, 'don't take them that way up the street. You'll have to find another route.'

He suggested to the policeman that the pilgrims should all be assembled inside the church and not be allowed out until further notice. He found a young priest and asked him to fetch a doctor. Then he took Father Kennedy with him and returned to the scene of carnage. The priest knelt down and began whispering the words of extreme unction as best as he could. Lady Lucy appeared to give moral support to her husband. She looked away quickly when she saw the blood-drenched body, the red flow gushing out over the stone, and stared down at her feet. A thin stream of blood was now nearing her shoes. A scallop shell seemed to be floating in the blood inside the stone coffin. Inspector Léger was making notes in his police book. There was a sweet almost sickly smell in the air. In the distance you could hear the voices of the children, complaining about their shortened visit to the statues and the church, wondering what could have happened at the far end of the abbey. They imagined many things, but not murder.

Powerscourt stared sadly down at the third body dispatched on the route to Compostela. Stephen Lewis the solicitor from Frome would not be going on any more train rides across southern France and taking lunch in agreeable hotels. Powerscourt tried to work out a connection, any connection, between his latest corpse and the two earlier victims but found that he could not. Lewis would write no more wills for the citizens of Frome, their secrets secure in the safe behind his desk. He would supervise no more the affairs and the accounts of the local Dramatic Society who had been urging him for years to take a small part in one of their productions but had always been turned down. Mrs Lewis would sit alone now on her terrace on the summer evenings, with no more gossip and anecdote from the town to entertain her.

An elderly man who looked as though he had seen all the sins of the world approached with a bag. Dr Bisquet, he said to no one in particular, medical practitioner in Conques these past thirty-five years. What have we here? He knelt slowly down to examine the body. Powerscourt thought flippantly that you could almost hear the knees creaking.

'He's dead, of course,' he said in a matter-of-fact voice as if he saw death every day, like the sunset. 'Instantaneous, mind you. That must have been a blessing. One vicious stroke right across the throat from behind delivered with great force. Monsieur, I show you.'

The doctor seemed to have identified Powerscourt as the principal player in the little group. He stood directly behind Powerscourt, so close that Powerscourt felt the grubby wool of his jacket on his neck. The doctor shot his right hand to the far side of Powerscourt's neck and slashed it across to the other side.

'That's all it would take, monsieur. The knife must have been very sharp. You find the knife, yes? Not yet? Never mind. It is too late for the poor man here.'

The Inspector sent a man to search the surrounding area.

'Could you say anything about the height of the killer, Doctor?' asked Powerscourt. 'Would he have been taller than his victim? Could he have done it if he had been a couple of inches shorter?'

Powerscourt was hunting through his memory for the relative height of the pilgrims, the remaining pilgrims, as he reminded himself bitterly.

'That is an intelligent question, monsieur. I'm afraid I cannot give a definite answer. It would have been easiest if our murderer had been taller. If he had been of the same height it would have been perfectly possible. A little shorter and it would have been difficult but not impossible. For the dwarf, or the little person, they could not have done it.'

'And the blood, Doctor? Would any of the blood have stuck to the murderer's clothes?'

'Ah ha!' said the doctor, who was a great devotee of detective stories in his leisure hours, although he was careful not to tell his patients. 'There are a number of ways of stabbing a man to death. If you stab upwards from below the heart, that is a very certain killing stroke. Many would-be murderers don't understand that it is best to strike from below so the knife goes in under the chest bones. Strike from above in a downwards direction and the blow may not be fatal. Our victim may survive. But with this method here, the rapid slit across the throat,' the doctor mimed the action once more, 'the murderer may not have any blood on his clothes at all. He will look like everybody else. There we are.'

Powerscourt looked down at the dead body once more. What had been a human being that morning had turned into a bundle of clothes that might have been left out for the rag and bone man. The blood was still dripping out.

'Do you know the name of the dead man?' The doctor looked once more at Powerscourt. 'You do? Good, perhaps you could come back to my surgery where we can fill in the necessary forms for the authorities with one of these policemen. I will arrange for the removal of the corpse. I will send some kind of shroud so the citizens and pilgrims of Conques do not have to look at something to remind them of their sins and their own futures. We will all end up dead some day.' The doctor looked as if he told this to his patients on a regular basis. Powerscourt did not think they would find it reassuring. 'Let us pray that we do not end up like this.'

As they filed past the front of the abbey Powerscourt found himself wondering which side of the great tympanum Stephen Lewis had gone to on his final journey. Was he perhaps in hell, with the devils and the prongs and the halters and the roaring fires? Or was he clothed in white, accompanying the elect into heaven, checking perhaps that they had all left their earthly affairs in order before they set off? On balance, Powerscourt thought, Stephen Lewis, the solicitor from Frome, would be with God's chosen. Even in heaven, he reminded himself, they must need lawyers.

13

Powerscourt found the great doors into the Abbey Church of Sainte Foy closed on his return. The pilgrims were huddled together, sitting on the ground on the opposite side of the square, guarded by two policemen, like prisoners being taken to the guillotine. Inspector Léger shrugged.

'We have had a visit from the Mayor while you were away,' he said. 'The pilgrims are not welcome here in Conques, he told us. No hotel will give them rooms. Nobody will serve them food. Even the bar up the street will refuse their custom.'

'He said they had defiled the town,' Lady Lucy cut in, 'that a place of God had been turned into a charnel house by people pretending to be pilgrims. I think he runs the wine shop, this Mayor, Francis. He smelt of drink. You could see imaginary rows of onions hanging from his neck and a beret on his head, if you know what I mean. And he had a priest with him.'

Powerscourt wondered suddenly if the priest was a regular customer, checking to see if the Mayor's wares could be turned into the blood of Christ.

'And he said more of the same, the priest,' Lady Lucy went on. 'Pilgrims not welcome, pilgrims desecrating one of the holiest sites in France, pilgrims defiling the memory of one of her greatest saints. Nothing but sinners and a murderer in the priest's view. We are meant to leave here within the hour.'

'I see,' said Powerscourt wearily. 'Was Father Kennedy any use? Didn't he try launching an appeal to Christian charity, to the stuff about forgiveness of sins?'

'I'm afraid the Father was too preoccupied with consuming some of the creamier products of the bakery up the street, Francis. He tried but it was no good. You can't take anything seriously if it comes from a man with his mouth full of éclair.'

'He got his order in before the Mayor arrived, did he?' said Powerscourt. 'He must have been quick off the mark.'

'He was,' said Lady Lucy sadly. 'The Inspector has had a conversation with young Alex Bentley about accommodation. They think the best plan is to return to the Auberge des Montagnes in Espeyrac for this night. It would be too far for us to travel on to the next place where he's booked hotels.'

'What about the funeral?' asked Powerscourt. 'Aren't the pilgrims allowed to bury their dead? Can't they even see Stephen Lewis put in the ground and say their farewells?'

'The authorities will bury him,' said the Inspector. 'The priest assured us that they will give him a proper burial in the town cemetery. They don't want Father Kennedy anywhere near the service, they said. The poor man can't be buried by a glutton in a dog collar.'

Powerscourt turned and looked at the terrible fate of the stone glutton in the tympanum seven centuries before, being pulled towards a fire under an enormous cooking pot, the fire of hell.

'We should go now.' The Inspector took command, searching the top of his head once more for the vanished hair. 'I have told the pilgrims they are to march in single file. They are not allowed to talk to each other. It should only take a couple of hours.'

Back they went, back past the cobbled streets and the half-timbered houses, back through the Porte du Barry and over the Roman bridge pilgrims had crossed in their thousands centuries before. Those earlier pilgrims, Powerscourt thought, would have left Conques with their spirits high, inspired or terrified by the Last Judgement and the fate of the figures in the tympanum, astonished by the golden wonder of the statue of the saint, blessed by the mystery of the Mass. These pilgrims of 1906 were fleeing Conques like Lot and his family in the biblical story of Sodom and Gomorrah. If they looked back they would be turned into pillars of salt. Then he remembered that one important part of the story was the wrong way round. In the Bible the refugees were fleeing from the cities of iniquity, Sodom and Gomorrah. Here, on the road to Senergues and Espeyrac, Conques, the city behind them, was totally innocent. Iniquity lay among the pilgrims.

All through the early afternoon the pilgrims marched in silence, lost in their own thoughts or contemplating their sins. Michael Delaney knew what to do with the hotelkeeper to secure their lodging for the night. He felt sure that word of the latest murder would reach the hotel before they did.

'Offer him double what we paid the night before,' he said to Powerscourt as Espeyrac and its spire came into view once more. 'That should keep the fellow quiet.'

Shortly after they arrived the Inspector and Powerscourt began another round of interviews. Where exactly were the pilgrims when the schoolchildren arrived? Could they put a cross on the page with the drawing of the square the Inspector had produced from memory? Did they see Stephen Lewis go round to the side of the building? Did they see anybody go with him? How well did they know Lewis? Had they ever met him before? Had they seen anybody come back from the part of the church with the fateful coffins? As he wrote down the answers in English while the Inspector wrote them in French, Powerscourt found that his brain had moved off somewhere else even as his pen raced across the page and his voice translated from French into English and back into French again. He had done this so many times already. Perhaps he and Lucy were on an interpreter's course and this was the final exam, though a part of his brain told him it was certainly not the final test. They might be only halfway through. Maybe they would get a diploma at the end, whenever and wherever that might be. Then he noticed something else, something that worried him very much. The harsh words of the Mayor and the priest of Conques had made the bond between the pilgrims even stronger. They looked at the Inspector as if he was an enemy and at Powerscourt as if he might be an ally who would turn traitor and desert the cause at any moment. There was an air of hostility towards the policeman that there hadn't been in Le Puy. Powerscourt wondered if the pilgrims were telling them the truth. He wondered if they would lie for a fellow pilgrim even if they thought he might be a murderer. His investigation, never easy in this case, was growing more difficult all the time.

There were more problems later that day when Jack O'Driscoll, the young newspaperman from Dublin, asked if he could have a word in the hotelkeeper's office. The reporter looked anxious.

'Please forgive me for troubling you, Lord Powerscourt,' he began. 'I've got something on my mind.'

For a brief second Powerscourt felt hope flooding through him. The young man knew who the murderer was. Jack O'Driscoll had the answers. A day or two more and he and Lucy could go home to their children.

'You remember I'm a reporter, Lord Powerscourt, with one of the big papers in Dublin?'

Powerscourt thought he knew what was coming. He had been expecting it. 'Of course I do, I remember you telling me all about it.'

'It was my editor who sent me here,' Jack O'Driscoll went on. 'He said it would be good for me. They've always been good to me on the paper.'

Powerscourt thought that the customary cynicism of the newspaperman had not yet wormed its way into the O'Driscoll soul.

'Now I think I'm letting them down, Lord Powerscourt, so I do.'

'And why is that?' asked Powerscourt with a smile.

'I think you know just as well as I do.' O'Driscoll grinned back, a rather naughty grin. 'Here we are sitting on one of the best newspaper stories of the twentieth century. I promised you before that I wouldn't do anything or write anything without your approval. Well, I would like to ask you to reconsider, I really would.'

'What do you think has changed since we spoke about this before?' Powerscourt wasn't going to make the young man's life too easy.

'It's obvious, Lord Powerscourt. Forgive me if I talk in newspaper speak for a moment. The last time we had one dead body, thrown off the twisting path up to that little chapel in Le Puy. One murder, even of an Englishman or an Irishman, in foreign parts doesn't rate too highly. Small para in the news round-up on an inside page at best. Two deaths in the south of France, a dead American added to the mix, that's better. Mysterious murders. Corpses sent floating down French rivers in the middle of the night. That might get you half a page and a lot of words, four or five hundred, maybe more. But three! Three dead men, sent to their end by a maniac who leaves scallop shells on the bodies of his victims. It'll be the best murder story since Jack the Ripper stalked the tenements of Whitechapel all those years ago. Think of the ingredients, Lord Powerscourt. American millionaire. Dying son saved from death by a miracle. A pilgrimage paid for by Croesus for members of his family. A pastry priest from Manhattan, keener on his stomach than on the salvation of souls. Some of the most sacred places in France. A Black Madonna. A stolen saint. Three victims all killed in different ways. A famous Anglo-Irish investigator and his wife, summoned from London to solve the mystery. The pilgrims themselves, a dying man, another on the staff of a senator in Washington, another on the run from his creditors. What a cast! What a story! The Psychopath from Le Puy!'

Jack O'Driscoll paused, and took a deep draught of the beer he had brought with him.

'And how would you tell the story?' Powerscourt asked.

'I thought about that this afternoon as a matter of fact,' the young man said. 'Nothing like being force-marched along the road like a bloody convict to concentrate the mind. Originally I was going to write it up as one very long story. Then I thought of the boys in the circulation department. There's nothing they like better than splitting a story up. If they thought they could get away with it, they'd carry the reports of the football matches on successive days rather than the whole thing on the day after the game. Make the readers hungry for more, they say down in circulation. Make them want to buy the paper again the next day. Then we'll sell more copies, charge more for the advertisements. They'd love this story, Lord Powerscourt, they'd just love it. Maybe I could write one general piece at the front about Mr Delaney's son and the decision to make the pilgrimage. Some colour stuff about the pilgrim routes through France. Warning in the last paragraph that things are about to go terribly wrong as they reach Le Puy. Murder starts in tomorrow's paper. Reserve your copy of the *Irish Times* now, that sort of thing. Then it's a dead body a day. The Scallop Shell Murders, I quite like that for a title. What do you think, Lord Powerscourt?'

Powerscourt smiled. 'When you put it like that, it is indeed a tremendous story, even if it does deal with the death of people we know. And I can imagine how anxious you must be to see the story in print before anybody else gets wind of it. By all means, write the story if that is what you think best. But I must ask you not to publish it, not yet any rate.' Even as he spoke Powerscourt was desperately trying to think of an argument that would convince the young man to hold his fire.

'Of course I shall pay great attention to your views, Lord Powerscourt.' Powerscourt knew immediately what that meant. If Jack O'Driscoll decided to publish, his views would be politely ignored.

'Let me tell you what I think would happen, Jack.' Powerscourt pushed out the Christian name, like an exploratory pawn. 'There would be a tremendous fuss. The other papers would have to decide whether to ignore it, because it came from a rival, or to send their own reporters out. English papers, French papers, American papers, the route to Compostela would soon be as packed as a Fleet Street pub. And what would happen then? I think the French would throw us out. A few dead pilgrims in holy places, that's a minor irritant. France mocked because its detectives cannot solve a crime, the murderer still on French soil, there would be an outcry. And these pilgrims, who you know far better than I, would they not be cheated of their mission? Michael Delaney would not have offered proper thanks for the salvation of his son. Shane Delaney with the dying wife, how is he going to face his Sinead when he comes home without fulfilling his goal, and her hopes of a miracle to save her life, however improbable they might be, are dashed to the ground? A bitter cup that would be for Mrs Delaney. And what of the others whose motives are less clear? Are they to be denied what they hoped for from the pilgrimage? And all for a few newspaper articles which might make your name but would be soon forgotten when another scandal came along to knock it off the front pages.'

Powerscourt wondered if this would work. He felt that only an appeal to the wishes of his fellow pilgrims might succeed in stopping the young man and his story. To his astonishment Jack O'Driscoll laughed.

'There's a very old sub-editor on the paper, Lord Powerscourt, who's always telling us not to take the business of journalism and newspapers too seriously. Remember it'll be wrapping up somebody's fish and chips or lining their knicker drawers tomorrow, he says. You're right about Shane Delaney's wife, of course. She's much more important than the words in a newspaper article.'

The young man looked sad all of a sudden. Powerscourt couldn't decide whether it was because of Mrs Delaney or because he was going to have to postpone publication yet again.

'Why don't you write as much of it as you can?' he suggested. 'It can't be easy to get the tone right first time round.'

Jack O'Driscoll looked at him carefully. 'I might just do that, Lord Powerscourt. But tell me this, do you know who the murderer is now?'

'Not yet,' said Powerscourt delphically. As the young man took his leave he wondered if he had said the right thing. 'Not yet' implied that he might be on the verge of a breakthrough. He didn't want word to get round the pilgrim grapevine that he was on the verge of solving the mystery. That might not be good for his health. Maybe he should have said that he hadn't a clue. But that might find its way into the newspaper article and he would be made to look a fool. One other thought struck him as he went in search of Alex Bentley. He wondered if young Jack O'Driscoll might have too soft a heart for ultimate success in his chosen profession.

Lady Lucy Powerscourt was having a very different sort of conversation with another of the pilgrims, Christy Delaney, the young man from Ireland due to go up to Cambridge in the autumn. Christy had asked Lady Lucy to take a walk with him. He wanted some advice.

'Now then, Christy.' Lady Lucy smiled at the young man as they left the village and headed up the twisting road towards Entraygues. 'How can I help?'

The young man took a deep breath. 'I'm in love, Lady Powerscourt, I'm sure of it.'

Lady Lucy resisted the urge to laugh at his solemnity. I shall have to be very careful, she said to herself. Love can be a very serious business when you're all of eighteen years old and in a foreign country.

'Might I ask who the young lady is?'

'You may,' said the young man. 'It's Anne Marie, the daughter of the hotel owner here in Espeyrac. You must have seen her, Lady Powerscourt. She helps out in the hotel and waits at table sometimes in that black and white uniform they all seem to have.'

Lady Lucy had indeed seen Anne Marie. Even Father Kennedy had been observed staring at her as she carried away the pudding plates or served the vegetables. The girl was a beauty, tall and slim with dark hair and light brown eyes. She had a distinguished air about her as if she might have dropped in from some fashionable salon in Paris or St Petersburg. 'She is very beautiful,' said Lady Lucy. 'But tell me, Christy,' she resisted the urge to remind Christy how young he was, 'have you been in love before?'

'I have not,' the young man replied proudly. 'This is my first time.'

'Well, that can be wonderful, being in love for the first time. Sometimes it can be painful too, mind you. What makes you so sure – that you're in love, I mean.'

Christy Delaney thought hard for a moment. 'It's quite hard to describe, I think. I feel elated and excited every time I look at her. I think about her all the time. I hardly noticed the time walking back from Conques this afternoon. It's just – exhilaration, you know, Lady Powerscourt. You must remember what it's like falling in love with somebody.'

Lady Lucy didn't say that she was still in love with her husband. 'I do remember, Christy, it is all very exciting. Sometimes you think you're going mad. Have you spent a lot of time with young ladies? Do you have any sisters at home?'

'That's just it, Lady Powerscourt. There are five boys in our family. And the school I went to was all boys. So I don't suppose you could say I was experienced in these matters.'

'And how can I help? It's very flattering to be taken into your confidence like this, and I'd be delighted to help in some way if you think I could be of service. How good is your French, for a start?'

Christy explained the primitive phonetic system evolved in ordering rounds of drinks. He wondered if it could be adapted to affairs of the heart. He pulled a notebook and pencil out of his pocket.

Lady Lucy laughed. 'Let's see what we can do. Does she know your name for a start?'

'I don't think so.'

'*Je m'appelle Christy. Vous êtes Anne Marie, n'est-ce pas*?'

'Could you say that again?'

'*Je m'appelle Christy. Vous êtes Anne Marie, n'est-ce pas*?'

Lady Lucy peered over his shoulder as he wrote in his notebook. 'Je ma pell Christy. Voo zet Anne Marie, ne-sup-pa?'

'Good, Christy. Perhaps you'd better tell her you're Irish. I think the French would prefer the Irish to the English. *Je suis Irlandais. Je suis Irlandais*. But this isn't going to make for a very long conversation. What else would you like to say?'

'I thought I might ask her to come for a walk with me. Then we could point at things like trees and roads and say the words in our own languages,' said Christy seriously. He made a trial run and pointed suddenly at a group of animals in a neighbouring field. 'Sheep,' he said firmly. 'Sheep.'

'*Mouton*,' Lady Lucy replied.

'Moo tong,' Christy wrote in his book.

'*Voulez-vous faire une promenade avec moi*? That's 'would you like to come for a walk with me?'

They worked their way through How old are you, I am eighteen, Have you always lived here at the hotel, I am going to university, What is your favourite colour, How many brothers and sisters have you. Christy had filled four pages by the end. Suddenly he stopped learning his lines and asked, 'What if she doesn't like me, Lady Powerscourt? What shall I do if she is in love with somebody else already? She must have hundreds of admirers.'

'You're a very presentable young man, Christy,' said Lady Lucy, feeling about a hundred years old. 'The French have a word for it. It was the motto of the Three Musketeers now I come to think about it. They came from somewhere near here originally. Courage, dash, it says, always dash. *L'audace, toujours l'audace.'*

'Low dass,' Christy scribbled quickly, 'two dewars low dass.'

Powerscourt was highly amused when Lucy told him of her encounter with Christy back in their house in the hills that evening. 'Chair,' he said, pointing. 'Book. Cup. Bottle. Plate. Wife. You missed the exciting part back there in the hotel, my love. The Inspector has been summoned to a big meeting in Figeac first thing tomorrow morning. Nobody is to leave the hotel until he returns. Maybe they're going to deport us all.' He smiled suddenly. 'Pack. Train. Boat. Long journey. Not come back. Goodbye. Now then, let's be serious for a moment. I want you to look at this form, Lucy, and see if you think I've left anything out. I'm going to get all the pilgrims to fill this in immediately after breakfast. It's a long shot, a very long shot. See what you think.'

He handed Lucy a single sheet of paper. It was a sort of questionnaire. Name, it said at the top. Date of birth. Brothers' and sisters' names and dates of birth. Place of residence. Previous places of residence if appropriate. Parents' names and dates of birth if known. Brothers and sisters of father. Brother and sisters of mother. Place of birth of parents. Grandparents' names and dates of birth if known. Grandparents' place of birth if known. Brothers and sisters of grandparents if known. Great grandparents' names and date of birth if known. Place of birth if known.

'My goodness me, Francis, you're going back a long way. Methuselah, date and place of birth. Parents' names and dates of birth if known. What do you hope to achieve by this?'

'I said it was a long shot, Lucy. I think we all agree that the answer to the mystery lies somewhere back in the past. We've had conversations with the pilgrims about their history but we didn't write it down. Johnny Fitzgerald and Alex Bentley's brother are, we hope, ferreting about in the Delaney past to see if there are any skeletons in the cupboard or maybe how many skeletons there are. We've got Alex Bentley's stab at a family tree, though he says it's incomplete. When we've got this, if the pilgrims can remember as much as I would like, we may be able to make some connections. It's a fishing expedition, if you like, with a very poor rod in very choppy water.'

'Could I make a suggestion? Why don't you leave a blank space at the bottom for them to put in any other details about their family. It doesn't have to be important. You know how most families have myths about their past, the great auntie who kept pigs in the front room, the uncle who could walk on his hands, that sort of thing. That might be useful.' Lady Lucy paused and looked carefully at her husband. 'You realize, Francis, that the murderer is going to fill this in too?'

'I do.'

'You don't suppose the murderer will think you might be on to him?'

'What if he does?'

'He might change the batting order, Francis. You might be the next on the list.'

14

Johnny Fitzgerald found it very strange being back in the ordinary Ireland rather than in the great houses of the Protestant gentry where he had stayed the year before. Macroom was still the same small Irish town as all the other small Irish towns he had known when he was growing up. The main square was there with the tall spire of the Protestant church and the grocer and bookmaker with bars attached. The shops were selling the same stuff they had sold when he was growing up all those years before. There was a drunk lolling against the wall of the pub on South Street. There had always been a drunk somewhere about the town. The children still trooped off to the Christian Brothers and the convent for a proper education in the pieties of Irish life. The wall of the demesne ran along one side of the square. Through the ornamental gate with the one-legged lion, wounded by an inebriated young revolutionary in some earlier uprising, the road snaked its way through the woods past the lake to Macroom Castle, home, he presumed, to one Jonathan Henry Osborne. And to his wife, Mary Rose Osborne, née Lennox. Johnny knew he would have to ask somebody as casually as he could if they still lived there. He hoped he could keep his voice steady when his hour came. He wondered if there were any children. He realized with a start that any sons and daughters might be almost grown up now, conducting their own love affairs, breaking other people's hearts. And what did Jonathan Henry Osborne do with his time? Was he a conscientious landlord, improving his estates, looking after his tenants? A hunting, shooting and fishing landlord forever out in pursuit of fox or fish? Perhaps he had died in the saddle or been accidentally shot in his coverts. Maybe the widow Osborne would be waiting for him, a relief after years in black.

Johnny had established his headquarters in the O'Connell Arms, a handsome building at the top end of North Street. From his bedroom he could just see into the grounds of Macroom Castle. Nothing moved. Nobody was taking a walk through their property. No children could be heard playing in the grounds. Perhaps they had all gone away. Johnny decided to jump his fences as soon as he could. He bought a drink for the landlord in the lounge bar of the hotel, the walls lined with pictures of horses, rickety tables that had seen better days scattered round the room like patients waiting for the dentist.

'That's a grand day we're having now,' said the landlord. 'They say it's going to rain tomorrow.'

The weather, Johnny remembered, was often the overture to most conversations in Irish bars.

'Let's hope it doesn't last,' said Johnny, keeping the meteorological ball in play.

'Have you come far?' said the landlord.

'I've come from London as a matter of fact,' said Johnny.

'That's the divil of a long way,' said the landlord. 'We had a lad from the town here two or three years ago who went to London, so he did.'

'What happened to him?' asked Johnny.

'Didn't last. He came back a week later, Declan Dempsey. He said he couldn't stand the noise and the huge numbers of people. He's a regular in this bar on alternate Wednesdays after the cattle sales. If he has too much porter he'll tell you all about London. There isn't a customer here who hasn't heard the story fifteen or twenty times.'

'Tell me,' said Johnny, taking a very large draught of his Guinness, 'are there people still living in the big house up there?'

'Up in Macroom Castle? There are indeed. There's Mister Jonathan and his wife and a herd of children. Why do you ask?'

'I knew a man in the Army who used to stay there years ago,' Johnny lied. 'He said they had very good parties.'

'We wouldn't know about that,' said the landlord. 'We're not invited.'

'Could you tell me this, seeing you're a knowledgeable sort of man about the locality,' Johnny plunged on, 'is there anybody round here who knows about the history of the place, a local historian if you like? A friend and I are writing a book, you see, and we need some information about Macroom's past.'

'A book, do you say? Who would want to read a book about Macroom's past, for God's sake? Nothing ever happens here. People are born, they get married, they die. That wouldn't even fill a page.'

'The book's mainly about the famine,' Johnny said. 'We thought we should write it while there may still be people alive who can remember it.'

The landlord crossed himself. 'The famine. Mother of God. It was bad in these parts, very bad. But perhaps you knew that. That'd be a fine thing to do, writing a book about the famine. Nobody'd buy it, mind you. Not round here. Not in Ireland. We're still trying to forget the whole thing. We had a young priest here years ago who formed the theory that the reason the locals drank so much was that they were trying to forget what had happened to their ancestors.'

'Seems rather a complicated reason for liking a drink,' said Johnny, finishing his pint and ordering another. 'He's not still here, is he, the priest?'

'No, no. He gave up. He did manage to enrol most of the adult males in that you can't have a drink thing they have, the Temperance League or whatever it's called. One day he happened to pop in here for a glass of water or something and found the whole lot of them knocking back the porter in the public bar. He never got over that, Father Bell. The boys told him they'd only joined up to make him happy, they never intended to go dry at all.'

'Poor man,' said Johnny, 'can you imagine what it'd be like never having a drink? You'd never get through the day.' He took another liberal helping of stout to calm his nerves.

'You were asking about the local history and stuff,' said the landlord. 'I tell you now the fellow you want. Brother Healey, he's your man. He teaches history up the road at the Christian Brothers and he's always described as a mighty scholar. They say he once had an article published in the *Cork Examiner*.'

'And where would I find him?'

The landlord looked at his watch. 'Here,' he said. 'He's regular as clockwork. After school he goes back to the house and marks the homework and polishes his strap or whatever they do. Sometime between six and six fifteen he pops in here. Two glasses of John Powers and he's away again. I've never seen him take any more and that's a fact.'

'Perhaps he joined the temperance lot too,' said Johnny. 'I think I'll take a walk now. I'll be back in time to meet the Christian Brother.'

Johnny knew he was torturing himself. He could perfectly easily have stayed in the hotel bar and chatted to the landlord. Instead his legs carried him, almost without his knowledge, to the gates of the big house. He stood there for a moment, staring up the drive. I'm like a love-struck schoolboy, he told himself, lurking outside his girl's house in the hope of seeing her. He wondered briefly about walking up to the house and knocking on the front door. A butler would open it. Johnny Fitzgerald, the butler would proclaim, and he would be ushered into the presence. What would he say then? What would she say? What would the husband say, if he was there? It was all too embarrassing. Johnny was nearly back at the hotel when he heard a carriage rattling up the street. As he turned to look he caught a glimpse of a hat, only a hat, not the face he had kissed so passionately all those years before.

Brother Healey was a small Brother of about fifty years, plump now and with small eyes, holding tightly on to his whiskey glass as if somebody might come and take it from him. Johnny introduced himself and explained his mission. He gave a more elaborate version of his legend about the reasons for his visit this time. He and a friend, he told the Brother, were writing a book about the famine. They had been commissioned by a very rich American called Delaney who was particularly interested in the Delaney family, many of whom he believed had perished in the years of hunger. Did the Brother know anything about these Delaneys? Would he care for another shot of John Powers to lubricate the brain? Brother Healey did care for a freshening of his glass as he put it.

'Delaneys,' he said, savouring the word as if it were another variety of whiskey, 'there are a whole lot of Delaneys buried there in the field outside the town. It's not a period I know a great deal about. I'm rather better on Cromwell and the redistribution of land, myself. But I know a man who is an expert on the famine. It's rather late in the day to call on him now, I'm afraid.'

'But it's only a quarter past six,' said Johnny.

'I know, I know,' said Brother Healey. 'I wouldn't wish to speak ill of the fellow. But he begins to take a drop of refreshment very early in the day, if you follow me. Before breakfast, I believe. The woman who looks after him says it's the drink that's kept him alive. She says he's so pickled in John Jameson that no disease could get near him. But he's the man for you. I've got the first two lessons off tomorrow. I'll take you round to him then. You see, he's well over eighty now. He lived through the bloody famine. He survived.'

Powerscourt thought you could tell which pilgrims had done well at school by the way they filled in his forms. There was a certain amount of pen-sucking in some quarters. Waldo Mulligan polished his off in no time at all and stared out of the window. Christy Delaney, the young man in love, was also well ahead of the pack. He wrote the name Anne Marie on his hand over and over again. Girvan Connolly, the man on the run from his creditors, seemed to be writing an essay in the extra space provided. He was now on the other side of the page.

Powerscourt wondered what you would do if you were the murderer. Would you tell the truth? Would you make up a totally fictitious past? Could one tell if a person was lying from words written on a page? It would be, he realized, much easier to tell if a person was lying in a conversation than it would be reading a sheet of paper. What would I do, if I were the murderer? he asked himself. A clever murderer would know that he, Powerscourt, had no means of checking out the information. He could invent a totally fictitious past and a totally fictitious family. Maybe the whole thing was a waste of time.

The pilgrims began to drift away after they had finished. Inspector Léger's men watched their every move. One of these men is a murderer, Powerscourt reminded himself, one of the most daring murderers he had ever encountered. He wished there was some test he could give, other than this one, like those chemical experiments he dimly remembered from his school days where things turned blue or green when confronted with another substance.

At last they were all finished. Powerscourt took the papers up to Alex Bentley's room and together they began turning them into family trees, horizontal and vertical lines joining up the Delaneys spinning their way down the pages. Then he remembered the local vineyard. The owner had been taking his evening meal at the table next to the Powerscourts the evening before and had shouted a very loud invitation to visit him in the morning as he left. Normally Powerscourt would have declined but he had promised to go and his head was weary with family trees. 'I'll just pop over for half an hour or so,' he said to Alex Bentley. 'Can you tell Lady Lucy where I've gone?'

The last of the morning mist was clearing as he set out on the half-mile walk to the vineyard. Thin wisps could be seen disappearing very slowly when you looked at them. A bird of prey, buzzard or kite, was circling high in the sky. It was going to be a beautiful day. Monsieur Leon's vineyard was on top of a hill. On the right-hand side the vines ran down the slopes in orderly well-tended rows. On the left the hill became almost a precipice, tumbling down towards the Lot, the waters dark in the shadows.

Powerscourt knocked on the door of the house and found no reply. In front of him was a set of steps with the word *cave* or cellar written on a piece of wood above the entrance. From somewhere down below he thought he could hear music, a rather tinny sort of music. As he reached the bottom of the steps he saw that he was in quite a large cave. In the centre a feeble electric light tried and failed to illuminate all the interior. There were racks and racks filled with wine bottles reaching from floor to ceiling. The music, he realized, was the Marseillaise and it must be coming from a musical box by one of the enormous wooden vats at the far end of the cellar.

Powerscourt headed towards the noise, his footsteps echoing off the stone floor. The music changed. Now it was playing 'The Star-Spangled Banner'. Maybe it was one of those sophisticated machines that could play three or four different tunes. One of the vats had a sliding door cut into the front, presumable to make the cleaning out of the lees easier. Powerscourt stepped inside.

And the rockets' red glare, the bombs bursting in air,
Gave proof through the night that our flag was still there.
O say, does that star-spangled banner yet wave
O'er the land of the free, and the home of the brave?

Powerscourt hummed the words to the himself as he knelt down to inspect the little box. Some distant memory told him that the most sophisticated of these machines were manufactured in Switzerland. Just as he had it in his hands the light went out. Then he heard a rasping noise. The sliding door of the vat was moving. There was a harsh clang as it closed and a bolt was rammed home. Then another one. The music stopped. Powerscourt was trapped in the dark inside a wine vat over ten feet tall with no means of communication with the outside world. The winemaker Mr Leon seemed to have disappeared.

For a moment he cursed himself for his folly. Why hadn't he stayed with his family trees, drawing innocent lines of dead Delaneys across the page? Something told him that his ordeal had only just begun. There would be something else. He prayed that it wasn't rats, rats about to be released into his wooden tomb through some secret opening. All his life he had been terrified of rats, rats runnning all over his clothes, patrolling across his face, scratching at his hands, biting, clawing, driving him slowly insane.

Then he heard his fate. It wasn't rats that were to mark his passing. At first he thought it might be condensation coming off the roof of the wooden vat. There were drips falling on to the floor. The drips turned into a slow trickle. A couple of them landed on his head. Then he knew. This wasn't going to be Ordeal by Rat. It wasn't even going to be Ordeal by Water. It was going to be Ordeal by Wine. There must be some sort of funnel or entrance up there through which the murderer had released this slow trickle that seemed to be growing more powerful by the second. Presumably there was a link to some other container that was now being emptied all over him. He couldn't get out. He doubted if anybody would hear him shout, if there was anybody out there in the cave who was listening. He remembered some English king who had always delighted junior students of history by dying in a butt of malmsey. Well, unless he was very lucky, he, Powerscourt, was going to drown in a vat of wine. He hoped flippantly that it was good quality stuff. He didn't fancy drowing in *vin ordinaire*. He wanted to pass away to *Premier Cru*, maybe even *Grand Cru*. He wondered where Johnny Fitzgerald was. So often in the past he had thought that the two of them would die together on the battlefield.

Powerscourt patted his pockets to see what feeble weapons he might have at his command. He had left his pistol in the little house in the hills. He doubted it would have served him well even if he had it. The bullets might ricochet off the staves and kill him on the rebound. He had a book of matches. This vat, soaked in wine for heaven knew how many years, would never burn, and even if it did, he would burn with it. He had a clasp knife, complete with two blades and a corkscrew. The one thing he didn't need in here, he told himself bitterly, was a bloody corkscrew. The stuff was lapping at his ankles now. He bent down and picked up the music box. He placed it on a ledge level with the top of his head. He felt for the button or the handle to turn it on. The Marseillaise sounded forth again. He could meet his end to the song of the men marching from Marseilles to Paris in 1792. He would have a suitably French end.

He tried shoulder-charging the walls of his tomb. His only reward was a bruised shoulder. Then he began feeling with his hands along the wooden staves used to build the giant barrel. The cooper who made it would have known all about how to make it waterproof. He tried inserting the stronger blade of his knife into the overlap between the planks. Nothing happened. He wondered if he could make a hole, just a little hole that would let the wine escape. It was up to his calves now. A quick bend down and a dab of his fingers told Powerscourt that he was going to meet his maker in a sea of red rather than a sea of white. Jordan river, for him, would be *rouge* not *blanc*. He began working with his knife at the wood about halfway up the side of the vessel. He realized that the corkscrew might be more useful in trying to gouge out tiny sections of wood. With a knife in one hand and the corkscrew in the other he launched a furious assault on the walls of his tomb. The music box played on.

> *Aux armes, citoyens!*
> *Formez vos bataillons,*
> *Marchons, marchons!*
> *Qu'un sang impur*
> *Abreuve nos sillons . . .*

Powerscourt sang along in French to raise his spirits. He remembered that the soldier who wrote the words in a single night was a captain of engineers. Maybe some of his skills could be transferred to Powerscourt's hands.

> To arms, citizens!
> Form up your battalions,
> Let us march, let us march!
> That their impure blood
> Should water our fields . . .

Lady Lucy felt cold when she heard about her husband's trip to the vineyard. She could sense danger. She thought of the road between the hotel and the vineyard. She remembered the words of the Inspector – 'We're only letting the pilgrims out one at a time. No pairs, no groups. If they want to kill themselves instead of one of the others, so much the better.' The killer might be lying in the wait for her Francis. She remembered all the times in the past when Francis had gone out on potentially dangerous missions accompanied by Johnny Fitzgerald as friend and protector. Now he was on his own. And they were up against one of the most ruthless murderers they had ever encountered. If the murderer began to see Powerscourt as a threat, she felt sure that he too would be killed. She remembered Sherlock Holmes's advice to Dr Watson when he was telling him how to cross London without falling into the clutches of the evil Professor Moriarty: 'in the morning you will send for a hansom, desiring your man to take neither the first nor the second that may present itself'. Francis, she thought, had jumped heedlessly into the first one.

She rushed to find Inspector Léger. Together they ran up the road to Monsieur Leon's with Lucy praying as she went that her husband would still be alive when she got there.

The wine was well over his knees now. Powerscourt thought that he had only five or ten minutes left. The music box, obviously a deeply patriotic machine, had worked its way through all seven verses of the Marseillaise. Now it was playing 'God Save the King' at a very rapid speed. Powerscourt wondered if he would die happy and glorious. His hands were still hacking feverishly at the wood. His indentation was about an eighth of an inch deep. He didn't know how thick the planks were but he doubted he had enough time. He realized suddenly how difficult it would be to effect a rescue mission. Anybody walking into the cave would think everything was normal, the bottles parked neatly in their rows, the great vats standing to attention at the end. Nobody would ever know he was inside one of them. He hoped the music box would carry beyond the curved walls of his prison. He thought of Lucy and the years ahead they might never enjoy together. He thought of his children growing up without a father. He thought of his first wife Caroline, drowned with their little son in a shipwreck on the Irish Sea. He thought about the murderer in his present case and that drove him to yet more furious efforts with knife and corkscrew. If there was one thing that made him angry, it was the thought of being beaten. This bloody murderer, he said to himself, is not going to kill me. I won't have it. As the wine rose to his waist and filled his pockets he began shoving the corkscrew into the wood as if it was a cork in a bottle. He thought he could drive it in another eighth of an inch. There was still a long way to go. There was now a musty smell in the vat of death, heady fumes rising from the liquid. Powerscourt realized he might be forced to drink the stuff at the end. An imaginary waiter appeared before him. Would Monsieur like to try the wine?

Inspector Léger and Lady Lucy were halfway there now. The hill had slowed them to a walking pace. Inspector Léger was mopping his brow with a blue handkerchief, freshly ironed, Lady Lucy observed, wondering about Madame Léger and life in the Léger household. Some of her anxiety had transmitted itself to the policeman. He patted his pocket from time to time, making sure his gun was still there. A small group of clouds passed overhead, obscuring the sun. A cart, laden with manure, passed them going the other way. On either side the vines were ripening slowly.

The wine was at Powerscourt's heart now. The musical box had moved back to the American national anthem. He was beginning to feel dizzy. His clothes were sticking tightly to his body. He could feel the energy ebbing away from him as his fingers still hacked at the wood of his prison. He cursed the murderer. He thought he was about to cry.

Lady Lucy and the Inspector were only a couple of hundred yards away. Lady Lucy was panting, holding on to her side. She knew she couldn't slow down. A terrible memory came back to her, of her husband lying wounded, shot by a killer in the Wallace Collection in London's Manchester Square and hovering close to death. He lay in a coma, and she recalled all too vividly the thought that he was going to pass away in front of her and she wouldn't even know he had gone.

Perhaps he's dead already, Lady Lucy said to herself, for her anxieties had grown on the journey, and I wasn't there to say goodbye. Very quietly she began to weep.

Powerscourt thought he was making progress at last: the wood at the end of his corkscrew felt slightly different. It began to yield a little. He though of prisoners in their cells in the Tower of London in Elizabethan times trying to saw away at the bars of their prison. The wine was by his shoulders now. Every time he rammed his corkscrew into the wood there was a swell in the liquid around him. At its height the red tide washed up to his ears. His music box was back on 'God Save the King'. Powerscourt thought the Dead March from *Saul* might be more appropriate. Very quietly he began to sing the last verse:

> From every latent foe,
> From the assassin's blow,
> God save the King!
> O'er him thine arm extend
> For Britain's sake defend,
> Our father, prince and friend,
> God save the King!

Inspector Léger and Lady Lucy had reached the winemaker's house. They took a lightning tour. They peered into the darkness of the cellar and the Inspector went back into the kitchen to search for matches. God only knows, he said to himself, where the bloody light switch is. Lady Lucy stood halfway down the steps straining for a noise or a cry or the sound of some stray dog barking by a human body.

One more attack with this corkscrew and I might be through, Powerscourt said to himself, bracing himself for a mighty effort. The music box now gave forth a rather high-pitched rendering of the Marseillaise. Maybe the fumes of the wine were affecting its inner workings. In went the corkscrew, Powerscourt turned it as hard as he could. It was getting somewhere. Then it was through. There was a tiny hole in the side of the vat. Powerscourt began to smile. But as he watched the wine trickle out, he knew that it was no good. His trickle was less, far less than the flow coming in from above. He might have postponed his doom but only for a few seconds. And then he saw that something else had gone terribly wrong. In his last round of pushing, turning and twisting he had broken the corkscrew. The vital part of it must be lying on the floor outside. The wine was up to his neck. The fumes were much worse. He thought he would pass out before he died. He would never see Lucy again.

After what seemed an eternity Inspector Léger found some matches. He left the winemaker's kitchen looking as if it had been ransacked by a burglar in a hurry, drawers thrown on the floor, cupboards emptied, a whole row of saucepans tossed aside. Lady Lucy clutched his arm as they made their way down the steps, enormous shadows flickering now across the sides of the cave.

At the bottom the Inspector paused to light another match.

'Listen, Inspector,' said Lady Lucy suddenly, straining forwards to catch a noise. 'Listen!' Together they tiptoed forwards away from the bottles towards the tiers of great vats at the end.

'It's the Marseillaise, for God's sake,' said the Inspector, 'and its coming from that great vat over there!'

'And look,' said Lady Lucy, 'do you see, there's a trickle of wine coming down the side!'

The Inspector knew what to do. One of his uncles kept a vineyard in the Loire. He raced over to the vat and pulled back the bolts on the sliding door. A torrent of wine knocked him backwards on to the floor. Lady Lucy dodged to one side. The music box was still playing. And then, very unsteadily, like a man who has been drinking for days, his clothes dripping red on to the floor, his hand still clutching his clasp knife, his face deadly pale, came the staggering figure of Lord Francis Powerscourt.

'Lucy,' he said, his voice thick from the fumes, 'I'm so glad to see you.' And with that he fainted into her arms.

15

Shortly after nine o'clock in the morning Brother Healey took Johnny Fitzgerald to meet Sean McGurk, the eighty-year-old veteran of the famine. The Christian Brother stayed for a cup of tea and then left to do his marking. McGurk was a little over five feet tall and his face was lined like a parchment map. His front room had three armchairs, a fire, a couple of book-cases and pyramids of empty bottles of John Jameson. Johnny did a quick count and reckoned that with twelve empties on the first row, ascending to the summit by eleven, ten, nine and so on to the single bottle at the top, there were seventy-eight John Jamesons in each pyramid. He wondered if the number seventy-eight held some symbolic significance for the priests of ancient Egypt or the distillers of Dublin. And there were seven pyramids stretching out from the side of the fire to the opposite wall, a total he thought to be over five hundred.

'How long did it take you to drink that lot, Mr McGurk?' asked Johnny Fitzgerald. There was another bottle and a jug of water on the rickety table by the old man's chair. Pyramid builders, Johnny reckoned, must work all day.

'One pyramid every two months or so,' said Sean McGurk. Christ, said Johnny to himself, that's over a bottle a day. He was amazed the old man was still alive. The medical fraternity would have said survival was impossible at those rates of consumption.

'You're looking well on it,' said Johnny cheerfully. 'It must help to keep the days at bay.'

'It does that,' McGurk smiled and the lines on his face grew ever deeper. 'Now then, Brother Healey said you wanted to know about the famine here in Macroom. Is it any particular district or any particular workhouse or any particular family you're interested in?'

Johnny explained about his book, commissioned by a rich Delaney in New York to find out about his ancestors. He almost believed the story by now.

'There's one thing I must ask you before we start,' said McGurk, taking an enormous gulp of John Jameson. 'Please don't go asking me about my own experiences in those terrible times. I swore to God I would never talk about it again after I had three Americans here two years ago it was this August. Four days they spent here, staying in that hotel where I'm sure you are, and they wouldn't leave me alone. "Surely there's something else you can remember, Mr McGurk," they started saying halfway through the second day and they carried on like that for another forty-eight hours. I got through two and a half bottles of medicine the evening they left and that's a fact.'

'It's Delaneys I'm interested in, Mr McGurk,' said Johnny. 'I'm sure your experiences are fascinating but I'll settle for Delaneys.'

The old man hobbled to his bookcase and brought down two blue school exercise books. 'I've written up all my discoveries in these little volumes,' he said, carrying them back to his chair. He took another draught of medicine. 'I've been talking to survivors of that dreadful famine for over thirty years now. Somebody had to do it, you know, and I've always liked history. It was my best subject at school.'

The old man began looking through his books. 'Daly, Davies, Davitt, Davy, that's no good, here we are, Delaney.' He took another swig to help his reading. For a moment there was silence in the little room. Johnny wondered what was coming.

'I'm not sure your man is going to like this very much,' said the old man, looking up at Johnny. 'I don't think he'll like it at all.' He carried on reading.

218

'Right,' he said at last. 'Here goes. Are you sure you won't be taking a drop?' He nodded at the bottle. Johnny declined.

'Before the famine,' McGurk began, peering at his handwriting as if he had never seen it before, 'there were a lot of Delaneys in these parts, mostly around Clonbeg down the road. Poor they were, terribly poor, living on the potatoes off their tiny holdings in those dreadful cabins we all lived in during those times. There were three Delaney families with over twenty children between them living in poverty and one family who had done rather better for themselves here in Macroom. They had a fair bit of land, the Brian Delaneys. When the potato crop failed the starving ones turned to their cousin for help. Brian Delaney refused. He wouldn't give them a penny or a potato. Then the time came when they were all going to have to go into the workhouse. By this stage going to the workhouse was virtually a death sentence, the fever and the dysentery were so bad people were dropping down inside the workhouse gates. One of the poor wives managed to reach Brian Delaney in his house. They say he wouldn't even let her through the door in case she infected his family. He gave her nothing. They all died. Or rather I think they all died.'

'What do you mean, you think they all died?' said Johnny, thinking that perhaps a glass of John Jameson might be rather welcome now.

'Well, this is the strange thing,' said the old man, pausing to pour himself a refill, 'they managed to keep some sort of records in these parts, records of the dying, I mean. Maybe the workhouses got paid for the dead as well as the living. In some parts of the country they've no records of the dead at all, it's as if the poor people had never been here at all. We know there were twenty-four Delaneys, men, women and children, brought into the workhouse. But there are only records of twenty-three of them dying. One of them managed to get away, to survive, though God knows how they did it.'

'Do you know which one it was, Mr McGurk? Man, woman, boy, girl?'

'That's a very intelligent question,' said McGurk. 'It was a boy of about twelve years.'

'Do we have a name?'

'I'm afraid not.'

'Do you know what happened to the Brian Delaney family? The bad ones? Are their descendants still here?'

'They're not. I don't know if there was bad feeling against them but they left for America a couple of years after the famine.'

'I don't suppose you know which part they went to?' said Johnny.

'I'm afraid I don't,' the old man replied, closing his book. 'Are you sure you won't have a drop to keep me company before you go?'

'That's very kind of you,' said Johnny, wondering what size of glass the old soak would pour him. He stared in astonishment as the bottle was tipped up into a fresh tumbler. Couple of inches, standard measure in an Irish bar, four inches, double, six inches, treble, eight inches and the recipient would probably fall down. McGurk stopped just after eight. 'I hope that's not too small for you,' he said. 'I can't see much point in a half-empty glass myself.'

Johnny could see why Sean McGurk might not be at his best by the evening. As he thanked the old man and left him a five-pound note for his pains, he wondered if the historian would live long enough to build another pyramid of empties. Maybe he could be buried inside one, like the Egyptian kings all those years before. Making his way back to the hotel, just on the right side of sober, he saw a well-dressed woman walking down the street towards him. Johnny's heart began to pound and he didn't think it was the whiskey. People can change their hairstyles, he said to himself, their faces change of their own accord, but their walk remains the same. Coming down the street towards him, less than fifty yards away now, was Mary Rose, once the love of his life, now the wife of another.

Two hours after his escape from the cellar, Powerscourt was discussing his ordeal with Lady Lucy as they walked from the little house in the hills down to the Espeyrac hotel. The Inspector had discovered the winemaker bound and gagged in a barn beside his house. He told the policeman he had no idea who his assailant had been.

'That invitation last night was so loud that anybody could have heard it, anybody at all,' said Powerscourt, smelling his collar anxiously to make sure his clean clothes didn't also reek of drink.

'But why should the murderer decide to kill you now?' said Lady Lucy. She wished more than anything that she could spirit Johnny Fitzgerald to her husband's side. The knot of anxiety that tormented her when she knew Francis was in danger was churning round inside her. 'What has changed in the last day or so? He could have made the attempt a long time ago.'

'I've no idea. Maybe it was saying to Jack O'Driscoll that I don't know who the murderer is. I think I said not yet. Maybe that got around among the pilgrims. Maybe the murderer interpreted not yet as meaning that I was on the verge of a breakthrough.'

The hotel keeper greeted them anxiously as they reached the Auberge des Montagnes. 'Monsieur, monsieur,' he said in a worried tone, 'Mr Delaney is most anxious to speak with you. Immediately. And this cable came for you first thing this morning, monsieur. I'm afraid it seems to have been opened by mistake. I'm truly sorry, monsieur. Let us hope the message is not important?'

'Do you know who opened it?' said Powerscourt sternly.

'I'm afraid not, monsieur, it was lying on the front desk in the reception. I suppose anybody could have read it.'

Powerscourt didn't think anybody could have mistaken the name Powerscourt for the names of any of the pilgrims. Delaney, Mulligan, O'Driscoll, Flanagan, even a Frenchman would not be likely to mix those up. So, maybe the enemy was reading his post. He, Powerscourt, had often opened other people's mail during his years in Army Intelligence. But then, he said to himself, Johnny Fitzgerald and I always covered our tracks. Nobody would have known we were reading their letters and sealing them up again. That way, you kept the advantage. Once the enemy knew you were intercepting their messages, the exercise lost all its value and could even become counter-productive if your opponents arranged to have false information sent to themselves through a third party. This could completely fool the interceptors, who would believe it to be genuine. Then the tables would be turned indeed. Powerscourt stared down at his cable. An intelligent man, he reckoned, could have sealed it up again quite easily, or sealed it up so the recipient could not be sure whether it had been tampered with or not. He wondered if the message was so dangerous for the murderer that he had to take immediate action, that his own position was now so exposed that he didn't think about sealing it up again.

I don't suppose I'll ever know the answer, he said to himself, leading Lady Lucy to a seat in the sunshine some hundred yards from the Auberge des Montagnes. The message came from Franklin Bentley, Alex's brother who worked for a law firm with offices in New York and Washington. 'Some progress,' it began. 'Copies of book on Delaney's life that was pulped years ago may still be at large. Total of four sent to London dealers before Delaney intervened. Publishers presumably hoped for sale to Americans in London. New York firm that published it went bankrupt years ago. No records found so far. Presume you investigate London end. Waldo Mulligan believed by rumour to be having affair with colleague's wife. Not clear if sent away by senator who knew about it, or left in fit of morality.

Morality fit unlikely behaviour in Washington DC. Uncon-firmed, very unconfirmed rumour that Michael Delaney was married before the arrival of the second wife, mother of James. Not clear what happened. Wife dead? Couple divorced? Delaney bigamist? Inquiries continue. Good luck. Franklin Bentley.'

'God bless my soul,' said Powerscourt, and handed the cable over to Lady Lucy. 'I'll say this for Alex Bentley's brother, he's a good worker, and a quick one.'

The sun was bright overhead as Lady Lucy read the message. 'Do you think we'll be able to find one of those books in London, Francis?'

'I suppose we'll have to wait until Johnny gets back,' said Powerscourt sadly. 'I would love to get my hands on a copy of that book. Let's hope he makes good progress over there in Ireland.'

'I've got a second cousin, twice removed mind you,' Lady Lucy put in, 'whose husband works in publishing. I think he's a director of some firm or other only I can't for the moment remember which one. I'm sure he'd be able to help, Francis.'

Powerscourt had always known that whether he ended up in heaven or hell a selection of his wife's relations would be there to greet him and demand the latest news about other members of the tribe. He hoped they might be closer than second cousins twice removed.

'We don't have an address, though, do we, my love? If we were in London I'm sure we could find out in a matter of hours but it's not so easy over here. Let's wait for Johnny. I'd better go and see Michael Delaney, Lucy. I don't think he likes to be kept waiting.'

Two policemen were on duty in the hall of the hotel. Another one patrolled the ground floor. Yet another wandered in and out of the bedrooms, not bothering to knock before entering, just marching in as if he had a search warrant. Michael Delaney was drinking coffee in his private sitting room looking out over the valley.

'Good day to you, Powerscourt,' he said, inspecting an enormous cigar rather doubtfully. 'Sorry to hear you might have been killed over there. The Inspector told me about it. Bad business. It must go with the job in your line of work, I suppose. Rather like going bankrupt in mine.'

He paused briefly and lit his cigar. 'Now then. We're all to stay here for another day. Only allowed out one at a time as before. There's some damned conference this afternoon in that place Fidgack or whatever it's called. Church, police, mayors along the route, a couple of local congressmen – deputies, I think they're called – have got in on the act. I'm not invited. I just told the Inspector to remember that whoever is being killed, they're not Frenchmen. No apparent danger to the local citizens if you ask me. But I've had an idea, Powerscourt. I'd like to hear what you think about it.'

'Fire ahead,' said Powerscourt, watching as a plume of smoke floated out towards the hotel flower bowl.

'You'll remember how it was in the Wild West,' Delaney continued, 'or if you don't remember, you'll surely have read about it. When the sheriff and the authorities wanted to catch a villain, bank robber, cattle rustler, murderer, that sort of character, they used to put up a poster in the town. Wanted, Dead or Alive, that sort of thing.'

Powerscourt thought his brains must have been addled in the wine cellar. He couldn't see where this was leading.

'And under the dead or alive section, they'd put Reward, Five Hundred Dollars, or whatever they could afford. Greed's always a good motive for betrayal, my friend, I've seen that so many times in business. So why don't we put up a notice here in the hotel, offering a huge reward to anybody who provides information that leads to the apprehension of the killer? Money only handed over on conviction, mind you. I'm not going to put my hand in my pocket just because some fellow comes in with a tall story. What do you think?'

'It's certainly ingenious,' said Powerscourt. Lady Lucy or either of Powerscourt's elder children could have told Michael

Delaney from that opening remark that Powerscourt did not think this was a good idea. 'How much money were you thinking of?' he continued, playing for time.

'A colleague of mine in New York tried this once when somebody in his firm was leaking business secrets to his competitors. He reckoned it had to be pretty big to work. What do you say to fifty thousand dollars?'

'Fifty thousand dollars?' Powerscourt was amazed at the size of the sum. 'Why, Mr Delaney, a man might not need to work again if he had that sort of money!' He knew there was no point in asking if Michael Delaney could afford it.

'Well, at least he'd still be alive to enjoy it if we got our man. So would a lot of other people. So would you, Powerscourt, come to think of it, after this morning's escapade.'

'Well,' said Powerscourt, 'I think it deserves serious consideration, your proposal, Mr Delaney, I really do. I'll have to see what the good Inspector thinks about it. We are on his turf, after all. I do have one reservation, I have to say. In those days in your Wild West, when people rode around on horses with gun belts and big hats and rifles strapped to their saddles, there were characters called bounty hunters, I seem to remember, who made a living out of catching the wanted men, the dead or alive people. And sometimes, in their enthusiasm, they might finger the wrong man in order to get their hands on the cash. Is that not so, Mr Delaney?'

'Early version of free enterprise, bounty hunting,' said Delaney. 'All part of the American way of life, get your hands on as many dollars as you can. I don't see your problem.'

'It's this. What happens if five or six of these pilgrims all decide to finger one of their colleagues to pick up the fifty thousand? They make up stories about their companions, a different person every time. The Inspector and I have to check them out. In the meantime the real killer continues undetected because we are following a whole lot of false leads.'

'Forgive me for saying this, Powerscourt, but your investigation isn't exactly proceeding at lightning speed at present, is it?'

'Nobody is more conscious of that than I am,' Powerscourt replied, 'that is absolutely true, and it is perfectly proper to remind me of it. But let me talk to the Inspector, Mr Delaney. I'll get back to you as soon as I can. I do think I have earned the right to have some say over the way this investigation is conducted, mind you. After all, I could have paid for it with my life.'

Johnny Fitzgerald felt his face turning red, maybe even purple. Mary Rose, the girl he had proposed to all those years ago, the girl who had rejected him in favour of another, was now but ten feet away. Christ in heaven, he muttered to himself, this is worse than battle with the shells going off and the guns firing and the dervishes yelling their battle cries. Mary Rose took the initiative.

'Goodness me,' she said brightly, 'it's Johnny Fitzgerald, isn't it? I'd have known you anywhere. How are you, Johnny? What are you doing in these parts?' Mary Rose spoke calmly as if she were talking to an old school friend she hadn't seen for years. Johnny was in turmoil.

'I hope you're well, Mary Rose,' he stammered. 'I'm here on business.'

'Really?' said Mary Rose. 'You're not still in the Army then?'

'No, I'm not.' Johnny was sure his face was still lighting up the street. Two middle-aged ladies on the other side of the pavement slowed their walk to funeral pace to catch as much as they could of the conversation between the lady from the big house and the stranger. Word would go round the town before lunchtime, but it was unlikely that even the most far-fetched explanations would be as bizarre as the truth about the meeting of the former lovers.

'How are the family?' Johnny couldn't bring himself to speak her husband's name.

'They're all fine,' said Mary Rose. 'I've got three boys and three girls now. Jonathan's just been made Master of the Hunt, you know. He's got rather plump with the passing of time, Jonathan has. I tell him it's the cream. We have to find bigger horses to carry him every year.'

It was the word Jonathan that finished Johnny off. Even after all those years he could still see the cold print in the marriage columns of *The Times*. Jonathan still alive. Jonathan still married to his Mary Rose. Jonathan plump. Jonathan Master of the Hunt. Jonathan taking too much cream. Damn Jonathan. Damn him to hell.

'You'll have to excuse me, Mrs Osborne.' Johnny was stammering again, and stepping past her as he spoke. 'I'm in a great hurry. I've got to get back to London. My business won't wait.'

'But won't you come to lunch? Won't you come to stay? I'm sure the children would love to meet you. They're always interested in everybody's past.'

But her invitations were in vain. Johnny was striding up the street the way she had come as fast as he could. 'Wait, Johnny, wait!' she called after him.

Johnny just resisted the temptation to shout at her that waiting was the one thing she hadn't done for him in the past, that she had promised to wait for him until his return from Army service but had betrayed him and his love and his offer of marriage with another instead. Wait indeed. Jonathan indeed. Too much cream indeed. Johnny didn't wait. He headed for the railway station as fast as he could and waited two and a quarter hours for the next express to Dublin. He was leaving Ireland as fast as he could. He would wait no more.

Christy Delaney felt his French was improving. He knew now the word for tree. He knew the word for leaf, for cow, for sheep, for grass, for horse, for mouth, for face and for nose and for eyes. In some dim recess of his brain he was beginning to grasp noo, voo, too, eel and el. Somme was not a river in the north but had something to do with the word to be. His first proper encounter with Anne Marie as she cleared away the plates after lunch in an empty dining room had gone well. He had learnt her name and been informed that she would go for a walk with him later that day. Christy did not know it but Lady Lucy had smoothed his path by having a word with the girl's mother.

'Mightn't he be a murderer, like all the rest of them? I don't want my girl being involved with a killer, heaven forbid,' had been the reaction of Marie Dominique, the mistress of the hotel.

Lady Lucy had assured her that she didn't think Christy was a murderer. 'He comes from a good family in Ireland, as far as I can make out,' she continued innocently. 'I believe they own a lot of land.'

'Do they, indeed,' replied Marie Dominique. 'I see. How very interesting.'

Their walk had taken them up into the hills. They had sat on the grass and looked at the view and into each other's eyes. They made another date. Christy decided that he needed to improve his vocabulary yet further. He resolved to set up another tutorial with Lady Lucy. It was just one word he was interested in this time, the word for love.

16

Cable from Johnny Fitzgerald to Lord Francis Powerscourt:

Have found the story about Delaney family in famine years. Old man married to whiskey bottles has interviewed surviving locals. Three poor Delaney families, one better off. Potatoes give up ghost. Poor Delaneys on verge of giving up ghost. Appeal to richer Delaney family. They refuse aid of any kind. All twenty-four poor Delaneys repair to workhouse and die of plague, dysentery, despair etc. But one survived. Boy, about twelve years in 1846–48. Fate, country of residence unknown. Richer Delaneys later went to America, possibly unpopular with surviving locals. Reckon this survivor would be in late sixties, early seventies. Unknown if he had any children. Unknown place of residence. Obvious motive. Do you have any elderly pilgrims who look as if they might have fled the famine? Regards, Fitzgerald.

P.S. Am feeling remarkably unwell. Met Mary Rose, that woman I wanted to marry, walking up the street in Macroom. Fled the field. Have not felt so strange since I won all that money at the Derby years ago. Usual solace being applied. JF.

Cable from Lord Francis Powerscourt to Franklin Bentley:

Earlier message most helpful. Many thanks. Am anxious to discover more about Delaney's first wife. Did they meet and marry in New York? Or did he come to NY from some coalfield or oil-rich place where he made first fortune? Suggest newspaper cuttings library might have article about Delaney having arrived from Pittsburgh or Ohio or some other industrial place. Long shot. If it works suggest seek details of earlier Delaney life. Catholic church in wherever he came from? Also any more details of the man Delaney robbed in New York with his fraudulent share dealings? Man alive or dead? Children?

Life looking up here in southern France. No new murders for forty-eight hours. Regards, Powerscourt.

Cable from Lord Francis Powerscourt to Johnny Fitzgerald.

Cable most welcome. Sorry to hear of meeting with Love's Labour's Lost female. Trust medicine will aid recovery. Need information on book written about Delaney's past. It was called *Michael Delaney, Robber Baron*. Originally published in New York 1894. Contained juicy details about manifold sins and wickednesses of Delaney past life. When Delaney heard of it, he bought up entire stock and pulped them. But four escaped the pyre. Sent to London dealers, presumably for potential sale to rich Americans engaged in finance. Name of dealers unknown. Suggest you approach my financier brother-in-law William Burke in City of London for advice on which bookshop might have ordered such a thing. Chances of them having records very remote. You could try Hatchard's in Piccadilly as rich Americans might have lived in those parts. If all else fails maybe antiquarian bookshop like Beggs in the Strand. Book may hold key to solving entire mystery. Regards, Powerscourt.

Cable from Johnny Fitzgerald to Lord Francis Powerscourt:

> Bad news from William Burke. Says most unlikely book
> would have been sent to City district. City men read
> balance sheets, bills of exchange, promissory notes, share
> offer documents, annual reports, bulletins from Lloyd's
> of London. Not books. Not books about obscure Americans
> years ago. Any reading financiers would have bought in
> West End. Setting out on voyage of discovery to Picca-
> dilly. News to follow. Regards, Fitzgerald.

As he inspected his messages Powerscourt knew there was
one avenue he had to explore, an avenue he had been
dreading. The man who knew most about Michael Delaney's
past was here, Michael Delaney himself. He had, after all,
organized the pilgrimage. But Powerscourt doubted if he
would tell him the truth. He found Delaney inspecting a pile
of cables of his own.

'Steel stock going up, Powerscourt, oil too. I've got big
interests in both. I'm a lot richer today than I was yesterday!'
He looked up from his armchair in the private sitting room.
'Can I be of assistance? Is there any news about the French
pow-wow? Might we be able to leave soon?'

Powerscourt assured him that there was no news on that
front yet. 'I wanted to ask you a few questions about your
past, Mr Delaney.'

Even as he spoke Powerscourt could see the brows tightening,
a slight look of menace crossing the Delaney countenance.

'Can't see what my past has to do with anything,' he said.
'You're here to find out about what's happening now, for
God's sake.'

'Mr Delaney, before you were married to the late Mrs
Delaney, mother of James, were you married to anybody else?'

Delaney laughed. Powerscourt had always thought of
laughter in this kind of questioning as a tactic, a means to gain
time for the brain to work out the most appropriate lie.

'No, I was not!' he said, and Powerscourt wondered if the tycoon was going to hit him.

'And are there any business dealings in your past that might have left somebody with a grudge against you and members of your family? Forgive me, sir, but I have to eliminate all possible lines of inquiry.'

'The answer is no, again, no.' Powerscourt thought that the tornado might have abated into a severe storm. 'Of course I have made enemies. You must have made enemies, Powerscourt. It's inevitable in a cut-throat world. But I do not believe any of them would be so stupid as to take time out to order a series of murders on a family party on pilgrimage in the south of France. The whole thing's ridiculous.'

Johnny Fitzgerald had made inquiries in Hatchard's. They had been going for a couple of hundred years, after all. No, they could not help him. Their records did not go back that far. And with an order of only four books it was unlikely that any booksellers in London, however carefully their transactions were logged, would be able to help him. They directed him, first, to The Antiquarian Booksellers in the Charing Cross Road and, if that failed, to Beggs Brothers in the Strand. Johnny was beginning to think that the proverbial needle might be easier to find. He had drawn a blank in the Charing Cross Road and was walking into Beggs with a heavy heart. A charming young man greeted him at reception. There was only one person in the firm who might be able to help, Mr Macdonald. If Johnny would care to wait for a moment? Johnny Fitzgerald sat down under a painting of the Rising of Lazarus in very melodramatic colours. It was as if the miracle had to be shouted from the rooftops. He expected Mr Macdonald to be an ancient greybeard who had served the firm all his days. The young man led him down two flights of steps into an enormous basement, lined with bookshelves, and there, seated at a large desk at the far end, was a very thin middle-aged man with fading black hair and spots of dandruff littered all over what had once been a fashionable suit on the streets of London about 1885.

'Welcome, you are welcome indeed!' said Macdonald 'I believe the youth said your name is Fitzgerald. You're not related by any chance to the Fitzgerald who translated *The Rubáiyát of Omar Khayyám*? Any first editions of that work would be most valuable.'

'Alas, no,' said Johnny Fitzgerald with a smile.

'Pity,' said Macdonald, brushing a wandering piece of dandruff from his shirtsleeve. 'Let me tell you about my area of competence here. I love books, Mr Fitzgerald, I always have. I've always preferred them to people as a matter of fact. Perhaps that's why I never married. I don't like daylight much either. That's why I am content down here. My late father, God rest his soul, left me a large collection of books and I've been adding to them ever since. I believe I own first editions of most of the major English novelists since the middle of the eighteenth century. But I digress. Here, I am the record keeper. I keep details of all the major sales and purchases we make. I file the obituary notices of the rich in case they have valuable libraries which may have to be sold for tax reasons. I recommend to our young men the auctions they ought to attend and the works they should obtain for us and at what price. I am the memory of Beggs Brothers, here in my basement, a living archive! How can I help you?'

'I am interested in an American book that came out about twelve years ago, in 1894 I think, Mr Macdonald. Only four copies of the book were sent over to London by the New York publishers. I do not know where in London they were sent. Coming here is a long shot, a very long shot indeed.'

'But you have come to the right place, Mr Fitzgerald! Here at Beggs we like long shots. My late father, God rest his soul, seldom went to the race meetings, but when he did he always used to bet on the long shots. He claimed it was much more profitable than backing the favourites. Do we have a name for this book? And do we know what became of the American copies? We have contacts in the United States who could help you, Mr Fitzgerald.'

The bookseller smiled at his customer. Johnny saw that his teeth were almost yellow. Perhaps it was the lack of fresh air. Another small cloud of dandruff escaped from his head and floated to the floor.

'The book was called *Michael Delaney, Robber Baron*. The Michael Delaney in the title was a rich businessman who did not like the thought of what might be in the book. So he bought the whole lot and pulped them.'

'My goodness me,' said Macdonald, 'does that mean these four copies are the only ones left in existence? They might be worth a fortune today. What a splendid puzzle you have brought me, Mr Fitzgerald! Now then, let me see.'

He turned and opened a cupboard behind him. Johnny saw that it was filled with row upon row of great ledgers that might have been used for the accounts of some mighty insurance company.

'Each one of these contains the record of a fortnight. What we bought, when it sold, what the price was, whether we reordered any more from the publishers. Did you say 1894?'

'I did.'

Macdonald began rummaging through the past. 'Forgive me for the delay,' he said. 'I'll let you know once I've found anything.'

Five minutes passed, then ten. There were occasional grunts from Macdonald. 'Don't despair,' Macdonald advised after a few minutes, 'it just takes time, and time, as my late father, God rest his soul, used to say, is the one thing we can never hurry.'

Johnny looked round the bookshelves and wondered if Macdonald had read all the volumes in this basement room. Perhaps he had. There was a comfortable-looking chair in the corner, by a powerful lamp. Maybe Macdonald neglected his filing and archiving duties when he was on his own and buried himself in Plato or Plautus or Petrarch. He could always hear the footsteps of anybody coming down the stairs and return to his desk.

'Yes! Yes! Yes!' Johnny Fitzgerald thought Macdonald sounded as if his long shot at the races had just turned into a winner. 'They were here! *Michael Delaney, Robber Baron*, four copies, received from New York, the fifteen of October 1894! See the beauty of the archives and the ledgers!'

'And what happened to them, Mr Macdonald? Don't tell me that you still have one or two of them here?'

'All gone,' said the archivist, turning back to face Johnny once more, clutching an enormous ledger in his right hand. 'There are none left. But I'm not through yet, Mr Fitzgerald. Did you say how much you would be prepared to pay for one of these *Robber Barons* if we could locate one?'

'I don't think price would be an issue,' said Johnny loftily.

'If we sell these books over the counter, you see, we have no idea who bought them. But consider this. Most of the population of these islands do not live in London, thank God. They may live in the Home Counties or in East Anglia or anywhere at all. Well over half of our customers are country members, as we call them. They write in, asking us to find a book or to recommend some of the latest history works, whatever it might be. We oblige. But with these customers we do keep records of the purchases, filed by both book and customer.'

Macdonald, accompanied by another snow flurry of dandruff, disappeared back into his cupboard. 'You see, Mr Fitzgerald, we often find that some of the books our country customers buy are sought after by other clients. Maybe they have gone up in value. The customers can resell the books at a handsome profit if they wish.'

He reappeared with another enormous ledger and riffled through the pages. '*Michael Delaney, Robber Baron*,' he said triumphantly, 'bought by a Mr Ralph Daniel, 4 Royal Crescent, Bath. Pity he lives in Bath, mind you. My late father, God rest his soul, used to warn me about places beginning with B. Bath, Biarritz, Brighton. Fast, he used to say, fast, very fast.'

'You don't by any chance know if this Mr Daniel is still in the same place?' asked Johnny.

'But we do, Mr Fitzgerald, we do. Only last week he ordered some works by that man who writes about the sea, Joseph Conrad. Would you like me to write a letter of introduction for you?'

'Please do,' said Johnny, 'and could you write it now? If I'm lucky I could be in Bath tomorrow morning.'

'God bless my soul,' said Macdonald, 'the book is unknown and unloved for years and you have to track it down in twenty-four hours. You must want it very badly.'

'Let me tell you, Mr Macdonald,' said Johnny Fitzgerald, 'and I'm not joking. This book may be a matter of life or death.'

Lord Francis Powerscourt and his wife were sitting on the terrace outside their little house in the hills. The French authorities had still not decided what to do with the pilgrims.

'Lucy,' said Powerscourt, staring at a herd of sleek cattle in a field opposite, 'let me try a few theories on you about what's going on.'

'Of course.' Lady Lucy put down her lists of family trees which she had been reading as if she were about to take an exam in them. She was used to these sessions by now. They often involved her husband walking up and down their drawing room in Markham Square, ticking points off with his hands as he went.

'Theory number one, and this does seem quite possible, is that we are dealing with a madman, a psychopath who has come on pilgrimage simply to kill as many people as he can. Now he's well on his way, he can't stop. He'll just keep killing until somebody catches him.

'Theory number two goes something like this. The real victim was the first one, our window-cleaning friend from

Acton who was sent to meet his maker scarcely off the train. But let's suppose something goes wrong. Maybe he's seen leaving the hotel with the victim minutes before the murder. Whoever saw him, if that's what happened, has to go. So they are sent on a river cruise down the Lot. Maybe two people saw him, or maybe the third victim saw him go out in the middle of the night to put his second victim in the rowing boat. He's for it. On this theory we could have come to the end. But there's one flaw in it. There are probably dozens of flaws for all I know.'

'The flaw being that we know of nobody who might want to kill a man who spent his working life going up and down ladders?' asked Lady Lucy.

'Precisely, Lucy. How right you are. You see, we have assumed all along that the murders must have something to do with Michael Delaney. Perhaps they haven't.'

'But you'd have to say that he was the most likely person to provide the key. I don't think you make that many enemies with your mop and bucket. Well, people might get cross if you overcharged them, or left their windows smudgy, but they wouldn't want to throw you off the side of the Rock of Ages.'

'Which brings us back to Michael Delaney. Let's take things in chronological order. Theory number three takes us back to the goings-on at the time of the famine. There must be lots of stories about people abandoning their relatives to save themselves, like pushing them out of the lifeboat because it was too full. But it's a very long way from one survivor, if he did survive, and a man with a grudge against Delaney. Why wait all this time, if you're that lone survivor? And if you were the son of the survivor, why would you wait all these years?'

'Maybe', said Lady Lucy, 'he didn't know about the New York Delaney and all the other Delaneys until Alex Bentley began looking for them. If you lived on the edge of some rain-drenched Irish bog you'd hardly know what was happening in Dublin, never mind the other side of the world. And I think there's another flaw.'

'What's that, my love?'

'Well, if you look closely at these family trees you realize something fairly obvious. One single Delaney couldn't have produced this pack of cousins and second cousins we have down at the hotel. It's impossible given the way reproduction works. There were lots of other Delaneys who will have gone from Ireland to England or America in those times.' Lady Lucy looked down again at her family trees, handwriting legible and not so legible, letters large and letters small, some of the words in capitals, some of them underlined. 'We've got Delaneys here from Macroom and Mullingar and Newport and all over the place.'

'You forget', said Powerscourt, keen to hang on to the shreds of his theory before it was completely demolished, 'that it was Maggie Delaney herself who mentioned a saga of betrayal and death in the famine years in Macroom, the place where Johnny has just been to confirm the story. Anyway, let's mark that theory as doubtful. Theory number four is that it has to do with the ruined businessman, the one Delaney stole all the money from. Let's suppose he ends up poor, a broken man, and his son sets out to take revenge, inspired again by Alex Bentley's researches. This too suffers from the why wait until now problem. I don't think we're doing very well here, Lucy. Theory number five says it has to do with the hypothetical earlier marriage, though how that fits in I have no idea. It could be, of course, that one of these pilgrims is actually a hired killer, sent by some person or persons unknown, to commit these crimes. But that's not very likely either.'

'If it's any consolation, my love, I get more confused every time I study these family trees. Some, maybe all of these people are related to one another, we just need to go one more generation back. But that's the bit they don't know about. Do you suppose, Francis, that somewhere, probably in Ireland, there was once a prototype Delaney, the first one of all, from whom the rest are descended? I like to think he looks something like Michael Delaney does today.'

'Not quite sure how the first one gets here, if you see what I mean, Lucy. No mention of Delaneys in the Garden of Eden as far as I know, Adam, Eve, Cain, Abel, Delaney doesn't sound quite right, does it, so there must have been a time when there were no Delaneys in existence at all. But I have no idea how the first one arrived. The only thing we can be sure of is that there are now three less of them in this world than there were a month ago. And, unless we sort ourselves out, their numbers may shrink even further before we're through.'

Early next morning Powerscourt and Lady Lucy were wakened by a frantic knocking on the door just after seven. Alex Bentley had borrowed a bike from the hotel and was panting slightly from his exertions.

'You're to come at once,' he said, 'please. It's chaos down there at the hotel.'

'There hasn't been another murder?' said Powerscourt, pulling a shirt over his head.

'No, no,' said Bentley, 'it's not as bad as that. The Inspector is there and about half a dozen of his men. They've brought four police wagons that look as though they take prisoners to jail or to court or something like that. The Inspector says, I think, that we are all to leave in half an hour, bags packed, that sort of thing, stuffed inside these wagons like criminals!'

'And how is Mr Delaney taking all this?' asked Powerscourt.

'Not well, sir, not well at all. I couldn't have translated most of what he shouted at the Inspector and that's a fact. I didn't know he could swear like that. He wants you, sir, now if not sooner. If you care to take the bicycle down the road I'll escort Lady Powerscourt when she's ready.'

'But I am ready, Mr Bentley.' Lady Lucy smiled at her young admirer. 'Men are always surprised when women can dress themselves in the morning as fast as their husbands. I'm sure we won't be packed away in one of these carriages. I wouldn't miss this for the world.'

Powerscourt set off at full speed towards the Auberge des Montagnes. From well over a hundred yards away he could hear shouting. The Inspector sounded as if he was replying in kind to the American.

'I'm going to telegraph to the American Ambassador!' Delaney yelled. 'I'm going to get word to our President – God knows the man owes me a favour or two . . . ' Powerscourt could hear every word as he entered the village. There followed a sound that might have been a table being thumped.

'Powerscourt!' shouted Delaney, as the investigator strode into the dining room. The pilgrims were huddled together by the door into the kitchens, whispering to each other. Maggie Delaney was fingering her rosary beads at Olympic speed. Father Kennedy had obviously decided that the only prudent course of action was to eat as much breakfast as possible in the shortest time. He seemed, Powerscourt noticed, to have opened negotiations with the waitress for fresh supplies of bread and jam. Inspector Léger shook him by the hand in the manner of French morning greetings. Perhaps he had shaken hands with them all.

'Good morning, Lord Powerscourt. Communication has been difficult this morning. The young man, Bentley, he tries hard, but I do not think he understands everything. Let me explain to you what is to happen. Then perhaps you could translate it for the pilgrims.'

Inspector Léger spoke for a couple of minutes. Powerscourt could feel the wrath of Michael Delaney surround them all, like a lion's breath. Powerscourt grabbed a cup of coffee and looked round at his audience.

'I do not know how much you have gathered of what the Inspector has told you. I would ask you to remain calm, however difficult the circumstances. Our French friends can be very stubborn when they feel like it. Hostility and complaint can only make things worse for the present. The position is this. This is what the authorities, temporal and spiritual, have decided to do. You are to leave here in twenty minutes, with your bags packed. The four carriages outside will take you to the railway station at Figeac. Each carriage will have a policeman in it to secure your safety. From Figeac a special train, open only to people in this room, will take you on your way. Your train will take you along the route traversed by the pilgrims all those years ago. As a gesture of goodwill, you will be allowed to stop and visit a couple of places of special historic or religious interest on the route.'

There was a muttering among the pilgrims. They seemed to be asking Jack O'Driscoll to speak for them. Powerscourt held up his hand. 'I haven't quite finished,' he said. 'The train will take you to the Spanish border where you will be placed under the care of the authorities in the province of Navarre. The Inspector here does not know what they will decide.'

There was a brief moment of silence as Powerscourt sat down. Lady Lucy and Alex Bentley slipped into the room and went to stand by Michael Delaney. Powerscourt thought you could feel the temperature rise as the tycoon got to his feet.

'I am an American citizen,' he began. 'Five of us here are American citizens. We are a free people under the law. Our ancestors crossed the Atlantic to enjoy freedom, democracy and free enterprise. These others are citizens of the British Empire, subjects of King Edward, people who believe in fair play and natural justice.' Powerscourt felt this was boardroom Delaney, maybe businessman advocate Delaney making his case before some vast concourse of investors, politician Delaney. 'You have no rights at all to carry out these actions, to treat us as if we were criminals. I said before and I will say it again, I intend to let the American authorities at the very highest level know what is going on. You may have precipitated an international incident here this morning, Inspector. Neither the American public nor the British public like to hear of their fellow citizens being ill treated by Johnny Foreigner. You may have packed your finest off to the guillotine in covered carts in days gone by, Inspector, but you cannot do it to us here today. I refuse to go along with this plan. Now, let others speak.'

The Inspector whispered something to Powerscourt.

'The Inspector wishes me to inform you,' he said mildly, 'that the authorities in the Revolution did not send people to meet Madame Guillotine in covered carts. The carts were open so the people could see and rejoice at their oppressors' fate.'

Delaney grunted. Jack O'Driscoll rose to speak. 'Like Mr Delaney, I do not like your plan, Inspector. But I suspect we may, in the end, have little choice but to accept it. Could you tell us where we are to sleep on our journey? Or are we to be locked up in this special train for days at a time?'

Once more the Inspector spoke rapidly to Powerscourt. 'You will be locked up all right, my young friend,' Powerscourt translated, 'but not in the train. Accommodation has been arranged for you in the police stations and the jails of France along the way. Insalubrious perhaps, but safe. Nobody will be murdered in them. Single cells for all. Accommodation for Miss Delaney in the local hospital.'

There was uproar in the dining room. Even Father Kennedy stopped eating at the thought of being locked up for the night with a bucket for company.

'I'm not going to put up with this!'

'I'm going home!'

'Damn the French!'

'This is monstrous!'

Once more the Inspector whispered to Powerscourt. He pointed at a large bag at his feet, though the gesture did not reveal what was inside. Towards the end Gallic gestures punctuated his words, a shrug of the shoulders here, a wave to the right with one hand, a wave to the left with the other, regular checkings on the vanished hair. Now Powerscourt understood. He rose to his feet once more.

'Ladies and gentlemen,' he said, 'the Inspector left out one very important part of his message. You seem to think you have a choice. I'm afraid, after what the Inspector has just said, that you do not. Three people have been murdered so far on this pilgrimage. In his bag the Inspector has warrants from an investigating magistrate to arrest everyone in this room on suspicion of murder. If those warrants are served, it would be up to the magistrate to decide whether or not to grant bail. He could decide against it. In that case, everybody is marooned here, possibly in the county jail, until the case comes to court. That could take months. They still have another option, to put everybody on the special train, but send the train to Bordeaux and put you on the first boat out of France. The French authorities have given you, in effect, three choices. Continue by train to the Spanish border. Continue by train to Bordeaux. Or stay here as murder suspects until the killer is apprehended and the case heard in the French courts. I don't think it is a very difficult choice, but it is yours. And I feel the Inspector is in earnest with his time limits. If you fail to meet them he will open his bag and bring out the warrants.'

Michael Delaney resumed his unusual role as tribune of the people. 'Let us put it to the vote, ladies and gentlemen, as we did before. All those in favour of staying here.'

No hands rose.

'All those in favour of Bordeaux.'

No hands rose.

'All those in favour of the Spanish border.'

The bull fight and the prospect of Rioja drove them on. All voted for the Spanish option. Powerscourt and Lady Lucy watched them go, the younger ones dispatched to different carriages in case of rebellion on the way.

'Moissac, Lord Powerscourt, Moissac, the most beautiful cloisters in the world,' said the Inspector. 'For the time being the authorities have provided me with an interpreter. I do not know how long he will be able to stay. The Cardinal Archbishop of Toulouse was particularly anxious that the pilgrims should take spiritual refreshment there. We shall see you there at eleven o'clock in the morning in two days' time. Obviously we shall watch over the pilgrims' visit to one of the special places on the route to Compostela.'

'I take my hat off to the French authorities, Lucy,' said Powerscourt to his wife as they breakfasted in a deserted dining room, 'they've really been very clever.'

'What makes you say that, my love?' asked Lady Lucy.

'Well,' said Powerscourt, 'think about it. They've virtually deported the pilgrims for a start. You couldn't get them out of the country quicker from here than by the Spanish border or Bordeaux. And they've washed their hands of the murder too. Just think of the headaches if they had served those warrants. Pilgrims to accommodate for a start. How long would it take to find the killer at Conques? Heaven knows. They've simply passed the parcel, certainly out of here, probably out of France. And they're allowing the pilgrims little treats, like a morning out at Moissac. It's all very smart.'

'Have you been to Moissac, Francis?'

'I have not, Lucy. I look forward to it. I've always adored cloisters. Such quiet peaceful places.'

PART THREE

ESPEYRAC—FIGEAC—MOISSAC—PAMPLONA—SANTIAGO DE COMPOSTELA

My Sword I give to him that shall succeed me in my Pilgrimage, and my Courage and Skill, to him that can get it. My Marks and Scars I carry with me, to be a witness for me, that I have fought his Battles, who will now be my Rewarder ... As he went, he said, Death, where is thy Sting? And as he went down deeper he said, Grave, where is thy Victory? So he passed over and the Trumpets sounded for him on the other side.

Mr Valiant-for-Glory, *The Pilgrim's Progress*

17

The city of Bath is graced with some of the most beautiful architecture in Britain. Georgian streets, Georgian squares, Georgian terraces rise in elegant and restrained splendour up the hill above the river Avon and the railway station. There is even an astonishing creation called The Circus, a perfect circle of grand town houses ranged round a garden in the centre. Johnny Fitzgerald tried to remember what he could about the place as he set off from his train up to Mr Daniel's house. Regency bucks, he thought, dressed in those gorgeous long coats with a stock at the neck. A man called Nash who had been the arbiter of taste in late eighteenth-century Bath, and had lived openly with a woman who was not his wife. Balls. Assignations in the Roman baths or the Assembly Rooms. A marriage market discreetly carried out behind the shuttered windows of Gay Street or Golden Square. Whores by the score drawn to the place by the needs and the purses of the fashionable, the twin magnets of men and money. Johnny thought he would have rather liked it here in Bath in those times.

The door of 4 Royal Crescent, the most elegant street in an elegant city, was opened by a young butler who showed him into an enormous drawing room. Portraits of earlier Daniels lined the walls. Johnny was staring at a spectacular eighteenth-century beauty in a pale blue dress when he heard a door close behind him.

'That one's a Gainsborough,' said the man. 'Everybody gets transfixed by that painting. Allow me to introduce myself, Ralph Daniel.'

'Johnny Fitzgerald.'

'She came to a bad end, I'm afraid,' Daniel went on.

'Bad end?' said Johnny.

'Sorry, the Gainsborough girl. She married into a very respectable family here in Bath, then she eloped with some American playboy. He abandoned her out in the wilds of Indiana or some other place in favour of a younger woman. Nobody knows what happened to her in the end. Forgive me, I gather you have come to see me about a book. Macdonald didn't say which one, he's always very cagey about things like that. How can I help?'

Johnny Fitzgerald handed over his letter of introduction. He had rehearsed various stories in the train on the way down, all of them lies. Ralph Daniel was a slim gentleman of about forty-five years old, clean-shaven and blessed with a winning smile. Various pieces of military memorabilia, a curved dagger on a table, a photograph of a group of officers with Daniel in the centre, told Johnny that he might be in the presence of a military man. Retired colonels, he dimly remembered, had always been fond of Bath. Suddenly Johnny felt tired of his fictions, of wearing other people's clothes, as he put it to himself.

'Forgive me this question, Mr Daniel: are you or were you a military gentleman?'

'Yes, I was, but I don't see what it has to do with this book.'

'It's just easier speaking to a fellow soldier, if you see what I mean. You know the rules. I'm going to tell you a story, Mr Daniel, if you have the time to listen. I was going to tell you a pack of lies about this book, but I think you deserve better than that. The book in question came out in the last decade of the last century. It's called *Michael Delaney, Robber Baron.* Can I ask you first of all, have you the read the thing?'

'The book?' Ralph Daniel smiled. 'I don't think I have. It was my father who ordered it, you see.'

Johnny was relieved to hear that this father did not come with God rest his soul attached.

'We'd better make sure, first of all,' said Daniel, 'that I still have the book in the house. No point in you telling me a story if I don't have it. I'm not sure where it is, now I come to think of it. I know I have seen it somewhere. It came with a dark green cover. I do hope my wife hasn't tidied it away. She's a terrible one for tidying things. Then, of course, she can't remember where she put them. If you wait here, I'll see what I can do. There's a book about the British Army in India that's just come out on that little table by the window which might interest you.'

A couple of minutes later Daniel was back, grinning, with a book in his hand. 'This is it here,' he said, '*Michael Delaney, Robber Baron*. Your journey hasn't been in vain. The wife had tidied it away, as a matter of fact. She'd transferred it and a whole lot more she didn't like the look of out of the main library up to the reserves in the attic.'

He looked inside the book. 'I don't think anybody has ever read it,' Daniel said. 'The pages haven't been cut. Now then, tell me the story behind it.'

Johnny explained about the fate of the original work in America, pulped on Delaney's orders. He stressed that all his information came second-hand. He told Daniel about the murders in the south of France. He told him what he knew about the progress of the investigation, that Powerscourt was working on the theory that the reason for the murders might lie deep in Delaney's past.

Ralph Daniel was fascinated. 'So, if I understand you correctly, the reason Delaney wanted the book destroyed was that it contained shameful secrets about his behaviour in the past? And that one of those secrets might explain this horror story on the pilgrim trail today?'

'Exactly,' said Johnny Fitzgerald.

'Well, then,' Ralph Daniel handed the book over, 'you'd better have *Michael Delaney, Robber Baron* right now. Do with it what you will. I would be pleased if I could feel that a book from my house had helped to solve a murder mystery.'

'Can I pay you for it?' asked Johnny.

'Don't be silly. Of course you can't. Do get in touch when the investigation is over and we can work out what to do with it. May I ask what you propose doing with it now?'

'I'm not sure,' said Johnny thoughtfully. 'You see, if I read it and tell Francis what I think are the most important bits, I may miss something. I don't know as much as he does. I suppose I could post it to him, or I could take it over to France myself.'

'Well,' said Ralph Daniel, 'you found out about the book yesterday, you came here today. Why not keep moving? I don't think I'd rest easy in my bed putting a *Robber Baron* in the post. Of course ninety-nine times out of a hundred the book would get there safely. But there's always the one that didn't. And it sounds as if your friend is moving about a great deal. You don't want the book mouldering away at some hotel or poste restante in Auch when your friend has moved off to Burgos or somewhere.'

'You've convinced me. I'll go today. I'll travel through the night if I have to. Thank you so much for your assistance and your advice, Mr Daniel, I am most grateful.'

'Think nothing of it,' Daniel replied, escorting Johnny to the front door and the full sweep of the Royal Crescent, 'and God speed on your journey. I hope it contains what you are looking for, *Michael Delaney, Robber Baron.*'

'It says here, Francis, that there's a tympanum, one of those arched doorways with statues and things, at the Abbey of St Peter, the place with the cloisters.' Lady Lucy Powerscourt was reading from a little guide to Moissac she had borrowed from their hotel. It was two days since the pilgrims had been locked away in the Black Marias on the journey to their special train. Powerscourt and Lady Lucy were due to meet them in a couple of hours' time.

'Another tympanum, Lucy? I think I could become quite attached to tympanums, you know. Maybe I should write a book on them one day to go with that cathedral volume. I wonder if this one has as many horrible sinners as the one at Conques. I rather hope not.'

Powerscourt and Lady Lucy were walking up the slope above the river Tarn. The river, Lady Lucy had remarked, was probably as wide as the Thames going through London. 'It's another Last Judgement, Francis.' Lady Lucy stopped about fifteen feet away from the church door. 'Based on the Book of Revelation. This is pretty dramatic stuff, my love: "Behold. A throne was set in heaven, and one sat on the throne. And he that sat was to look upon like a jasper, and there was a rainbow round about the throne, in sight like unto an emerald. And round about the throne were four and twenty seats: and upon the seats I saw four and twenty elders sitting, clothed in white raiment, and they had on their heads crowns of gold."'

Lady Lucy paused for a moment. 'Here we go, Francis: "And out of the throne proceeded lightnings and thunderings and voices: and there were seven lamps of fire burning before the throne which are the seven Spirits of God."'

'Don't think the sculptor bothered with the fire and the weather bit, Lucy.' Powerscourt was now standing by the south door of the abbey. It was set in a deep splay rather like a jaw, with the sides serrated like the central sections of human back teeth. In the centre was a pillar wreathed with lions. Above that was a lintel of rosettes. Two rows of fleurs-de-lis ran right round the central section, which was dominated by Christ, the largest figure in the group with his right hand raised in blessing. He sat, holding a scroll in his left hand, surrounded by a lion and an eagle and other beasts symbolizing the four evangelists. The twenty-four elders mentioned in the Book of Revelation were all seated, holding medieval musical instruments that looked like primitive violins, or goblets symbolizing the prayers of the saints, a medieval chamber orchestra come to Moissac with their own refreshments. They sat in three tiers, with fourteen on the bottom row, six in the middle and four in the top. All were looking up and across at the figure of Christ, and the sculptor had demonstrated his abilities by giving each head a different angle, a different tilt across and upwards.

'Look at their legs, Francis.' It was Lady Lucy who noticed it first. Each pair of elders' legs, like each head, was different. Some were held close together, some were wide apart, some were folded one on top of another, some were twisted away from the body almost at right angles. But it was the face of Christ that fascinated Powerscourt. This Christ was lord and master of all he surveyed. He was bathed in majesty. His gaze travelled out of the tympanum, out over the valley of the Tarn, out over France and the known world towards the eternal and the infinite. He might have been placed on earth, carved in stone, but his kingdom stretched out into the next world.

But there was another statue that fascinated Powerscourt. It enthralled him. Its beauty was such, he told Lady Lucy later that evening, that he felt ravished by it. On either side of the south door there was a saint, presumably by the same hand that produced the tympanum above. On the left was St Paul, looking businesslike with a bible. On the right was St Jerome, a figure who did not look as if he belonged in the world of 1120 when the abbey was built. He belonged in another century altogether, hundreds of years in the future. He might even, Powerscourt thought, belong in the present. This St Jerome looked about thirty years old. His body was long, dressed in a flowing tunic, and he carried a scroll in his hands. The face and the beard and the long moustaches were all intertwined, with delicate grooves of hair that looked so soft you wanted to stroke them. His eyes, in so far as you could tell nearly eight hundred years after the sculptor finally laid down his chisel, seemed to look inward. The face was delicate, dreamy, almost feminine. Powerscourt had to remind himself that it was carved from granite, not the softest of materials. This was a man of sorrows, acquainted with grief. He looked as if he might be carrying all the sins of the world on his shoulders. The face and the expression could have been those of Christ himself, carrying his cross to his own version of the Last Judgement to the place which is called Calvary where they crucified him, and the malefactors, one on the right hand and the other on the left. It was the modernity of the face that haunted Powerscourt, who described it to himself as a symphony in melancholy.

Halfway between the abbey and the entrance to the cloisters there was a clatter of wheels and the reassuring noise of horses' hooves on cobblestones. The pilgrims had arrived. They clambered round Powerscourt and Lady Lucy like excited schoolchildren released to liberty at last after a long period of detention. And they complained. They complained about the solitary confinement in the police cells. They complained about the food. They complained about conditions in the train, where they alleged the sanitary arrangements weren't fit for pigs. They complained about the French police and their total failure to understand a word of English. The Inspector and his men shepherded them as gently as they could towards the cloisters, the Inspector confiding in a whisper to Powerscourt that he would be very relieved when they were all over the border. The prisoners had evolved their very own means of revolt. They refused to speak to him through his interpreter. They refused to speak to him at all, even in their own language, except, he thought, to swear at him. That, he said, was the only thing capable of bringing a smile to their faces.

They were just inside the cloisters when they were overwhelmed. A never-ending procession of young men in black cassocks marched in and pushed the pilgrims out of the way. Trainee priests, Léger said to Powerscourt, come to Moissac on a Sunday morning to see how their predecessors had lived in former times. Powerscourt thought there was no danger of the south of France being short of curés and monsignors and bishops in the years ahead. He thought there were over two hundred of them, maybe three hundred. The beauty of the cloisters was obscured by a black cloud of bodies. The pilgrims virtually disappeared behind a sea of cassocks. Two older men, also dressed in black, hopped over the little parapet at the bottom of the pillars and made their way into the middle of the grass in the centre. Behind them an enormous cedar tree offered shade to monks and visitors. The taller man, obviously the supervisor or tutor to the young men, introduced his colleague, a professor of history from the University of Bordeaux, a tubby little man scarcely over five feet tall but with a deep penetrating voice that had obviously been trained to reach the back of the biggest lecture hall in his university. He began by telling them about the foundation of the abbey. After five minutes he had reached the time of Dagobert's son Clovis the Second who was apparently King of Neustria and Burgundy in the year 650. Powerscourt had to whisper a reply to Lady Lucy that no, he had no idea at all where Neustria was. After ten minutes things were looking up at the abbey when rich property owners Nizezius – possibly an early version of Michael Delaney, Powerscourt thought – and his wife, who was actually called Ermintrude, shelled out thirty thousand acres of land in the Garonne along with all the churches, mills, serfs, settlers and freemen thereon in 680. That seemed to reawaken interest in the young ordinands, whose eyes had been glazing over at the long litany of dead abbots and dead princes. After fifteen minutes the professor introduced a character called Louis the Pious who took the place under his protection. And so it went on. And on, Powerscout said to himself.

The sun was moving round the pillars, changing the areas of shade and light and the colour of the brick. Powerscourt felt a moment of relief when he realized that the history lesson might stop when the professor reached the 1100s when the cloister was built. The professor did indeed reach the year 1100. But he did not stop. He knew about architecture too, the professor, and he was not going to miss this opportunity of sharing his knowledge with the seminarians.

Powerscourt stared across at the opposite gallery. He could see about half a dozen pilgrims penned against the pillars but no more. He couldn't see anything at all to his left or right. He presumed the rest were trapped round the other galleries. West gallery, the professor said, and now he was describing the sculptures on the capitals, the top of the pillars. Number two over there, he went on, the sacrifice of Abraham and Isaac. That took a minute or two. Some of the capitals were decorative, with no sculpture at all. These merited only a brief mention. Then there was Daniel in the lion's den. Another couple of minutes. Powerscourt began doing some serious mental arithmetic. He reckoned there must be about eighty capitals with sculptures. One minute each and that meant an hour and twenty minutes. Make it a minute and a half and that was two hours. Surely the little man couldn't go on that long. God in heaven.

Across the grass Powerscourt saw that Inspector Léger might have been making similar calculations. He was wriggling free from a scrum about four deep. There was a certain amount of pushing and shoving and then he was lost to sight. Powerscourt wondered if he should join him. After a couple of minutes the resurrection of Lazarus at pillar number nine was on the menu. Powerscourt thought that if Lazarus knew he was going to be brought back to life here and now with this interminable lecture in these cloisters he might decide to stay where he was. He saw the Inspector again making his way across the opposite gallery. He was looking worried. After a couple more minutes the professor was pointing to an inscription on pillar number twelve which referred to the construction of the buildings in 1100 when Dom Ansquitil was abbot. The Inspector was making frantic gestures to Powerscourt to join him. Then, paying no attention to the senior clergy in the centre, he hopped inside the cloisters and made his way very slowly along the four galleries. Powerscourt decided to join him.

'Count the pilgrims,' the Inspector whispered.

Michael Delaney and Alex Bentley were sandwiched in between a couple of very tall ordinands. Jack O'Driscoll and Christy Delaney were squashed against a pillar. Maggie Delaney was closer to Father Kennedy than she would have thought proper. The rest were scattered around the cloisters in various degrees of discomfort. Inspector Léger and Powerscourt did their rounds twice. The professor had reached murder with the story of Cain and Abel at pillar number nineteen. The Frenchman drew Powerscourt into the street outside. The church bells were tolling the Angelus. There was a small crowd in front of the tympanum.

'How many did you make it?' asked Léger.

'Twelve,' said Powerscourt, beginning to feel rather sick.

'So did I.'

'How many do you think there should be?'

'Thirteen,' said the Inspector. 'God knows I've counted the buggers often enough these last two days, on and off the train, in and out of the cells.'

'Could he have escaped? Run away in all the confusion with the priests?'

'No, he couldn't. One of my men is on guard just outside.'

'Could he be in one of those rooms off the cloisters?'

'We'd better go and see.'

18

By the end of the north gallery they came to what had been the refectory. It was completely empty. Next door was the Chapelle St Ferréol with some ancient sculptures but no living pilgrims. The professor had reached the story of David and Goliath from the first Book of Samuel at pillar number twenty-two. Along the east gallery was a series of empty chambers, full of dust with cobwebs circling out from the walls. Powerscourt began to wonder if they hadn't just miscounted the pilgrims. One of them could have been hemmed in by the taller men in black till he was virtually invisible. The south gallery backed directly on to the side of the church but at the corner where it met the west gallery there was a set of stairs leading upwards.

'Come on,' said the Inspector, 'if he's not up here we can't count. We'll have to go back to school.'

The steps led them into the upper chamber, an extremely tall room with great slim arches. Strips of light were flooding in through a series of openings on an upper level. One side of the room looked directly into the church. Anybody up here could eavesdrop on weddings or baptisms down below without being seen. The vaulting was supported on twelve square ribs radiating out from a central keystone. The room was deserted. Powerscourt and the Inspector tiptoed round it in opposite directions. Then there was a muffled cry from Inspector Léger.

'My God!' he said. 'After all the precautions we've taken, there's been another murder!'

Powerscourt turned round and joined him. At the bottom of a little flight of steps there was a huddled shape. It looked as though somebody had taken all their clothes off and dropped them on the floor. Even in the shadows they could see drops of dark blood oozing from the back of what had once been his head. Lumps of grey matter that might have been brains, Powerscourt thought, were lying on the floor. One hand was still at the back of his head, as if trying to ward off the vicious blows that killed him.

'Look,' said the Inspector, pointing to dark marks on the pillar above them, 'it seems somebody smashed the victim's head repeatedly into the stone. He might have been gone after a few blows. It must have been like a pummelling from a giant hammer, poor soul. Do you know who he was, Powerscourt?'

Powerscourt peered down at the remains of a human being dumped on the floor of St Peter's Abbey. 'Connolly,' he said quietly, 'Girvan Connolly, related to Michael Delaney on his mother's side. He was on the run from his creditors, Inspector, but I don't suppose they found him here. Whatever his misdemeanours, however large his debts, he hadn't deserved to die like this.'

'Could you wait here till I send one of my men up? I'm going to put a man at the bottom of the steps too. All too late, of course, but at least nobody's going to see him till the doctor gets here. And I'll tell the priest in charge of all those young men to get them out of here. That'll be a relief.'

Powerscourt stared sadly into the body of the church. The technique, he realized, was the same in all four murders. God, he thought, there have been four of them and my presence here has been a complete waste of time. Come with me, my friend, up the steps to the Chapel of St Michel in Le Puy, or to the river bank on the Lot, or to the back of the church in Conques, or to this upper chamber, come and I'll tell you a secret. You're going to like the secret very much. There was indeed a secret waiting for the person who went with the killer; their own death, always surprising even in more peaceful surroundings. And what was the secret, or the bait? Was it blackmail perhaps, or the promise of some rich pickings from Michael Delaney?

His thoughts were interrupted by the arrival of one of Inspector Léger's policemen who crossed himself vigorously when he saw the bloodied bundle that had been Girvan Connolly and began saying a series of Hail Marys.

Something in the Inspector's face must have alerted Monsignor Michelack, the priest in charge.

'It is something serious up there, Inspector, is it not so?'

'Yes, I'm afraid it is,' Léger replied.

'It is not a sudden illness or you would be running for the doctor. Am I right?'

The Inspector wondered briefly if the Monsignor was not in the wrong profession.

'It is a dead man?' Michelack whispered. 'Another of these murders?'

The Inspector realized that most of the clergy of southern France must know about the chequered progress of the Delaney pilgrims, their passage marked by blood and sudden death. The Church after all had been deeply involved in the discussions about what to do with them.

The Inspector nodded sadly. The priest crossed himself very slowly and deliberately. He closed his eyes and said a brief prayer. Then he turned to address his students.

'Gentlemen,' he began, 'I have a sad announcement to make. In the midst of life there is death. Death came this afternoon for one of these pilgrims in the upper chamber here behind me. Murder strikes in one of the most beautiful buildings in France. Before we go I want us to say the prayers for the dead. I want you to form up in ranks of four abreast. We shall progress round the cloisters in the manner of the monks of old, saying the same prayers they would have said for one of their own, fallen asleep in his cell perhaps, or passing away from old age as he worked in the fields.'

The young men were very solemn as they fell into their ranks. The Monsignor placed himself at the head of the column. He walked slowly, his hands joined together and pointing to the ground. He spoke quietly as he led the young men in their devotions.

'Hail Mary full of grace, blessed art thou among women, pray for us now and in the hour of our death, Amen.'

Two hundred young voices joined him in the Hail Mary. The pilgrims had prostrated themselves against the walls. Powerscourt and Lady Lucy watched from the entrance to what had once been the monks' refectory, a place of physical rather than spiritual sustenance.

'Absolve, Lord, we entreat you, the soul of your servant from every bond of sin . . .'

Only those near the front of the procession could hear the words of the Monsignor. For the rest the seminarians' voices took over.

'. . . that he may be raised up in the glory of the resurrection and live among your saints and elect, through Jesus Christ our Lord.'

Powerscourt thought this must be a profound experience for these young men. They will have read in their history books all about the daily life of the monks of centuries past, the seven services, the prescribed ordering of each day in God's service. Now they were living out one part of it. Surely they would never think about monastic life in the same way again. Today, for them, the past had, quite literally, come to life, walking in order round the four galleries of the Moissac cloisters.

'Incline your ear, oh Lord,' the Monsignor went on, 'to our prayers in which we humbly entreat your mercy, and bring to a place of peace and light the soul of your servant . . .'

Maggie Delaney, standing very still against a wall near the Pillar of Cain and Abel, was weeping for the beauty of the procession and the soul of Girvan Connolly, sinner and corpse.

'. . . which you have summoned to go forth from this world,' the young men carried on, 'bidding him to be numbered in the fellowship of your saints through Jesus Christ our Lord.'

Powerscourt remembered his earlier conversation with Connolly as they walked the pilgrim trail, the pots and pans that wouldn't sell, the sheets that collapsed after the first use, the debts that closed around him as death had enveloped him this afternoon. He didn't think Connolly would have much in common with the saints.

'Hear us, oh Lord,' the Monsignor looked as though he could go on praying for ever, 'and let the soul of your servant profit by this sacrifice, by the offering of which you granted that the sins of the whole world should be forgiven, through Jesus Christ our Lord.'

Half of the cloisters were in shadow now. Shafts of sunlight sent bands of brilliant light across the black of the seminarians. The bricks were glowing pink or almost white. Powerscourt watched in astonishment as the pilgrims began to join the rear of the procession. Brother White, Christy Delaney, Charlie Flanagan and Jack O'Driscoll formed themselves into a line of four and joined the seminarians at the end of their column.

'Our father which art in heaven, hallowed be thy name . . .'

Now the rest of the pilgrims fell into line and progressed round the cloisters with the men in black, with only Maggie Delaney left on the sidelines.

'Thy kingdom come, thy will be done . . .'

Lady Lucy was whispering to Powerscourt. 'Should we join in too, Francis? What do you think?'

Powerscourt shook his head. 'I think not, my love. Not our cloisters, not our religion, not even our pilgrimage.'

'On earth as it is in heaven . . .'

The sound rose above the cloisters and into the blue skies

above. Christy Delaney was crying now. So was Wee Jimmy Delaney, his huge frame racked by sobs.

'Give us each day our daily bread . . .'

Lady Lucy was holding her husband's hand very tightly. Inspector Léger in the corner was now flanked by a man with a bag who might be a doctor and a couple of orderlies with a makeshift stretcher.

'And forgive us our trespasses, as we forgive them who trespass against us . . .'

Beads of sweat were forming on the Monsignor's upper lip as he processed round the cloisters for the last time. Behind him the young men kept their places, eyes down, hands still.

'And deliver us from evil, for thine is the kingdom, the power and the glory, for ever and ever, amen.'

Monsignor Michelack led his men right out of the cloisters, still keeping their ranks of four apiece, and into the square to wait for their transport. Inspector Léger marched the remaining pilgrims out too, pausing for a quick word with Powerscourt.

'I'm sorry,' he began, 'I meant to ask you before but I forgot. I have lost my interpreter. I would be very grateful if you could accompany me on the train. I've ordered a couple of extra carriages. Maybe these pilgrims will talk to you more easily than they would to me, my lord. We won't be asking you to spend the night in the cells with them, mind you.'

Powerscourt said they would be delighted. The doctor and his assistants, the melancholy apparatus of death, hurried off to the upper chamber to remove the body. Lady Lucy went to see if she could offer comfort to the pilgrims. Silence returned to the cloisters of Moissac.

Powerscourt watched as two burly French policemen carried Girvan Connolly's body down the steps at the northeast corner of the cloisters. At the bottom they placed the corpse on a makeshift stretcher and carried it away to the cathedral square where a Moissac ambulance would take it to the Moissac morgue and into the care of the doctors. Beyond the wall he could still hear sounds of weeping and lament as the remaining pilgrims mourned the loss of yet another of their number.

Powerscourt was now completely alone. Eternal silence had returned. And he had seen this afternoon something approaching a miracle. No monks had walked round these four galleries since the revolutionary upheavals of 1793. But today, he had seen with his own eyes a great column of religious, processing round as their predecessors would have done eight hundred years before, saying the prayers for the dead. The cloisters, Powerscourt thought, were unmoved by murder and violent death. Built in their original form about 1100, they had survived the Black Death, the Crusades against the Cathars, the Hundred Years War, the Wars of Religion, the Revolution and the Terror. One more death would not affect them. As he looked at the four great arcades flanking the central garth – the grass space in the middle where a fountain or a spring had been centuries before – he tried to remember what the fussy little local historian had struggled to tell his party earlier that day. Twenty pillars each in the east and west sides and eighteen on the north and south. So the cloisters were nearly square. The pillars alternating between single and double columns. The great cedar towards the north arcade that would have given shade in the summer. And up here – the chubby Frenchman had grown quite animated at this point – 'gentlemen, the glory of Moissac! What makes it most unique! The capitals at the top of the pillars! In these middle times, they had the sculptures on the top of the pillars, seventy and six of them, no, showing leaves and foliage and all the different scenes from the Old and New Testaments. For the monks this would have been like a book to read as they went about their work, a book to inspire them and keep them to their callings. And the pilgrims, my friends, the pilgrims would have read them as we read newspapers today!'

The rattle of wheels and the clap of horses' hooves told him that the body must now be on its way to another resting place. The sun was advancing slowly but relentlessly along the south arcade, highlighting the pillars and the capitals in red and gold. Powerscourt wondered if the stones had a message. Perhaps they were as remote as the broken statue of some long dead Egyptian potentate, buried in the sands in the Valley of the Kings . Modernity, he thought, would probably want to sweep them all away and build something new, something relevant to the times. The cloister, indeed, had only just survived an early encounter with modernity when the engineers of the new Bordeaux to Sète railway had wanted to knock the whole complex down and replace it with gleaming modern railway tracks. It had taken a great campaign to deflect them and even now, as Powerscourt heard the rumble of an approaching express behind him, modernity shook parts of the building every time a train shot past. Powerscourt walked slowly round the cloisters, a voyage out of light into shadow and back into light again and thought about the monks and the abbots who had spent their lives here centuries before. The men who walked here then didn't think about the future, they thought about eternity.

The dull browns burnished into light pink, the weathered red brick wrapped around the cloisters, the great tree reaching up into a deep blue sky, they spoke to Powerscourt of a profound peace. He would always remember these cloisters, the deep stillness they conveyed even when the arcades were full of chattering pilgrims, the all-pervading calm, their austere and timeless beauty. He heard footsteps advancing towards him from the south gallery. Lady Lucy was coming to join her husband in his deliberations. As she walked along the row of pillars, the sunlight was dancing in her hair.

There were two telegrams waiting for Powerscourt when he and Lady Lucy returned to the hotel. The first was from Johnny Fitzgerald and was unusually delphic for Johnny. 'Am coming in person to join you on holiday in south of France. Bringing one of Knightsbridge's finest lost and found. Shall expect detailed report on best local vintages for immediate consumption. Fitzgerald.'

'My love, what on earth is one of Knightsbridge's finest lost and found?' Lady Lucy had been reading the message over her husband's shoulder.

Powerscourt laughed. 'It's a primitive sort of code, Lucy. Look at the first letters of the words after "bringing" and you'll see it says "book". Johnny must have got hold of a copy of that old book about Delaney, the one that was pulped all those years ago. And he's bringing it himself. Maybe he didn't like to trust it to the post. Anyway, he should be here soon. I think that's tremendous news.'

Lady Lucy was more thrilled than she let on. She had always been very fond of Johnny Fitzgerald. He had been best man at their wedding, scarcely recovered from a bullet wound in the chest. But when he was there, she felt Francis was safe. Johnny looked after him as he had looked after Johnny for years now. It was as if a blanket of security was about to be thrown over her husband.

The second telegram came from Franklin Bentley in Washington. 'Have located young Delaney,' it said. 'Early years in Pittsburgh, city of steel. Have located local priest who may remember him. My employers have given leave for me to go there tomorrow. Suspect they want to curry favour with Delaney, take his account away from Smith Wasserstein Abrahams up in New York.'

'Well,' said Powerscourt, 'things may be looking up.' A faint outline of a plan to catch the killer was forming in his brain. It depended on his having Johnny Fitzgerald by his side. And, for once, he wasn't going to breathe a word of it to his wife.

After dinner they went out to have coffee and drinks at a series of wooden tables at the back of the hotel. This small square had once been the stable block and indeed there were still a number of horses and a few carriages to be seen. A bearded man could be observed lying under the bonnet of a very large and very expensive-looking motor car, a rag in one hand and an oil can in the other, swearing violently from time to time as he encountered further mechanical problems.

It was Powerscourt who saw them first. Flying high above them was a positive armada of small birds, swallows and martins and swifts, with their scythe-like wings and short forked tails. They looked as though they were on parade, medieval knights on tournament duty perhaps, armour burnished, lances polished, standards cleaned till they glowed in the sunlight, trotting along the green field to impress a sovereign or delight a mistress. Hundreds and hundreds of the birds passed overhead, the noise of their wings mingling with their cries and the traffic of the town. Somewhere out of sight, Powerscourt thought, they must wheel round and return, drawn for some unknown reason back to the little square that started as a stable block.

He remembered the excitement in his household the previous year when reports reached England that two Americans had invented a machine that could fly. This was no Montgolfier balloon that had carried the French into the skies before their Revolution, dependent on the wind, uncertain of navigation, symbolic of veering and abrupt changes in political direction. This American contraption, when it was more fully developed, would fly where man wanted it to go. The wings, unlike those of aviation pioneer Icarus, would not melt if taken too close to the sun. Powerscourt's eldest child, Thomas, had been fascinated by the flying aeroplane. He bought all the newspapers and magazines he could find that contained articles about it. Daily for nearly a month, his father recalled, Thomas had announced at mealtimes, all mealtimes, that he was going to fly one of these devices when he grew up. His sister Olivia, almost as excited as Thomas at the prospect of flying machines, announced that she wasn't going to bother to learn how to fly the things. This, she implied, was a rather menial task, like mending broken motor cars. Rather she would travel in state and in style, seated in luxury by one of the windows, taking small but sophisticated sips of Kir Royale, a concoction Olivia had been allowed a minute mouthful of in France the year before and regarded as the epitome of chic.

Then the pattern in the heavens above changed. No longer were the birds flying in huge formations, hundreds and hundreds to a regiment. Now they were coming in small attack platoons, fifteen or twenty at a time. Before they had sailed high above the buildings. Now they dived straight for them, only turning away at the last possible second. They skimmed along the sides of the stables a few feet from the solid bricks that would have crushed their skulls. The birds, swifts mostly, Powerscourt thought, headed directly for the chimney tops, twisting out of the way with inches to spare, screaming as they went. There were dark birds, totally black, in the line-up now, which he suspected might be bats. Wave after wave of them came in their demonic flight, skirting along the sides of the square. No human brain, he thought, could have made the lightning calculations needed to tell the birds to turn away from the walls and the turrets now or they would be obliterated. This was, quite literally, for these swifts and swallows and martins, a dance of death.

He looked over to his right and saw the birds still turning and twisting and racing and shrieking and diving across their arena of the roofs of the stable block.

When he turned his gaze back to the hotel, everything had changed. The little birds had stopped, or moved on. Perhaps God or some other celestial seneschal had blown a whistle to announce the end of the match. In their place, high above the playground of the swifts and the swallows, a couple of ravens were beating a regular and steady path across the skies. Pay no attention, they seemed to say, to the frantic antics of these small swifts and swallows. We are the serious characters round here. We shall always be with you. And in place of the shrieking of the little birds he could hear Lady Lucy's voice asking him if he had gone deaf, surely, she had been trying to talk to him for at least a minute, and did he want another drink before the bar closed up for the night.

Powerscourt and Lady Lucy were sipping their coffee in a corner of another hotel dining room the next morning when a great shout disturbed the breakfast peace.

'Francis! Lucy! The top of the morning to you both!' And Johnny Fitzgerald, holding a large dark brown bag very tight in his right hand, strode across the room. He embraced Lady Lucy and held Powerscourt in an enormous bear hug. Only then, as the relief flooded through him, did Powerscourt realize how much he had missed his companion in arms. Lady Lucy felt happier than she had done since she came to France. Francis would be safe now.

'Coffee,' said Johnny, seating himself down, still holding on to the bag and signalling to the waitress, 'I could do with some coffee. I feel it's too early for a drink, even for me. Now then,' he tapped his holdall significantly, 'I've brought you the Crown Jewels, Francis. I had to go all the way to Bath to get it, mind you. I think this is the only copy left in England.'

'Have you read any of it, Johnny?' asked Lady Lucy.

'I've got to page one hundred and fifty. It's a very strange book. The subtitle is *The Seven Deadly Sins of Michael Delaney*, and each of the seven chapters deals with a different crime. Maybe the author hoped it would be serialized in one of the weeklies, a sin a week for a month and a half. But it's as if the author is two completely different people. The beginning of each chapter is full of detailed financial stuff I didn't really care about, then at the end he turns into a sort of hellfire preacher man and rants and raves away about how wicked Delaney is and how he is sure to be punished in this world or the next.'

'And are the crimes bad enough, Johnny, for people to want to kill all his relations?' asked Powerscourt.

'Depends on how bad you think all these financial mis-demeanours are, I suppose,' said Johnny Fitzgerald, rummaging around in his bag. 'You know I could never understand anything about money – the financial pages leave me in such a daze that my wits can only be restored by a glass or two of something.' Johnny handed the book over to Powerscourt who noticed that Johnny had wrapped the cover in plain brown paper so that nobody would know what he was reading.

A glance inside told him that the author was a Robert Preston, one-time reporter with the *Wall Street Journal*.

'Well,' he smiled at his wife and his friend, 'let's hope we find some answers in here. Wouldn't it be odd if the solution to these murders came all the way from Bath.'

19

The pilgrim train was now six carriages long, four for the pilgrims and two extra for the Powerscourts laid on by the Inspector. Léger had called at the hotel soon after Johnny's arrival to tell them they would be leaving at eleven o'clock.

'I've done all the paperwork,' he said wearily to Powerscourt, 'I've filled in all the forms. I've arranged for the funeral. I had a frightful time with the local police and the Mayor and everybody, mind you. They kept saying these wretched pilgrims should be held here in Moissac, pending further investigations. I asked them how many more dead bodies they wanted on their doorstep. Then they said I couldn't take the suspects out of the area. I asked if they wanted hordes of newspapermen crowding round their damned cloisters – said I was going to make an appeal via the gentlemen of the press for information from the public that might lead to an arrest. I even, God help me, talked about a reward.'

'Would you have done that, Inspector?' asked Powerscourt.

'Certainly not,' said the Inspector with a grin. 'I'm hardly likely to want to advertise our failure to find the murderer. But they weren't to know that. We'll conduct the interviews as we go along. If the pilgrims won't talk to me or to you, Powerscourt, I'm going to tell them they may never get out of France. They could be locked up in a cell for years while the case is investigated. As it is, I've talked to the railway authorities. They've put a newer and faster engine on the train. The quicker the pilgrims are out of the country the happier I shall be.'

Failure. Our failure. Failure. My failure. Powerscourt wondered if this would be his last case, the shame and ignominy of failure finishing off his reputation for good. His mood was not improved by a summons to see Michael Delaney who seemed to have appropriated one of the extra carriages as his own. The train was now moving towards the south at considerable speed. Johnny Fitzgerald was looking at the birds out of the window, swearing quietly when their speed prevented him from making a proper identification.

Delaney seemed to have obtained a fresh supply of cigars. The great fat one he was smoking now was of a type Powerscourt had not seen him smoke before. He seemed to be in a filthy mood. Powerscourt wondered if his famous temper, admirably held in check until now, was about to explode.

'Ah, Powerscourt,' he said, sounding rather like a headmaster Powerscourt had once known, 'sit down.' He took another mighty puff on his cigar. 'In my line of business, Powerscourt, we have to keep an eye on the managers we put in. Are they doing their job properly? Are they fiddling the books? Are they succeeding in bringing in loads of profit for the firm, that sort of thing. Are you with me up to this point?'

Powerscourt said yes, he thought he could manage it so far, thank you.

'One of the hardest jobs our managers have to perform in the unforgiving world of commerce is to turn around companies that are failing, losing money, losing me money. Let me tell you a story, Powerscourt. Let's suppose I've just bought a little railroad company in upstate New York. It's not doing well, but there is a lot of potential. In goes the manager, who comes with very high recommendations and references, the best in the business and so on. And he fails. The company is not turned round. It continues to go down the pan. And what do I do? In my innocence I believe that it is not his fault, that

271

he deserves another chance. So I send him to save another company, a ferry business operating out of Long Island Sound that should be making money hand over fist. Again he fails. The citizens of Long Island Sound are not crowding on to his ferries, they're travelling on the other bastard's boats. So what do I do? Like a fool, I keep the man on. This time I send him to a printing works that should be flush with dollars with people buying more newspapers and so forth. But no. For the third time the man fails. The order books of the printing works are no better than they were when he came, they are worse. Three times now this man has failed me, he's failed himself, he's failed to fulfil his part of the American dream that all businessmen are free to make as much money as they can. I give him one last chance. Another train company. Maybe he was unlucky the first time. Maybe this time all that praise for his abilities will come good. Maybe or maybe not. The fool fails again. So what do you think I should do with him, Powerscourt? You know all about people with superb references and recommendations, after all.'

'I think that's entirely a matter for you, Mr Delaney.' Powerscourt thought he knew what was coming. Under normal circumstances it might be possible to move away from such sulphurous encounters. On a train there was no escape.

'Quite so, Powerscourt. Now let us suppose we have a different sort of problem. Let us suppose a rich American decides to sponsor a pilgrimage to Europe as a thank-you to God for the saving of his son's life. God does you a good turn, you do God a good turn back. And let us suppose there is a suspicious death, almost certainly a murder. The French police appear to be hopeless. You launch a search for the finest investigator in France and England who is fluent in both languages. You hire the fellow, perfectly charming, lovely English manners, delightful wife, and with no more clue about finding the killer than the man on the moon. Does he find the murderer of the first victim? He does not.'

Delaney's voice was rising.

'Does he find the killer of the second victim? No, he does not.'

Delaney was shouting now. He banged his great fist on the table in front of him. His cigar had been abandoned in his wrath.

'Does he find the murderer of the third victim? Of course not!'

Another thump on the table. Powerscourt thought the engine driver and his assistant at the front of the train must be able to hear every word by now. Thank God they wouldn't understand any of it.

'Three bodies now, laid out on cold slabs in the French morgues,' Delaney ranted on, hardly able to control himself, 'so does the great detective fare any better with the next one? You'd think it should be easy by now with the number of suspects dropping by the day, wouldn't you? Does he catch the killer of victim number four? No, he does not. I might have been better off employing nobody at all.'

A final thump on the table. Powerscourt said nothing. He wondered if it was going to come to blows. Delaney was a couple of inches taller and a great deal heavier. He looked as if he might pack a fearful punch. But he stayed on his bench. It looked as if the anger was ebbing from him. He picked up his cigar again.

'Five days more. That's all. If you haven't caught the man by then, you're off this train and out of my sight. And I'll spend whatever it takes to blacken your reputation in the newspapers back there in England. I've done it in New York, I'm sure I can do it in London. Now get out and get on with it before I shout any more.'

Powerscourt had been in real fights in real battles that were much worse than this. But he knew that for his own self-respect he could not let these insults pass.

'You're perfectly entitled to your opinion, Mr Delaney, of course you are. But let me tell you this. I may not have caught the murderer yet but I am absolutely certain of one thing. If you had told me the truth about your activities in the past and the enemies you have made throughout your long life in business, the careers you have broken, the men you have destroyed, then I am sure the murderer would have been apprehended by now. Your actions, maybe so far back in the past you have almost forgotten them, are what lie behind these terrible deaths, I'm sure of it. Think about it, Mr Delaney. If there is anything you wish to tell me, I shall be in the next carriage. Good morning to you.'

Delaney picked up his cigar and blew a great cloud of smoke at Powerscourt's retreating back as if it were a flame-thrower. He stared moodily out of the window.

Powerscourt found he was shaking slightly as he told Lady Lucy and Johnny what had happened.

'Bloody man,' said Fitzgerald. 'Maybe the murderer will sort him out. Serve him damn well right, being rude to Francis.'

'That's a little uncharitable, Johnny,' said Lady Lucy. 'We shouldn't wish anybody dead, I'm sure, not even Mr Delaney. You'll survive, my love, you've survived much worse before.'

'Well,' said her husband, 'it was a lot better than being stuck in that wine vat, I can tell you.'

The Inspector arrived in search of an interpreter. Powerscourt suggested Lady Lucy should accompany him. The pilgrims might open up more with the wife than they would with the husband. Maggie Delaney had been befriended by two young pilgrims, Jack O'Driscoll and Christy Delaney. They had come to feel sorry for her, usually left on her own, with nobody to talk to apart from the inter-minable rosary beads. They had been teaching her card games, snap and gin rummy and pontoon. The elderly lady showed a remarkable talent for poker, bluffing her way to victory, her suspicious old eyes never giving anything away.

Powerscourt himself returned to *Michael Delaney, Robber Baron*. He had reached page forty-five without any revelations that might make a victim commit murder. His right hand fiddled with the paper knife as he read on.

Inspector Léger and Lady Lucy realized after two or three conversations that the pilgrims were still not going to co-operate. Jack O'Driscoll muttered that he was going to write all this up in his newspaper when he reached home. Charlie Flanagan was working on another wooden carving as he spoke to them, punctuating his answers with deft strokes of his knife that set alarm bells ringing in the Inspector's brain. Yes, they had been in the cloisters. Yes, they had been crushed up against the walls when the seminarians came. No, they had not seen anybody leave to go up to the upper chamber. No, they had not seen Girvan Connolly at all. That didn't mean he wasn't there, just that that they hadn't seen him. That was all they could remember. Yes, they had been in the cloisters. Yes, they had been crushed up against the walls when the seminarians came. Pilgrim after pilgrim repeated exactly the same story in the same words, with the same air of prisoners being interrogated by a hostile power. Lady Lucy could see how united they had become, bonds formed in adversity, together against the foe that was depriving them of decent beds and a glass or two of beer in the evening. They were besieged, Lady Lucy felt, huddled together inside the thick walls of the ruined French castles that were so frequent in these parts. They would parley with the enemy heralds but they would not come out and they would not surrender.

Inspector Léger checked his hair again on the way back to the Powerscourt carriage. It was hopeless. Just a couple of days, he said to himself, and he could return home to Lucille and the vegetable patch he tended with such care. Lucille was hopeless with crops, they always went wrong when he wasn't there.

They found Powerscourt in a state of considerable excitement. He had reached page eighty-six of the book and thought he might be on to something. He explained the complicated history of *Michael Delaney, Robber Baron* to the Inspector.

'Now then,' he put the book in his lap, 'how about this. I'm not sure how long ago all this was, the author has forgotten to put a date on it, but it must be way back in the past. I won't read all the relevant passages, we'd be here all day. Michael Delaney owns a small railroad leading out of the city into upstate New York. It's nothing special. But he realizes that if he could get his hands on another line, they would complement each other and make a great deal of money. This other line belongs to a man called Wharton, James Joseph Wharton. Why don't we amalgamate the two lines, says Delaney. We'll both be better off. I think this Wharton may have inherited the business from his father. He was a bookish sort of fellow, apparently, not sharp like Delaney, spent a lot of time in the New York Public Library. Anyway, Delaney says he'll handle the paperwork, sort everything out for the new company that's going to own the lines. The only thing is, he puts all the shares in his name. Wharton only finds out after the new company has been floated on the New York Stock Exchange. By then it's too late.

'He hires some lawyers, as Americans always do. But they aren't very good lawyers. Delaney hires better ones. Delaney always does. He swears Wharton agreed to let him put all the shares in his name. Delaney wins. Wharton has lost his livelihood. Listen to what the author says about his fate: "Deprived of his livelihood by the rapacious frauds of one he supposed a friend for life, bereft of funds to support his wife and son, he turned for solace and consolation where so many have turned in times of trouble and tribulation, to the temptations of the demon drink."' Powerscourt looked up at Johnny Fitzgerald and shook his head sadly. '"Wharton's health, never strong even in the good times, began to decline. He was banned from the New York Public Library after being sick over a rare volume concerned with the early settlements in Virginia. He began to have hallucinations and blackouts, the punishment sent by nature for alcohol abuse. Had the unfortunate man seen sense and taken the pledge, even at this late stage, as his priest and his wife continually urged him, he might yet have been saved. There was a young son whose early impressions of fathers were of people who fell down the stairs and smelt bad. The house had to be sold to pay for the drinking. The family moved into humbler accommodation where Winifred, the wife, who thought she was marrying upwards into a higher social class, felt ashamed of her position. When she discovered that the money she thought was destined to pay the rent was going to the liquor store instead, she left him and went back to her mother. Three days after that, James Joseph Wharton blew his brains out. Only three people attended the funeral at a pauper's grave. Michael Delaney was not one of them."'

'Does he say what became of the boy, Francis?' Lady Lucy leaned forward to stare at her husband. 'Did the mother marry again? Would the boy have a different name now?'

'The book doesn't say, Lucy. That's the end of a chapter. The next one deals with matters a few years later. It may come up further on in the book but I doubt it. What do you think of it as a motive for murder, though?'

'Well,' said Johnny Fitzgerald, 'it'd be fine as a motive for killing Delaney, but he's still here.'

'Maybe', said the Inspector, thoughtfully, 'he nurses a grudge, hatred, not just for Delaney but for all the members of his clan. But without a name it is very difficult.'

'I shall have to wire to our friend in Washington. And I must give him all the poste restantes where we may be stopping. Inspector, do you think you could arrange for the train to stop briefly in the next town? And could the pilgrims be permitted a night in a hotel rather than a night in the cells? I have a plan to put before the three of you. It is very dangerous. I know you will not like it, Lucy. But it might just enable us to catch our man.' Powerscourt had reluctantly decided that, however much he might want to keep the plan a secret, he could not keep it from his wife.

The shadows were long as the pilgrims were marched from the train to their hotel, the d'Artagnan, in the little town of Aire-sur-l'Adour. Aire was graced with a cathedral with a saint buried in a white marble tomb in the crypt. Edward the Confessor, Powerscourt dimly remembered, had signed a treaty here with some French bishop. And there was the Adour, another of those rivers that grace the towns of France. The hotel was right on the waterfront, four storeys high and looking as if it might have been a barracks or a convent in earlier times. On the first floor a ledge ran right along the frontage, joining the balconies that gave the more fortunate visitors their own private view of the Adour.

The pilgrims were chattering happily, some looking forward to the meal, others to the beer and wine, the older ones rhapsodizing about the joy of clean sheets and a proper pillow. Father Kennedy hoped the Hôtel d'Artagnan had some decent puddings. As the pilgrims dispersed to their single rooms on the third and the fourth floors, Lady Lucy had a long conversation with the hotel housekeeper. It was her husband, she explained. He suffered from a chronic back condition, poor man, and needed special arrangements in his bed. Did the housekeeper have large bolsters? She did? Could Lady Powerscourt have one, maybe even two if they could be spared? While the housekeeper scurried off to her linen cupboard Lady Lucy noticed a couple of wigs lying on a small table by the window. Previous clients must have left them behind. She couldn't think of how they might be helpful to a man with a chronic back condition, but she still whipped them into her pocket before the housekeeper returned. Lady Lucy declined the housekeeper's kind offer to carry the bedding upstairs and make the necessary installations. Lucy would do it herself. There was so little, she assured the housekeeper, that she could do to make her husband's life more comfortable, this was one duty she could perform for him. Lying flat on the back for fifteen minutes three times a day, the housekeeper passed on the local medical wisdom as Lady Lucy disappeared at full speed up the stairs, that's what had cured the butcher's chronic back condition only last year. Maybe her husband the milord should try it.

Jack O'Driscoll had been passing on more of his recently acquired French. They were quite near to Bordeaux, he told them knowledgeably, home to the finest red wine in the whole of France.

'This is how you order it, boys,' he said. 'Oon grond vare de van rouge.'

Other pilgrims made experimental flights with Jack's phrases and were indeed rewarded with fine glasses of red. Johnny Fitzgerald, who had always been regarded as a friend by the pilgrims, was holding forth at one end of the bar, an expensive bottle in front of him. 'It's my belief', he told the company, 'that my friend Powerscourt has solved the mystery at last. He's writing a report up there in that big bedroom above the front door with the enormous balcony. He won't tell anybody about what's in it. I doubt if the wife knows. But he did say he was going to present it to the Inspector in the morning.'

For the pilgrims, freedom beckoned. Release from jail is always welcome, even if the sojourn has only been for a few days. The young ones hoped they would soon be free to walk the pilgrim route once more, for the walking had taken possession of them and they felt diminished when they couldn't do it. One or two of the others thought they could go to Mass in the morning and pray for their immortal souls. That, after all, was what had brought them on this strange journey in the first place. They grew elated and drank more red wine. Dinner was uneventful, Powerscourt looking preoccupied and pausing every now and then to make some more notes in a black book he had brought to the table. Lady Lucy's eyes scanned the diners. One of them was a murderer. One of them had tried to kill her Francis. But the faces gave nothing away.

When the last of the apricot tarts had been cleared away, Powerscourt and Lady Lucy went up to their room. Powerscourt stepped out on the balcony and watched night falling slowly over Aire-sur-l'Adour. Lady Lucy was fiddling with the bolsters, waiting for the signal to start work. Down below Powerscourt could hear the noise of laughter from the bar. He stared at the street in front of him, wondering if he could see any sign of movement. Then the noises off began to die down. Outside their room he could hear the pilgrims making their way upstairs. Inspector Léger had a man on every landing, ordered to watch through the night. Silence fell over the Hôtel d'Artagnan.

'Time to work your magic, Lucy,' said Powerscourt. The bedclothes were whipped off each bed in turn. Bolsters and pillows were deployed to imitate the curve and the shape of the human form. Lady Lucy's model, if that was the right word, was the way her Francis slept at night, back curved, legs drawn up slightly at the knees. She replaced the bedclothes, ruffling them furiously as she did so, to make it look as if the sleeping figures had tossed and turned in the night. Then she looked at her husband.

'Would you like to be brown or fair, my love?' she said, turning the two wigs over in her hands.

'Brown,' said Powerscourt with a smile, 'definitely brown.'

Lady Lucy stepped back to check her handiwork. She ruffled the pillows once more. 'That's about as good as I can make it, Francis.'

'Looks pretty good to me,' said Powerscourt, pulling out the light bulb and putting it in his pocket. He picked up a suitcase. They closed the door very carefully and tiptoed as quietly as they could down the back stairs and out into the little square behind the hotel. They crept along a couple of back streets and rejoined the road by the river a couple of hundred yards from the Hôtel d'Artagnan. Here was another room reserved for them in the Hôtel Mousquetaire. Powerscourt had booked the room at the same time he made the reservations for the pilgrim party. The hotel manager had been warned that they would be late. Their room was very like the other one with a balcony looking out over the river.

'How long before you go back, my love?' Lady Lucy was feeling very nervous.

'An hour or so, I'm not sure,' said Powerscourt.

'You will take great care, Francis? We don't need any heroics. The Inspector's men can look after the rough end of things.' Even as she spoke Lady Lucy knew she was wasting her energies. If there was a rough end of things then Francis would be in the thick of it.

Just after midnight Powerscourt kissed his wife goodbye. She held him very tight, reluctant to let her man go. 'Good luck, my own love,' she said, 'I shall be waiting for you.'

Powerscourt made his way back to the Hôtel d'Artagnan very slowly. He was thinking about Alexandre Dumas's legacy, hotels named after him in this little town and all over France, small boys all over Europe acting out the adventures of his characters in bedrooms and parks and back gardens. He remembered reading *The Three Musketeers* as a child. His father had found him a wooden sword and he used to charge around the lawns and shrubberies of Powerscourt House having long battles with his enemies. There was a lone fisherman on the river, his lines draped over the back of the boat, drifting downstream with the current. Above, the sky was ablaze with stars and the moon was nearly full. He worried about Lady Lucy, left behind with the musketeers and with no knight errant to protect her.

On his way in he nearly bumped into the Inspector, tiptoeing down the stairs. They did not speak. There was a long corridor running the length of the hotel on all three upper floors. The bedrooms were off to the left. Every twenty yards or so there was a small alcove set back into the wall where a man would be virtually invisible to anybody coming towards him, a murderer at large in the night hours. Powerscourt's position was in one of these niches, some twenty yards from the door of his room. Johnny Fitzgerald was twenty yards behind Powerscourt towards the stairs. At each end of the corridor there were stairs to the next floor or the floor below. The two former soldiers were united again, waiting for another battle as they had done so often in the past.

Powerscourt was squatting on the ground, his eyes fixed on

the further set of stairs. He wondered if this most difficult case might be about to end. He thought briefly about taking Lucy away somewhere when it was all over. Perhaps they could complete the pilgrim route and go to Santiago de Compostela and stand beneath the Portal de la Gloria in the Cathedral of St James.

Johnny Fitzgerald was trying to remember the names of the *Premiers Crus* of Bordeaux, the most majestic wines in France. Château Lafite Rothschild, Château Latour, Château Margaux he said to himself, where the hell was the other one? Johnny was fairly sure there were only four of them. He tried to imagine one of those wine maps the tourist industry are so fond of with vineyards marked out by little bottles. Château Haut-Brion, he remembered at last, and it wasn't even in Bordeaux, it was in Graves to the south of the city.

One o'clock passed. Very faintly from the ground floor Powerscourt heard the chime of a ghostly clock, striking out the hours in a ghostly hotel. Only it wasn't a ghost they were waiting for tonight, crouching in the dark, but a killer who would come with a knife or a piece of wire to commit another murder. Inspector Léger was worrying about the vegetables in his garden. He suspected his *haricots verts* would be beyond revival when he eventually reached home. His wife would shrug her shoulders as she always did and proclaim her innocence, saying she had carried out the written instructions the Inspector always left behind. He never reproached her. She failed because she gardened without love, the Inspector believed. He thought it odd how the plants and the flowers always seemed to know when they were unloved and then just pined away.

Lady Lucy wondered about going out on to her balcony and looking back to the d'Artagnan. She decided against it. She tried to work out at what time of night she would commit a murder. One o'clock, probably too soon, she felt. Late readers might still have their lights on and hear you creep by in the corridor outside. Two o'clock? Three o'clock? Surely only an insomniac would be still awake at such an hour. Three thirty, she decided, that would be a good time. Just over two hours to go. She shivered slightly and wrapped a shawl round her shoulders. She said another prayer for Francis.

Two o'clock passed and then three. Powerscourt had eliminated three people from his inquiries in his mind. That left five suspects in the frame. Suddenly he wished the murderer would hurry up. Sleep was washing over him and he didn't know how much longer he could hold out against it. He tiptoed over to Johnny Fitzgerald and made a couple of signs with his fingers. Johnny nodded. He, Johnny, would have to watch both sets of stairs until Powerscourt returned. He was just going outside for a breath of air.

Powerscourt crept down the stairs and out into the street. Nothing stirred in Aire-sur-l'Adour. The nocturnal fisherman seemed to have gone home, or drifted further down the river. Perhaps he would have fish for breakfast. Powerscourt breathed deeply. The air was soft, almost like velvet. A slight breeze was whispering through the trees. He shook his head vigorously and returned to his position.

The Inspector had carried out a major review of the dispositions in his vegetable garden. Next year, he thought, he would try everything in a different place. He dreamt, as he often did, of fruit trees, with apples and pears and plums growing on his own land. But he knew his garden faced the wrong way and the trees would not prosper in his little patch. Perhaps Lucille and he should move house for a south-facing garden. He rubbed at his calves. Much more of this, he said to himself, and I'll get cramp.

Four dim, distant chimes told the watching three that their vigil would soon be over. Powerscourt wondered who would be who from Alexandre Dumas's *The Three Musketeers*. Johnny Fitzgerald would be Porthos, all drink and swagger. He, Powerscourt, would like to have been d'Artagnan, but he felt, if he was honest, that he might be more like Aramis, liable to gloom and fits of melancholy. The Inspector would have to be an unlikely d'Artagnan, the first d'Artagnan in living memory to be losing his hair.

Lady Lucy had nodded off in her chair. She awoke shortly after half past four. She looked round wildly for Powerscourt but he wasn't there. What was happening back there at the hotel? Had the murderer been apprehended, caught, literally, in the act? Were Powerscourt and Johnny Fitzgerald even now toasting their success in the hotel bar with the Inspector? Lady Lucy thought that would be very unfair, leaving her up here with her terrible knot of anxiety, far from the celebrations. She said another prayer for her husband.

Shortly after six they could hear noises down below as the hotel staff began to prepare for another day. It was hopeless now, Powerscourt said bitterly to himself. No murderer in his right mind would set out on a killing spree with the hotel maids liable to walk past him in the corridor. He went over to the Inspector and led him and Johnny Fitzgerald into Powerscourt's bedroom. He replaced the light bulb he had taken out all those hours before. What they saw left them speechless. The floor had turned virtually white with feathers. They lay in heaps beside the two beds. They were scattered like confetti all over the floor. Some of them had drifted upwards and stuck to the walls. The housekeeper's bolsters were no more. They both had great knife slits in their sides. The two wigs had been slashed and lay in fragments, nestling incongruously among the fallen feathers.

'*Merde!*' said the Inspector.

'Mother of God!' said Johnny Fitzgerald.

'Look,' said Powerscourt, pointing to the balcony door which was wide open, the cold air of dawn flooding into the room. He strode out on to the balcony.

'He must have nerves of steel, our murderer,' he said. 'He must have made his way down from his floor on to a balcony, then crept along that ledge to our room. He must have been in his stockinged feet so as not to make a noise.'

The Inspector looked down at the ledge, just visible in the

light from the bedroom. 'That's right, that's how he must have come. What fools we've been, fools, all of us. We have five, no, six people on duty inside and not a soul outside watching the front of the hotel. And he's got away with it too!'

Powerscourt thought there had been a great deal of violence used on the bolsters and the wigs. Maybe the murderer was venting his frustration when he realized there were no humans in the room or in the beds. Lady Lucy would have perished too, if she had been there. Both bolsters had been ripped to shreds, great gashes spoiling the linen. He walked back to the balcony. A new day was dawning over Aquitaine. There was a slight shimmer of mist lying over the river which would soon dissolve in the morning sun. The birds were singing merrily, chattering to each other in the branches of the tall trees by the Adour. One or two people were already about in the street. It looked as if it was going to be a beautiful day. For Powerscourt, making his sad way back to Lady Lucy, it was yet another failure. His plan lay in tatters on the bedroom floor, ripped to shreds like the housekeeper's bolsters. The murderer was still at large to kill again. On Michael Delaney's timetable he had four days left to find the murderer. Four days, or face a lifetime of failure.

20

They reached the Spanish border in the middle of the afternoon. Lady Lucy spent much of the time asleep, hands folded neatly on her lap. Johnny Fitzgerald was reading a small book called *The Birds of Europe*, checking out what he might find in Spain. Powerscourt continued with *Michael Delaney, Robber Baron*. As they moved out of France the landscape was dominated by the jagged peaks of the Pyrenees, blessed with many waterfalls and home, as Johnny informed his companions, to large numbers of vultures and brown bears. Inspector Léger came to say his farewells. He wished Powerscourt all the luck in the world with the rest of his investigation. He was to telegraph immediately once the mystery was solved. He was gallant with Lady Lucy, saying what a pleasure it had been to meet her. As he led his men out of the border station, he took them first into the nearest bar.

'I'm going to buy you boys a drink, maybe two,' he announced. 'We've got rid of those bloody pilgrims at last. Thank God I didn't listen to those fools in the Town Hall in Moissac or we'd still be there. France is well shot of them.'

'Do you know who the murderer is, sir?' asked one of his men.

'I haven't a clue. I don't think our English friend has either. Let's hope the pilgrims kill each other before they get to Santiago.'

The Spanish Inspector spoke perfect English. His name was Felipe Mendieta, son of an English mother who had fallen in love with a Spanish waiter and married him in Spain. The father Mendieta had now graduated to owning his own restaurant. The tapas, his son assured them, were the finest in Navarre. He brought a priest with him, Father Olivares, who opened religious negotiations with Father Kennedy in Latin. The Spanish authorities, Inspector Mendieta assured them, took the same position as the French as far as the pilgrims were concerned. This train would take them all the way to Santiago. Nobody else would be allowed on board. Overnight accommodation would once again be in the town jail or the police cells, whichever could accommodate them. Maggie Delaney would be accommodated in hospital or nunnery as before. It was for their own safety. The Spanish authorities were most anxious that the pilgrims, having endured so much on their journey, should find spiritual satisfaction at the end. Inspector Mendieta trusted that the presence of Father Olivares would lend spiritual comfort. Powerscourt and his party were, of course, free to come and go as they pleased.

The Inspector made his way down the train to make himself known to the pilgrims. There was a sudden cry from Powerscourt. 'Listen to this,' he said, 'here's another Delaney crime! This author doesn't treat the subject chronologically, he treats it by industry. We're in oil now. This must have happened twenty or thirty years ago. Delaney and two other people, Richard Jackson and Ralph Singer, buy up an oil concession in Ohio. Delaney runs it. He tells the other two after a year or so that it's no good, the prospector teams haven't found anything, they're not going to get rich this time. So they all agree to sell out to a company called Michigan Oil. So far so good. Three months later Jackson and Singer discover that the owner of Michigan Oil is none other than Michael Delaney. And, surprise, surprise, the land in the concession is dripping with oil, it's worth fortunes. Delaney has cheated them; God, he's a bad man. I'll have to ask Father Kennedy if he can be forgiven this many sins.'

'What did the other two characters do, Francis?' asked Johnny Fitzgerald. 'Did they drink themselves to death like the other fellow in New York with the socially ambitious wife?'

Powerscourt held up his hand while he finished the chapter. 'Jackson and Singer never recovered from this betrayal, the man says. Their business careers failed. One ended up working for the US Mail and the other one earns his daily bread as a clerk in a hardware shop. This is what the man says: '"Think of how their careers might have been different if they had not been defrauded by this wicked man. Think of the turn their lives and the lives of their families might have taken had they not been swindled out of what was rightfully theirs. Think of the sad end to their days, when the American Dream, for them, turned into the American Nightmare, the promise of a better future that is the birthright of all Americans turned to dust in the earth of Ohio. Think of yet another crime entered in Delaney's ledger of wickedness, think of the misery his greed has brought on those who cross his path. Think of what his fate may be."'

'Children, Francis?' asked Lady Lucy. 'Any sons who could have lived on to take revenge?'

'The book doesn't say,' said Powerscourt. 'This is like all the other possible shades from Delaney's past. Why wait so long? And why, if you want to do away with Delaney, do you kill all these others first? I don't think it adds up,' he said sadly, putting the book down on the table. 'There is one thing about *Michael Delaney, Robber Baron*. It makes you look at the man in a totally different light.'

They were pulling away from the mountains now. The train stopped at a tiny station in the middle of nowhere and a message was handed over to Inspector Mendieta. He laughed as he rejoined the Powerscourt party at the back of the train.

'The pilgrims are going to be happy on their night in Pamplona!' he said with a smile. 'The town jail is full, the police cells are full, so my boss has kicked a load of people out of one of the town's finest hotels to put the pilgrims on the upper floors.'

'Is there a crime wave in the town?' asked Johnny Fitzgerald.

The Inspector laughed. 'You could call it a crime wave, I suppose. Today is Tuesday, the tenth of July and Pamplona is in the middle of Fiesta, or Festival. People come from all over for the bullfights and the religious services and the parties and the bands and the excitement. And, I nearly forgot, for the running of the bulls. Fiesta is held at the same time every year, from the sixth to the fourteenth of July. Because all the thieves and pickpockets in southern France and northern Spain know these dates, they come too for their own festival of crime. Every year the jails are full at this time. The hotel will probably have its own share of bands and jugglers and other entertainers passing through this evening. Even though the pilgrims will not be allowed out, the fiesta will come to them. The patron saint of Fiesta is San Fermin. Among other things he is the patron saint of wineskins. They sell in the thousand at this time for people to refill at the little wine shops in the side streets. They say some people don't go to bed at all for the entire duration of the festival.'

Their dinner later that day in Pamplona seemed to consist of tens of courses, served at irregular intervals. Johnny Fitzgerald maintained that the waiters popped out into the street for half an hour or so between courses. A brass band came through, some of the musicians swaying slightly as they blew. A team of jugglers danced their way through the tables, the lemons flying over the diners' heads. A pair of troubadours serenaded them, the boy playing the guitar and the girl singing the sad song of her only true love, a matador who perished in the ring through thinking of her rather than concentrating on the bull which gored him to death. Throughout the proceedings, as dish followed dish and the rough local red flowed on, the Inspector's men never left their posts, eyes fixed on the exits to the dining room, hands never far from the pistols in their belts. The Inspector himself was by the main door, sometimes conversing with the kitchen staff or the waiters, sometimes checking on a list of names in the dark blue notebook he brought out from time to time. The pilgrims were all named in his book and a series of little ticks by the side of each one showed that Inspector Mendieta had recorded their presence.

Shortly after five o'clock in the morning Powerscourt woke to an urgent tapping on his door. He grabbed his pistol from the drawer beside his bed and opened the door a fraction.

'You must come at once!' the Inspector whispered. 'Some of the pilgrims have escaped! They are not in their rooms! My man has been bound and gagged and cannot remember for the present exactly what happened. Join me by the front desk in a moment.'

Powerscourt wondered if he should wake Lady Lucy. He left her a short note instead. 'Some pilgrims escaped. Gone to look for them. Love, Francis.'

He collected Johnny Fitzgerald on the way, Johnny protesting about the early hour and wondering if any of those wine shops would be open yet. The Inspector told them the bad news. It seemed as if the younger ones had managed to escape. 'Wee Jimmy Delaney's gone, so has Charlie Flanagan and Waldo Mulligan and Christy Delaney and Jack O'Driscoll, five of them altogether, all the younger ones.'

'Have they taken their things with them?' asked Powerscourt. 'Has all their stuff gone from their rooms?'

'That's a very good question, my lord, I didn't think about it.'

'Let me go and look,' said Powerscourt, 'I know what most of their packs look like.' With that he sprinted up the stairs to the top floor. There were still revellers in the streets outside, maudlin songs floating through the open windows of the hotel. All the pilgrim packs were still there. That was a relief, he said to himself as he raced back down the stairs. Or was it?

'Their belongings are all still there,' he said. 'In one sense that is good for they obviously intend to come back here at some stage. Perhaps they've just gone to join the party. But in another sense, Inspector, nothing could be worse. In every single murder on this journey the victim has been lured away by the killer, up a hill of volcanic rock, over to the side of a river, out to the back of a church, up to an upper room in a set of cloisters, and every time the killer strikes. All of those pilgrims bar one are in deadly peril, and that one is the murderer. Where easier to kill than in the streets of Pamplona in the hour before dawn when another body lying in the street will not arouse any interest? Even if there is blood flowing it will be taken for wine. We must search the whole town until we find them, Inspector. Pray God that the missing five come back alive!'

'Lord Powerscourt, forgive me.' A hotel porter had materialized from behind the front desk. 'This came for you yesterday morning. We forgot to pass it on. Our apologies.'

Powerscourt was about to stuff it in his pocket but something told him to open it. He skimmed rapidly through the contents. It came from Franklin Bentley in Washington. 'I have news from Pittsburgh,' the message began. 'Thirty years ago Michael Delaney lived there. He was married with a son aged two. When the wife was three months pregnant Delaney walked out and went to live in New York. Wife died in childbirth. Baby stillborn. Priests and nun contacted many relations in hope of finding somebody who would take on the boy and bring him up.'

Outside a drunk was singing in the street. Powerscourt had no idea what was coming next. 'Nuns even offered to pay for him to be taken back to England or Ireland or wherever a willing Delaney might be found. One nun volunteered to escort him across the Atlantic to a new home. But there were no willing Delaneys. There was no new home. They all refused to bring up a child who was a member of their family. The boy was eventually adopted by a devout Catholic couple with no children of their own, and here is a strange coincidence. The priest who gave me this information said I was not the only person to ask him for news about the boy

Delaney. Six months ago a very angry man had been to see him who had discovered adoption details in his father's papers after his father died unexpectedly. He went to the priest for confirmation of what he had discovered. Reluctantly the priest backed up the details. I myself had to make a generous contribution to the Church Missionary Society before he divulged all. This man was indeed the little son Michael Delaney abandoned. He had been given the surname of his new parents. He left the priest an address in Washington to send any further information that might emerge. His name is Waldo Mulligan. Hope this information is useful,' Bentley concluded. 'Something tells me you will not be looking for any more research on this side of the Atlantic. Warm regards, Bentley.'

'Sorry for the delay,' Powerscourt said to his colleagues. 'Inspector, Johnny, we have a name at last. If your men find Waldo Mulligan, Inspector, arrest him immediately. We haven't time now for me to tell you why, but I am virtually certain he is the killer. Now, we must find the pilgrims before he kills again.'

'I will fetch more men,' said the Inspector. 'I suggest you try in that direction over there, my lord. That is the area where the running of the bulls takes place. And quite soon too. If I were a young man, tired of being cooped up by policemen, that is where I would go.'

Powerscourt and Johnny Fitzgerald set off in the dark. Five prisoners had escaped. In an hour or two the bulls would be loosed to charge down the streets of Pamplona. The streets were wet from the night rain. Watching them from the darkest point behind the hotel Waldo Mulligan set off in pursuit of them, careful not to be spotted, his right hand holding very firmly on to something in his inside pocket.

Powerscourt lost Johnny Fitzgerald five minutes after leaving the hotel. He shouted his name but there was no answer. He was now in a great press of people, almost all of them young, heading for the start of the running of the bulls in Santo Domingo Street. The dawn was coming and he saw that nearly all of the young men were wearing white shirts and bright red scarves round their necks. Some of the older ones wore red sashes round their waists. They had the forced gaiety, Powerscourt thought, of young men about to go into battle. He had seen it so often before, a mixture of bravado, excitement and a fear that you would never admit to except to very close friends. Young men had to keep up a show in these circumstances, they couldn't let people see they were frightened. Many of them held rolled-up newspapers in their hands to deflect the bulls' attention. They told jokes or made plans to meet their girls after the run.

Powerscourt found himself thinking about an angry Waldo Mulligan conferring with the priest in Pittsburgh. He told himself to concentrate on the events ahead or he could end up killed or injured while his mind had wandered off to Washington. He could see now that parts of the route were lined with double rows of barriers with a small gap between them to allow runners to escape or medical staff into the route to remove the wounded. There was a clattering up above as people in houses with balconies crowded on to them drinking great cups of chocolate to keep warm.

Waldo Mulligan had manoeuvred himself into a position three or four people behind Powerscourt and almost invisible to him. It was ten to seven in the morning. Powerscourt and the others were held in by police barriers keeping the runners in their place. There was no escape now.

The running of the bulls in Pamplona has an ancient history going back to the days when the bulls were brought into the town to fight in the public square, which was also used as a bullring. In modern time the bulls are brought in at eleven o'clock the night before and kept in a corral. Six bulls make the run accompanied by one group of eight oxen with bells round their necks and followed by a further three oxen to sweep up any stray bulls on the route. Each bull weighs about twelve hundred pounds and can run at fifteen miles an hour, faster than most humans. For the bulls this is their first exposure to masses of people and to loud noise so they can become disoriented. If that happens they can turn dangerous. The route starts at Santo Domingo on a slope that favours the bulls as their front legs are shorter than the hind ones. After about three hundred yards the bulls enter the Plaza Consistorial Mercaderes for a stretch of a hundred yards or so. Then there is a sharp right-hand turn of ninety degrees called the Estafeta Bend which leads into the longest stretch of the route, the Calle Estefeta, a narrow street three hundred yards long where the only protection is in the doorways. Then there is a short stretch called the Telefonica where the double barriers come into play, acting as a funnel. The bulls are slower now, approaching the *callejon* or lane which leads into the bullring. There the runners are told to fan out along the side of the bullring while the bulls are corralled again, ready for the bullfight later in the day and death in the afternoon.

Powerscourt was trying to remember what he had been told years before about the *encierro*, the running of the bulls. It didn't last very long, he seemed to recall. Only the brave or the foolhardy tried to run with the bulls for as long as they could before they slipped off to one side. Some reckless souls, he thought, started their run near the end and tried to time it so they just beat the weary bulls into the ring. Above all, he remembered, it may be many things, an ancient ritual, a trial of manhood, a test of nerve, but it's not a race. There was no medal for the first runner or bull into the ring. Above all it showed the same Spanish obsession with death that marked the bullfight itself. There it was usually the bulls who died. Here on these narrow streets with the crowds behind the barriers and up on their balconies it was the humans who were more likely to perish. The prospect of sudden and violent death brought that extra frisson to the spectacle.

Waldo Mulligan was just two paces behind Powerscourt now.

He could trip him up, or shove him into the path of a bull. It was five to seven. The young men began to sing to San Fermin to ask for his protection. 'We ask of San Fermin, for he is our patron, to guide us in the bull run and give us his blessing.' They waved their rolled-up newspapers and shouted 'Viva San Fermin!' in Spanish and in Basque. At three minutes to seven they sang it again.

Suddenly Powerscourt turned round. His eyes locked on to those of Waldo Mulligan as surely as a matador might lock eyes with a bull in the ring. Powerscourt knew. He knew that Waldo Mulligan was the killer. Worse, looking at Mulligan, Powerscourt was certain that Mulligan knew that Powerscourt knew that he, Mulligan, was the killer. The prayer rang out for a third and final time. Powerscourt joined in where it talked about guiding us in the bull run. Mulligan was going to try to kill him in the next few minutes. Death would come for him in the morning.

Lady Lucy felt helpless when she realized Francis had gone in pursuit of the missing pilgrims. She wondered what she should do. If she went out on to the streets she could be another potential victim. She remembered the two bolsters hacked to shreds in the hotel in Aire-sur-l'Adour. She opened the doors and went out on to the balcony. The sun was high in the sky now. It was going to be a beautiful day. She could hear the noise of the running of the bulls but she could not see it. Lady Lucy didn't know that her husband was in deadly peril, and not just from the twelve-hundred-pound bulls.

Johnny Fitzgerald too had been sucked into the event, but further down the course from Powerscourt. He had made friends with a man with a couple of wineskins tied round his waist. Johnny thought the day was beginning to look up already.

At seven o'clock precisely the clock of San Cernin struck the hour. A rocket shot up into the sky, announcing that the mighty gates of the corral holding the bulls and the oxen had been opened. The police removed the barriers that had held the runners in. The *encierro* was under way. Powerscourt's group began to run, not very fast, down Santa Domingo towards the Plaza. Other braver or more foolish souls waited to run as long as they could with the bulls in this opening stage. You could hear them before you saw them, Powerscourt thought, a rumbling noise like thunder getting closer or the pounding noise the closest spectators heard as the horses came round the last bend in the Derby.

As he looked round he saw that Waldo Mulligan was right behind him and trying to trip him up. Very suddenly Powerscourt turned and smashed his elbow into the centre of Mulligan's mouth as hard as he could. Mulligan stumbled and held his hand to his face. The crowd was so tightly packed that he only slipped back a little, but he was no longer directly behind Powerscourt. Looking back again Powerscourt saw the bulls for the first time, dark brown brutes running as fast as they could, threatening to trample anybody who stood in their way. They were about twenty yards behind them now. Mulligan, swearing to himself, had returned to a position behind Powerscourt. Again he tried to trip him up. Then the crowd behind carried him to the right-hand side of the course. Powerscourt had been edging to his left, to the side of the street, away from the centre where the bulls were running. They had reached the Estafeta Bend now and the bulls were ahead of them now, two young men running just in front of them at top speed waving their rolled-up newspapers in the air.

Then disaster struck. The cobblestones were slippery. The largest and fiercest-looking bull slipped on the wet surface right at the edge of the ninety-degree bend. He fell slowly to the ground, less than ten feet from the crowd. The bull didn't seem to know how to get up again for it took him the best part of a minute. He looked around sadly. All his companions had disappeared. He staggered towards the centre of the street.

Runners swerved left and right to avoid him. He straightened himself up at last and seemed to Powerscourt to have an expression that said, Somebody is going to pay for this. Powerscourt pressed himself up against a wall. Some of his companions flung themselves to the ground and curled up into human balls. Powerscourt had often been in positions of extreme danger in his military service, under attack from mounted Pathan tribesmen on the North-West Frontier, strafed with shell fire in the Boer War, climbing up dangerous mountains for a night attack in India. Never had he been as frightened as this. The bulls were so big and so stupid. Anything could happen. This one, stumbling about in the wet street, might soon be close enough to shake hands or shake horns.

There was a scream from one of the balconies. The surrounding crowd had fallen silent, holding on to each other in their fear. Was the bull strong enough to break through the barrier? Would he soon be amongst them, goring as he went? The bull turned, still disoriented, and went back towards the other side. Powerscourt saw Waldo Mulligan shaking his head and trying to make himself invisible pressed against the barrier. Younger, fitter or more frightened people were climbing over the top of the fences, helping hands waiting to lift them to safety. Maybe it was the movement that tipped the bull over the edge. He stared at Waldo Mulligan. Mulligan looked at the bull and raised his fists to cover his face. The bull may have taken that as a hostile act. A couple of steps and the bull bent down. He gored Mulligan just above the groin, the horn ripping deep into his body, and flung him backwards to land on the cobblestones of the Calle Estafeta.

Blood was pouring onto the street. The crowd was screaming. Mulligan's blood, almost the same shade of red as the scarves and the sashes, dripped across the cobblestones. The bull glowered at Mulligan as if thinking of a second goring to reinforce the first. Powerscourt remained pressed against his wall. The bull lumbered down the edge of the barrier where the crowd were now running away as fast as they could; he was looking for another victim. A group of cowherds with long sticks who were policing the event forced the bull back into the middle of the road and down the street to rejoin his companions in the bullring. Four medical orderlies raced through the gap in the barriers and put Mulligan on a stretcher. They carried him down to the hospital in the bullring. The staff there were used to gored people. They saw them virtually every afternoon on the days of the bullfights. Another rocket shot up into the morning sky. The bulls were all in the bullring. It was four minutes past seven.

Lady Lucy could sense the excitement as she looked at the crowds streaming past her balcony, heading for the bullring to hear news of the victim. When she went downstairs to the reception a porter with a little English told her that an Englishman had been gored running with the bulls. He pointed her in the direction of the hospital. Lady Lucy found she could not hurry as she would have wished. The crowd, sombre now, the high spirits before the start ebbing away like Mulligan's blood, was so thick that all she could do was to allow herself to be carried along. Was it Francis? Was it Johnny? Were they even now breathing their last, their insides ripped to shreds by the horns of a bull, and she wasn't there to hold their hands and stroke their faces?

Running as fast as he could, dodging in and out of the crowd, Powerscourt forced his way into the hospital. He had to speak to Mulligan before he died. He explained his position to a doctor who spoke French, that he was investigating four murders, that he believed Mulligan to be the murderer, and that he must speak to him before he died. If he died. Wait till we have looked at him, said the doctor. Inspector Mendieta appeared, panting, to add local weight to the foreigner's pleas. They sat on hard chairs in a little waiting room. Pictures of bullfighters and bullfights filled the walls. It was growing hot in the Pamplona hospital. A couple of flies were buzzing around the ceiling. There were no pictures of the bulls' victims who were carried here on what proved all too often to be their last journey.

'You can have a couple of minutes,' the doctor said, 'no more. He may not last that long.'

Mulligan was heavily bandaged right round his middle. His dark eyes looked up at Powerscourt, filled with pain that turned to hatred.

'I think you should tell us the truth now,' said Powerscourt, speaking very quietly. 'Did you commit the four murders? You don't have to speak if that's too painful, you can just nod your head.'

Mulligan's eyes travelled to and fro between Powerscourt and the Inspector, coming to rest on a painting of the Virgin on the wall. Maybe it was the Madonna that did it. He nodded his head, slowly but unmistakably.

'Are you Michael Delaney's son? Were you planning to kill him at the end?'

Again Waldo Mulligan's eyes came to rest on the picture of the Mother of God. Pray for us now and in the hour of our death, Amen. Another nod.

'Were you planning to kill all the pilgrims? Because they too were Delaneys?'

Mulligan grew agitated. His eyes searched for the doctor. His face turned even paler.

'Gentlemen,' said the doctor, 'I'm afraid you must go now. The patient is becoming disturbed. If you wait outside I will tell you more in a moment.'

They passed a priest coming into the ward as they went out. The last rites had arrived for the man from Washington. They would never know how many pilgrims Mulligan intended to kill. They would never know whether he picked his victims at random as the opportunity presented itself or whether he had a predetermined list of targets in his mind. Half an hour later the doctor came back to tell them Mulligan was dead. He made the sign of the cross.

Walking back to the hotel, Powerscourt suddenly realized the full import of what he had just seen. He thought back to Franklin Bentley's telegram. Waldo Mulligan had plotted his revenge on the relations who had abandoned him and the father who had deserted him. Mulligan must have thought the pilgrimage was his lucky break, the perfect opportunity to take his revenge with all those Delaneys collected in one place like lambs to the slaughter. Michael Delaney had launched this great venture as a thank you to God for saving the life of one son. He did not know that another son had travelled in his party halfway round the world on a deadly mission of retribution for events thirty years before. Nemesis travelled from the New World to the Old. The pilgrimage had been ruined by murder, the pilgrims travelling by day in a sealed train and sleeping most of the time on the floor of police cells or the unforgiving concrete of the local jails. Now it was clear that another of Delaney's sons had come out of the past to kill him and nearly succeeded. James was the son who was saved in the New York hospital under the picture of St James the Great. Waldo Mulligan was the other one, abandoned all those years ago in Pittsburgh. His life had not been spared. It was ended early on a Wednesday morning by the horns of a bull from Pamplona.

21

Everybody was back in the hotel by half past eight that morning. The other pilgrims had been rounded up partying on the streets or drinking in some of the bars that never closed during Fiesta. Powerscourt had all the pilgrims assemble in a private room on the first floor. The Inspector joined them. Michael Delaney was wearing a very bright suit of yellow check today. Alex Bentley worked his way round so he could sit next to Lady Lucy at the top table. Johnny Fitzgerald wondered if anybody would notice him taking the occasional swig from his new wineskin. He hoped to be able to spend a day or two in the mountains soon, looking for vultures.

Powerscourt rose to his feet. He was finding it hard, as he had told Lady Lucy five minutes before, to believe that the case was over. It was finished. Normal life without wine cellars and bodies in cloisters could resume. He was sombre as he began.

'Ladies', he nodded to Maggie Delaney, 'and gentlemen, I have both good and bad news for you this morning. I have to say I think the good outweighs the bad, but you must decide that for yourselves. We have another death, I'm afraid. Waldo Mulligan took part this morning in the running of the bulls. I'm sure you have all heard of it by now. He was unfortunate enough to be in the wrong place at the wrong time. One bull got detached from the rest. I am told they are at their most dangerous when they are disoriented and separated from their companions. Waldo Mulligan was gored by the bull just above the groin. He died of his injuries shortly afterwards in the hospital in the bullring. A priest was with him at the end.'

Powerscourt did not mention that Mulligan had tried to kill him, to trip him up beneath the hooves of the bulls.

'That is the bad news. The good news is that there will be no more murders. Waldo Mulligan confessed to me before he died that he was the killer. He was responsible for all four deaths. The Inspector here was with me at the time. He can confirm it. The special trains, the nights in the cells should all stop now, once the Spanish authorities give their approval.'

The Inspector said that he hoped to complete the formalities by that afternoon. There was a moment of silence, as if all this was too much to take in at once. Then there was a torrent of questions. When did Powerscourt know that Mulligan was the killer? How had he found out? Did he think Mulligan would have tried to kill more people? And, the most regular of all, why had Mulligan done it? What was his motive?

Michael Delaney rose to sum up the views of the pilgrims. 'Could I say first of all, Powerscourt, how grateful we are to you for having solved the mystery. I may have spoken harshly to you the other day but I take back everything I said. And could we ask you to tell us something about your investigation?' Powerscourt felt reluctant. Then he told himself that these pilgrims had lived with the threat of death for a long time. One short walk with the killer might have been enough to end their lives. But he felt, even after their row a few days before, that he should spare Michael Delaney.

'I will do that, Mr Delaney,' he said, 'but could I suggest that you do not stay with us now? There are some matters you might not like to hear in public. I would be perfectly happy to give you the details in private later on this morning.'

'Nonsense, man, I've got nothing to hide.'

Oh yes you have, Powerscourt said to himself, wondering if Delaney had blotted out large sections of his own past.

'Really, Mr Delaney, I do think it would be better if I spoke with you in private.'

'Nonsense, man, I'm not scared of what you might have to say.'

Powerscourt wondered briefly if he should not give the details of Delaney's past crimes. Then he reflected that that would not be fair to the pilgrims. Delaney had been given his chance.

'The first murder, the one that brought me here,' he began, 'was that of John Delaney, pushed, I believe, off the volcanic rock path of St Michel to his death. The poor man was scarcely off the train from England. Any suggestion that he might have suffered from vertigo was banished from my mind when I learnt from England that he was employed as a window cleaner. There was no motive that I could see. You will recall that Lucy and I asked you to fill out various forms about your ancestors, that we tried to engage you in conversation about your parents and grandparents. We were looking for connections. There were none that we could find.

'The second murder was another apparently motiveless crime. So, it seemed, was the third. So, it seemed, was the fourth. They did have one thing in common. This was a murderer who operated on the spur of the moment and at lightning speed. If he saw a chance to lure one of his victims away from the rest of the party, a walk by the river at night perhaps, a look at the upper chamber at Moissac cloisters maybe, he would seize his moment the instant it appeared. Out would come the knife or the blows against a pillar and the deed would be over in a matter of minutes. There was one possible interpretation that did present itself to me from this modus operandi. It seemed to me unlikely that the victims were pre-determined. There wasn't a plan to kill Patrick MacLoughlin or Stephen Lewis or Girvan Connolly. The victim could as easily have been any one of you here, if you had been in the right place for the killer to strike. If the opportunity arose, the nearest pilgrim would do. If this theory was right, there were two possible explanations. One, that the man was a serial killer in the manner of Jack the Ripper, that he killed at random because he enjoyed it or derived some strange satisfaction from the act of murder. The other was that the victims were all killed because they were Delaneys, that the murderer had a huge grudge against every Delaney he could find. You might ask why, in that case, he didn't kill Michael Delaney himself and have done with it. My answer, and this, I have to say, is supposition on my part, is that he did intend to kill Michael Delaney, but as his last victim, not his first.'

Powerscourt paused to take a sip of his coffee. The pilgrims sat spellbound. Jack O'Driscoll was taking notes. Christy Delaney was scribbling away too, though Powerscourt felt it might be a love letter rather than an account of his theories.

'All along, all through this case, I have thought that the answer lay somewhere in the chequered past of Michael Delaney. I did, of course, ask him if there were any skeletons in his cupboard. He denied it. So I have had inquiries made in both Ireland and America about events in Michael Delaney's past. Let me tell you about them in chronological order. The first of these events took place during the worst years of the Irish famine. Most of the Delaney family in County Cork were starving. Their potatoes had failed, like everybody else's, they had no savings and no crops to plant for the future. Their only option was the workhouse. And almost everybody who went into the workhouse at that time never came out again. But, not far away, there was a family of more prosperous Delaneys. They had money and food to spare. Time and time again various of the poor Delaneys made appeals for help to their richer relations. Time and time again they were refused. Twenty-four Delaneys went into the workhouse. Only one, a boy of about twelve, survived. All the rest perished. The richer Delaneys subsequently emigrated to America. Was it possible that the lone survivor, or his sons, traced Michael Delaney as a descendant of the family who had let their relations die? It seemed to me that this was a very long shot. There were too many variables and too many unknowns. And the time scale was too long. Corsicans or Sicilians might be able to sustain a vendetta over a period of over sixty years, but I doubted if the Irish would be able to manage it.

'Maggie Delaney mentioned a book written some years ago about the organizer of this pilgrimage called *Michael Delaney, Robber Baron*. Delaney was so alarmed at the prospect of this book being published about him and his alleged misdemeanours that he bought up every copy and had them all pulped. Nobody ever got to read it. What Delaney didn't know was that four copies had been sent to England. Johnny Fitzgerald managed to track one of them down and it is now on my bedside table upstairs. There were two pieces of deception that could have given rise to a mighty hatred of Delaney. On the first occasion he pretended to form a joint railroad company with a man called Wharton. Only it wasn't a joint company at all. Delaney put all the shares in his own name, cutting the other man out altogether. The company prospered but Delaney's so-called partner did not. His other ventures failed. Wharton took to drink. He failed to service his debts. His wife left him. Then he killed himself, leaving one small son as survivor. This son would now be in his thirties. But there were doubts in my mind as to whether he could have been the murderer. Why had he waited so long? Why take the trouble to come all the way to France when he could have hired a couple of killers in New York City to murder Delaney? And surely such a killer would begin with Michael Delaney himself? Why go to the trouble of killing all the other pilgrims? The same objections, I thought, applied to the children of the other people Delaney supposedly swindled in an oil prospecting business.'

Lady Lucy had been casting surreptitious glances at Michael Delaney as her husband ran through the chronicle of his crimes. His fingers were drumming nervously on the table in front of him. His face remained impassive. He might, she thought, have been sitting through a rather disagreeable board meeting where the results were not as good as had been expected. She wondered if he guessed at what was to come. Johnny Fitzgerald winked at the pilgrims and took an enormous draught from his wineskin. Then he passed it over to the pilgrims. Thirsty work, he felt, listening to Powerscourt describing his theories.

'It was only very recently that I came across the most promising line of inquiry. It transpired that thirty-odd years ago Michael Delaney had been married for the first time. He was then living in Pittsburgh. They had a son and then when Delaney's wife was expecting their second child he walked out without warning and without leaving any means of support for his family and went to New York, where few questions are asked about newcomers. The wife died in childbirth and the baby, a little girl, was stillborn. The little boy, aged only two, was an orphan. The priests and nuns who looked after him tracked down every relative they could find and asked them to take on the lost child and bring him up as one of their own. Suffer the little children to come unto you. They wrote to Delaneys in America, in Ireland and in England. The Delaneys all refused. Every single one of them said no. The little boy was adopted and took on the surname of his adoptive parents.'

Powerscourt paused and took another sip of his coffee. Out of the corner of his eye he could see that Michael Delaney was totally still, as if he had been turned to stone. Father Kennedy had his head in his hands. The wineskin was circulating regularly among the pilgrims. They could just hear another band striking up on the street outside.

'Here, in this news from Pittsburgh,' Powerscourt was speaking softly now, 'at last was a motive for killing as many Delaneys as you could. They, or their families, had, after all, refused to take you in. Here was a motive for killing Michael Delaney, the father who had abandoned you and caused the premature deaths of your own mother and sister. This was not Oedipus killing his father when he did not know who he was. This was a son deliberately setting out to murder his own father. There was a person of the right age in the pilgrim party and that was Waldo Mulligan, born Waldo Delaney, son of Michael. He tried to kill me at the running of the bulls this morning. Just before that our eyes met, and I knew and he knew that I knew that he was the killer. He confirmed as much in the hospital before he died.'

Powerscourt sat down. There was a rumble to his left and Michael Delaney rose to his feet. For a moment Powerscourt wondered if he was going to defend his conduct, but he merely asked Father Kennedy to accompany him. There were, he said, things he wished to discuss with the priest. The pilgrims watched him go, his bearing still erect, his head held high. Nobody spoke. Delaney's departure seemed to leave a hole, a vacuum in the room, as if some of the air had been sucked out. It was Jack O'Driscoll who broke the silence.

'That is all very clear, Lord Powerscourt,' he said, 'but could you answer me a question? You've been here all the time. Yet you were also making inquiries in Ireland and America. How did you manage that?'

Powerscourt smiled. 'Good question,' he said. 'Johnny here did all the work in England and Ireland before he joined us. He actually brought the book *Michael Delaney, Robber Baron* with him. And I had a very intelligent young man working for us in America but I didn't like to mention it in Michael Delaney's presence in case he decided to make life awkward for our man when he returns to the States. It was Alex Bentley's brother Franklin, who works for a law firm with offices in New York and Washington. He did the devilling over there, he found out about Delaney's first marriage in Pittsburgh.'

'Lord Powerscourt.' This time it was Charlie Flanagan from Baltimore. 'This is a lot to take in all at once. We're going to have to consider whether we carry on with the pilgrimage or not. But could we ask you one more favour? Would you and Lady Powerscourt and Johnny Fitzgerald be the pilgrims' guests at dinner this evening? No Father Kennedy, no Michael Delaney, just Alex Bentley and ourselves?'

Powerscourt assured them that he and Lady Lucy would be delighted. He would be most interested to hear what they decided about the pilgrimage. Johnny Fitzgerald headed a delegation towards the latest Fiesta celebrations and the nearest bar.

'That all went well enough, Francis,' said Lady Lucy as she led her husband off to their room. 'But tell me this, my love, what do you think Michael Delaney is going to do?'

'I really don't know, Lucy. Maybe they go through emotional upheavals like that every day on Wall Street, I don't know. I don't know enough about his religion, but I should think he's going to make his confession. He's got quite a lot of sins to get through, more than most people I should think. But if I know Michael Delaney, there'll be more to it than absolution. He'll be offering to hand over more money for schools in poor areas, more funds for more medical research, more support for priests and nuns, that sort of thing.'

'Do you mean that he's going to buy his way out of trouble, Francis?'

'Of course I do. All that stuff about it being easier for a camel to pass through the eye of a needle than for a rich man to enter the kingdom of God is for the innocent and the naive, if you ask me. If you're rich enough, you buy up all the camels, you buy up all the needles and you've already put down a deposit for buying heaven.'

Dinner with the pilgrims that evening was a boisterous affair. Maggie Delaney was not there. Thirty years of dislike of her cousin Michael had been washed away by the day's revelations. She was going, she told Lady Lucy, to see what comfort she could bring him in his time of trouble. Families should stick together after all. So it was the young men who set the tone for the occasion, behaving like children just let out of school on the last day of the summer term. They had ordered up a great round table in the upstairs room where Powerscourt had addressed them that morning. Powerscourt and Lady Lucy were at opposite sides of the circle with Johnny Fitzgerald halfway between them. As they made their way through stuffed red peppers and salt cod, suckling pig and sheep's cheese from the mountains, the pilgrims plied them with questions about their past investigations, about their children, about their houses in London and Ireland, about their plans for the future. Shortly before midnight the pilgrims exchanged glances. There was a sudden banging of forks on the table and loud cries for silence. Christy Delaney, now wearing the white shirt and red neckerchief of the festival of San Fermin, rose to his feet. He looked, Lady Lucy thought, absurdly young.

'Lady Powerscourt, Lord Powerscourt, let me welcome you to this dinner here tonight. And why I should have been chosen to speak for the pilgrims I do not know. These other characters are older, and possibly wiser, than me and they should all be making this speech instead of me.' Christy stared in mock severity at his colleagues. Lady Lucy thought they had chosen well. Christy had charm, he had grace and he had a voice that some women would have happily listened to all day long.

'My first duty', he carried on, 'is to thank you for keeping us alive. It has been a very difficult time for everybody, but we're still here, you're still here and the pilgrimage is still out there.' He waved in the direction of the street where the noise of revelry was reaching new heights. 'We have spent most of the day talking about the pilgrimage, about whether we should go on or not. I am instructed to let you know what we have decided. I think I can speak for everybody here when I say that pilgrimage takes hold of you in ways you never expected. It becomes a part of you, or you become a part of it. I know I speak for everyone here when I say that it has played and continues to play a central part in our lives. So we are not going to turn round and go home. That would devalue the meaning it has come to acquire in our hearts. So we go on, we go on to Santiago itself where the pilgrim trail ends. And, Lord Powerscourt, Lady Powersourt, Johnny Fitzgerald, we ask you to join us on our journey. Come with us across northern Spain through Burgos and Leon and Rabanal del Camino to Santiago itself. Walk with us through the heat and the dust and the flies. Lend us your company on the last stages of our journey.'

The young man stopped suddenly and looked at Powerscourt and Lady Lucy.

'Please come,' he concluded. 'You'd make us all very happy.'

Powerscourt rose and had a whispered conversation with his wife.

'Thank you, Christy,' he said finally, 'thank you all so much for your kind and generous offer. I'm going to have to say no, I'm afraid, though there could be a consolation prize. Lucy and I would be coming with you on false pretences, you see. From the moment you set forth from Le Puy you were on pilgrimage, a spiritual mission for many no doubt, layered perhaps with faith and thoughts of penance and absolution and forgiveness. No doubt you have found other things as well on your journeys. You are looking for spiritual sustenance of some sort. I came here looking for a murderer. Our motives are completely different. And we have young children back in London that we do not like to leave for too long. But I make you an offer, an offer of friendship if you like, of companionship. One of the great occasions in the pilgrim route happens in the cathedral in Santiago on the fifteenth of August, the Feast of the Assumption of the Blessed Virgin. I believe there are special rituals to welcome the pilgrims who arrive on that day. Lucy and I will see you there. We will return to England and come back to meet you all again. What do you say?'

The pilgrims cheered. 'Santiago!' they shouted. 'August the fifteenth!' 'Feast of the Assumption!' 'Santiago!'

Several hours later, as Powerscourt and Lady Lucy were making their way to bed, they were intercepted by an excited Alex Bentley. 'I thought you'd like this,' he grinned. 'Father Kennedy is overjoyed, saying it is one of the greatest days of his life!'

'Why is that?' asked Powerscourt.

'Simply this. You're going to enjoy the news. Michael Delaney has agreed to pay for two new foundations to be run by the Church.'

'What's so special about that?' said Powerscourt, 'I thought Michael Delaney sprinkles his money about like holy water all the time.'

'This time it's for a home for abandoned mothers, deserted by their husbands. And a new orphanage to be run by nuns, large enough to cope with most of the orphans on the eastern seaboard of the United States.' Alex Bentley paused for effect. 'And they're both going to be in Pittsburgh.'

A month later Powerscourt and Lady Lucy and Johnny Fitzgerald were walking across Santiago towards the cathedral. Lady Lucy was sporting a new hat in pale blue from Bond Street. It was Wednesday, the fifteenth of August, the Feast of the Assumption of the Blessed Virgin Mary, and Santiago was treating itself to a holiday. The service was due to start at eleven o'clock. Lady Lucy was very excited about another guidebook she had brought with her from Hatchard's in Piccadilly.

'Do you know, Francis, that the whole story of St James may be a myth, fiction even?'

'How do you mean?'

'Well, the story goes something like this. I don't think my dates will all be right but never mind. St James comes to Spain and preaches the Gospel some time after the Crucifixion. Then he goes back to Rome and is martyred, poor man, by having his head cut off. This is where it starts to get a bit odd. Somehow or other the body of James and his head are brought back to Spain in a stone boat, to Padron down the road from here. And then nothing is heard of him for about seven hundred and fifty years. Absolutely nothing. No pilgrimage, no statue, no churches, it's as if he's never been. Then the Spaniards are having a lot of trouble with the Moors and the Infidel. They need a patron saint of Spain to rid the country of the invaders. So, my author implies, the church authorities remembered the stories of James in his stone boat. Behold! A body is found! It is pronounced, heaven knows how, to be that of St James in person! And he becomes a mighty warrior, able to defeat whole armies of Moors single-handed. His name becomes a great battle cry, Santiago Matamoros, James the Slayer of Moors. The cathedral is built here at Santiago. The whole pilgrim industry starts up and never looks back. It was all very convenient.'

'It's a good story anyway,' said Johnny Fitzgerald.

Powerscourt looked up at the cathedral believed to contain the bones of St James, towering above them. 'It looks pretty solid to me, Lucy. Who ever says myths have to be true anyway? What about the Son of God who came down to earth to be crucified and to rise again on the third day so that his followers could eat him in church every Sunday?'

Lady Lucy laughed. They were walking up the nave now, greeting their friends the pilgrims who were already in position, arranging to meet for lunch afterwards. They found outside seats halfway up the transept. There were still ten minutes to go before the service. Powerscourt noted the memorabilia of the saint, the scallop shells, the great statue of St James himself, which had been encrusted with gold until French soldiers stripped it off and carried it away to Paris during the Napoleonic Wars. Looking upwards he saw that each century had left its mark on the original construction, elaborate statues, soaring pillars, delicate carvings.

The service for the assumption of the Blessed Virgin Mary in the Cathedral of St James in Santiago de Compostela began. Sonorous Latin rolled across the transept and down the nave and echoed around the roof spaces far above. Every pew was filled. The congregation knelt and rose and knelt and rose again. Priests and bishop in scarlet and purple moved purposefully around the high altar. There was a handsome young man standing beside Michael Delaney, the son James whose miraculous recovery from illness had led to the pilgrimage. Now he had joined his father and the other survivors at the end, a father's pride apparent to all every time Michael Delaney looked at his son. Powerscourt found himself thinking of the Last Judgement in the tympanum at Conques, the depiction in stone of the sins which could send a soul to hell, greed, adultery, pride, the glutton about to be roasted in some infernal cooking pot, the kings without their crowns about to suffer the torments of the damned. He thought of the fallen, John Delaney, his body bouncing off the volcanic rocks from the path to the top of the chapel of St Michel in Le Puy. Pray for us now and in the hour of our death, Amen. He thought of the trainee priest, Patrick MacLoughlin, his corpse sent down the Lot in the middle of the night to be found by schoolboys in the morning. He thought of the pilgrims he had met again that morning, their eyes bright, their faces tanned by the long march from Pamplona, now at journey's end here in the Cathedral of St James. He resolved to hold a pilgrims' dinner every year in London for the survivors. The young men, his young men, as he now thought of them, could relive their days in the vast open spaces of the Aubrac and the roasting plains of Spain. He thought of Stephen Lewis, cut to pieces behind the great Abbey Church of Conques. Hail Mary Mother of God.

The worshippers were beginning to come forward now to receive the sacrament, Maggie Delaney leaning on the arm of her cousin Michael, still trying to buy his way into heaven. Powerscourt remembered what he had said to Lucy a month earlier, and felt he had been right when he had spoken of the rich buying up all the camels and establishing a monopoly on needles. He thought of Girvan Connolly, feckless, burdened with debt, a man on the run from his creditors, who still did not deserve to meet his doom in the upper chamber at Moissac, his head smashed to pulp against the stone pillars. He thought of Waldo Mulligan. Forgive them, Lord, for they know not what they do.

His young men were coming forward to the altar now, on this, the culminating moment of their pilgrimage. Wee Jimmy Delaney and Brother White were raising the chalice to their lips. Blood of Christ. Body of Christ. Take this in remembrance of me. Powerscourt touched Lady Lucy's hand and smiled at her. He wondered how they all felt, now they had finally reached journey's end. Were their sins forgiven? Would God grant their prayers to heal the sick and make the blind see and the deaf speak?

Shortly before one o'clock the service was drawing to an end. But the ritual was not. An air of excitement ran around the cathedral. A group of eight men, dressed in dark red robes, assembled at the top of the nave, opposite the altar. They brought a great silver-plated censer over to be filled with a mixture of charcoal and incense. This was the Botafumeiro, literally Smoke Expeller in Galician and Portugese, and it was only brought out on special occasions. No priest or acolytes walked among the congregation waving this thurible about from side to side. It was too big, five feet high and weighing almost two hundred pounds. It was attached to a system of ropes that led down from a pulley in the dome and it would swing across the transept, almost from one door to another, pouring incense over the altar as it went, swooping over the heads of the congregation.

When the censer was filled it was brought back to the red-robed men, each of whom now had a rope in his hands. These were like bell ringers' ropes except that, rather than each rope being connected to its own particular bell, they were all connected to the master rope shooting up towards the dome at one end, and to the Botafumeiro, gleaming in the light, at the other. There was a certain amount of shuffling about and then one of the red-robed men took the thurible out into the centre of the transept and gave it a push. It was, Lady Lucy thought, exactly like somebody giving a send-off shove to a model boat at the Round Pond in Kensington Gardens. Then the red men seized their ropes and pulled, bending a long way down as they did so. The censer began to swing in longer and longer arcs, forty feet up, fifty feet up, sixty feet up, higher and higher towards the ceiling.

Then disaster struck. The man opposite Powerscourt, who had been swaying about as if he were a human thurible, suddenly tottered out into the gap between the pews, directly in the path of the censer. It was moving away from him as he lurched out. But it looked certain to hit him on the way back. Quite what impact a two-hundred-pound Botafumeiro travelling at over forty miles an hour would have on a human skull Powerscourt did not know. He shot out into the gap to try to bring the man back to safety. Lady Lucy stared at the scene in horror. The censer had turned and was shooting towards Francis at great speed. In a moment he might be dead. Johnny Fitzgerald dived from the edge of his pew and tackled Powerscourt, rugby style, just above the knees. Powerscourt and the reeling man crashed to the ground. The Botafumeiro shot over them on its journey to the other door. Johnny Fitzgerald put his arms across the others. He didn't want them rising to their feet only for the thurible to smash into their faces on the way back. The men with the ropes appeared to change their routine to bring the thing to a halt sooner that it would under normal running. A priest ran over to make sure nobody was hurt. In a matter of moments all three men were back in their seats.

'My God, Francis,' said Lady Lucy, brushing the dust off his jacket, 'we come all the way to Spain on a murder investigation. Five dead men, four pilgrims and a murderer later and you've solved the mystery only to get yourself nearly killed by a giant block of incense.'

Johnny Fitzgerald was more philosophical. 'Bloody country this, Francis, if you ask me, the buggers are obsessed with death,' he whispered. 'If you don't get gored at the running of the bulls, you may catch it in the bullring. And if you're still alive after that the smelly monster on the ropes will knock the back of your head off. Thank God Waldo Mulligan never got acquainted with this Botafumeiro thing – he'd have killed off half the congregation.'

The pilgrims were filing out of the cathedral now. Powerscourt thought they had been valiant against all disaster, Jack O'Driscoll and Charlie Flanagan and Christy Delaney and the other survivors. No discouragement had made them once relent their first avowed intent to be a pilgrim. They had struggled on through death and sealed trains and nights on the floors of the police cells of France. They had indeed been beset round with dismal stories of murder in the afternoon and sudden death in the morning. Perhaps, Powerscourt thought, they knew now, all of them, after this long journey towards God, that they, at the end, would life inherit, that they would fear not what men say, that they had laboured night and day, To Be a Pilgrim.

EPILOGUE

The Powerscourts received regular reports on the pilgrims' progress back in the world they had left behind. Only Christy Delaney, now surrounded by the courts and libraries of Cambridge, proved an indifferent correspondent. And then in early December there came two letters from France, one from the Mayor of Le Puy, the other from the Secretary to the Cardinal Archbishop of Toulouse, the worldly cleric through whose archdiocese they had passed earlier that year. Mr Jacquet of Le Puy informed them that the two fountains were in position with the appropriate inscriptions and hoped that the Powerscourts would be able to visit them when they were next in the south of France. Business in the butcher's shop, he told them as an aside, had never been better. The Archbishop's interest was more general. He wished to know what had befallen the surviving pilgrims. Powerscourt suspected he wanted material for a sermon on the benefits of pilgrimage and the workings of God's grace on His faithful servants. But he pulled out a couple of sheets of his finest writing paper and began his story of the outcome of the long journey from Le Puy-en-Velay to Santiago de Compostela.

He began with Michael Delaney. Delaney had not let himself be affected in any way by the revelations of his past sins in the Pamplona hotel. He had simply ignored them, bulldozed his way past them and carried on with his life and his work. If he felt any remorse he did not show it. If he felt any guilt it was not apparent. His son James was now safely installed at Harvard and enjoying himself. If there was one noticeable change in Delaney's behaviour it was that he was giving ever more money to charity. The institutions for orphans and single mothers in Pittsburgh were expected to open in the New Year. In his home city of New York he was giving enormous sums to Catholic education. And, in conjunction with the Church, he was establishing a new travel facility called the Catholic Pilgrim, to organize pilgrimages to Santiago where the journey would be planned every step of the way, with different options for walkers and train travellers. Alex Bentley was the managing director and spent much of his time in France and Spain.

Jack O'Driscoll had indeed written a long account of the pilgrimage for his newspaper, which was successfully syndicated all round the world. Jack turned down job offers in Manchester and London, saying he preferred to stay in the country he knew, where his family and friends were. Charlie Flanagan was being so successful at selling model ships that he thought he would be able to save enough money to go to college and train as an architect. He still had all the drawings he made in Europe, neatly stored in large folders. Sometimes on quiet days like a Sunday afternoon he would open them out and take himself on an improbable journey back to the façade of the cathedral in Le Puy or the cloisters of Moissac, scarcely able to believe that he, a young man from Baltimore, had travelled all that way and seen these glorious buildings.

Shane Delaney had reported great news, wonderful news, news fit for a miracle if it lasted. Two weeks after he returned home, his wife Sinead, who had been dying slowly from cancer, appeared to recover. Her energy came back. She visited her family. Shane took her for a holiday to Weston-super-Mare. She had never seen a beach or a pier before or stayed in a hotel. Their seven days there in the Strand Hotel, she told her husband, had been among the happiest of her life. Then they returned to Swindon. Two weeks later the disease returned. The end was close. She died, Powerscourt told the Archbishop, in early October. Willie John Delaney, the man dying on pilgrimage from the incurable disease never expected to reach Santiago. But he did. He never expected to last out into the autumn. But he did. Maybe it was the cold that saw him off. Five of his fellow pilgrims attended his funeral in the second week of November.

Brother White gave up teaching altogether. He retrained as an accountant in a reputable firm in Guildford where the numbers and the ledgers held no temptations for him. Maggie Delaney had abandoned her little apartment in New York with its box files of clippings from the business pages of the *New York Times* and gone to live with her cousin Michael in his palace in Manhattan. The worldly air of the great town house and the people who passed through it made her a less crabby personality. Father Kennedy had put on weight during the pilgrimage. His Bishop did not think that a portly priest was the right man to tender to the spiritual needs of the rich of Manhattan. He sent him to a poorer parish in New Jersey but replaced him with a former Wall Street banker who had seen the light and joined the priesthood. At least, the Bishop said to himself rather cynically, the rich will now be told how to make their charitable donations as tax efficient as possible.

Powerscourt kept the most dramatic piece of news till the end. The letter from Pittsburgh had been addressed to Lady Lucy and she had cried when she read it. Marianne Delaney, beloved little sister of Wee Jimmy, appeared to be recovering her sight. She was still dumb, she was still deaf, but she could see. The sight might never be perfect and the doctors did not know how far the recovery would go. Lady Lucy remembered Wee Jimmy saying that the family couldn't expect everything, but any improvement would be a blessing. Well, improvement there had been and Wee Jimmy reported that the little girl was so excited that she could now see her parents and her brothers and sisters and marvel at the flowers in the park. Every day brought fresh wonder as Marianne saw more people and more places for the first time. Wee Jimmy had brought her back a scallop shell, symbol of the pilgrimage to Santiago, and she could now see it as well as touch it. It was one of her most treasured possessions. The family and the little girl were overjoyed. It was a gift from God. Wee Jimmy's pilgrimage to Santiago had borne fruit in the sight of his little sister. The Promised Land across three thousand miles of the Atlantic Ocean, Powerscourt wrote to the Cardinal Archbishop, had always been represented to the famine refugees from Ireland and the poor of Europe as a place of hope, the country of the American Dream. Now, perhaps, the story of the pilgrimage was ending as it had begun, with an American miracle.